Sarah,

Thank you for reading!

You are enough. You are loved.

Hugs,

Joy Palmer

weddings, willows, and revised Expectations

V. JOY PALMER

WhiteFire
—Publishing—

This is a work of fiction. All characters and events portrayed in this novel are either fictitious or used fictitiously.

WEDDINGS, WILLOWS, AND REVISED EXPECTATIONS

WhiteFire Publishing
13607 Bedford Rd NE
Cumberland, MD 21502

ISBN:978-1-946531-15-5 (digital)
978-1-946531-14-8 (print)

Dedicated to Sandra Thompson and Faye Hawes.

*Gram, I think our bookish family can be laid at your feet.
I know you would have been one of my biggest fans.
I love you. I miss you.*

*Faye, I hear you every time my daughter hugs
one of her dolls and says, "Baby!"
You changed our lives for the best.
I love you. I miss you.*

Prologue

A great philosopher looks at his various struggles as fodder for his innovative thinking, but, since I am not a great philosopher, I look at my struggles as something akin to stepping on a bee the size of a Komodo dragon. Painful and horrifying. Like I said, I am not a great philosopher. I'm a hairdresser who usually misspells innovative.

Correction: I *was* a hairdresser. Now I'm not sure what I am.

So, yeah. I'm not sure how to begin this. Maybe if this chair weren't grinding my tailbone to dust, I'd be able to think straight and tell you this story. I always complained to Gram about this chair. She would just say that I was sitting in it wrong. No amount of shifting, however, relieves the pain. Or maybe that's just the hole in my heart. Cheery, right? Well, I've never been a sunshine and rainbows girl.

I should get a grip and start at the beginning. What expression isn't already coined by a multimillion-dollar movie franchise? Oh, never mind. As Solomon would say, "There's nothing new under the sun." Also a cheery thought. I'm just full of those today.

Anyway. On a cold November night, after three days of labor, a happy couple welcomed their beautiful baby girl into the world. They just knew this little angel had great things in store for her. Then eleven minutes later, I was born. Once again, the happy couple imagined their second darling babe's future, sure it would also be great and wonderful.

I know what you're thinking. It's the same thing I think every day.

Boy, did I prove them wrong.

But let's skip ahead to my—our—fifteenth birthday. Because I blame everything happening right now on that day.

I glance around the willow grove. Courtney is standing by the present table, sipping a cup of punch. It looks like Queen Courtney is holding court, surrounded by all the popular, smart, and perfect boys and girls. She laughs and tosses her glossy hair over her shoulder. The way the boys stare, I'm convinced it contains some type of drool-inducing spores.

If I tried to flip my hair, I'd probably fall over.

Whatever. I roll my eyes like the "average" teenager I am and keep searching.

For him.

Gram set up our fifteenth birthday party in my favorite place, the willow grove. Courtney said we should just do it inside, in the kitchen, but I begged and begged. The idea of a fluttery party in the willow grove on a warm summer day just seemed enchanting. And it is. Our theme is purple because we couldn't agree on a color, so Gram picked one for us. Twinkle lights—thanks to an extension cord—and streamers sway in the breeze. Tables with purple tablecloths dot the field surrounding the grove. People mill around, laughing, eating, and just enjoying one another's company.

Where is he?

I have no idea why Chance McFarland and his father have been coming around so much. Gram hasn't told us—yet. But I have the feeling it's important. What I do know is that my heart feels like it will fly with the birds whenever Chance talks to me. A scary condition (especially because I'm afraid of heights) that I've been living with for a year, ever since the new, joint junior high and high school for the county opened its shiny steel doors.

Still no luck. I might just eat my body weight in cake today...

When Chance said he'd be at our birthday party last week—and I don't want to be dramatic or anything—I thought I was going to die. Be still my heart! He actually winked at me when he said it too.

I search the throng of teenagers, pretending that I'm engrossed in organizing the cookies on the snack table.

Did Joe Cutly seriously try to do a mohawk?

Whoa, step back! That's a lot of fuchsia.

Oh, look. Another one of Gram's friends dyed her hair blue. Hope Gram isn't next.

Anxiety thrums in my stomach, and I finger my locket. Seriously, where is he? Maybe he's not coming. Oh, man. He's not going to come, is he? If he doesn't come, that's all I'm going to remember about today. Whenever I look back on this birthday, there's going to be a big black smear on this otherwise wonderful memory.

However, like the lovelorn fool I am, I keep searching for him.

Finally, I see him. Chance leans against a willow tree. Despite the fact that his back faces the crowd, I see him reach down, pluck a blade of grass, and pop it into his mouth. Apparently, he's trying to be all cowboy. Why do guys do that? He knows this is New Hampshire, right? Not exactly the Wild West.

I start toward him, prepared to tease him about the grass chewing.

Except a hand clamps down on my shoulder.

Um, creepy. Fight or flight? Fight or flight?

"Hi, Apryl. I just wanted to catch you and wish you a happy birthday."

Oh, it's Chance's dad, Mr. William McFarland. "Thank you, sir."

He smiles and reaches for a cookie. Laugh lines crinkle all over his tan, weathered face, especially around his eyes. He rambles on and on, but I don't hear what he's saying. However, the way he's studying me makes me feel self-conscious. I smooth the black lace on my dress skirt in an attempt to calm the anxious feeling trying to overtake me like the hives I get when I eat shellfish.

How long do you have to wait until it's no longer considered rude to leave?

I think it's been long enough.

I'm just about to excuse myself when I see a girl saunter around the trunk of the willow tree Chance continues to lean against. He takes her hand.

I can't feel my face.

"Apryl, did you hear me?" *Mr. McFarland asks.*

"Wh—What?" *I feel like I just lost a slap bet, face stinging from seven or eight smacks.*

Mr. McFarland follows my gaze and nods. "Ah..." The breeze flicks at his full head of salt-and-pepper hair.

I lean against the table. My hand grapples for something to hold. My brain only registers that I've stuck my hand into something sticky when the unknown substance glues my fingers into a half-curled position. I am so dumb. Of course he's with another girl. He's always with another girl.

"Ah, that son of mine. Barely sixteen years old and flirting with every girl he can see."

Yeah, I can see it too.

"I remember what it was like to be young."

Oh, boy.

"I understand he wants a girlfriend."

Clearly. I look at my jelly-covered hand. Gross.

"I just wish he'd go for a different kind of girl." Mr. McFarland looks at me, his brown eyes piercing me where I stand.

Gulp.

A different kind of girl?

Am I a different kind of girl?

"Those girls aren't good for him. He needs a girl who can understand the kind of legacy we're building. And don't think I haven't noticed the way you guys spend time together. You certainly seem to get along." His eyes pierce me once again because he knows. I thought I had been playing it cool. But cool doesn't have permanently rosy cheeks.

"Um. Yeah." I swallow.

"Good. That's good." He fixes me with his dagger-like stare once again. "Don't you think?"

"Yeah, I do."

He clears his throat. "Yes. I agree."

Then he smiles. Only it's not a nice, knowing, shared-secret kind of smile. It's the kind of smile that would make a happy baby wail for their mom.

"Yes, I think Courtney is a good match for him."

Once again, I can't feel my face. But that only lasts for three seconds. Then it burns like lava as shame, humiliation, jealousy, and mortification consume me alive. If I could get away with it, I'd rip my locket off and throw it at someone.

"She's just the kind of girl Chance needs. I intend to make sure he's spending time with a proper young lady." He places his hand on my shoulder once again, and I swear it weighs a hundred pounds. "You understand what I'm saying, young lady?"

Oh, yeah. I understand. I nod, my neck stiff and my head wooden.

"So, please, stay away." He gives me one more pointed look before walking over to another group of partygoers.

There it is. I'm not good enough for his son. I'm no good. I'm not a proper young lady. A girl forever destined to be average.

And who would ever want average?

Chapter One

"Let me say this again, so clear that every senior citizen with a hearing aid in a two-block radius will hear me and be able to repeat this a week from now." I pause for dramatic effect. "No."

"You're not the bride," Izze singsongs. She does a side-to-side head bob that sends the shoulder-length curls she's been growing out bouncing.

"Bridezilla," I grumble.

Kaylee holds up the offending magazine. "This hairstyle is beautiful."

Courtney takes the magazine from her, studying the picture like it's the Holy Grail for her law exam. "It's not that bad, Apryl."

"Not that bad? Not that bad!" I sputter in mock horror. How can I aptly express my disgust? Would clawing my own eyes out be too dramatic? Perhaps hacking my hair off with the butter knife in front of me would send the message.

Izze starts waving her arms all over the place. "It's classic."

I grab the magazine. "It's old-looking. Been there, done that. Don't you want something new? Romantic? Creative? Something with curly tendrils and pretty flower appliques?" We're gathered at Izze's cousin's café, Whipped Cream, planning last minute details for her bridal shower. At least we were. Somehow the conversation had dissolved into an argument about hairstyles for the wedding.

Izze stares at me like I just spoke gibberish to her. So do Courtney and Kaylee.

I sigh. "Courtney, please turn around."

She takes a sip of her black (gag) decaf espresso before answering. "Not happening."

Before the somewhat-aggressive words can form on my tongue, Kaylee takes the clip out of her red hair. She runs her fingers through the pin-straight tresses. "Okay."

With my purse slung over my shoulder, I walk around the table and start braiding, looping, and pulling her hair into a masterpiece fit for royalty. Alas, I'm still waiting for Kate Middleton to tell me that I am her one and only stylist. Her loss.

I pull another bobby pin out of my purse—I keep a plastic bag full of these little miracle workers in there at all times—and curl and pin the last strand just above her right ear.

"Wow." Izze gingerly reaches out her hand to touch it.

"And that's just what I can do with a few pins."

"And she's oh so humble about it." Courtney rolls her eyes, and I bite my tongue to keep the sisterly comebacks to myself.

"All right. Let's get back to planning the bridal shower." Courtney clicks her pen in a way that means business. "Let's talk about games."

I stifle a groan. Bridal shower games and I do not get along. I tune in and out of this inane conversation for the next twenty minutes. I glance at Izze. She looks happy. Really happy. Like, light-glowing-from-her-espresso-colored-eyes happy.

That's right, peeps. My always-the-bridal-consultant friend is finally a bride. And just for the record, she is not marrying an accountant. For too many months I thought Miles was an accountant, not a financial consultant. Either way, he works with numbers. That seems pretty accountant-y to me. But after Izze threatened to throttle me, I stopped asking to borrow his calculator.

And just so you can note it on the official record, he has five calculators.

My phone starts to ring in my purse. I pull the dinky thing that barely passes for a smartphone out of my second-hand purse. It's vintage—I found it in my grandmother's antique shop the last time Courtney and I visited her.

"Apryl." Courtney's critical tone pulls me from the memory.

"We aren't supposed to be using cell phones. Remember? I said no cell phones."

"It's Gram's ringtone, Courtney. Get a frozen chamomile tea, would you?"

"What does frozen chamomile tea—and by the way, yuck—have to do with your grandmother calling?" Kaylee asks.

Courtney rolls her eyes. "It's her way of saying relax, take a chill pill, calm down."

"I'm going to use that," Izze says.

For some reason the call went straight to voicemail. I listen to the message, dread filling my body from the top of my blue-black hair all the way to my black- and silver-painted toenails. As a man's voice fills my ear, panic and fear wrap around my heart. I don't hear anything other than seven terrible words:

Your grandmother is in the Keene hospital.

"Courtney, Gram is in the hospital. We've got to go. *Now!*"

My twin sister starts shrieking and asking all sorts of questions, but I don't have any answers. Her blue eyes, which are slightly darker than mine, are wide with panic. I shove my phone at her while I gather our stuff. Izze and Kaylee spring into action, trying to help me pick up our junk while Courtney mutters "Where is she?" over and over again to the man in my phone.

"Finally!" Courtney grabs my arm and pulls me out the door with her. "I'll drive."

"We're praying for you!" Izze yells.

"Let us know if you need anything!" Kaylee shouts.

"Thanks," I mumble too quietly for them to hear me.

"Someone has until the end of *You've Got Mail* playing on the waiting-room television to tell us what's going on, or this entire hospital will suffer the consequences. And Meg Ryan is about to meet her cyber crush only to discover Tom Hanks, so you don't have long." I've been in a glare-off with the receptionist in the emergency room for over an hour, and my patience is wearing thin.

The boney woman puts a hand on her waist. "Ma'am, there's nothing I can do."

My chest hurts and not just from the fact that she called me "Ma'am." I'm only twenty-four!

"At least let us go back there! We drove all this way—" In other words, twenty minutes—"and we have the right to see her. We're her immediate family!"

"I'm afraid I can't let you."

"I am going to sue this entire hospital! My sister over there is a lawyer." Well, almost a lawyer, but the receptionist who bears a striking resemblance to Ursula the Sea Witch doesn't need to know that. I wave my arm behind me to indicate Courtney, who is Lamaze breathing in a chair across the room, legs crossed and jiggling with nerves. She paints the picture of competent lawyer right now, doesn't she? At least she isn't brown paper bagging it.

The woman narrows her eyes and speaks through clenched teeth. "Please sit down. I will do my best to get someone to talk with you. But it's crazy back there, so it may take some time."

With a huff, I storm across the waiting room and sit beside Courtney.

"No luck," Courtney states.

"We're going to sue them."

"What?" Her eyes are wide with horror. "You can't joke about lawsuits in a hospital! That's like...like..."

"Like screaming 'Bomb!' at a TSA convention?"

She stares at me for a moment. "I don't think that's the expression."

"I don't use clichés."

We both fall into worried silence. There were no details in the message that I can remember. Zippo. Zilch. Nada. Nothing. However, I'm not sure I remember anything other than those seven horrible words. So here we sit, borderline homicidal.

"She's not going to die, Apryl." Courtney's whispered words should be reassuring but they're not. Sometimes people die. We both know that. And now we're sitting in my least favorite place in the world. The place where our lives were devastated forever.

I squeeze my eyes shut against the memories. When I open them again, it's just in time to see a tall, broad chested man with arms the size of my head walking out of the waiting room. I do a double take.

Chance McFarland.

Thankfully, I'm distracted by another man in light blue scrubs who walks into the waiting room and stops at the receptionist's desk. He talks with her quietly, and Ursula the Sea Witch points at us. I hold my breath as he approaches us.

"Are you Charlotte Burns's granddaughters?"

"Yes!" we shout in unison like creepy twins from a horror movie.

"Follow me, please."

He leads us down a hallway, and for a moment I think he's taking us to the little room, the bad news room, the same room from seventeen years ago. He walks right by it, though, and waves his ID badge in front of a sensor on the wall that opens the doors to the ER. My heart relaxes. He leads us through the chaotic maze and finally stops in front of a room with curtains for walls.

He pulls back one of the curtains for us to enter. "The doctor will be in to see you shortly."

Gram lays in a bed in the middle of the curtained room. I immediately rush to her left side, and Courtney rushes to her right. I take her withered hand gently in mine, afraid it might break.

This is too much.

She's fast asleep. Peaceful even. I wouldn't think there was anything wrong with her if not for the wires and machines connected to her. Oh, and the huge brace on her from the waist down.

A man in dark blue scrubs and a lab coat steps into our billowy room. "I'm Dr. Scott, the attending physician on your grandmother's case." He gives us that patented doctor smile. Seriously, they must take a class in med school on how to smile like that. Entitled *The Perfect Calming Smile* and taught by stinking Dr. Smile himself.

"What happened?" Courtney exudes calm, cool, and collected now. You would never have known she hyperventilated to the beat of Taylor Swift's "Shake It Off" just minutes earlier.

"Charlotte fell down the stairs and suffered a hip fracture,

which is a break in the thigh bone—the femur—of your hip joint."
He walks over to the one actual wall in the room and begins
drawing a picture on the dry erase board mounted there. As he
draws, he gives us mini-lecture on ball and socket joints. Apparently the hip is one.

As he recapped his marker, Dr. Scott's expression remains
grave. Like a funeral plot. "To be blunt, it was a bad break with
multiple fractures. There was a break approximately two inches
from the hip joint and another fracture four inches from the hip
joint. And the femoral neck fracture, the break closest to the hip
joint, is cutting off blood supply to the head of the thigh bone.
She's going to need surgery. Tonight. My team is preparing the
OR now."

"Is this a dangerous surgery?" I whisper, unable to take my
eyes off my precious grandmother.

"There are risks to every surgery, but this is the only course
of action. We'll be performing an internal repair. The plan is to
insert screws into the bone to hold it together while it heals." Dr.
Scott sets the marker back onto the board's attached tray. "Dr.
Rothman, a colleague of mine, will be assisting in the surgery."

I blanche at the words "screws" and "bones." Judging by
Courtney's pale face, she's feeling nauseated as well.

Dr. Scott points to one of the IVs leading into Gram's pale
arm. "As you can see, we're keeping her well-medicated, but I
suspect it's made her drowsy. It usually does. We went over the
risks and benefits with Charlotte before the meds knocked her
out, and she gave permission for us to keep you two informed."

Two men pull the curtain aside. The bigger man with white
bushy eyebrows turned to Courtney and me first. "We've come
to transport Charlotte Burns to pre-op."

"Excellent." Dr. Scott looks at us again. "I'll speak with you
after the surgery. One of the nurses will show you the way to the
OR waiting room."

Courtney and I stand there helpless as the doctor exits and
the transport guys unhook our grandmother. Without a backwards glance, they wheel her away.

I didn't say goodbye.

A nurse arrives and smiles at us with sympathy. "Can I show you to the OR waiting room?"

"No, thanks," I mumble. "We know the way."

Courtney and I leave the ER and walk down the bland, lifeless hallways to the waiting room. I stop and grab my sister's arm. "I'm going to run to the bathroom and to get some junk food. You go get us some good seats. Try to score us one of the couches. Take it with force if necessary. I think we're going to be here awhile."

"Okay, fine." Courtney sighs. Not in a way that says she's annoyed with me but rather in a way that says she's drained by all this. Physically, emotionally, and spiritually drained.

She's not the only one.

I go to the bathroom first, only breaking down a little bit in the stall. At least I thought it was only a little bit. My lobster-red face, however, says otherwise. My pale blue eyes look eerie in this light. My blue-black, naturally straight hair falls a couple inches past my shoulders in a way that normally highlights my high cheekbones but now just highlights that I've been honking like a dying seagull. Attractive image, is it not?

I need Starbursts and Snickers and about a thousand bags of chips. I'm thinking Cool Ranch Doritos.

I leave the bathroom and punch the down button for the elevator. It dings, and the doors open. I step inside mindlessly. The doors are about to close when a large, rough hand inserts itself between them.. The doors open again, and inside steps Chance McFarland.

This was *not* happening. "Get off the elevator," I growl.

"Going down?" He completely ignores my demand, and the doors slide shut behind him. Totally and stinking fantastic.

"Get. Off. The. Elevator." I desperately push all the buttons trying to get the elevator to stop.

"Can't." He leans against the opposite side of this stupid, tiny enclosed chamber. His long legs seem to take up all the available space.

"Why are you here?"

He shrugs.

"Why?" I snarl.

Once again, he shrugs.

"At least acknowledge that I'm speaking to you!" I'm filled with visions of flicking him in the forehead.

"Once upon a time you told me to stay out of your way. I thought that would include not speaking to you."

Twit. Twit. Twit.

"I think that would have included not riding in the same elevator as me." I fiddle with my antique gold locket, rubbing my finger over the familiar floral pattern. It's my nervous, anxious, angry habit. It's nothing short of miraculous that I haven't rubbed it smooth. "And by the way, you're speaking to me now."

"I don't see why you seem to hate *my* guts, but it's certainly your prerogative."

"I don't recall ever saying that I hate your guts. But you're right, I do *not* like you."

Chance raises an eyebrow. "And the reason would be?"

"Sometimes you just don't like people." Never in a million reasons will I tell him the *real* reason.

"Perhaps the smell of motor oil repulses you? Most women turn their noses up at it, but I never took you to be a prissy girl," he drawls.

I flinch.

Chance's eyes are lit with the knowledge that he knows he struck a nerve. Oh, man. That's it. Crossing the four feet separating us, I prepare to engage in verbal warfare. And maybe one of those old movie slaps.

That is, until the elevator jerks to a stop and the lights flicker out, leaving us in total darkness. The sudden halt sends me flying into Chance's broad chest.

My face smacks into a cloth-covered brick wall, and my scathing comments disappear from my brain, replaced with one thought and one thought only:

Who knew that Chance would have abs like that?

Chance caught Apryl in his arms but, at the force of her impact, lost his balance. They both crashed into the ground, with

Apryl landing right on top of him, the top of her head knocking him in the jaw.

He spat out a mouthful of silky black hair. "Get off me."

She scrambled to get off him but tripped on his outstretched leg in the dark, this time punching him in the jaw.

"Ow." He rubbed his aching jaw.

"I can't believe this," Apryl moaned as she rolled off of him. "I'm going to die in an elevator. It's just like that wretched ride."

Chance rolled his eyes, thankful that she couldn't see him in the dark. "I'm fine, thanks."

"What are you sputtering about?"

"My jaw that you nailed twice. What are *you* sputtering about?"

"That ride at Disneyland...or Disney World. I can never keep them straight. Anyway, I've never actually been on the ride."

"Then how would you know it's wretched, as you put it?" Chance shook the chin-length, blond hair out of his eyes. He usually only wore his hair in a ponytail when he was working, but he sure wished he had that leather band with him right now.

"Because I saw a video of it. Regardless, we're going to die in here." Apryl kicked and banged the walls of the elevator. She screamed over and over, "Help! We're stuck in here!"

Finally, when his eyes were starting to adjust to the darkness, she collapsed onto the ground again. Where were the emergency lights in this thing? "I don't want to die." She reminded him of Donkey in *Shrek*.

"I think you should get a grip," he mumbled.

"I can't believe I'm going to die in here!"

"We aren't overly dramatic, are we?" Chance studied Apryl, huddled in the opposite corner of the elevator. Her knees were drawn to her chin, and she was rocking back and forth. Oh, great. She was on the verge of hysteria, and Chance had never been fond of dealing with hysterical women. "Why don't we talk about something else?"

"Should we take a musing look at our lives or talk about the bucket lists we never got to complete?"

Oh, brother. "How's your grandmother?"

"She was taken to surgery just before I got stuck in this hanging coffin."

Man, she really did not let an idea go once she got it into her thick head. Of course, Chance knew that from firsthand experience.

"Wait." Apryl picked up her head from where it rested on her knees. "How do you know about my grandmother?"

"You can't be serious."

"Not often, but yeah, right there I was being legit. I'm not exactly in the mood to joke around."

Chance popped his jaw. There. That would help. "I brought her here. I called you. I stayed with her, waiting for you and Courtney to get here. Took you long enough, by the way."

"There was a lot of traffic on the highway." Silence filled the air while she paused, her fingers tapping her knees in a quick rhythm. "Were you there when the doctor talked to Gram about the risks?"

He shifted uncomfortably. "Um...yeah."

"Is it bad?"

"There are always risks." What was he supposed to say? Yeah, there were risks. Blood clots. Bleeding. Infection. Problems with anesthesia and delayed healing. Not to mention all the long-term problems that could arise. The doctor, however, made it clear that the benefits far outweighed the risks. The chances of survival without the surgery...

"Thanks for inspiring confidence." She tried to infuse her normal edge into the sarcastic comment, but her voice broke on the last word.

Chance stifled a groan and let dropped his head into his hands. He just wasn't cut out to deal with women. Crazy mood swings and lots of crying. That's why he was never in a relationship long enough to deal with those particular feminine traits. He rubbed his scruffy face with both hands. To make the situation even worse, her crying was justified. He should comfort her. He fished around in his pocket. His hand wrapped around a thick cloth. Was it the cloth he used to wipe grease from his hands? He took a whiff of it. Nope. Should be good to use.

"Here." He tossed the cloth to her.

Apryl caught it midair. "Uh, thanks." She proceeded to wipe her face then sniffle even more.

"Just blow your nose already! Stop trying to be polite." Oh, that earned him a look worthy of death.

Apryl lifted the cloth like she was about to blow her nose then shrieked. Next thing Chance knew, his peace offering had smacked him in the face.

"Why would you give me your sock?" Apryl shrieked in disgust.

Chance held it up for inspection. It was indeed his sock. Whoops.

"Eww! Did you take that off your foot?" Apryl wiped her tongue on the sleeve of her sweater.

"For crying out loud, woman! Why would I do that? And why are you wiping off your tongue? Did you lick the sock?"

Apryl said, "Because you're my nemesis." at the same time Chance said, "Because I'm your nemesis."

"Saw that one coming." He sighed. This crazy firecracker was too much. Had always been too much.

"I swear, if we get out of here alive, you are going to regret that."

Chance sighed. So much for brokering a temporary peace treaty between them.—Wouldn't want things to get too boring. His father was right—Apryl was as unhinged as ever. When they got out of here, Chance would happily go back to avoiding her. The woman was so fiery she burned blue. He'd be willing to bet that was why her hair had a bluish tint to it.

Her fire.

Chapter Two

Some people look at hospitals as their saving grace. I look at hospitals as the breeding ground for paranoia. It takes a perfectly happy family who believes in fairy tales and happy endings and then delivers a gut-punching introduction to the cruel, bearded, beady-eyed reality.

Courtney and I are camped out in the ICU waiting room, pretending to sleep. But let's be honest—we aren't even trying.

I shift on the long, uncomfortable bench the hospital tries to pass off as a cushioned couch. The clock with the annoying tick that hangs above the door seems to hesitate before striking seven. As if it doesn't want to usher in the new day.

So reassuring.

Chance and I were stuck in the elevator for almost three hours before the hospital workers rescued us. I kissed the hand of the worker who helped me climb to the higher of the two floors we were stuck in between. Some paramedics examined both of us while the tech guys tried to figure out what went wrong. One of them theorized that someone pushed too many buttons. I nervously cleared my throat when Chance shot me a meaningful glare. Thankfully, he didn't rat me out.

Sitting up, I gently shake Courtney. "We have to clean up our mess, or that rude woman from housekeeping is going to bust us."

"Yeah. She wasn't happy to hear that we would be sleeping in here."

This hospital seems to come miraculously alive at seven in the morning. Seriously, it goes from being dark and quiet to bursting with activity. Nurses report to their stations, joking around with each other while doing the morning report. Doctors clump together and walk from room to room doing rounds as if they are auditioning to be the new face of *Grey's Anatomy*. Housekeeping wakes everyone who sleeps in the waiting rooms by yanking the blankets off them. Families with forced smiles arrive and buzz the nurses for access to see their loved ones who are in the ICU.

Courtney and I sit up and gather our belongings strewed across the floor. I throw away the trash and tuck the remaining junk food into my purse. I nod at Courtney, and she goes to buzz the nurses. We decided last night in the middle of our tossing and turning that Courtney would handle the nurses now. I supposedly threaten them too much.

"Come on, Apryl," Courtney says as the automatic door unlocks. She holds open the door to prevent it from relocking. We duck through the doorway and walk down another hallway that is even narrower than the previous hallways, if that's possible.

We stop in front of room 117. Gram's room.

"I can't believe they wouldn't let us see her all night," I mumble.

"The night nurses claimed she was still heavily sedated and shouldn't be disturbed."

"Meaning there was some type of problem with Gram, and they didn't want us to be in the way."

Courtney doesn't argue with me. There's no way to know. And I'm too combative. Huh, maybe I was threatening the nurses too much. Insight.

Stepping inside the room, I want to upchuck all the Skittles I ingested during my sleepless night at the sight of Gram, hooked up to even more tubes and monitors than she was before the surgery. The doctor told us last night that the surgery was successful, but that she would need to be in the hospital for one to two weeks.

The memories are much too close to home, but I thank God that Gram doesn't look that bad. Regardless, it's scary seeing her like this.

Gram's eyes blink open and she moans. "Ourtne. Epri."

Uh, I think that's us.

She tries again. "Courtney. Apryl."

"Hey, Gram," I say softly.

Courtney pats her shoulder. "Love you, Gram."

"Love. You. Both."

It's kind of freaking me out how hard it is for her to talk. Is that normal?

As if reading my mind, Courtney pats her shoulder again. "I'll be right back," she says before darting out the door. Leaving me alone.

Don't panic. Everything's ok. Do not panic.

"Hop."

What?

I look around, trying to find something that will help decipher her new language. "What?"

"Hop," she says more forcefully this time.

So I hop.

Gram frowns at me.

I point at her. "You said hop!"

"No! Hop!"

"I did hop!"

Courtney comes back into the room and stands next to me. "Are you okay, Gram?" She looks at me and lowers her voice. "The nurse said it's normal. She had a tube down her throat all night because she had a reaction to the anesthetic. It made her really sick."

"Hop! Hop! Hop!" Gram looks desperate and close to tears.

"Hop," Courtney mutters to herself. "Do you mean shop?"

Gram nods quickly.

"Your shop?" I ask.

"Yes," Gram croaks.

"I'm sure it's okay, Gram."

"Go. Ee. Hop."

"Go see the shop," Courtney translates.

Gram nods. "Yes."

"Gram," I interject. "We're going to stay with you."

"Must. Go." She looks frantic again.

Courtney swings her head to look at me. "Just go see the

shop. Make sure it's okay. I'll stay here. Make sure she's okay. Deal with the nurses," she says through clenched teeth.

I open my mouth to argue with her, but let's be honest. I hate hospitals. As much as I want to be here for Gram, I don't want to be *here*. I nod.

Courtney looks at Gram, her voice exuding a calm and soothing effect. "Gram, Apryl is going to go check the shop. I'm going to stay here with you today, and if you're doing okay, then I'll go back to the house and spend the night with Apryl."

Gram nods her head. "Yes. Yes. Yes."

So.

How long do I wait?

Courtney and Gram both give me pointed looks. "Go!" Gram squawks.

"Okay, okay." I lean over to kiss Gram on the forehead. "I love you, Gram."

"Love. You."

Bright sunlight akin to a fire poker in the eye blinds me as I turn down the winding driveway to Gram's house—the home of our youth. The thirty-minute drive to Riven, New Hampshire from the hospital in Keene felt more like a reenactment of *Around the World in Eighty Days*, the way it takes me from one world to another. It's a blessing that Gram was transferred to the Keene hospital since the small, local hospital in Riven wasn't equipped for the procedure.

I purposely take the back entrance and the longest way to Gran's house to avoid the bane of my existence, the thorn in my side, the sore of my eyes.

"Oh, happy days," I mumble.

In case you haven't realized that most of what I say is sarcastic, allow me to clarify—these are not happy days.

I catch sight of the willow grove on my left. Those beauties stand like sentries, watching over my grandmother's property. Looks like the blossoms are already gone for the season thanks to the unseasonably warm winter and spring. Hundreds of slender branches with their tiny pale green leaves flow to the ground like cascading water. A gentle breeze dances through them as if inviting the willows to waltz with her.

Oh, I do love that willow grove.

A faint squiggle that looks like a giant toddler took a crayon to Gram's immaculately landscaped lawn meanders into view. I follow the twists and turns of the rushing river and spot the familiar huge Victorian house. Actually, I'm not sure that *huge* is an accurate description. *Wayne Manor* might be more appropriate. Four floors (including a full basement), turrets on either end, and gorgeous woodwork that marks each floor, window, and door fills my vision. When I was young I use to pretend that Gram lived in a castle whenever Mom and Dad took us to visit. After Courtney and I came to live with Gram, she renovated the house, turning the first floor into the base of operations for her antique shop specializing in everything from chandeliers to furniture or clothing, complete with a fancy office.

The fancy office was very important to Gram.

Parking my borderline rust-eaten car that will not pass inspection this summer in front of the door to the shop, I take a deep breath.

Why is everything so hard? Why can't some things just be easy?

Pushing the car door open, I climb out and freeze.

Do you sense it too?

Something is not right.

Tiptoeing toward the lilac-painted front door with Willow Grove Antiques written in faded green lettering, I take the hidden key out of the secret alcove on the top of the doorframe. The door creaks open, and I can almost hear the instrumental buildup like I'm in a horror movie. This is the part in the story where everyone screams, "No!"

Everything looks normal.

Except for the demon eyes staring at me from the top of the wardrobe in the middle of the showroom.

"Ahhh!" Stumbling backward, I try to remember what Sandra Bullock taught us in *Miss Congeniality*. Drat! What was it? I can't remember so strike a ninja pose instead.

"What are you doing?"

I whirl around, throwing my leg out to kick my attacker. Except that move doesn't work. To avoid taking out the stained-glass lamp balanced precariously on a cloth ottoman, I pull my leg back in, like an Olympic figure skater. But my foot catches on the rug, and I land on my rear end.

And my tailbone shatters into a million pieces. At least, I assume it does, judging by the way fire climbs up my spine.

No time to mourn the loss of my ability to sit properly. I grip my purse like a weapon. All the junk in there will finally be put to good use. "Who's there?"

An impossibly tall form steps from the shadows and materializes into Chance.

This is a horror movie.

An impish grin stretches across his tanned face. "Do you always pretend to be James Bond when no one is looking?"

This guy's cracked. Anyone watching could clearly see I was a ninja. "For your information, I was a ninja. Ninjas sneak and strike when no one is watching." I move my purse to my side, but I don't take my hand off of it. I may still need it. "Besides, that move was clearly figure skating material."

"Well, I think you wrecked the curve." His annoyingly full lips—seriously, men should not have lips like that—morph from grin to smirk.

Grr. "Why don't you just coo 'toe pick' already."

"What?"

"*The Cutting Edge*." He stares at me blankly. "It's a movie." Nothing. He doesn't even blink. Maybe I should use one of those little laser lights that doctors use to check for signs of cognitive function.

Enough of this. "Why are you here, Chance?"

He strides forward and sticks out his hand. "Why are you unleashing your inner Zelda?"

I look at his hand, practically snarling at it. "There's a creature on top of the wardrobe." I stand up by myself and point to the last known location of the monster.

"Gremlins?"

"You're hilarious."

"Maybe it was a terrible, flesh-eating Morlock."

"Just stop."

"Or maybe it was your grandmother's cat."

My grandmother's...cat.

Oh, the shame. He's right. I don't even have to say the words for the foul taste to fill my mouth. "I suppose it *could* have been Miss Jeremiah."

You're wondering about the name, right? Well, Gram thought she was getting a boy cat, per the assurance of the sales clerk in the pet store. For a couple weeks, she called the cat Jeremiah. Turned out that when Gram took Jeremiah to the vet, *he* was really a *she*. So Gram just added "Miss" to her name and said the matter was settled.

I speak through clenched teeth, "Why. Are. You. Here?"

"To feed the cat. Check the store. Scare away varmints. Make sure the basement isn't flooded."

Varmints? What is this? A John Wayne movie? Ugh. "Well, I'm here now. Your services are no longer required."

"Really? Do you know where the cat food is?"

"Do I know where the cat food is? Are you kidding me? I used to live here!" Of all the nerve! What a cocky, twittering twit!

I brush past Chance, careful not to bump into his abs of steel lest I dislocate a shoulder. Flinging open the door that conceals the stairway from customers, I stomp up the stairs and burst into the kitchen. The kitchen, living room, laundry room/pantry, and a full bathroom are on the second floor. Five bedrooms and another full bathroom are on the third floor.

Turning left, I jaunt through the kitchen into the laundry room/pantry. My confident walk that resembles Alfalfa going to pick up Darla skids to a halt.

Uh oh.

Please, God, don't let him be behind me.

"Ahem."

Dandy.

"Give me a minute. I'll remember."

Closing my eyes, I pretend that I'm like the Robert Downey Jr. version of Sherlock Holmes. I imagine the counters, cabinets, and shelves on the right—the pantry side. Then I imagine the left side with the washer and dryer, the baskets of laundry stacked next to them, and the overhead shelves running the length of the wall.

My eyes pop open.

Giddy, I saunter to the pantry side and open the third door from the left of the lower cabinets. It's not right in front like it used to be. I reach in farther, going so far that I think my arm has been eaten by the cabinet like some sort of sacrificial offering. In other words, I may be stuck in here.

"Apryl."

I attempt to look at him from my odd vantage point. All I see are legs. Legs that are so annoyingly toned that you can see the man-calves through the coarse structure of blue jeans. I brace my hand against the back wall of the cabinet so that I can attempt to move from my knees to a crouched position.

Did something just touch my hand? I shiver.

Lord, please keep the spiders at bay. Away from my hand. And from crawling up my sleeve. And into my hair.

Pop.

I look up again. Chance has popped the lid off a metal can of nasty cat food. Miss Jeremiah bolts into the room and starts rubbing against his legs. He dumps it into a little bowl in the corner. Miss Jeremiah devours it like she hasn't eaten in days.

Has she eaten the last few days?

"I've been feeding her," Chance says in response to my unasked question.

"Where did you find the food?"

"Your grandmother moved all the cat stuff over here." He points to the last cabinet on the right.

"Oh." Something occurs to me. "How have you been getting in to feed her? Do you have a key?"

"Yes, she gave me one a while ago."

"Why?"

"Because of the rental agreement. We have an arrangement."

Of course they do. Nine years ago, shortly after our miserable fifteenth birthday party, Gram gave us some big news. She was having some money problems; however, she never told us the details, us being kids and all. Her solution to this problem: rent out the guest house and barn on the southern tip of her property to one Mr. William McFarland. Chance and his father moved in, and Mr. McFarland renovated the barn into an auto mechanic shop, McFarland and Son Auto Repair.

And life got so much more complicated.

About three years ago, Mr. McFarland retired and moved out, and Chance took over the business.

Not that I was paying attention to what happened with him or anything.

"Like a handyman?"

"In a way. Only I'm supposed to help with things pertaining to the business too, like moving and delivering heavy furniture." Instead of hanging free around his face like the last time I saw him, Chance has half of his chin-length, blonde hair pulled back. His hair was never this long in school. It's...um, different. In a distracting, surfer boy way.

The news that Chance and Gram have some fancy addendums in their rental agreement doesn't surprise me. However, I'm too worn out to deal with this particular nugget of information right now. I make a mental note to tell Courtney. This seems like something that would be right up her alley.

"Well, okay then," I say, sarcasm dripping off of me like I bathed in it...which I kind of do. I know what you're thinking, but it's a one-of-a-kind fragrance made by yours truly. It's not sold at Bath and Body Works. Sorry. "Courtney and I will check it out to make sure it's all official. Start recording what you do and when you do it. You know, for the books. Until then, you can leave."

"Talking to you is like getting one giant hug." He rolls his eyes. His eyes are...weird. We're going to go with weird. At the moment, they're the color of green fields surrounded by the golden haze of a setting sun. Yesterday, they were a lighter green, almost like moss.

"Only if you like to hug boa constrictors."

"Well, I've never been a fan of snakes," he drawls like a Midwestern boy.

I catch his underlying meaning. Oh, right. Like I'm the snake in this room.

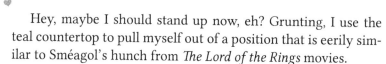

Hey, maybe I should stand up now, eh? Grunting, I use the teal countertop to pull myself out of a position that is eerily similar to Sméagol's hunch from *The Lord of the Rings* movies.

I wipe my palms on my thighs. Why does being around him still do this to me? "Bye."

He holds up his hands. "Hey, it's not like I wanted to be here." He turns around and clambers down the stairs. I can hear him muttering, "Crazy, ungrateful woman," the whole way down. The door slams shut a moment later.

Good. Because it's just too hard to be near you.

After Chance left, I cleaned up the house a little. Dusted some of the antiques and furniture. Changed the litter box—yuck. Washed the dirty dishes hogging the sink and kitchen counter. I called Courtney to check on Gram, who was insisting that I stay the night at the house. News that made me delirious with joy. Then, because I'm nosy, I decided to take a look at Gram's ledger. Study her profit and loss statements. And I found...

Nothing. But mostly because I can't read a ledger to save my life.

However, if the "Past Due" notices stacked up nice and neat next to the ledger are any indication, Gram's hemorrhaging money.

I stare blankly at the Bible app on my phone.

My heart feels heavy.

Gram has a broken hip. She had major surgery. I'm physically being thrown into Chance at every turn. And now I find out that Gram's business is going under. Again.

"What do we do, God? I'm really asking here. What do we do?"

A dog howls. Not exactly the answer I wanted.

The white screen of the phone is like a bold statement. A light in the darkness. The messenger of hope. I'd been reading through Romans in my Bible reading. And what verse slaps me in the face today when I open the Bible app?

That's right. The twenty-eighth verse of Romans chapter eight. It was even the verse of the day, for crying out loud!

"And we know that for those who love God all things work together for good, for those who are called according to his purpose."

Can I tell you something that might make me the worst Christian in the world?

I'm not sure I believe this verse.

So what do you do when you're not sure God is in control?

Country music blared from the radio. Blake Shelton sang about love and God as Chance closed the hood of the 1958 Ford Pickup truck he was restoring. Country music had been his guilty pleasure for as long as he could remember. Not that there was anything wrong with it, but most of his old friends didn't associate their mountainous, "hillbilly" lifestyle with the ballads of country crooners.

He wiped his greasy hands on his jeans—they were probably already stained beyond repair—before rubbing the back of his neck. A groan escaped as he caught sight of the antique clock—a gift from Charlotte Burns—that hung over the door.

Time could not pass any slower.

It was only ten o'clock on a Friday night.

The trouble with being a nice guy is that nice guys don't have any fun.

He used to *have fun.* Perhaps too much fun. Then when Chance totaled his previously priceless 1958 Ford Pickup while driving home one night, God called to him. He'd been out all night four wheeling with some buddies before driving home at dawn. His eyes slipped closed for a second then jerked open to see a moose in the middle of the road. Chance had swerved, gone off the road, and ended up wrapped around a pine tree.

He'd woken up in the hospital without a scratch.

Sometimes he wished he had gotten a few broken bones or a serious injury. Even just a scratch would have done the trick. Something—anything—that he could see and feel to remind him in moments like this why he left his old lifestyle and rededicated his life to God. Chance glanced at the half-assembled vehicle in front of him. He supposed that was why he continued to build this new truck. To remind himself.

A couple hazy memories from the accident had come back eventually...and one clear memory at 3:17 a.m. in the hospital. God's ironic way of giving him a scratch to remember.

Chance grabbed his soda from the windowsill. He unscrewed the cap and savored a long sip of Coke, relishing the way the liquid burned and then soothed his dry throat. He finished the bottle and went to throw it in the trash when a light across the yard caught his eye. Since his garage windows faced the northern side of the one-hundred-acre property, he could just see the light in the big house that could rival Bruce Wayne's estate.

Yeah, he'd always liked Batman.

Must mean Angry Apryl—the nickname he'd given her when they first met—was still awake. And possibly staying for a while.

He had known Apryl and Courtney since high school. While Courtney had been a cheerleader, student body president, salutatorian kind of girl, Apryl had been withdrawn and almost depressing. She had never been emo or goth, but she had never mirrored her sister's peppy enthusiasm for life.

She was, however, excellent at debate.

Chance had enjoyed a verbal sparring match with her so much that he would purposely take the opposing side in school, no matter what he thought about the subject. He'd wound up in some interesting debates. The debate about why chick flicks appealed to guys as well as girls had been particularly aggravating because he'd ended up watching *A Walk to Remember*, *While You Were Sleeping*, and about a dozen other girly movies just to make his point. He'd also lost.

A rueful smile tugged at his lips. One thing was for sure—whenever Apryl was around, conversation was never dull.

He tossed the empty soda bottle into the can across the room. Since it looked like she'd be around awhile, he might as well have some fun. Chance could always get a rise out of her. Okay, new plan.

"Let the games begin."

Chapter Three

"**H**ave you seen this thing?"

I grab the eighteenth-century bowl out of Izze's hands.

"Yes."

"What is it?" Her dark brown eyes light up. She's expecting it to be something dainty and delicate.

"It's a bleeding bowl."

I can't help but laugh at the look of horror that covers her face.

"Eww!"

I roll my eyes. "Well, where did you think the blood went when doctors bled their patients? Into a bowl. Otherwise, there'd be a huge mess getting in the way of what was really important. You know, saving a life."

"I prefer not to think about it." Izze wrinkles her nose.

Courtney and Miles come out of the office. Miles scribbles into a notebook as Courtney talks fast enough to rival an auctioneer.

My sister called in the cavalry.

Courtney didn't get home—I mean, she didn't arrive at Gram's house—until after midnight. She said that Gram was fine and had ordered her to go rest. When I told her about the ledger, she insisted we look at everything before going to sleep.

As you can see, we're cut from the same nosy cloth. Well, we are twins. We're bound to have *some* things in common.

After three hours of pouring over the ledgers, the rental agreement, and overdue bills, Courtney declared that she would call Miles in the morning. Surely he would know what to do. I'm not being dramatic. She said those actual words.

And while I know Miles is a genius in his own right and skilled at helping failing businesses, judging from the look on his face, I'm not sure there's anything he can do to help Gram. His glasses seem to magnify the regret in his blue eyes.

Courtney's words from the night before echo in my mind. *"We cannot let Gram's business fall apart. It's unacceptable and I will not accept anything less than the best."*

Well, dear sister, sometimes things don't go according to your perfect plan. There will be roadblocks and flat tires. Sometimes things fall apart and break. You of all people should know that. But Courtney has never been one to settle when life throws rotten tomatoes. Perhaps that's the reason our lives are on such different tracks.

Izze grabs a teapot off a bookshelf, pulling my attention away from them. "This is adorable!"

Courtney says something to Miles, but I can't hear her. I force a smile and return my attention to Izze. "Yeah, that's one of my favorites." It's over, Courtney. Let it rest.

Miles tugs at his shirt collar. "Without full access to her finances, I don't have a complete picture. If you can get her to agree, I can try to help." Miles clears his throat. "Otherwise, I don't know what I can do."

See? Miles agrees.

What? You have to read between the lines to see what he's really saying. But trust me. He agrees.

"Do you think this would go with my wedding theme?"

Izze is still holding onto the teapot with the pale pink roses. "Yeah, I think so. It works with the shabby-chic theme. There's a matching vase too."

Izze squeals. "Where is it?"

I sidestep to the left and squeeze behind a bookshelf. Stretching on my tiptoes over a wingback chair, I pull open the top draw of a standing dresser. Holding up the aforementioned vase, I say, "Right here."

Izze's mouth hangs open in amazement. "How did you find that so quickly?"

"Gram is quirky. She has weird organizational habits. Plus, I put it there."

"This place is worse than Mrs. Kim's Antiques in *Gilmore Girls*," Izze mutters.

"I'd say it's about the same."

Izze points up. "Mrs. Kim didn't have a ceiling full of chandeliers."

I grin for real this time. Gram has a weakness for chandeliers. About six years ago she was convinced they were going to sell like hot cakes. She invested in sixty rewired antique chandeliers and had them all professionally hung from the ceiling. "To be showcased," she had said. Fifty-four of them are still hanging from the ceiling.

I shrug. "I'll give you that."

Izze marches over to her fiancé. "I'm buying these for the wedding."

Miles frowns. "Why?"

"Because it's adorable and works with our theme."

Courtney nods her head, mahogany waves dancing to the beat. "It does."

"I really think you should stop telling people this is *our* theme. It's all you," Miles says.

Izze huffs. "You said, 'Baby, whatever you'd like.'"

"Because my theme is making my future wife happy," he growls, but the mirth in his eyes says he's just teasing her.

"Well, these will make me very happy. They're going on our table."

"Wonderful."

Courtney reaches for the vase still in my hand. "I never thought of using these for something like a wedding. That will look so pretty."

"You should put chips in it," I add.

Courtney scoffs. "Why on earth would she do that."

"Because it's not a party without chips." I grin at Izze. "Especially Ruffles. Original flavor, of course. We wouldn't want to stain our dresses." I wiggle my fingers for emphasis.

"Of course." She grins in return.

I tilt my head, and the blue-black tresses that I should have pulled back into a ponytail fall into my face. Swiping the offenders behind my left ear, I say, "You know, I bet Gram wouldn't mind if you borrowed them for the wedding."

"Say what now?" Miles lifts an eyebrow.

"I said you guys could probably borrow some stuff to help decorate for your wedding. It will really give it that vintage feeling."

"That's a great idea!" Courtney exclaims. I can tell by the sparkle in her eyes that she really does think it's a good idea.

Wow. My sister agreed with me. Mark this day in history!

Izze tucks a stray curl behind her ear. "That doesn't seem fair. You could lose a potential sale if it's not here when you're open for business."

"Possibly. We're not exactly getting a stampede of shoppers right now."

Izze raises a beautifully thick eyebrow. She and Miles really have that eyebrow thing down. "How do you know that?"

"Because we're open right now. Been open all day." I point at the door where the OPEN sign faces the great outdoors.

She gasps.

Courtney winces. Another nail in the truth coffin.

"And because I've seen the current ledger, I know when the last sale occurred."

Miles strokes his chin. Almost like he's thinking.

My cheeks flame from embarrassment. I can't even run Gram's business for her. I know it's not my fault, but guilt scrambles in my stomach regardless.

"Uh..." I clear my throat. Like a lady, of course. "Gram's mentioned a few times that she's loaned pieces out to friends for events. I don't think it'd be a big deal."

Izze opens her mouth to reply, but Miles holds up a hand.

"I have an idea."

Gram stares at us for two minutes without blinking.

Then she coughs.

I sneeze.

Courtney shifts in her seat, breaking Gram's concentration.

Gram refocuses and proceeds to stare at us again.

For the record, this is not my idea. I tried to talk them out of it, but once Miles announced his brilliant idea—and yes, I did say that sarcastically—there was no stopping them.

Gram opens her mouth. Shuts it. Oh, great. More staring. I hate awkward silences. Courtney loves them. Loves to stare someone down until they break. Must be the future lawyer in her.

"What?" Gram finally asks. There's a hallelujah chorus in my head because the silence is over. Then I realize something.

I cough and glance at Courtney. Gram didn't dismiss the idea outright, which means she's considering it. Based on the gleam of victory in Courtney's cornflower blue eyes, she knows she has a shot.

Yes, she. I still think this is all madness.

My stomach turns and flipflops, and I don't think it's due to the stench of antiseptic. I rub my locket, longing for its familiar comfort. Alas, even the locket seems to be failing me now.

Courtney takes a deep breath. "So, first off, we should say that we are sorry for going through your ledgers. We saw the overdue bills and got worried."

Seriously, can you see the lawyer in the way she presents things?

"Well, that was wrong." Gram nails us each with a look that sets me squirming in the hard, plastic chair tucked into the corner of her hospital room. Funny how one well-placed look can make you feel like a little kid again, isn't it?

Gram continues, "Please explain your friend's idea again, though. He's a business manager?"

"Sort of. He specializes in marketing and finances," I say.

Gram just nods. Has my strong, capable grandmother always looked so...fragile? The full impact of what she's been through hits me all over again. I just can't even...wow. Sitting in a hospital bed, surrounded by beeping monitors and IVs and hospital food, wearing one of those dreadful, open-back gowns would take a toll on anyone, but the feisty spark in Gram's eye is gone. /That terrifies me more than anything else.

Courtney leans forward in the chair. Her right leg rests on her left one and it's bouncing. She's excited. "Miles thinks that we should make the switch from an antique shop to a wedding venue decorating service."

We? Uh-oh.

"Why?" Gram's blue eyes crinkle like she's trying to figure out where the piece that looks like every other piece in the jigsaw puzzle goes.

"Well, you yourself have said that tons of people ask to borrow your furniture for events," Courtney points out.

She nods. "Some have even offered to pay me. But I'm too old to be doing something like that."

"But we aren't!" Courtney exclaims as she waves her hand back and forth between us.

Little rocks form in the bottom of my stomach.

"No, I suppose you're not," Gram says.

"It would be perfect, Gram. Wedding venue decorators are in high demand, and you have so much variety in the shop."

Oh, sister. Do you like the subtle sucking up?

"Why just weddings?" Gram shifts her gaze from Courtney to me.

Courtney kicks my foot at just the right angle so that Gram can't see from where she's sitting in bed with five pillows propping her up. Courtney gives me a look that says, *Contribute to the conversation!*

"Well," I squeak. Ugh. I clear my throat. "Well, Miles suggested just weddings for now because he and Izze have a lot of wedding-related business contacts. But you, um, we could always decorate for other events too. Maybe. In the future."

Courtney adds, "Miles thinks weddings are the way to go."

"I like the idea of decorating for weddings," Gram says. Her eyes look to be lost in deep, faraway thoughts.

The little rocks in my stomach clump together to form one big rock.

Because the spark in Gram's eye is back.

Courtney bounces in her chair again. "And the best part is that we already have two weddings tentatively booked! One of Izze's coworkers is getting married in three weeks and was in full panic-mode after some of her other arrangements fell through. I took the liberty of having her look around, and she really liked what she saw. Then there's Izze's wedding the following month. If you agree to the idea then Miles can post an ad in the local newspapers."

"And this is really something you want to do? I won't be able to help you girls. To be honest, I was seriously considering closing the shop and selling the property. Maybe moving somewhere closer to you two. I thought this was God's way of backing up my thought process. The doctor told me that I'll be here another week at least and that I have many long months of recovery ahead of me. At this point, I would be turning the business and management over to you two," Gram says, studying us.

"Yes, we absolutely want to do this. Apryl and I talked about it for a long time." Courtney nods.

I muffle a scoff with a cough. She talked. I listened and was forbidden from disagreeing with her. Thankfully, neither one seems to notice my blunder.

Gram taps her saggy chin with her pale, wrinkled hand. "What about your schooling, Courtney? You won't be available to help very much during your exams. And what about when you become a lawyer?"

"I've got a new plan and it's perfect!" Courtney smiles. Trust her to already have a ten-year plan in place, one that she hasn't bothered to share with me. "I'm already going to school for business law. Eventually, I was thinking I could work as the lawyer for small businesses, including ours, in a small law firm. While it's true that I'll be busy in the coming months, I'll help whenever I possibly can. But I know that Apryl is more than capable of doing this."

I blink. I'm sure I look like an owl, just blinking away. I can't seem to stop it.

My sister just called me capable. I'm not sure she's ever said that. *Ever.* At the risk of sounding like Taylor Swift, never, ever, ever.

"What about your job, Apryl?"

"I took a long term-leave of absence." Courtney made me. "I explained that you had an accident, and that you needed help running the family business." Although, does it count as a family business when you do a complete revamp of said business? I guess it's still run by the family.

Gram studies me. "Were they okay with that?"

"Yes, they even said that I would always have a job there no matter how much time has passed." The ladies at Pin It Up Salon are amazing, especially the owner, Jayden. I will miss them. But not as much as I thought I would.

Surprising...

I'm not going to think about that particular detail right now.

"See! Everything's perfect!"

Gram ignores Courtney and gives me her truth-serum, no-nonsense, raised-eyebrows, sharp-as-a-hawk look. "Is this really what you want?"

I don't have the heart to tell her no. To smoother that spark. To devastate Courtney. Instead, I just nod my head. My throat swells from emotion; I'm just not sure it's positive emotion. But either I'm that good at lying (Sorry, God!), or they don't see my palpitating heart.

Courtney squeals and Gram takes charge. She starts telling Courtney things that she needs to do. Courtney, true to form, pulls a yellow legal pad out of her purse and starts writing down Gram's instructions.

I take a few deep breaths as I make a mental list of why this is a good idea.

I can do this.

I am capable.

The spark in Gram's eye grows even brighter.

I owe her everything.

Oh, this couldn't get any worse.

I spot Chance through the kitchen window walking toward the house.

Revised statement. *Now* it couldn't get any worse.

I watch him for a moment. His purposeful stride reminds me of the one-track focus of the giant ant I crushed with my heel earlier. Poor guy didn't see it coming.

I don't want to do this. As much as I dislike Chance and his family, this feels so manipulative.

Ugh. Even thinking the word leaves a bad taste in my mouth.

I want to hyperventilate, eat my body weight in salt and vinegar chips, and scream into my pillow. "I would rather do anything than this—even exercise," I whisper to no one. Or maybe to God.

What kind of idiot schedules something without any way to do it? This girl. And her sister. When we got home—er, back to Gram's house—Courtney looked at her schedule, shrieked, and said there was no way she'd be able to help with the first wedding.

In case you're keeping track, I have no way to transport the pieces to the wedding venue. I have no one to help me unload and set up the ceremony and reception space in an undisclosed amount of time. And because this bride just loved the idea of a chandelier, Courtney said we could absolutely hang some up in the reception tent. Which means I have no one who can help me rig a working chandelier because it just so happens that I am not an electrician.

But Chance is.

It was in that moment that my fate was sealed even though I spent the last two days trying to think of other options. But I knew what I needed to do. The only thing I *could* do.

I remember reading Bible story after Bible story as a kid where God would sweep in and save the day. Rams in bushes. Giant boats. Blind eyes that could see after you spit into them. Situations that were miraculously turned around at the drop of Heaven crackers.

But even then, I doubted Him. I doubted that He would help me.

"Well, God. Now's the time to prove me wrong. I need some sweeping."

The kitchen door croaks like a dying toad. "Well, hello, Angry Apryl."

Egyptian rats, man. "You send me this?" I mutter.

"What was that, darling?"

"It's about time you got here, grease monkey."

"Something wrong?" He doesn't address that he's an hour late, regardless of the fact that he said he would be available when I called him two days ago. Instead, his greenish-brown eyes travel over my face in a lazy pattern. My heart pitters-patters like the racoons that live in the attic.

Betrayal! I say to my heart.

Can you blame me? she says. *He looks like a hero from Greek mythology. Men should not be that yummy.*

Seriously, we cannot do this again!

"I'm fine," I say to him.

"Well, you know what they say 'fine' really means." Chance strolls into the kitchen, pulls a chair out, and lowers his six-foot, one-inch frame into the neon-green chair.

Gram was a fan of the seventies.

I stalk across the room and slap my hand against the oak table. "I don't give a zucchini tush what it really means. You were supposed to be here an hour ago!"

"I had to get the rent check."

"Swell."

He pulls it out of his front pocket and lays it on the table. Flecks of blue-green lint cling to it. Gross.

Chance looks at me. Expectantly. Like I've forgotten something.

"What?" I bark.

"You're the one who wanted to make sure this was completely professional. 'For the books,' I believe you said. That means I need a receipt."

I growl. Like the Beast. Chance smiles like Gaston. Arrogant twit.

I stalk to the office downstairs, and Chance follows me. The ledger sits in the top draw on the right side of the desk. I pull it out and scribble a barely legible receipt.

Chance leans against the desk. "Remember the flooded toilet in the shop that Courtney couldn't handle yesterday? Should you pay me for that? You know, for the books. I acted in a handyman capacity."

How does Bruce Banner keep from becoming the rage-filled, psychotic Hulk? Yikes, mixing superhero fandoms. Not good.

"Oh, and there's a lightbulb in my workshop that's not work-ing. You should probably take a look at it."

"Are you serious?"

"You know. For the books." He smirks. He's enjoying this.

Breathe deep, Swamp Thing (the DC Comics version of Hulk).

"Why don't you just change the lightbulb?"

"Well, technically since I'm the renter..."

"It's in your contract with my grandmother. As is the flood-ed toilet. Under the Repairs and Maintenance clause." Thank you for boring me with the renter's agreement for almost three hours, Courtney. "It's part of the reason your rent is dirt cheap."

He steps close to me. "I thought it was my devilish good looks."

I look him up and down, ignoring the salsa dance my heart takes to performing. "Eh. I've seen better." I'm not sure where but it must be true. Surely somewhere on God's green earth a man more handsome than him lives. Or lived. I'd settle for a dead man.

That sounded weird. Ignore that.

I can smell his musty cologne. He spends all day with dirty cars and motor oil, which means he didn't come straight from the garage to the house. I didn't even hear his rumbly truck come or go. This means he was probably with someone else. Someone else with a normal-sounding car. The familiar disappointment threatens to gut-punch me, but I file the information into the recesses of my brain. I can't let it show.

"Right." He winks. "Just admit that you need me."

"My grandmother thought she needed an errand boy, yes. I need you about as much as I need warts on my foot."

"Flattery will get you everywhere."

"But if you still need help with that lightbulb, I'll send a child over to help you."

"It's okay. I know my way around an electrical socket."

Ah, just the opening I need. "Would you know how to wire, say, an electric chandelier?"

"Say what now?"

"The ceiling of chandeliers downstairs."

His eyebrow quirks. "Yes, I know the ceiling of which you speak."

"Say I need to make one—" Ahem, or three—"of them work. Would you be able to do that?" My heart continues to pound but for an entirely different reason now.

He studies me for a moment, his eyebrow raised and mouth twisted. Clearly he's a little concerned that I'm a few nuggets short of a McDonald's Happy Meal. "I suppose I could."

"You just suppose? What happened to the man who could do anything?" I'm purposely goading him now. But I must know for sure.

Both eyebrows are raised now. His green eyes convey that he's accepted my challenge. And he's determined to win. "I can do it."

"Good. Mark your calendar for the Saturday the twenty-ninth."

"What? Think again. I'm completely booked that day."

"You're completely booked three weeks in advance?"

Chance spreads his hands in front of him. "What can I say? People come to the best."

"You mean those old ladies who come to stare at your backside don't know that there's better mechanics in this town, let alone this state?"

"Don't pretend you haven't done the same thing."

I can't help but blush at the implication. Hopefully, he will think it's from rage. There's a reason he's called me "Angry Apryl" all these years. "If I'm watching you walk away, it's to determine if I can throw something hard at you and escape without being caught."

"You have a way with the compliments. Really. Makes a guy feel—"

"You can feel? I'm flabbergasted. Oh, you probably don't know what that word means."

He rolls his eyes. "I can't. Sorry. Well, sort of sorry. You know, I'm really not sorry at all." He starts for the door again.

That invisible hand squeezes my heart again. Time to pull the trigger.

"You have to help me." I keep my words calm, even, collected.

I am completely in control. Or at least pretending to be. "It's in the renter's agreement. Under the Rental Discounts clause."

Chance stops. Turns around. Glares. "What?" he asks through clenched teeth.

The artic temperature of his words hit me, and I step back. Wow. Ice, ice, baby. "You know exactly what I just said. You have to help me. Courtney and I spent hours going over the renter's agreement. Quite bizarre really, but you and I both know that this is nonnegotiable. In exchange for that joke of a rent check, you handle your own repairs and maintenance as well as the labor for Gram's repairs and maintenance. In addition, you are always available to help with any needs of Gram's business." Gram, bless her heart, made sure that the rental agreement legally covered everything lest someone insinuate something fishy with the arrangement.

It's so ironclad, Sheldon Cooper could have written it.

He scoffs. "Or what? Tell me, what will you do?"

I march up to him and poke him right in the middle of that brick wall masquerading as his chest. "Or I'll evict you. You'll have to find a new place to set up shop. When you lose your business, you'll remember this conversation. Then you'll think, 'Gee. What if I had helped Apryl instead of acting like a narcissistic he-man? Maybe I wouldn't have gone bankrupt and ruined my father's legacy. Oh, golly.'"

That annoying tan on his high cheekbones fades. Because he knows I'm right. Even if Gram hadn't put us in charge of everything, she put our names on the rental agreements in case something ever happened to her. Legally I'm able to terminate the agreement with little notice.

Chance crosses his muscled arms and clutches his forearms like he's trying to keep himself from punching the wall.

Maybe I should just level with him. "I need help." My voice breaks a little. I hate having to ask for help. Again. Least of all from him. "We're transitioning from an antiques shop to a wedding venue decorator."

"A what?"

"We're going to decorate weddings with the antiques from the shop. It's our last hope." Oh, I sound like Princess Leia. "Please. I just need you to help me transport, install, set up, and tear down. That's all."

"Oh, that's all," Chance growls lowly, like a wolf about to strike. So much for being nice and honest with him. Okay, honest.

"Yes," I say forcefully. "That's all. Whenever we have a wedding."

"I guess it never occurred to you not to take a job you were ill equipped to perform." Sarcasm and disdain drip from his every word.

Actually, it occurred to me about a million times. But I don't tell him that.

It's a stare-down, folks. I hold his gaze, trying to look tough, but in reality, I'm pleading with my own eyes. His gaze softens just a bit.

"Apryl," he starts again, but I cut him off. I can't let him say no.

"Look, I'll make your options really simple. If you won't help, consider this your eviction notice."

The wolf growls again. He could rival Jacob from *Twilight*. His eyes—completely green now—burn and shoot bits of molten emerald at me. I swear I can hear the blood pumping through the veins in his neck.

"For how long?" he finally asks.

"For as long as I need you."

"All right," he huffs.

"Okay, well... Thanks?" What am I supposed to say? I just forced him into this. But my mom always said to say "please" and "thank you." Saying "please" didn't get me anywhere, but I can at least say "thank you."

"Don't bother thanking me. I'm not helping you out of the goodness of my heart."

So much for that. I won't make that mistake again. "Then goodbye."

He sizes me up again. "Well, I was right about one thing."

I frown. Right about what?

Chance scoffed. "I always knew you needed me."

It's almost like he knew just how badly those words would sting.

Chapter Four

Apryl was having a meltdown.

A sigh escaped Courtney's lips. Why would being here, helping Gram, be so hard for her? Courtney had wracked her brain for hours trying to figure it out, and so far, she was emptier than Izze's coffee pot.

Okay, so Apryl had always maintained this façade of running away.

But why?

One thing was for certain—Courtney definitely poked the dragon when she asked if Chance had agreed to help.

"Agreed?" Apryl had shouted. "Yeah, he agreed!" Then she had stomped up the stairs. Courtney hadn't seen her again until this morning. And her frosty demeanor had not thawed.

Luckily, hot chocolate sounded good to Courtney.

Courtney strolled through the sliding doorway at the hospital. She didn't like leaving Gram alone all day, so she tried to stop by whenever possible. A quick update every morning. Five minutes before class. Between classes, if possible. On the way home at the end of the day. To share a cheeseburger that the nurse Apryl affectionately named Ursula had tried to confiscate.

Okay, so it was a wonder Gram hadn't banned her from the hospital.

Today Courtney planned to conduct a marathon study session in Gram's hospital room. She figured a hospital was as good a place as any to study. Certainly, as boring.

She looked around the emergency room. It was, ahem, a little early—six o'clock in the morning to be exact—so the main entrances weren't opened yet, meaning Courtney had to enter through the emergency room. It was a little busy, so she sat down and waited to ask the nurse to buzz her though the door that led to the main part of the hospital.

Her phone buzzed.

> *Hey, babe! I miss you, too! Today is a little crazy.*
> *Can we meet tomorrow for dinner? It may or*
> *may not include your favorite cheesecake.*

Courtney smiled then bit her lip. He was canceling—again. Dallas seemed to cancel plans at least once a week, but he always made up for it the next day. It didn't bother her—at least, it hadn't at first. Now, though, it was beginning to. Mostly because she never knew why he was canceling. It was starting to seem a little suspicious.

Or maybe that was just her inner *I've-watched-too-many-television-dramas-with-cheating-men* paranoia talking. He was studying to be a lawyer too—that's how they met. She should cut him some slack.

Right?

Right.

A loud bang that reminded Courtney of glasses shattering and silverware crashing drew her attention to the doors the hospital staff ushered emergency patients through. A woman came running out of the doors. An IV pole had been knocked over and was being dragged behind her.—Ouch! Courtney ached just looking at the poor woman.

"Marta, come back! Please let the doctors help."

"No!" yelled the woman Courtney presumed was Marta. She shook with sobs and terror as another woman put her arms around her. Courtney's heart broke a little.

"Marta, it's okay. Joan and I will be here the entire time."

Courtney froze. That voice. She would know that voice anywhere. It was the voice she had fallen asleep thinking about every night for almost a year.

She searched the crowed room until she spotted him leading the hysterical woman back through the double doors.

Dallas.

"Hey, earth to Courtney? Aren't you always the one telling me to focus?"

Courtney blinks. "Sorry."

My sister is being very weird, and I can't take it anymore.

My eyes narrow as I study her. "What's your damage?" I lean forward at the kitchen table where we had been discussing the list of items to bring to the wedding for Izze's coworker, who shall henceforth be referred to by her Christian name, Roxanne.

"Nothing. Just drop it."

"Are you having doubts?"

Her startled eyes shoot up to me. They even look a bit guilty. "Wh—What do you mean?"

"Are you having doubts about what we're trying to do with the shop and for Gram? Because it's a lot. Anyone would understand." I know I certainly do. My heart flutters. Am I hopeful? Nervous? Disappointed? Will this craziness come to an end?

I don't understand myself anymore.

"No," Courtney emphasizes. "I'm not worried about that at all. This—" She waves her hands around the room—"is a good thing."

More heart flutters as disappointment and happiness dance within me. How is that even possible? "Then what's the issue? You've been moping for the last two days. Out with it. You clearly need to talk."

Courtney sighs.

I tap my index finger on the table.

This is why I wish I could read minds.

"Okay, I'll talk." Courtney looks around as if fearing the walls can hear her. She leans forward and lowers her voice. "You know how I was at the hospital the other day?"

I whisper-hiss, "Agent Burns, use the proper code!"

Courtney glares. "Apryl, be serious."

"You be serious! There is no one here but us. Talk in a normal voice!"

"I saw Dallas at the hospital!"

"Your secret boyfriend? Is he okay?" Yes, Courtney's secret

boyfriend. She's been dating him for almost a year, and no one has met him yet. Which is just ridiculous.

Not that I'm bitter about that or anything.

"Yeah. I mean, I think so."

"What's that supposed to mean?"

"I've been avoiding him."

"Courtney! What if he's hurt or sick? Don't you think he deserves the support of his secret girlfriend?" I can't quite help the sarcastic emphasis on the word "secret."

"He wasn't…It's just…I think he lied to me…about everything."

"Okay," I say slowly. "That is a little mind boggling. But maybe you should just talk to him about it. Maybe there's a reasonable explanation…" I wave my hands around, mimicking her. "…for everything."

"I don't know what to say!" She moans and smashes her head into the tabletop.

"How about, 'Hey, dude, what's going on?' What *is* going on? You never actually said."

"I was starting to think he was cheating on me," she says quietly.

The words hurt my heart. As much as my sister drives me crazy, I would never wish that on her. I would probably Carrie Underwood the car of any guy who would dare do that to my sister.

"But I'm not sure that this is any better," she says, huffing.

"Uh, why?"

"Because he's been lying to me for months! Why hasn't he explained this…whatever this is?" Courtney throws her hands out in exasperation.

"I don't know, especially because I don't know what you saw, but there's no excuse for lying. A lie is a lie. But you guys have been together for a while. Talk to him. Don't just shut him out."

She's silent for a long time. "Yeah, you're right."

"Thanks." Ah, fuzzy feeling in my heart, I like you.

"I guess it was bound to happen eventually."

I pat her hand and get up. "Nice moment over."

My favorite place in the world.

The willow grove.

I'm sitting in a tree in the middle of the grove. This is my spot. It's probably the best tree of the lot and absolutely perfect for climbing. I feel like I'm in a fairy world up here. In fact, the branch I'm sitting on has a gnarly looking knot where I used to make the perfect fairy house when I was little.

The earthy scent of moss fills my lungs. That it's eleven thirty at night and inky black doesn't detract from the beauty of this sacred place. The moon casts an iridescent glow on the pale green leaves of the willow trees, lighting them up like the lights of the fairy village I used to dream about as a child.

I also used to dream about being kissed out here. Never happened, but it's such a romantic spot. Seemed like the perfect place for a first kiss. Mine, however, was from Allen Reinhart, my boyfriend of two weeks, next to the trash can in the freshman hallway. We were busted by the hall monitor and given detention. He broke up with me the next day with a note in detention. For which we were given another week's detention.

My love life lacks a lot of love.

Twigs crunch nearby.

Suddenly visions of murderers fill my head. Courtney watches way too many cop shows, and she has clearly filled my head with paranoia.

The crunching stops directly underneath me.

"Well, God," a deep voice says, "I'm not doing too good."

Chance. Chance is out here. Underneath my tree. Praying.

The fifteen-year-old girl inside of me squeals. I mentally slap a hand over her mouth.

"I'm angry. I'm tired. I feel beaten down. I want to forget everything that's happening right now so badly that it scares me. And probably worst of all, I want my old life back."

I know he's angry and complaining to God, but the way he's talking to God, like God is right there next to him, makes me really jealous. I've been a Christian most of my life, and I have never felt that way.

I lean forward a little.

What? Oh, don't look at me like that. It's not like I can help eavesdropping.

"Help me, God."

He says those three words made up of nine little letters in such a quiet voice that I have to lean forward even more.

Which results in me slipping from my precarious perch.

"Ahhh!"

Branches scrape my arms as legs as I fall. A chunk of hair catches on one, but it's not enough to stop my cascade through the leaves. My scalp burns where there once was hair, and I prepare myself for the second shattering of my tailbone.

Strong arms catch me.

But not my dignity. My dignity crashes to the ground like Humpty Dumpty, never to be put back together again.

"What are you doing?"

I realize my face is buried in his neck.

Oh. Man.

"Uh. Uh. Uh." I can't stop stuttering. Where are my words? Of all the times for me to be struck mute, now is not the time!

"Apryl?" Concern edges onto Chance's expression, pushing the anger right off his face.

My mouth hangs open. Maybe I am injured?

Speak! I scream at myself. *Nothing you could possibly say would make this situation any worse!*

"You smell good."

Surprise flashes over his face.

And apparently, I was wrong. So very wrong.

"Thanks," Chance says, graciously ignoring what he can of my social blunder,—for now. I fully expect him to bring it up very, very soon. "Mind telling me what you were doing eavesdropping in a tree in the middle of the night?"

"I wouldn't say it's the middle of the night. Say someone sleeps eight hours a night, and they don't go to sleep until ten o'clock at night, then the middle of the night for the average person is two in the morning. Not eleven thirty." Ah, Rambling, my long-lost friend, we meet again.

Now he glares at me.

"I'm sorry, Chance. I honestly wasn't trying to listen to you. I used to spend a lot of time here before I moved out. It's my spot. I love it here. I would come out here to think and uh, pray too. I needed some of that tonight due to all of the craziness, and I couldn't sleep. I wasn't trying to intrude. Some might say you were intruding on me, but I wouldn't say that! Because you had no idea that I was out here. Courtney would probably say that. And I did not mean to sniff your neck. That was weird. And I'm sorry. Again." That was a lot of hot air. I try to replace it, sucking in as much of the cool spring air as my lungs will allow.

"Wow," he says slowly. "I'm not sure I've ever heard you talk like that."

"Like what?"

"All breathy."

"I'm sorry," I say again.

"I'll live. Will you?"

I touch my burning scalp with great care. "My dignity won't, but the rest of me will. Thanks to you."

"You're welcome." He flashes his signature smirk.

"Uh, do you think you can put me down now?"

"I thought girls liked to be held by strong men who smelled good." Chance wiggles his eyebrows but sets my feet on the ground.

I stick my index finger towards his moonlit face. "We will not speak of that ever, ever again."

He smirks. "I always knew you liked me."

"You're so full of yourself."

"I saved your life, and you repay me with insults?"

"You and I both know that that is not an insult. If I wanted to insult you, I'd insult you." I brush twigs and leaves from my clothes.

"Now that sounds like Angry April." Chance reaches out and untangles something from my hair.

My heart nearly stops with the realization that his hands are in my hair. "What are you doing?" Am I breathless? No, not breathless. I just had a near-death experience. I'm recovering. So, okay, maybe a little breathless, but an acceptable breathless.

Chance presents a small branch with six leaves to me. "You

should save that. Use it to show the world that you fought gravity with a tree. And lost."

"Thanks. How very philosophical of you," I mumble, praying he doesn't see the red tint to my cheeks.

"Well, I'm sorry for startling you. I don't like you a lot right now, but I wouldn't try to kill you." He holds up three fingers representing the Boy Scout hand sign. "Scout's honor."

Should I tell him what really happened? No, I think I've been humbled enough for one night.

God, I was humble enough. We didn't need this incident to occur.

"You were never a Boy Scout," I say instead.

"You don't know that."

I raise an eyebrow at him. "Yeah, I do. We practically grew up together."

"Yes, those were fun times. Almost as fun as now." He rolls his eyes. "Although, telling everyone that you said I smell good will definitely be fun." A wicked grin lights up his annoyingly handsome face.

"No! You can't tell anyone!"

"Oh, I'm going to tell everyone." The grin stretches even further across his face.

"Please don't," I plead. "That's cruel."

"Almost as cruel as you threatening my home, livelihood, and everything my father has worked towards because you need a traveling handyman?" Oh, ouch. His pointed look burns almost as much as my scalp.

"You know the situation," I say quietly. "But for the record, I am sorry."

Chance scoffs.

"Really." I look into his golden green eyes. How can they still be so bright when it's so dark outside? "I am sorry. I didn't want to do that to you, but I really was desperate. Gram and Courtney are convinced this will work. And I owe Gram everything. I have to do this for her. That's the truth."

Here's the thing about being vulnerable—it's awful. Seriously awful. It's the emotional equivalent of walking onto a battlefield with no armor and the knowledge that the archers are three-time Olympic gold medalists.

And this is the most vulnerable I've been in a long time.

Chance clears his throat and looks at the ground. "I guess I can understand that. I know a thing or two about the weight of family loyalties."

I blink. I was not expecting that. I was expecting an emotional arrow to hit my heart. "Thanks."

"I still don't like it."

I frown. His voice drips with extra caustic venom, like he realizes he made himself vulnerable to my poison-dipped arrows and he needs to defend himself with a hard deflection.

Which is why I now sound a little harsh. "I understand. I'm no happier to be stuck with you than you are to be stuck with me. But can we try to make the best of this situation?"

Chance snorts in derision. "How do you suggest we do that?"

"If you promise to lay aside your bitter attitude then I'll lay down my verbal sword."

He scoffs and folds his muscular arms across that brick chest of his. "I highly doubt that."

"I'll still have the knife."

"Of course you will." Chance rolls his eyes.

"And I promise we'll hire someone as soon as possible to replace your traveling handyman function. Or we'll close our doors and sell the property. But then you and your daddy will have a whole new set of problems." I ignore the startled look on Chance's face and stick my hand out.

His warm one envelopes mine. "I'll try."

"And so will I."

Chance watched Apryl walk away, the last fifteen minutes replaying across his mind and leaving him a bit shell-shocked.

Why? Why would he be shocked?

Chance stalked back to his apartment. In the distance, an owl hooted. The wind stirred, carrying the faint scent of skunk on it. Great. That was the last thing he wanted to deal with.

Taking the porch steps two at a time, Chance tugged the door open.

All he had wanted was to pray.

Well and the other stuff. A part of him still wanted that too. But the bigger part—he sane, forgiven, and redeemed part of him—didn't want it, and that's what counted the most.

Right?

Chance paced back and forth, an unsettled feeling gnawing at him. Finally he went to the kitchen and stuck his head under the facet, cranking the cold water on high.

Breathe.

This anxious feeling had settled on him with an unearthly vengeance while talking with Apryl. Because he meant what he said to her. He knew all about the weight of family loyalties. Loyalties demanded to be heard. Loyalties were always right. Loyalties always won the battle because without your family, what would you have?

His father's words from their dinner meeting before he'd met up with Apryl and her outrageous demand ran through his mind. *"It's not an option. We have one course of action or we fail."*

And the possibility of failing was not an option.

"This is everything we've been working toward, Chance. We can't let it slip through our fingers. Remind her that we're still willing. It's our empire at stake."

His father didn't understand that Chance was content with finetuning the path they had cleared long ago. Chance didn't need an empire. He didn't need to prove himself. Frankly, he couldn't care less what people thought. Well, most people. Like it or not, he *did* care what his father thought, and Chance *did* want to make him proud. Unfortunately, making William proud required doing things his way.

The cold water started to work its magic, and Chance flipped his head back and forth , spraying water droplets all over his kitchen. Oh well. They would dry.

He glanced at the bundle of paperwork on his kitchen table. Paperwork with details and numbers and estimates dotted with water drops. An expansion. A remodel. A brand-new building. Quotes from vendors and leads on antiques just waiting to be restored and showcased.

His father's dream.

It didn't matter that his father had retired, handing over the official reins of the business to Chance. William McFarland still viewed *McFarland and Son Auto Repair* as his business, something that had started to grate on Chance, though he would never say as much to his father.

Chance pulled a bottle of water out of the refrigerator. It helped to cool the burn in his throat.

His unexpected conversation and truce with Apryl ran through his mind while he absent-mindedly flipped the bottle. A smile tugged at his lips. It was amusing how Apryl thought he smelled good, and her horror when she realized her face was pressed into his neck was downright comical. He wouldn't tell the world, but boy, he was going to enjoy harassing her about it for the next...okay, well, forever.

His smile faded as her words and sultry voice sounded in his ears again. *"Or we will close our doors and sell the property."*

He took another gulp of water, hoping it would cleanse him of the slightly guilty feeling. He didn't need to feel guilty. They had done nothing wrong. *He* had done nothing wrong.

Someone, however, should tell that to the guilty feeling gnawing its way through his insides and growing stronger with each passing moment.

Because it meant she didn't know.

Chapter Five

The day has arrived.

And the heavens are crying.

I stare out the window at the pouring rain, strong winds, ear-piercing thunder, and startling lightning. It's like the universe is screaming, "Don't do this! You will regret it!"

The thing is, that's exactly what I've been saying.

The thunder shouts as if to drive the point home.

"You don't need to convince me," I mumble. I let the white eyelet curtain from my pretty princess days flutter shut. My princess craze passed about a year after my parents did, and I found solace in the take-action attitude of a certain orphan-turned-superhero; however, I could never let the curtain go. It reminded me of my mother, who was all things pretty and princess.

I sigh. Eight hours. The wedding is in twelve hours, but thanks to a little arm-twisting, I have eight hours instead of the measly four to decorate.

By myself.

Okay, with Chance.

Courtney knocks and sticks her head into my old room. "Hey, just checking that you were up."

I ignore the unintended dig from my perfectly punctual sister. "Does six o'clock at night seem kind of late to start a wedding?" I rub my face. Six o'clock in the morning is also too early to get up for this night owl.

Courtney shrugs. "An evening wedding seems romantic to me. When are you guys leaving?"

I inhale slowly through my nose. Nauseous. I feel nauseous. Fan-flipping-tastic. "In the next thirty minutes."

"And hour to get there, then you'll have eight hours to set up, right?"

"Yup."

"And the wedding starts three hours after you guys are supposed to leave, right?"

"Yup."

"Is that cutting it close?"

My honest opinion? "Yup."

"Can you say anything other than 'Yup'?"

"Yup."

"Apryl!" Courtney growls.

I shoot my dear, well-meaning, but at this moment frustrating sister a glare. "Courtney. Seriously. I'm am stressed enough as it is. And I know your intentions are good, and I know you didn't intend to bail before the honeymoon had even begun, but I need to you to back off right now. I need you to be calming."

Courtney, to my complete surprise, nods. "Okay. Is there anything I can do to help?"

"Make me the biggest, nastiest coffee you can muster. To go." I'm normally not a coffee drinker—I prefer tea—but I need all the caffeine I can get.

Courtney actually salutes me. "You got it!"

Look at that, miracles do happen.

I run through the mental checklist in my head again. And again. And after another deep breath, again.

What am I forgetting?

So, this is why Courtney and Miles are always carrying around notebooks. Whoa. Insight.

I have boxes, crates, and at least ten plastic reusable shopping bags filled with bubble-wrapped antiques. Chance loads three bubble- and plastic-wrapped chandeliers into the back of his pickup truck.

It's now or never.

He walks in just then, and while he doesn't skewer me with a death glare, let's just say the forever frost hasn't thawed yet.

"This stuff too?" His voice is gruff as he eyes the sea of boxes.

"Will it all fit in your truck?"

"It's going to have to, isn't it." Not a question. A statement. A somewhat begrudging statement.

I might need one of those Eskimo parkas, because it's cold out here, baby.

Courtney saddles up to me and does that head tilt, hand-to-mouth thing we all did in junior high. Come on. You know what I'm talking about. When you were discussing your latest crush right in front of them. Anyway. "Someone is still peeved about you strong-arming him."

"That's why I leave the strong man stuff to you. You're better at the heavy lifting."

"You mean I don't alienate everyone."

"Isn't that what I just said?" The door creaks, announcing Chance's return from the truck.

He saunters into the room, takes in Courtney and me in our *girl talk* position, and raises an eyebrow. "The heavy stuff is loaded. You can help with the rest. Unless you just plan to supervise, *boss.*"

"*Apryl* is fine, but I also like *Lady of the Land*. Has a nice ring to it, don't you think?" I'm sorry. I'm trying not to be snarky, but he's not making it easy with that chip on his shoulder. And it is not a little chocolate chip. It's like a lifetime supply of Lay's pickle chips. "I'll be right behind you."

He shoots me a casual look, but his disbelieving grunt says it all as he saunters back to his truck. He has perfected the art of the saunter. It's not sleazy and overdone, but he never wavers in his confidence. Men all over the world should study his saunter. Okay, maybe not, because that would be weird.

Courtney raises her eyebrows.

I shrug. "Wish me luck."

"I'll pray for you."

I suppose I could have asked for that in the first place...

I sling two tote bags over each arm. Strong-arm? Yeah right!

The weight of these *delicate* antiques nearly rips my arms out of their sockets. Not that I'm being dramatic or anything.

Courtney holds the door open for me, so I half carry, half drag my lead weights to Chance's truck. He's standing in the back of the pickup, securing a tarp over the priceless possessions. Courtney walks silently beside me.

Chance looks up and sees my four bulging bags but, to his credit, doesn't say anything else. He just reaches down and hoists them up with no effort whatsoever.

Now *that* is a strong arm.

A sheen glistens on his forehead from the light sweat he's worked up from hauling and lifting. Real men sweat when they work. For that matter, so do women. But back to the men, or rather, the man in front of me. He tugs on the tarp once again, and the muscles in his arms flex, momentarily stealing my breath. And I don't know how I know this, since it seems like my eyes are glued to his arms and his attractive man-sweat, but the muscles in his calves happen to be very noticeable in those well-worn jeans.

Must. Stop.

Think about something else.

Famine... War... Creepy Elf on the Shelf dolls...

That's helping. I keep picturing the frozen, slightly maniacal look on the doll's face.

Chance hops down from the truck bed. "Time to hit the road."

"Well," Courtney says, sizing up the two of us. "Good luck." She catches my eye and mouths, *Don't kill each other.*

Yeah, I wish I could promise that, sis.

Chance glanced at the solemn woman riding in the passenger seat of his truck. Apryl had positioned herself as far from him as possible on the worn, faded green bench seat.

"I thought cooties died off in middle school," he mumbled.

"What was that?"

Apparently, he wasn't quiet enough. He blamed his father. He learned everything from him, and the man didn't know how to talk without his former military training raising the hairs on the back of the recipient's neck. It was his father's fault that he couldn't mumble.

"Nothing."

"Didn't sound like nothing."

Chance stifled a groan. "It was nothing."

"See, I thought cooties died off in middle school too, but it turns out that they can indeed survive well into adulthood in some certain primitive species. Usually men. Sometimes pigs."

What an awesome start to their working relationship!

"Oh, there's the occasional wombat too," Apryl continued.

"Well, so much for that truce," Chance countered.

He didn't look but he heard Apryl inhale sharply. Then silence. Though nothing *verbal* was said, he could almost hear the internal bashing of his name and person.

Chance merged onto the highway. Another forty-three minutes until they arrived at the country inn where the wedding and reception would take place, and Courtney had insisted they leave thirty minutes early. In other words, the chance of a verbal explosion was high.

They rode in silence for several minutes, the world flying by them in various shades of gray and brown. Even the sky was gray. Fantastic day for a wedding. At least it had stopped raining...for now. Chance imagined a hysterical bride at their destination.

Fantastic.

"Okay, you're right. I'm sorry." Her words sounded strained.

He knew he shouldn't. It wouldn't help. It would only make things worse—so much worse. He begged his body not to do it.

But...

He laughed.

Apryl, to her credit, kept her mouth shut. Albeit, her rosy lips were in a thin straight line but they were shut. Props to her.

"I'm really sorry, Apryl, but you were apologizing through clenched teeth." He chuckled again but cleared his throat, effectively diminishing his laughter.

She kept her gaze on the road before them, but man, the glare on her face could kill a possum.

He'd try again. "I'm sorry."

"It's fine," she mumbled.

Well, how could he doubt it with conviction like that? Chance refrained from shaking his head. That wouldn't help. He searched his brain for something to say. "Hey?"

Apryl turned to look at him and raised her eyebrows.

"Happy birthday." He glanced at the road for a moment then shifted his gaze back to her. Eye contact and all. "Well, belated, but that's better than nothing." Almost a year, so maybe he should have just waited until her actual birthday for this year. But in his defense, girls loved it when he remembered their birthday, late or not. *Work with me, Apryl.*

She didn't respond, unless you counted open-mouthed staring as a response. Which he didn't.

Okay, no progress. Might as well move back to his favorite persona—the goader. "Can I ask you something?"

She tilted her head toward him, sending her blue-black hair swishing to the right. Chance wondered if she knew that she did that whenever she gave someone her complete attention. "What?"

"Was it difficult not saying that I started it?" Poke.

"Was it difficult telling your *daddy* that I outwitted you?" Apryl hissed.

Chance clenched and unclenched his jaw. "You didn't outwit me."

"I didn't? My mistake. I thought—"

"Well, stop. You don't know what you're talking about." Because Chance hadn't told his father anything about this. And he had no plans to disclose this infuriating arrangement to his father. His father...

His father would go ballistic.

"Right," Apryl continued. "I would have no idea what I'm talking about. I only heard your overbearing father proclaim his dynamic plans for you day after day after flipping day. I know the speech by heart. I could pass any pop quiz on the subject."

"Seems like you're inordinately interested in me and my family."

"Just keeping my enemies close."

"Whatever. Let's just change the subject."

"Did I hit a nerve?"

"Look, just keep your opinions about my father to yourself. Okay?"

"Sure," she grumbled, turning to look out the window at the blurry landscape.

"Listen, my father isn't perfect. I know that—"

"Do you?"

"Will you be quiet for three minutes?"

Apryl pursed her lips together.

"I know that you never liked him."

"Oh, please," Apryl said while rolling her eyes.

"But attacking him is crossing the line," Chance finished with a hard edge to his tone. "Isn't there something in *the Bible* about loving your neighbors? Maybe you should try putting it into practice."

Apryl didn't actually speak. She didn't need to. Those flaming blue eyes of hers said that sooner or later he would hear her perfect rebuttal.

Also, Chance was pretty sure the right side of his face was melting thanks to her death-ray vision.

They rode in silence for several minutes before he shot her a strained version of his patented charmer smile. "I really did have a question for you."

"I'd rather just ride in strained silence."

"Do I need to remind you—"

"Nope." She sighed. "What? This is your last chance, McFarland."

Okay, time to tread carefully. Chance just needed to shift through her responses. Their last conversation had weighed so heavily on him that he needed to know for sure. "Why the last-ditch effort to save the shop?" He glanced at her, taking note of her startled expression and the guilty gleam in her eyes. She looked away.

"For Gram. It's for Gram," she finally said.

"Right. You mentioned that before, but at the risk of sounding like a conniving snake, why doesn't she just retire? I'm sure she'd love to spend more time with you and Courtney." Hint,

hint. He hoped his carefully constructed sentences would get Apryl to reveal what she knew about the situation.

"Yeah. She probably would, but..." Her words drifted out to the thoughtful sea, never to be recovered. She sounded emotionally exhausted.

Chance shifted his position. He felt like a complete cad for bringing this up, especially since he and his father owed Charlotte Burns an unpayable amount of gratitude. Without her, Chance didn't know what they would have done when his father's military career had come to an abrupt end.

"Hey, I'm sorry for bringing it up." He glanced at her again and met her sad eyes. "Let's play a game."

"What kind of game?" She pulled her navy blue thermos with the Patriots logo out of the cup holder.

"How about Twenty Questions?"

"Which Twenty Questions?" She took a sip of her coffee and made a face.

"There's more than one?"

"There's the one where you get to ask the person twenty questions about themselves." She licked her rosy lips.

Interesting. "Is it like truth or dare?"

"I'm sorry, I didn't realize I was riding with a thirteen-year-old girl."

Chance smirked but ignored the jab. "I'll take that as a no. And the other game is the one where one person thinks of something random and the other person has twenty questions to figure out what it is, right?"

"Yes." She took another sip and gagged.

"Let's play both, but we can start with the intrusive version. I'll ask you questions first."

"No fair! My mouth was full." She shot him a dark look, but whether it stemmed from annoyance or her apparent dislike of coffee remained unclear.

Knowing Apryl, it was probably annoyance.

"Too bad," he quipped. "Okay, first question: Why are you drinking coffee if you hate it?"

"The caffeine. I needed the caffeine," she moaned. "I like tea, especially chai lattes, but all Gram has in the house is decaffeinated tea in disgusting flavors like lemongrass."

Chance took note of the informational sign on the highway and changed lanes, passing a red Subaru that had seen better days. "Unacceptable. Coffee is life."

"That's what my friend Izze says. She thinks I should try it her way."

"What's her way?" Already, Chance didn't like the sound of this.

Apryl smirked, shifting her gaze back to the endless highway. "She drinks hers like a liquid candy bar."

"That... Well, adequate words to describe how disgusting that is fail me. One sugar and one tablespoon of milk is acceptable. No fancy flavors." To drive his point home, Chance took a long sip of his own classic roast coffee.

Apryl snorted. "Next question."

He swallowed and put the thermos back into the cup holder. "Okay, question number two—"

"Actually, it's number three," Apryl interjected.

"Fine, question number three: who is your favorite superhero?"

"Batman."

"Really?" Chance glanced at her. "Well, Apryl, I think we may have just found something that we have in common."

She shrugs. "It was bound to happen eventually. At the very least there was the fact that we are both living creatures."

"Sarcasm does not become you, Apryl."

"I highly doubt that. Ask your next question."

"Question number four and don't you cheat and say five just because I was shocked that you have decent taste in superheroes." Apryl laughed, but Chance continued. "Who is your favorite TV show and/or movie Batman?"

"George Clooney."

Chance blanched, jerking the steering wheel towards the ditch.

"What's wrong?" Apryl screamed, bracing herself against the dashboard.

"Sorry. I think I blacked out when you said George Clooney." He shook his head like a dog. "I'm good now."

"Oh, for crying out loud, I was just joking! Surely there are easier ways to kill me that don't require killing yourself in the process."

"The jerk was involuntary!" Chance laughed. "Who is really your favorite?"

"Christian Bale."

He pursed his lips and nodded. "Respectable, although not the best."

"Who's your favorite?" Out of the corner of his eye, he watched Apryl angle her head to look at him again, genuine interest on her face.

"Does this count as one of your questions?" Talking with Apryl like this was almost...fun. Weird. The feeling would probably pass soon enough.

"Just answer the question, dip wad."

And the feeling has passed.

"Ben Affleck."

"Gross!" she exclaimed, mouth gaping open. Where was a fly when he needed one?

"What's wrong with him?"

"He's not Batman!"

"Um, he's playing Batman in the movies, so I think you're wrong there."

"No," she said as she waved her hand around, trying to come up with an explanation. "No, he doesn't personify Batman. He's too much of a playboy."

"Exactly the point."

"What do you mean *exactly the point*?"

He grinned at her outrage. "He's the only actor that has been able to exemplify Bruce Wayne."

"Bruce Wayne isn't Batman."

"Do you even hear the words coming out of your mouth?"

"Be quiet." Apryl rolled her eyes. "Fine. Bruce Wayne is Batman in the sense that a man named Bruce Wayne puts on the cape and dons his girly mask, becoming Batman. But Bruce Wayne is just as much as a farce as Batman is. It's all a facade for those around him. That's not the real man underneath."

Truer words had never been spoken.

About him.

Chance shifted in the driver's seat, feeling like the truck's cab had caught fire. Would she notice if he pulled at his shirt collar? Time to change the subject. "You're crazy. Next question. Remember, you have to be completely honest."

Her laughter quieted and her complexion paled. Interesting. Looked like someone else felt uncomfortably hot. "If I don't like it, I'm not answering it."

"Those aren't the rules."

"You hadn't heard of this game. How would you know what the rules are?"

"The rules remain the same with any good question-and-answer game. You cannot skip a question. You must always answer truthfully. Failure to comply with the rules undermines the very foundation of the game. I don't make the rules; I just play by them."

Apryl crossed her arms across her stomach. "Oh, please."

"Hate the game, not the player."

"Whatever."

"Now who's the thirteen-year-old girl?"

Apryl huffed, "Oh, for crying out loud, just ask the question!"

"Earlier, when you didn't say that I started it even though I know that's what you were thinking, was that difficult for you?" He couldn't stop the rueful smile nor did he want to stop it.

Apryl rolled her eyes. "You have no idea how hard."

Okay, she should talk to him.

Talk. To him.

Talk.

To.

Him.

Courtney stared at her cell phone, a picture of Gram—her screensaver—starting back at her. The screen went black, and she pressed the HOME button for the thirtieth time.

Maybe texting would be easier?

Yeah, that seemed like a good idea. Courtney typed in her

password, pulled up the messaging app, and clicked onto Dallas's name.

Hey.

What next?

Hey. Why are you a liar?

Too aggressive? Okay, yeah.

Hey. I missed you a lot the other night. I felt a lot better when I saw you at the hospital.

Wearing man scrubs.

Big improvement.

Delete. Delete. Delete. After dropping her phone on the table and pushing it away, Courtney pressed her face into the tabletop, letting its coolness soothe her flushed face. If only something could soothe her soul.

Her heart fluttered.

Later. I'll deal with this later.

She stood, kicking the poor, unfortunate chair backward, and grabbed her coat and keys. After tromping through the house and locking the front door, she drove to the hospital. The entire drive there, a verse flickered in her head like a candy wrapper fluttering across the sidewalk on a breezy day.

"Come to me, all you who are weary and burdened, and I will give you rest."

Yeah, she knew the verse. It was the twenty-eighth verse in the eleventh chapter of Matthew. It was the first verse Gram had taught them and helped them memorize. It should help. It should comfort. It should soothe her flushed soul better than a tabletop to the face.

So why wasn't it?

She couldn't control anything in her world, so the very least God could do would be make the verse comforting! Was that seriously too much to ask?

Courtney turned right onto the road to the hospital, steering towards the emergency room/main entrance parking. Once she had secured the space after a brief but intense war with a sports car with an attitude problem, Courtney strolled into the building.

Maybe if she pretended she was fine and had it all together then everything else would get in line.

And people who had it all together strolled. The occasional hotshot sauntered, but Courtney couldn't move her hips like that.

The hospital surged with nine-to-five life, awakened from its nightly slumber, so Courtney had walked in through the main entrance. All around her people moved from one place to the next. She could almost imagine it was a beehive if it weren't for the everlasting smell of antiseptic and vomit.

"Ma'am, let me help you carry that."

Courtney's eyes slid shut. Why was he here? She hadn't talked to Dallas since the man-scrubs incident, but she really didn't expect to see him here today. Honestly, she had hoped that she wouldn't see him at the hospital ever again because then it would mean that she had just imagined it. She could live with that.

She opened her eyes. No, she wasn't crazy. There he was, his sapphire-colored eyes popping against the navy blue scrubs he was wearing . Dallas kneeled over an elderly woman in the café area, wrapping one of those thin blankets around her shoulders. As he helped her sit down, she said something to him that made him chuckle.

Then he looked up.

Right into Courtney's eyes.

His mouth opened, bearing a disturbing resemblance to one of those talking trout wall mounts. It would have been comical if it weren't for the guilt written across his face.

Dallas took a step toward her, and Courtney whirled around, stepping right into a mop bucket.

She shrieked and glanced over her shoulder. Dallas was talking to another man in scrubs and pointing at her.

"Are you all right, miss?" A woman in her mid-forties who wore a janitor's uniform watched her with a worried expression.

"I'm fine. I'm fine." Her heart beat against her chest in a wild pattern. Water soaked her shoe and sock. She didn't dare look down, lest she see any pretty pastel colors swilling around her foot. The smells, however, were not comforting.

"Courtney, hold up!"

"Well, I'll leave you to it." Courtney picked up her dripping foot and hopped twice to get away from the bucket and Dallas. Hopping seem like the best idea amidst her panicked adrenaline and mortification.

It wasn't.

She collapsed after two feet. A collective gasp filled the hallway, and a number of people asked if she was all right. Courtney thought she mumbled an answer, but she wasn't sure. She could almost feel Dallas breathing down her neck.

She needed to get out of here. Now!

So she did the first thing she could think of.

Please don't point out that this hadn't served her well so far. Desperation called the shots now.

Courtney ran for the nearest door, flung it open, and dropped to the floor. She pressed her back against the door so that if anyone looked through the glass pane, all they would see was an empty stairwell.

Please don't let him find me! Why she would pray that, she didn't know. You'd think she had run from a deranged serial killer, not the boyfriend she hoped to marry.

But if he couldn't trust her with something this huge and had lied to her for the last year then she couldn't rule out serial killer from his list of hobbies.

Courtney didn't know how long she had sat there. Long enough that her erratic heartbeat finally settled into a normal rhythm again. Long enough that her hands no longer shook from adrenaline. Long enough for Dallas to call seven times.

Her phone buzzed in the palm of her hand. Make that eight times.

Maneuvering onto her knees, Courtney popped up just enough that she could see the main hallway. He was nowhere to be seen.

Yes! She stood up, grabbed her purse, and pushed the release bar on the door.

The door didn't budge.

Oh. No.

She pushed, kicked, and body slammed the door. Nothing. Then she saw it. A chrome slot for keycards. With a lovely little sign saying that she was out of luck because she wasn't hospital staff.

When she got home, she was deleting *Grey's Anatomy* and every other doctor show from her Netflix queue. She didn't like medical dramas that much anyway.

Her phone buzzed again.

Courtney dropped to the floor once more. Pulling her knees up to her chin, she covered her face with her hands and growled. She would howl at that stupid keycard slot until she got what she wanted. She had all day.

Then she started to giggle. The giggles turned to full-blown laughter with tears, but the tears led to genuine sobbing. She couldn't handle this day getting any worse.

The heavy door slammed into her back, sending her sprawling onto her hands and knees. Pushing down her ire, she scrambled to her feet while saying, "Don't shut the door!"

At the same time a deep voice said, "Courtney?"

Dallas stepped into the stairwell, letting the door shut behind him. Courtney wiped her face, but she knew it would do no good. The cursed tears had already left their blazing trail down her cheeks and chin, coming to a final resting stop on her satiny lilac top.

They stared at each other for a several minutes. She didn't know what to say.

"I don't know what to say," Dallas said softly.

That made two of them. "Yeah." Courtney shrugged.

Dallas took a step toward her, but she took a corresponding step backward. Despite her desperate desire to hug him right now, she couldn't fall into a sweet embrace when confusion coursed through her.

"Why did you run away from me?" Dallas's voice was so soft, Courtney's poor eardrums strained to make out the words.

She shrugged. "I'm not really sure. It was my first reaction. To run away." Maybe she was more like her sister than she thought.

Dallas moved to the opposite wall and leaned against it, hands in his pockets. Warm air swooshed through the ceiling vents, filling the hallway. "I guess I understand. I've wanted to tell you for a while, but I kept making excuses."

"I saw you here a few days ago, in the emergency room with an upset, older woman."

Dallas nodded twice. "I knew there was a risk you'd find out when everything happened with your grandmother. But I kept avoiding the topic."

"You lied to me."

Dallas opened his mouth to argue then shut it. "You're right," he said, reluctance and regret filling his words. "I wasn't entirely honest. I'm sorry. Will you allow me to tell you the truth now?"

"How will I know it's the truth?" Courtney questioned, her self-righteous indignation bringing out her less-than-flattering side.

He ran his right hand through his sandy brown hair. "Courtney, I made a mistake. Yes, there's more to the story, but at the core, I am the guy you've known and trusted for the last year."

Was he? How could she be sure?

"*Ask him,*" a voice in her soul whispered.

"Okay." She softened her tone. "Tell me. What's the full story?"

She needed to sit. Courtney leaned against the wall, allowing it to guide her as she slid to the floor. Dallas mimicked her then crossed his long legs. Maybe four feet separated them, but the emotional equivalent resembled the Atlantic Ocean. Courtney bit her lip. Another unflattering trait, but that's what she did when anxiety threatened to break her.

He sighed. "Well, as you know, I'm going to law school to be a lawyer...but I plan to become a *medical* lawyer. I previously earned a BSN, a Bachelor of Science in Nursing, and my plan was to work for a few years, save as much as I could, and then go back to medical school. Then my mother got sick." Anger flashed across his handsome face, and he sighed again before continuing. "I saw how broken the medical system is and how corrupt some people can be. About a year after my mother passed away, I finally accepted that God was asking me to be a voice for others who are going through similar struggles and tragedies."

"Wow," Courtney whispered once she released her now-throbbing lip.

Dallas nodded. "That's my story. I'm still going to law school, and I work as a home health nurse. The woman you saw me with in the emergency room is one of my patients. She needed emergency care that night, and I was visiting her today before going to my other patient. I've only got two patients right now. Sometimes I have more, but I don't take on more than I can handle with my class load. My boss is really great about working with me. And... I'm rambling." He offered her a weak smile.

Courtney smiled in return then looked at the abstract star pattern on the floor tiles. She bit her lip again. This explained so much. At age thirty and brilliant, Dallas could already be a lawyer. Since he went to school part-time now, however, Courtney had just assumed he had worked for a while first and was paying his way as he could afford it. He'd always resisted speaking about his past, especially his mother's death. It made sense. But why didn't he tell her what his job was? That part made no sense at all.

Something inside of her hardened. Did it matter why? He'd lied.

"Courtney, I am so, so sorry. I...I hope that you can forgive me."

Courtney stared at the floor, her thoughts running in a jumbled pattern more abstract the pattern on the tiles.

"Courtney?"

She didn't answer him.

"Do you want to ask me anything else?"

"No."

"Do you want some time...to think about stuff?"

Courtney knew what he was really asking. *Is this the end?*

"Yeah, I do." she finally said.

Dallas sighed. "Okay."

They each stood up to leave, and her wet shoe squeaked against the floor.

"Courtney?"

She looked at him.

"Why is your foot wet?"

Oh, yeah. That. "I stepped into a mop bucket."

Dallas sniffed the air. "And the smell?"

"I didn't look to see what was in the bucket. That's rule number one, but I do know that I need to get a shower so I can scrub away the first three layers of skin," she said in a deadpan voice, void of all the humor such a statement would have contained before this, before everything changed.

"Ah. Well, I'm sure you'll feel a lot better once you've gotten that fixed," Dallas said awkwardly.

Yeah.

It would help.

Right?

Chapter Six

I, Apryl Burns, am a fantastic idiot.

Truly. Utterly. Completely. Undeniably.

Especially because I can't think of any more words to describe just how foolish I really am. Creative writing was never my best subject in school.

"It's not going to work, Apryl."

"Okay!" I throw up my hands. "I give! But we need to use the chandeliers somewhere."

Chance huffs. "I understand that but I can't hang all of them over the sweetheart table like a vintage disco ball, as you insist on describing it."

I hold up my right index finger. "Hey, I never used the words disco or ball."

"No," Chance grunts, manhandling the delicate chandelier so that it rests on the table. "I believe your exact words were 'like a glittery army of a thousand Lumieres on the charge to storm the castle.' Which doesn't make sense, by the way. I've seen *Beauty and the Beast*, and the possessed knickknacks were *defending* the castle."

"Tomatoes—"

Chance cuts me off, warning lacing his voice. "Don't you dare say 'ta-mah-toes,' Apryl Burns."

"Actually, I was going to say 'pah-tah-toes.'"

Chance groans.

Chance and I enjoyed a relatively nice ride to Rosebrook, New Hampshire, population one.

I mean, I'm assuming. It's the definition of a one-horse town.

Not one single stoplight decorates Main Street, and I use even that term loosely. No gas station, no grocery store, and no church. There is, however, a small brick building claiming the identity of both post office and town hall. Personally, I think that's an awfully big reputation for such a small building to live up to. Might give it a complex. Not to be mistaken with an apartment complex.

I need some potato chips.

Fifteen minutes after driving through—ahem—*town*, we came to a huge, beautiful resort boasting a country club, spa, golf course, and the gorgeous Rosebrook Inn, location of tonight's upcoming wedding and reception.

A posh man in a polo shirt and khakis greeted us immediately once we had navigated the immaculate roads to the inn's lovely whitewashed doorstep. It looked like he had been waiting for us on the wraparound porch covered with vines and flowers that encircled the railings, columns, and rafters in their entirety. He looked oddly out of place in his golfer apparel in this china doll setting.

And despite his professional, altogether normal appearance, something about him just screamed, "Run!"

"I've been expecting you," posh man had said in a low monotone.

Creepy. Creepy. Creepy.

Chance thwacked me on my arm and whispered that I needed to stop staring.

"He could be dangerous," I said.

"Then I'll use my brawn and protect us...or at least me. Your psychotic stare is only going to make him snap," Chance finished whispering right as creepy posh guy swung to face us again after examining Chance's pickup truck with apparent disdain.

After raising a bushy eyebrow at us, the man instructed us to drive down another road that would lead us to a large, white wedding tent. And then he disappeared just as mysteriously as he appeared. Chance claims he went inside, but one can't be too sure. Which is why I will wake up with a stiff neck tomorrow, a result of looking over both shoulders every seven minutes.

The backside of the Rosebrook Inn proved to be just as beautiful as the front. Fresh and colorful vines and flowers also covered the backside of the wraparound porch as well. Tall tables under a canopy of twinkle lights had been set up on the porch for cocktail hour while the bride and groom have their pictures done. The staff was busy setting up white wooden chairs facing the lake where the elegantly simple wedding would take place. To the right of where we were instructed to temporarily park loomed the huge white wedding tent.

That brings us to right now.

"I hate to interrupt your daydreaming, but what do you want to do?" Chance growls.

I fiddle with the locket at my neck. The locket I never take off. "I don't know."

"Well, shouldn't you figure that out? Better yet, shouldn't you have figured that out before you got here?"

"Dude, I know! Please don't keep reminding me that I'm not even six hours into saving my family legacy and failing horribly." I whirl around, sprinting from the tent as fast as my legs will carry me.

Not that I know where to go. It's not like I can quit, but the panicked feeling within my chest demands that I do something before I collapse onto the perfect green grass in a hyperventilating and/or vomiting mess.

I walk around to the back of the tent and spot a stone bench nestled into one of the small thirty-something rose gardens peppering the property. Walking to the bench and sitting down, I inhale the scent of freshly cut grass, pond water, and roses. Closing my eyes, I repeat the deep breaths, my heartrate gradually calming. The fragrance is so soothing that I forget to glance over my shoulder for any would-be attackers.

I don't hear the footsteps; I just feel the touch on my arm.

"Ahhh!" I scream.

"Stop screaming!" Chance hisses through clenched teeth while smiling and waving to the alarmed woman gardening about two hundred feet from us.

I press a hand to my chest. "What are you doing?" So much for calming my heartrate.

"I came to find you."

"Well, you found me," I sputter. "Now go away. I need to calm down. Again, thanks to you."

"I'm sorry," Chance blurts.

I wish life came with sound effects. I would make good use of the Screech button. "What? Why?" The gardener keeps her eyes trained on me. My voice must be a little louder than I realized.

"Because I was a little mean back there."

A little? That bite hurt! It could be the exception to that saying, "His bark is worse than his bite." Something I'm sure he learned from his father.

"It's fine." Because what are you supposed to say when someone apologizes? Regardless of the fact that I want to kick him in the shin, forgiveness is the Christian thing to do.

But man, just once I'd like to go with the kicking option.

"No, it's not." Chance sits down beside me, and the stone bench shifts in the soft ground from the added weight. "I know that you're new to this. I know that it was sprung on you. I know that you're learning as you go."

"Or failing as I go. Let's be honest, I'm not off to a great start."

"We'll get better."

We? Best to ignore that. I flick my knee. "I should have thought to tour the space with the bride before now."

Chance shrugs. "Eh, you live and you learn. I never would have thought to do that."

"You're a dude."

"That obvious fact shouldn't excuse me from everything."

I wave my hand. "Tomatoes—"

"Don't."

I grin. "Sorry." Not.

"Can I make a suggestion?"

"Go for it. I've got zilch."

"There are three raised high points in the tent from the main poles. Those would be the easiest places to hang a chandelier. They're already wired for exactly that."

"Wonderful. Even our saving grace isn't original."

"Stop whining."

"Oh, not being nice now. Got it. Go on." I nod my head for him to continue.

"We need to eat. We'll keep brainstorming over lunch."

"We don't have time for lunch," I say as my stomach rumbles with unladylike ferocity.

"I can't make *you* eat, but I need food. I am that weird, made-up word that means hungry and angry—"

"Hangry," I interject.

"Whatever. I am hangry at its worst."

"Sure, blame it on that." I stand up, brushing imaginary dirt from my backside. Seriously, does the staff dust the benches? That seems too far. We are outside, for crying out loud!

Not that I want dirt clinging to my rear. It's just the principle of the matter.

He rolls his eyes. "Come on. I saw a mom-and-pop sandwich shop on our way here."

Chance calls Mr. CreepyPosh, who gave us the number to his work cell phone in case we had an emergency. He informs him that we're getting some food and will be back in about forty-five minutes.

The man's icy stare follows us down the entire length of the driveway.

A few minutes later Chance pulls into the sandwich shop and we enter. The tantalizing smells of cinnamon and bread bombard my senses. The space is actually more like a café, flooded with natural light and decorated with lots of whitewashed wood and subtle touches of teal. The menu is small, consisting of only six sandwiches, an assortment of baked goods, coffee, tea, and little bags of snack-size potato chips.

I grab four bags of potato chips, but Chance doesn't say anything. Bless him.

I just blessed my enemy. How biblical!

A woman in a cute teal apron walks through a matching teal door, her arms full of small boxes. She shoots us a quick smile, sets the boxes on a shelf, and steps in front of the cash register. "Sorry about that. Are you ready to place an order?"

Chance looks at me and I shrug. "I think so," he says and orders a Rueben with extra Swiss cheese and a soda. I order a chai latte and an Asian wrap in addition to my chips and pay for my meal with the debit card from the expense account Courtney insisted on setting up.

The waitress hands us our drinks, and we sit down with them as she makes our sandwiches.

I take a sip of my tea before I open the first bag of chips—salt and vinegar—relishing the sound of the foil crinkling. I pop one into my mouth. You might not think that salt and vinegar chips go with chai lattes. You'd be right. But I simply don't care.

"I see you still have an obsession with potato chips."

"I prefer to think of it as a devotion."

Chance snatches a chip before I can slap his hand away. "Whatever you need to tell yourself, dear."

I ignore the endearment. It doesn't mean anything. It never does.

"Your order is ready," the waitress calls.

Chance grabs our food. My wrap looks delicious, and my mouth starts to water. But I don't take a bite. Gram taught us to say grace before breakfast, lunch, and dinner.

Chance shoots me a weird look.

"Grace," I stutter.

"Sorry," he says.

"Why?" I pop another chip into my mouth.

"I'm not used to saying grace. My dad isn't big on it."

I shrug. "No worries. Sometimes I forget too. Gram always said that grace didn't need to be a big and eloquent speech; it was our heart of thanks that mattered."

Chalk fills my throat at the mention of Gram, and a forbidden question—worms its way through my head. How many more times will I hear her utter those words before we sit down for a meal?

"She's okay, Apryl."

"Yeah." But that positive word doesn't hold a lot of belief.

"God's got her," Chance says, holding my eyes with his green ones, flecks of gold shimmering around his pupils. He takes a bite of his sandwich and moans in delight. "This is amazing."

I grin, thankful for the light change of subject. For the next five minutes we munch on our food, and I don't focus on the fear threatening to crawl up my back like a thousand spiders.

I lick a drop of peanut sauce off my thumb. I need more of this sauce in my life.

"So, think of any ideas?"

I set the remainder of my wrap down, appetite gone. "I think I should be a peanut sauce salesman."

Chance coughs. "I don't think there's a lot of work in that field."

"There will be once they hear my pitch. 'Ma'am, do you like peanuts? Do you like sauce? Why are you living your life with these wonderful things separate? *You* may as well be separate. Embrace the beautiful taste of peanut sauce today and be whole.'"

The waitress working at the counter snickers.

Chance takes a long drag of his soda. "Well, while you've certainly convinced me, I don't think we should leave that poor, hysterical bride in the lurch."

I wipe my hands on my napkin. "She'll only be hysterical when she sees that I've wrecked her wedding."

"I think you mean the reception. Hey, maybe it'll start to rain again, and you'll be saved."

I ignore him. "So until she knows that her reception has been demolished by my capable hands, I think we should revel in the beauty before us—peanut sauce."

"I think I should call you Mad Apryl because you're madder than the hatter."

"How very *Alice in Wonderland* of you." I rub my eyes. "Let's go over what we know."

"Okay." He opens my bag of barbeque chips and starts eating them. "I love barbeque."

I know.

I shift in my booth. "Well, we've got the chandeliers, and now we know where they'll be hung We have twelve teapots, twenty-four creamers, twenty-four sugar dishes, forty-eight teacups, and forty-eight saucers, all with a floral pattern on them for the tables. Twelve lace tablecloths in various shades of pink, yellow, and red. A red table runner with a gold rose pattern for the gift table. Four small, whitewashed tables. Four crystal vases. And a vintage cake topper." I tick the points off on my fingers. "That's it."

"The bride went through the shop and viewed everything that you had available?" Chance asks.

"She did but I feel like something is missing. There's no 'Wow!' factor."

"She didn't give you any directions?" Annoyance flashes across his face. "That seems a little ridiculous."

"She wanted the wedding to be elegant, but thanks to Izze talking us up so much, she said she wasn't worried." No pressure or anything.

"Then I'm sure it will be nice."

"It will be beautiful, but it's missing something," I say again.

"What?" Exasperation clings to his words, not that I blame him. I could turn the table into kindling with all my pent-up frustration.

I don't say anything this time. I don't know what. I just don't know.

"I'm surprised your grandmother has so many electric chandeliers. That doesn't seem antique," Chance says, more to himself than to me, but the words fling a toothpick at my brain, and it's just out of grasp.

"An antique is something one hundred years old or older," I say offhandedly as I try to grasp that stinking toothpick.

"Yeah, but electric chandeliers?"

"Electric chandeliers have been around since 1890, but I know for a fact that the chandeliers that Gram sells have been rewired according to current electric regulations."

That's when I grab the toothpick, and with it, an idea.

"Chance, do you know what size light bulbs the chandeliers take?"

He looks at me like I really did pull a toothpick from my ear. "No."

"Can we check? Also..." I smile for the first time in forever. "We need to find the nearest hardware store."

I fiddle with my locket.

"Calm down," Chance whispers to me.

Yeah, right!

Roxanne surveys the tent, turning in slow circles in the middle of the dance floor as the colored lights temporarily stain her white bridal sweats.

She turns to face me.

My breath hitches.

"It's perfect," she breathes.

"Really?"

Izze shoulder-bumps me, her coiffed hair and flawless make-up a stark contrast to her wrinkled, purple button-down shirt. "Look at this place! How could you not already know that it's amazing?"

Well, I admit, it is pretty cool.

The dance floor resides in the middle of the tent, underneath the highest point, with the tables arranged around it. Red, yellow, and pink lace tablecloths alternate. All the mismatched teapots, teacups, saucers, creamers, and sugar bowls are arranged on the guests' tables in the most cohesive way possible for the centerpieces, and the guests' favors are in the teacups on each table. The sweetheart table is across from the tent door, on the other side of the dance floor, covered in a beautiful pink table cloth and claiming its own little tea service centerpiece. Behind the sweetheart table are the four whitewashed tables with the crystal vases filled with roses in various hues, curtesy of the gardener that continued to check on me all day.

It looks like an elegant, massive tea party.

But perhaps the most amazing thing about this space is the lighting. While the chandeliers are similar in theme with their gold and bronze arms and dangling crystals, the light emanating from them is not. The chandeliers are suspended from the three highest points in the tent like Chance suggested. The middle chandelier, however, bathes the tent in a soft buttery light, the chandelier on the left beams with pink light, and the chandelier on the right dances with red light. The crystals refract the varied hues all over the tent like...well, like a vintage disco ball.

It's the "Wow!" factor.

"I don't know how I'll ever thank you enough!" Roxanne exclaims, tears gathering at the corners of her eyes. "How can I thank you?"

Is it awful to hope that she'll add a little something extra to the check as a thank you? "There's no need," I say because that's the polite thing to say to someone who's buying dinner for over a hundred people in a few hours.

I grin at Chance. We worked so hard, especially to make up for the time we lost trying to track down colored lights in the chandelier's respective sizes. But we did it.

And I did it.

And I only dry heaved once, so props to me.

Roxanne twirls on the dancefloor. "I can't believe it! It's even more beautiful than I had imagined!"

"Where did you get the idea for the colored light bulbs?" Izze asks, looking from Chance to me.

"It was Apryl's idea. She did great," Chance says, and the simple words send warmth down my spine. He catches my eye and winks.

Now I might as well be on fire.

I shrug and look at Izze. "It was missing something, but I didn't know what. Chance and I were talking about the chandeliers, and the idea popped into my head."

"Sounds like a God thing," Izze says, awe tinging her words.

I blink. Is it? Why hadn't that occurred to me?

Um...thanks, God.

Despite my awkward prayer, warmth floods me, a warmth more potent and expanding than anything Chance's winks have ever done to me.

Wow.

Izze bumps me with her shoulder again. "You guys are staying for the wedding, right?"

Oh, no. Why, no. No, we weren't. Sorry, but not going to happen. I glance at Chance, and his face registers shock and a fresh dose of annoyance. "I didn't think so."

Roxanne halts her imaginary waltz. "You have to stay."

My palms start to sweat. "No, no. This is your day. We'll be back tomorrow to pick up the pieces."

"Impossible." I jump at Mr. CreepyPosh's reappearance. "The tent will already have been taken down and returned tomorrow."

Izze sizes him up. "You're doing all that tonight?"

He nods once, concise and sharp. "Per our contract agreement."

Fabulous. Another detail that never occurred to me.

Chance huffs and walks out of the tent. The others are polite enough not to comment on his vanishing act. Mr. CreepyPosh turns on his heel, disappearing in just as eerie a way as he arrived. At least I can confidently say that he left this time.

Roxanne practically bounces over to me, but I'm going to ignore it since it's her wedding day and all. "Regardless, I want you to stay, and it will be easier in the long run for you guys. Driving back tomorrow would be a waste of gas money."

I try to reason with her one last time. "But we don't have any nice clothes with us."

"That doesn't matter."

Well, with logic like that. I hold back a sigh and force a smile. "Thank you. We'd be honored."

She squeals. "Wonderful! I'm so glad. Well, I need to get back, but thank you again!" She tosses me a wave before dashing for the doorway.

"Don't worry," Izze says.

"I'm not worried." Just stressed. Beaten down. Agitated. All of those things.

"Yeah, you are. I can read it on your face. But don't worry, I'll stay and help you pack up."

"Thanks," I mumble.

"It will be okay." She gives me a quick hug, then punctuates it with a sheepish smile. "I'm really sorry, but I have to get back." She gestures toward the inn. "I thought Roxanne's maid of honor was going to have a coronary when I said we were going outside." She rolls her eyes.

"Go. Be merry. I'll see you later."

She squeezes my arm before leaving me in the glorious tent by myself.

All by myself.

"What are you doing out here?"

Apryl whirled around, thrusting her key in front of her in a way that Chance could only assume was supposed to look threatening. Her aim, however, was better than he expected, and the key jammed into his water bottle.

Apryl gasped. "Chance, I'm so sorry!"

He looked at the bottle bleeding water. "Good thing you missed, because your aim is deadly," he said dryly. He tugged the key free and handed it back to her then set the draining water bottle on the ground a couple feet away from where they stood.

"I'm really not in the mood for your sarcasm," she grumbled.

"I meant it. I'm actually glad I had the water bottle, or you could have cut my hand."

She eyed him, skepticism filling her gaze. "What are you doing out here?"

"I believe I asked you that first."

"I needed some air." She turned and looked into the darkness.

"And I was trying to make sure some creep didn't sneak up on you."

"And how did that work out for you? Besides, I'm fine. I've got my trusty key." She held up her keys without looking at him.

"I'm going to ignore the fact that you just called me a creep."

She snorted. "More power to you."

Chance stepped next to Apryl, setting himself only a breath apart from her. Music, laughter, and colorful light spilled from the tent. Life and light in the middle of the darkness.

"Izze came to tell me that Roxanne and her husband will be leaving soon. Then we can pack up. Thought I should let you know," he said quietly.

"Well, I'm sure you're relieved." Her words held a little bit of a burn. A burn he probably deserved. He hadn't been charming company today despite what used to be written on the bathroom wall in the high school girls' locker room.

"I am." Chance ran a hand threw his hair. "A lot of things took me by surprise today."

"Yeah, me too." She glanced over at him. "For what it's worth, I'm sorry. I was even less prepared than I thought."

"We'll know better for next time."

She held his graze for a moment, vulnerability and fear and another emotion—longing?—fighting to be seen. Apryl looked away and fiddled with her locket, . the moonlight dancing across her face.

"Do you want to dance?" He didn't know where those words had come from, but the realization that he actually wanted to dance with her was what surprised him the most. She'd always been beautiful and clever, but her personal mission to despise everything about him had kept him at a distance. Even his father had noticed Apryl's unexplainable anger toward them, urging Chance to keep a safe distance.

Yet Chance wanted to dance with her. Had he fallen off a ladder while hanging one of those chandeliers? Was he lying in a hospital bed somewhere?

Apryl swung her body around to face him. "What?"

"Let's dance." He held out his hand for her to take. No turning back now.

She stared at his hand for several heartbeats, and then shook her head, taking a step back.

Ouch. His ego would hurt tomorrow.

"I'm not going to dance with you when I'm wearing jeans and a T-shirt covered in dust. It was embarrassing enough attending the wedding like this."

"We sat in the back. Besides, you look fine." Was it his imagination, or had she just flinched?

"Words every girl dreams of hearing, but I like to be dressed appropriately when I'm at a wedding. Instead, I was a sloppy wedding crasher." She gestured toward her clothes.

"Technically, we were invited."

"Dude, we crashed."

Chance grinned. "Maybe a little. Next time we'll bring a change of clothes."

"Next time?"

"Next time." He caught her eye, those baby blues unleashing

havoc to his nervous system. This was...alarming. He coughed. "You know, per our agreement."

"Right." Her clipped answer hung between them.

"It makes sense. Rather than lose a second day to traveling and tear down. And I bet we will run into the same issue other places if we tried to do it that way. Better to just put it in the agreement that we'll stay nearby or on site."

"That's true. I suppose I should have Courtney add it to the contract."

"And maybe we'll get some good food out of this deal." Chance rubbed his hands together like he did when he was a boy and ice cream was the most exciting thing in the world.

"I don't want other brides and grooms to feel like they need to feed us. That feels weird."

Chance swatted a mosquito from his bare forearm. "Some will offer. Some won't. Doesn't mean we can't hang out and enjoy the party, especially when we are invited, like tonight. We won't steal their food."

"I suppose. Maybe. We'll see." Apryl shrugged.

"Next time, bring a change of clothes." Chance stepped in front of her, resisting the strong, strange urge to life her chin and cup her cheek. "Because I want that dance."

Apryl's breath caught.

Before Chance could think or do anything else, loud cheers and a herd of people erupted from the tent, pushing them apart as the guests prepared to send the bride and groom off to wedded bliss.

Destroying their temporary bliss.

How rude.

Chapter Seven

*D*on't see me. Don't see me. Don't see me.

"Courtney!"

Walk faster. Walk faster. Walk faster.

"Courtney!" Dallas yelled. "Please! We need to talk."

Yeah, like they were going to have this conversation in the middle of campus with hundreds of college students wandering around them and witnessing all their drama.

Not. Happening.

"I don't have time right now," Courtney yelled over her shoulder. "I'll be late." Late for her bed, fuzzy pajama pants, and a pint of ice cream.

The sound of shoes slapping the pavement sent chills up Courtney's spine. She pushed past a group of students exchanging notes and ducked into the ally between the art history and political science buildings. She glanced over her shoulder, but Dallas was hot on her heels.

Thump. Thump. Thump.

Her heart went wild in her chest.

Dallas ran ahead of Courtney, whirled around, and caught her hand in his. His touch was gentle yet firm. And far, far too confusing. "Please," he said. She could almost smell the desperation on his breath.

"I...I don't know."

"We need to talk. I can't keep functioning in this...limbo. Are we together? Are we broken up? Is there a bounty on my head? I need to know." He let the strap of his backpack slide from his shoulder and fall to the ground.

"Dallas," Courtney huffed. "Come on. It's only been a week. I just need some space."

"Do you know what it means when someone says that they need space?"

"That they have an obsession with rockets?"

"That they want that person so far removed from their lives that no one would know if said person had been jettisoned into space."

"I think NASA would know."

"Courtney."

She yanked her hand out of Dallas's grasp and clutched the strap of her leather messenger bag in both hands. "What, Dallas? What do you want me to say? You lied to me! That's betrayal. How are we supposed to be a couple if you can't tell me the most basic facts about yourself? Doesn't seem that hard to share with someone what you do for a living or what you're working toward in your career."

"Do you think sharing my story with you was easy?" Anger darkened Dallas's eyes, turning them black. "Those were some of the worst days of my life. I would have hoped for a little understanding and forgiveness from my girlfriend of over a year."

"Funny. I would have hoped from a little honesty from my boyfriend of over a year," Courtney shot back.

Dallas growled. He turned like he wanted to walk away but stopped. Instead, he clutched his hands into fists so tight that Courtney heard his knuckles pop. Their ragged breathing filled the space around them, intensifying that claustrophobic feeling pinching Courtney's chest.

She should just leave.

But it appeared that her brain had decided to stop sending basic commends to her extremities. She'd get a brain scan—but wait, she'd have to go to the hospital and probably see Dallas again.

"Why, Dallas? Tell me why," Courtney finally said after an eternity of dead air.

"What?"

"I need to know why you would lie about that to me." Courtney shifted from her left leg to the right.

Dallas exhaled, slow and long. "I was afraid."

"Of what?"

"Of you. Of what you would say."

The only thing that would have shocked Courtney more would have been if Jesus had appeared and slapped her across the face.

"When we first started dating, you said...you said that you hated everything about hospitals and that you would never understand why someone went into the medical profession. That you wanted nothing to do with that life."

Courtney stared at him, and the conversation came back to her like in pieces.

"It was a stupid decision, but I was worried about what you would say. I was a licensed nurse, Courtney. I was going to be a doctor. And it's not like I had some great awakening; I'm studying to be a medical lawyer while I work as a home health nurse. Everything about me revolves around the medical field. For crying out loud, I read medical journals for fun!" Dallas exhaled again, leaving him looking physically deflated. He slumped against the brick wall for support. "Like I said, I know it's stupid. But when I heard your opinion, I went to fear. I thought you may not want anything to do with me."

"No!" Courtney exploded. She couldn't listen to another minute of this. "No, you don't get to pin this on me!"

"I'm not pinning it on you!"

"Yes, you are. You're trying to make it my fault that you lied to me."

"Did you listen to a word I said?" Dallas asked, his tone incredulous.

"I hate carrots. Does that mean you harbor a secret passion to live on a carrot farm? That's what your logic sounds like."

"You've got to be kidding me." Dallas smacked the building with his balled-up fist.

"I need to go." She brushed past him.

This time Dallas didn't try to follow her. Something that both infuriated and relieved Courtney.

But most of what she felt was a grief so tangible, Courtney thought it would smoother her.

I stare at the ceiling.

"Because I want that dance."

Each time I replay his words in my head, the inflection changes. Husky. Romantic. Condescending. Comical. Resigned. And now Chance's voice sounds like Bob Saget. Which is ridiculous. If Chance sounds like any celebrity, it would be Chris Pratt, leader of the Guardians of the Galaxy.

Oh, great. Now Christ Pratt is part of the conversation.

I groan and slap my hands over my ears to quiet the myriad of voices. Too bad they're all in my head.

I'd like a padded room for one, please.

It doesn't make sense to me. I'm not the kind of girl who draws Chance McFarland's attention. Unless we're talking negativity and scorn—then all of his attention is focused on me. But when it comes to slow dancing under a canopy of stars, Chance has always looked in any direction but mine.

I blink, and horror pools in my stomach.

Unless...

Unless he's bored. And he figures, why not have some harmless fun? All the old rumors from high school flood my mind. I mean, Chance had always been a church kid, but he'd also always been that guy who had a *good time*, if you know what I mean.

Who am I kidding? You'd have to be from an actual colony on Mars not to know what I mean. And I bet that particular sentiment is well-known in all space colonies, real or imagined. Well, this explains it. Like every other girl who's crossed paths with Chance McFarland, I'm just a game.

Mental slap.

Refocus... No. No, he wouldn't do that. The guy I heard talking to God so intimately wouldn't do that. He'd changed. He wouldn't do that...

Would he? What do you think?

The front door flies open and slams into the wall. The sound startles me so much, I simultaneously jump and try to stand, which results in me falling out of the faded green wingback chair.

"I can't believe him," Courtney shrieks.

I don't say anything as I clamber to my feet. One of two things will happen next. Option one: Courtney will rage (and by "rage," I mean she'll storm in and out of rooms while pacing like a prancing elf) until she wears herself out. Then she'll either apologize to the offended or forgive the offender. This is the usual course of action.

Option two: Courtney will ask for my advice. Option Two usually means that a meteor is hurtling toward earth in a *Deep Impact* kind of way before God flicks it aside at the last minute.

"I need to talk to you," Courtney says.

Meteor it is.

"What's up?" I resituate myself in the wingback like the dowager countess from *Downton Abby* might make an appearance next.

Courtney drops her messenger bag onto the floor and flops face first onto a velvet settee. After shrieking into the cushion (my poor eardrums), she rolls onto her back.

The dowager is less than pleased.

"Do you remember that thing I told you?"

"What thing?"

"The...the thing, Apryl. Remember?"

I search the dusty shelves of my brain. "Don't mistake spitting for blowing a bubble? No? Okay... Oh, never, ever eat beany weenie casserole when there's a possibility of kissing?"

Courtney covers her face. "No, Apryl." Her hands may muffle her voice, but they don't muffle the exasperation. "About Dallas. The thing I said about Dallas."

My eyes widen. "Do you mean?" I jump from my dainty perch. "I can't believe that guy! Well, don't worry about him. I'll make sure he knows he can't mess with my sister and get away with it." I smack my right fist into the open palm of my left hand.

"Apryl."

"That jerk will rue the day, Courtney! He'll rue it!" I start punching the air around me. This type of boxing is much preferred to wailing on that huge, heavy bag hung from ceilings in gyms. Zero pain.

I swing a little too hard, and my shoulder makes a pop that's almost as loud as it hurts.

Okay, some pain.

Courtney raises her eyebrows.

"I'm fine," I say while wiggling my shoulder in a circular motion. "I'm just preparing to make him rue the day."

"Rule?"

"No, rue. R. U. E."

Courtney shakes her head. "That's sweet but I don't think you could pound Dallas."

"Then I'll get Miles to do it! Izze will agree with me. No one cheats on my sister and lives to tell about it."

"Apryl, he didn't cheat on me."

My invisible boxing arena fades into oblivion. "He didn't? Then what happened?"

"He lied to me."

"I surmised that much. What did he lie about?" I sit in the wingback again, leaning back and crossing my legs.

"He lied to me about everything!" Courtney sits up, and the entire story tumbles from her lips. She ends with "Can you believe he's trying to pin it on me?"

Okay, I know that Dallas wasn't trying to pin the blame on Courtney. I can see that he was trying to explain why he freaked out and lied to her.

I know this.

So why would I choose to say this?

"Yeah, I can. Why wouldn't he? It's so much easier to make it your fault than accept the fact that he's a lying, scheming coward."

Please don't judge me.

Courtney harrumphs in agreement.

But I'm only just stepping onto the soapbox.

"Because that's what they do, right? They lie. They manipulate. They play you like a fool. And we are fools. We're fools for letting them do this to us."

In hindsight, I may have let my own issues color my thoughtful narrative.

"They who? Men?" Confusion furrows Courtney's brow.

"No," I say, gesturing like I'm a music conductor, "not specifically men. I mean people who think they can take way they want. Do what they want. And the rest of the world just has to bow to their whims. They think other people are games put on earth for their personal amusement. It's not okay and I've had it!"

I jump up, whirl away, and march to the front door, holy fire infusing my every step. I don't even stop to put on shoes lest the fire burn through the soles. And I like this particular pair of shoes. They have that memory foam that feels like a silky pillow for your feet.

"Where are you going?" Courtney yells.

"To tell—" I catch myself before saying his name out loud— "one of *those people* that their days of manipulating are over!"

North.

The answer to which way the storm was coming from.

More precisely, the large house where Apryl resided once again. It was a truth Chance lived and breathed. He never knew when Apryl's volcano would fire at him, when her twister would tear through him, when her angry winds would rip him to shreds. But he was always prepared. It was a motto by which he lived and breathed.

Be prepared for Angry Apryl.

"Chance McFarland!"

It seemed a storm had arrived.

"Chance McFarland, get out here this instant!"

Chance rolled his eyes and grabbed the plain black T-shirt from the workbench where he'd discarded it two hours ago when the temperature in his garage had gotten to an unbearable level. It may be spring, but the insulation in his garage made it feel like a tropical beach.

He'd just yanked the shirt over his head when the door slammed open.

"Thanks for the knock," Chance grumbled and straightened the hem of his shirt.

"How dare you!" Apryl stood just outside the door, as if she refused to cross the threshold into his presence.

"What?"

"You know what!"

"No... No, at the moment I'm pretty confused."

"Asking me to dance," Apryl said through clenched teeth.

Chance scoffed. "Are you serious?"

"Yeah. You don't get to just ask me to dance because you're bored. I'm not your plaything. I'm a person."

"My apologies. I thought you were a platypus."

"Pretty soon I'm going to be your worst nightmare."

"Is that a promise?"

Apryl let out a primal growl that, frankly, impressed Chance. The chick had some lungs.

"What is your problem? Most women find it charming when a handsome man asks them to dance." He leaned against the doorjamb. She wasn't wearing shoes. The sight of her pale little toes mingling with the grass while she stood there yelling at him, red-faced and steaming, brought a chuckle to his lips.

Not his smartest move.

"Are you *laughing* at me?" She spat the words at him.

Chance pursed his lips together. "No."

"This is exactly what I'm talking about! You people think laughing at someone when they're angry is acceptable behavior! That everyone else is here to bow to your whims."

"You people? I'm half German. Is that what you mean? Seems a little—"

"Don't finish that statement! That is *not* what I mean and you know it!" She stomped her foot for emphasis. Chance managed to hold in the snort of laughter that time.

"Could you finish a complete thought? I have no idea what you're talking about, Apryl."

Apryl buried her face in her hands. After taking a few deep breaths, she met his eyes again. "Chance, I am a person with feelings, and before you respond with whatever condescending comment is brewing in that thick skull of yours, understand that I am not going to fall in love with you just because *you* are working for *me*. I'm not a plaything. If you're bored, collect some stamps."

Chance snorted. "Have you ever loved me?"

Apryl opened and closed her mouth, but before she could respond, the rest of her proclamation registered in Chance's brain.

"What do you mean I'm working for you?"

She raised her chin in the air. "Exactly what I said." Defiance laced her tone.

"I don't work for you. For that matter, I don't work for anyone. I work with my dad. I work with your grandmother. I would rather hack my foot off with a steak knife than work for you."

"My grandmother"—Apryl enunciated each word—"put Courtney and me in charge. Therefore, you work for me. Get over your ego."

"You're one to talk."

Apryl threw her hands up. "You're just like him, you know that?"

"Who?"

"Your father." She said "your father" like it was a curse word.

Amazing how her particular gift for inflection felt like a slap in the face.

Brush it off. He shook his head, clearing away the sting from her comment. Saint or monster, he had told her not to attack his father.

"You know what? Good! I hope I am like him. My father provided for me, building a business with his own two hands that he could pass on to me. He was there for me when everyone else left. He may be rough around the edges and expect things done a certain way, but he takes care of his own."

"Yeah, his own." Apryl's eyes bore into his. "What about everyone else? Your father has no problem pushing around anyone who doesn't fall into that category, making them feel small and insignificant. He's a bully! I shouldn't be surprised that you're just like him since you idolize his every move."

"Stop!" Chance slashed a hand through the air. "You don't get to talk about him that way. Keep your opinions about my family to yourself because I don't want to hear your stupid junk anymore! Don't make me say it again."

Her anger pulsed through the air toward him, but she remained silent. Only their angry huffing spoke for them.

Apryl whirled around. "Don't ask me to dance again."

"Don't mention my father again!"

Chance slammed the door, not bothering to wait to see if she replied. He needed to repair the damage from her verbal storm. Now.

Otherwise, who knew what the light of day would reveal about the weak points of his shelter.

Chapter Eight

"A little higher on the right."

"How about you jump up here, Spiderman, and do it yourself?" I snarl. "Enough is enough! I swear with every fiber of my flabby, out-of-shape being—and that just means I have more fiber in my being than the average person—that if you make me move this banner once more, I will go full-on Joker crazy!"

Courtney holds up both hands in surrender. "Sorry. The banner is fine where it is."

"I thought so," I mumble as I climb down the ladder. I grab a bag of Lay's Classic style potato chips—my preferred comfort food when my mood runs hotter than lava.

Chance and I haven't spoken since The Dancing Confrontation. Two weeks and three days ago.

Every time I think about him standing in front of me, only mere inches separating us, or of the unmistakable husky quality to his voice as he said, "Because I want that dance," my emotional state explodes into a volcanic eruption of confused lava.

When I think about our last conversation, my anger threatens to decimate small villages like I'm stinking Pompeii.

My one bright spot proves to be Gram, who is finally coming home. Her blood pressure has been confounding the doctors for weeks, and they refused to let her leave the hospital until it had stabilized. But at long last, Mademoiselle Fate was lifting her head and gazing at us in passive interest.

Ever the optimist, aren't I?

Courtney surveys the WELCOME HOME! banner tacked over our grandmother's bed. "Oh, guess what! While you were at the hospital yesterday packing up some of Gram's stuff, we got another gig!"

Her perkiness makes me want to vomit. "Super."

"A little more enthusiasm, please."

I force fake cheeriness into my voice. "Sorry. Super, duper cool."

"Try again."

"Golly, Courtney, that's the coolest thing I've ever heard of, that is, since the invention of sliced bread." I add a little fist pump at the end. You know, to really sell it.

Courtney sighs. "I give. It doesn't matter how many times you say it, I won't believe you."

Fine by me.

"Do you want any details on when the wedding will be?"

"Soon, I'm sure." Because God is forcing me to breathe the same air as Chance as punishment for some dastardly crime.

Courtney ties a couple helium balloons to the bedposts. "Four weeks after Izze's wedding."

"Yippee." I pop another potato chip into my mouth. An idea pops into my head. "Hey, do you think you could call Chance with the details? And remind him about Izze's wedding. When to be there and all that. It would help me a lot."

"Sure, I can take care of those details for you," Courtney says, but her eyes narrow. "But why?"

"No reason." I try to keep my voice light while avoiding my sister's all-seeing gaze.

"Is this about the—"

"Knock, knock!" Kaylee calls from downstairs.

Saved!

As long as she doesn't get the others to gang up on me. Gulp. I shove another handful of chips into my mouth.

"Office!" Courtney yells.

"What?" Izze shouts.

"Office!" Courtney and I both yell.

"Who's Wallace?" Izze asks as she appears in the office doorway, followed by Kaylee.

"Office," I enunciate. Due to Gram's broken hip and the fact that she needs a walker to move around for the time being, we've spent the last twenty-four hours converting the office into a makeshift bedroom/living room combo. Nice and orderly in here, but the kitchen looks like the office upchucked on its favorite blouse.

Courtney runs over and throws her arms around Izze. "It feels like I haven't seen you in forever! It's so weird not being at the house with you guys. How's Miles? How was marriage counseling? Shocking? Well, anyway, you look older and wiser."

Izze blinks. "I'm not sure how to take any of that, so moving right along." She sets a container of pickle dip (the best thing in the world, in case you were wondering) on the folding table that we set up under the one window in the office.

Courtney sticks out her tongue at Izze.

I point at the dip. "Did you make that?"

Izze snickers. "That's funny."

"I did." Kaylee sets a cake carrier on the table. "Izze never remembers how much sour cream to use."

"It's my gift."

"I thought your gift was finding the perfect wedding dress for any given women." I pop the last chip into my mouth. Aww... Empty. Sad.

"That's my God-given talent. But God has gifted me—like an eternal birthday gift—with never having to make a meal."

We all stare at her.

"The mess makes me hyperventilate," she says.

"And you'd kill yourself in a gas explosion," Kaylee adds.

Izze nods in agreement. "God knew what He was doing."

"How are you?" I direct the question to Kaylee.

Kaylee narrows her emerald green eyes. "I'm fine. Why?"

"I feel like we left you in the lurch, moving out like that." Another reason why this situation isn't a good idea.

"Please. I'm fine." She shakes her head, sending her red hair into a frenzy.

"What about when Izze moves out?" Courtney asks.

Izze raises an eyebrow at Kaylee, also waiting for her answer.

"Don't worry about me. You guys focus on helping your grandmother and the plans God has for you. Hey, speaking of your grandmother, when does she get here?"

"Smooth," Courtney mutters.

Izze points at Kaylee, who ignores her. "This conversation isn't over."

"Any minute now." I grab another bag of potato chips from the box of essential supplies that I brought downstairs with me. I'll drop it. For now. Like Izze said, this conversation isn't over.

"Who's bringing her?" Kaylee pops the lid from the cake carrier, revealing the delicious-looking masterpiece. My mouth starts to water. Potato who?

"The ladies from her book club. One of them threatened to put the fear of God into me if I even tried to circumvent her plan." A swift kick in the behind, to be exact.

Izze chuckled. "How nice."

That's not exactly what I thought at the time, but okay.

"I can't believe your wedding is only eleven days away!" Courtney exclaims.

"Ugh," Izze moans.

I snicker. "That's a promising response from a bride right before her wedding."

"No, I just have so many last-minute things to finish. I was at my mom and dad's house last night, and I just burst into tears. And we were only figuring the final counts for the menu and what Mom will be making for the reception. It's not like they tried to give me the honeymoon talk. Not yet, that is."

Collective cringing fills the room.

Izze rubs her face, her olive skin looking extremely pale from lack of sun exposure. "I'm just tired and stressed. And so looking forward to a relaxing honeymoon. Miles finally told me that he rented a private house on the beach in Maine."

"That sounds nice," Kaylee says.

The music of the doorbell jingling fills the air. "Hellooo!"

The gorilla from *Tarzan* sings in my head, "The fun has arrived!"

We rush from the office to see Mrs. Firee and Ms. Erickson flanking Gram inside the shop. The three elderly women make up their book club/prayer group/Bible study. When Gram permanently brought us home after that awful day so long ago, these two women were already here and waiting with apple pie, hot chocolate, and fingers eagerly waiting to pinch our cheeks.

"Apryl! Courtney!" Ms. Erickson runs for me, pinchers at the ready.

"Hello, Ms. Erickson." I yank my head to the right and throw my arms around the dear woman in a hug. "It's great to see you!"

"You too, my dear!" Ms. Erickson settles for pinching my arms.

Yeah, that's going to leave a bruise.

"Move over, Ida!" Mrs. Firee exclaims in her typical style of brash meets gruff. "It's been ages since I've seen these babies."

I don't mention we weren't exactly drooling, colicky infants when we came to live with Gram. It's not worth it. One does not go head-to-head with Marge Firee, a former lieutenant in the U.S. Navy. She's also the woman who threatened me with her kicking prowess, if you hadn't guessed.

She gives me a solid squeeze and releases me, all business now. "Enough of that. We need to get Charlotte settled into her bed on the double. Where to?"

"We have her set up in the office," Courtney says.

"Why on earth did you do that?" Gram mumbles as she uses the walker to help steady her smaller-than-a-baby's steps.

"Charlotte, stop your hooting and hollering. You can't get up the stairs." Mrs. Firee passes a potted aloe plant to me. The woman has a tendency of bestowing plants on people for all occasions.

Oh, you got the job? Here's a nice fern.

Congratulations on your impending nuptials! Enjoy the roses.

You failed the test? Here's a cactus. Don't be prickly for too long.

She also matches the plant according to the situation. Apparently, aloe plants are for every situation that requires any type of healing because she's given me an aloe plant twice before—the first time was when I had a cold and the second time was at the start of puberty, when that cruel mistress claimed my face with horrendous acne.

I follow the caravan into the office. The spacious room now feels a little cramped. I shuffle behind the backpedaling Ms. Erickson and dodge Izze's swinging left elbow.

Gram continues to mutter as her soul-sisters help her sit on the bed. She grimaces, and a knife pierces my lungs. I imagine my lungs deflating as all the oxygen leaks out like when someone lets an inflated balloon fly around the room instead of tying it closed.

Courtney places a hand on our grandmother's shoulder. "Can I get you anything, Gram?"

Gram eyes the table of chips, sparkling juice, dip, and cake. "I'd like some of the pickle dip. And don't skimp."

Everyone chuckles as Courtney rushes to do exactly as Gram asks. I know my sister would wrestle King Midas and risk being turned into gold just to make Gram happy.

Thankfully, Gram isn't that sadistic.

We visit for several hours, and one by one, ladies young and old leave until it's just us and Gram.

"For crying out loud. It's after eight o'clock," Gram gripes as the phone rings. "People shouldn't call so late unless there's an emergency."

"Gram, it's only a minute past," Courtney points out.

"And what if it's an emergency?" I ask.

Courtney inches closer to where the phone rests on Gram's nightstand. "We should answer the phone."

Gram harrumphs. The phone rings for the fourth time.

"I'll answer and put it on speaker phone," Courtney declares. "Hello? Burns residence, Courtney speaking."

I shake my head. Only my sister still answers the phone like that. You all are lucky if I even bother to say hello.

"Hello?" an old voice warbles. "I'm looking for Charlotte Burns."

Gram jerks in her bed, shock flinging across her wrinkled features. "Alice?"

Alice? Courtney mouths.

"Gram's sister," I whisper.

Gram and her sister hardly speak. Great Aunt Alice lives in Oregon, and Gram claims it's the distance that keeps them from being in each other's lives.

But her voice cracks whenever she says her sister's name, so I've never quite believed her.

"Charlotte," Great Aunt Alice grunts. "How are you?"

"Broken hip. Weeks in a hospital bed. Terrible food. You know what it's like."

"Yes. I *do* know what it's like," the faceless voice retorts.

"Why did you call, Alice?" Gram's never been one to beat the whipped cream past forty strokes.

"Marge called me."

If Marge Firee called my long-lost great aunt, then she did so with fire that wouldn't be ignored.

Get it? Firee. Fire.

"Well," Gram says after an awkward moment, "it was nice of you to call. Goodbye." She signals for Courtney to hang up.

Courtney glances at me in panic, knowing as well as I do that these women can't end the conversation here.

"Charlotte," Great Aunt Alice's interjects with a level of force that stops Gram's forceful hand gestures. "I want to help. My grandson helped me do some research, and I've hired a home health nurse to help you during your recovery for as long as you need it. He starts on Monday."

Out of the corner of my eye, I notice Courtney stiffen.

Gram bristles at yet another reminder of her need to lean on the support of others (instead of the other way around), let alone from the sister she's hardly spoken to in who knows how long. She opens her mouth, but I shoot her the same look she gave me when Courtney chose the same pair of shoes as me so we could match in fifth grade.

She huffs again. After a couple deep breaths, Gram finally responds in a calm, somewhat thankful voice. "Thank you, Alice."

"You're welcome."

Static fills the line.

"I love you, Charlotte."

Tears glisten in Grams eyes. "I love you too, Alice."

The line goes dead.

"Are you finished murdering my expertly crafted dinner?"

Courtney looked up at her sister, who sat across from her at the table. "It's Spam and rice."

Apryl splayed her hands, indicating their partially eaten food. "It's not burned. And I added some special ingredients to it. Cumin. Red pepper."

She rolled her eyes. "Sure. Everyone knows that red pepper makes anything a five-star meal."

Apryl pushed the rice—if you could call it that—around on her plate. "Can I ask you something?"

"Maybe."

Her sister ignored her. "What did you say that made Dallas think that you hated everybody in the medical field?"

Here it was. The small detail Courtney had avoided sharing. "Well, I *did* say that I hated the medical field...and everything therein."

Apryl blinked. "Just like that?"

"Pretty much." Courtney shoved her food toward the middle of the table and turned to look out the window.

"Wow, Courtney! I get it now."

Her head swiveled back to look at her sister. "What?"

"No wonder he was afraid to tell you."

"I can't believe you're excusing his lie!" Anger bubbled up.

"Whoa!" Apryl held up both her hands, palms out. "I'm not. I'm talking about empathy. I can understand why he was scared. I'm not saying it was okay to lie."

"Then why does it feel the same?"

"Because he lied to you and that hurts. It broke trust."

Courtney crossed her arms on the chipped table and planted her chin on top of them. "What do I do?"

"I think you should talk to him again."

Courtney harrumphed. "Like you did with Chance last week?"

Apryl's eyes widened. "You heard that?"

Courtney nodded. "You're lucky we don't have any neighbors nearby, or someone would have called the cops for a domestic disturbance."

"My...relationship with Chance is hardly a display of domesticity."

"No kidding."

"Regardless, I think you should talk to Dallas. And soon."

Apryl's hands clasped hers. "I of all people understand why you said that. Be honest with him. It's a two-way street." She squeezed Courtney's hand.

"Like you've been honest with Chance?"

Apryl's face paled from its natural shade of alabaster white to the ashy white that usually only appears on the animated undead. "It's not the same thing."

"You could be honest with him."

Despite the bickering disdain that sometimes overtook them, Courtney and Apryl were each other's closest confidants. When Apryl had told her what William had said that day, Courtney spared no shortage of withering looks aimed at Chance's dad—that was all she could get away with on Gram's watch—while she tried to soothe her sister's battered heart. Although Apryl had never admitted it, Courtney knew how she felt about Chance. It was the twin thing.

"No," Apryl said forcefully.

"You don't think telling Chance what William said or how he's treated you since then would make a difference?"

"No. It wouldn't. Chance worships his father. There's no room for anything else with that in the way."

"Anything? Like what?"

Apryl shot her a glare. "Like honesty. And this conversation isn't even about me. It's about you. What are you going to do?"

"I don't know," Courtney moaned.

"Well, you better figure it out soon."

Soon... No kidding. Apryl had no idea just how soon.

Because it was Sunday night.

Courtney had a feeling. And while occasionally her feelings were wrong, this time they weren't.

She knew. She just knew. Oh, boy, did she know what was going to happen.

The ancient grandfather clock struck ten o'clock.

Gram's home health nurse would be here any second.

Courtney's pulse beat with a force that could probably be seen in addition to felt. Gram had already asked her if she needed to see a doctor. Thankfully, Apryl had left for the day to meet with the bride who would be getting married four short weeks after Izze. Apryl had insisted that she needed to tour the space and speak with the bride beforehand, and although Courtney was annoyed at first that she wouldn't be here to help with Gram, relief had flooded her when she realized Apryl wouldn't be here when Dallas showed up.

Because Courtney just knew.

A knock sounded on the door.

She flung it open.

Dallas sent her a sheepish smile from across the threshold. "Hey."

"Hi."

"How are you?" His voice was quiet, gentle, almost like he feared she'd bolt if he really showed this side of his world. He had Bambi Eyes. (Bambi Eyes, by the way, are a well-documented condition of the pupils, indicating stress, anxiety, and a fear so strong that the individual in question could flee given the slightest misstep. Symptoms include fidgeting, darting eyes, constant shifting, and spontaneous vomiting.) Given that Dallas had no idea what she wanted, the expression was justified.

The sad thing was that she didn't know what she wanted either.

Just that she wanted him.

"I'm fine." Not exactly lying. "Want to meet my grandmother?"

"As your boyfriend or as her healthcare professional?"

"Healthcare first."

His face fell.

Courtney reached for the hand not wrapped around the strap of a bulging duffle bag filled with medical supplies. "For now. Boyfriend...soon." She hoped.

He gave her a weak smile, but the Bambi Eyes disappeared. "Okay. Lead the way."

She took him to Gram's temporary bedroom. "Gram, this is Dallas. The home health nurse that Great Aunt Alice hired."

"Good morning, Mrs. Burns. It's nice to meet you." Dallas

gave her grandmother a firm handshake, something she knew Gram would appreciate.

Courtney watched in awe as her boyfriend—she hoped—charmed her grandmother for the next two hours with that personality that had drawn her in the first day she'd heard him speak in class. When they got into a heated, albeit friendly, debate with the class taking sides and cheering, Courtney knew she needed to get to know this man. Thankfully, Dallas had felt the same about her. He asked her out for their first date right after class.

"That was amazing," she whispered once they'd slipped out of her grandmother's temporary room.

"Thanks. I've always found it to be rewarding work." Dallas rocked back and forth on his heels. The tension from their last conversation hung between them like a giant black spider ready to pounce.

Courtney restrained herself from shuddering in response to the mental image. Shuddering would not send a good message to Dallas.

"So."

"So." Dallas raised his eyebrows.

"Can we talk?"

He studied her for a moment before nodding. "Okay."

"Okay." She lifted her lips into a nervous smile. Sweat pooled in her palms. "Follow me." What was wrong with her? She hadn't been this jittery since their first date. The upcoming conversation didn't need to hold *that* much power over her.

Courtney motioned for Dallas to follow her, and she held a finger to her lips. Gram had hearing that could rival Superman. She led him through the front door and around the left side of the grand house, stopping in front of a small gazebo. The scent of the river mingled with the hundreds of flowers Gram had planted around the space. But that scent—a scent that gave new meaning to flower power—wasn't what dizzied her senses.

Dallas didn't say anything as he stepped inside the gazebo. She watched him take in the elaborate carvings, crude etchings, and weather damage, waiting for him to catch sight of it.

"Renee Hart and Davis Burns." He ran this thumb over the date underneath their names, scratched into the old wood.

Courtney nodded. "My parents. Dad carved their names into the wood and then proposed to Mom here." Neither of them sat on the little benches in the gazebo that her father had made and painted himself. Instead they stood in the middle of the floor. Close but...not.

Dallas's lips quirked to the right. "Awfully sure of himself, wasn't he?"

"That's what Mom always said, but then she would smile and kiss him." Courtney shrugged. She felt Dallas's eyes on her, studying her, searching her, discovering her pain.

Waiting for her to share that pain with him.

Courtney cleared her throat. "I've told you that my parents died when I was seven, and my grandmother raised us after that." She risked a glance at Dallas, and he nodded confirmation. Or encouragement? "It was a car accident. We were with Gram when it happened. When she got the phone call, she rushed us to the hospital. And we waited...for weeks."

When Courtney didn't say anything for several minutes, Dallas spoke up. "Coma?"

She nodded. "Then their organs started to fail one night. Simultaneously. What are the odds of that?" She snickered ruefully. "The nurses and doctors pushed us out of the room. A few hours later, some doctor—I don't even remember his name or what he looked like—took us into a small room to tell us... I remember every detail of that room," Courtney whispered, avoiding his eyes.

"I'm sorry, Courtney. I'm so sorry." The emotion in his deep voice sent reverberations throughout her body, and unwelcome tears filled her eyes.

"I saw things in that hospital... I imagine anyone who's camped at the bedside of someone they love as an advocate and support person has a painful story of their own." She looked into his eyes again. "I know you do. But that's why I said...what I did. Those were the worst days of my life, and I just wanted to forget them. And achieving that meant having nothing to do with hospitals or doctors or medicine."

"Or cute medical lawyers," Dallas added with a sad smile. He cleared his throat, and a jolly breeze swirled around them in an attempt to liven the mood between them. "If I had told you in the beginning, would you have ended things?"

"I'd like to think that I wouldn't have. I kind of liked you, you know." Courtney quirked one side of lips but knew her eyes still held sadness. "But I don't know. It's not worth wondering about because we are where we are."

"And where are we?" Dallas's trepidation slipped through the facade of his even voice. His vulnerability melted her heart.

She took his hand and squeezed it. "We keep working through it."

"Is that what you want?" His eyes searched her soul.

Deep breath. "I want you, so...yes, I want to work through it."

Dallas rubbed her thumb with his. Heat radiated through her body. Was this what it felt like to swoon? At the moment, this small, gentle, seemingly inconsequential touch felt more impactful than the most passionate kiss she could imagine.

The nervousness within her exploded into a fit of awkward giggles. Dallas shook his head before his deep laugh joined her. Then he scooped her into his arms and twirled her around.

"So what now?" he asked when he'd set her down.

Courtney held onto his arm to steady herself against the world that continued to spin. Blink. Yeah, she was too old to spin like that. "I'd like you to come to Izze's wedding with me. As my boyfriend."

He raised his eyebrows. "Meeting your friends? And sister? Is this going to be stressful?"

"Most assuredly."

"Wonderful," he sighed, but a grin stretched across his lips. "What about meeting your grandmother?" He gestured toward the house.

"If you can survive my friends and sister then you can handle meeting my grandmother."

"Wait a second... Are you telling me that meeting your grandmother is going to be even more stressful than meeting your girlfriends?"

"Last year she chased a bear away from her hummingbird feeders with a weed whacker."

Dallas's eyes widened.

"Don't worry, I'll hide the weed whacker before we tell her."

He rolled his eyes. "That's real comforting."

"I thought so. It is her weapon of choice."

Chapter Nine

"**O**uch!"

"Sorry," I mutter through clenched teeth, concentrating as I put the finishing touches on my sister's low bun.

"Could you maybe not pull the skin off my scalp?" Courtney gripes, relaxing her shoulders.

Izze makes a face. "Gross. There shall be absolutely no talk of such things on this sacred day," she proclaims from where she sits in the oversized chair in the bridal room at our church. Kaylee kneels on the floor, busy painting sapphire blue polish on Izze's toenails, adding to the queen vibe Izze gives off.

Today is the day Izze and Miles tie the matrimonial knot, in case you hadn't guessed.

"Sound logic," I reply. "The world does revolve around you today."

"If anyone else said that, I would think they were calling me a bridezilla." Izze's head is covered in rollers to give her naturally curly hair a sleeker look, and her bridal sweats radiate an especially blinding light thanks to the harsh fluorescents in the room. Add those details to the fact that Kaylee is literally waiting on her hand and foot...

"Who says I'm not?" I wiggle my eyebrows up and down.

Relax, I'm just kidding.

Izze studies me for a moment. "You look like one of those creepy clowns that scar children for life."

"Anyone else and I'd think they were saying that my face resembles a creepy clown in a horror flick."

Izze grins. "Well, as long as we have an understanding."

I pull a couple hairpins out of my bag, sticking them in between my teeth. Then I grab my secret weapon—a piece of wood about as long as my hand that has a blunt hook on the end resembling one of Gram's latch hooks. Careful not to incite my sister's wrath once again, I slowly pull a few tendrils of hair from Courtney's bun.

Kaylee looks over. "Did you pull all of her hair out of the bun?"

"No."

She snorts. "Whatever you say."

I loop tendril after tendril, forming these adorable O's all over Courtney's head. I tuck the ends of each strand into the bun and secure them with more bobby pins. Then I take another lock of hair and wrap it around the base of the bun to hide that her hair resembles a pin cushion, securing it underneath with the twenty-seventh—not an exaggeration—bobby pin of the day. Last but not least, I use a tiny curling iron to style the tendrils that frame Courtney's face.

"Ta-dah!" I proclaim, taking a step back.

Izze and Kaylee both stand up to take a closer look.

Does Izze hate it? I could care less what Courtney says, since its Izze's wedding day. But if Izze wants to vomit just looking at it then there's a problem.

"It's my take on pin curls," I say after a moment. Izze really incorporated a vintage feel into her wedding theme, achieving shabby chic in a way that truly lives up to the name. I thought this reimagined version of a classic hairdo would work well.

Thought being the operative word.

"Dude, this is amazing." Awe tinges Izze's voice. Kaylee agrees with her, and even Courtney, after a thorough inspection, can't find any fault with it.

"Well, if there's one thing I know I can do, it's hair." I mean to say this lightheartedly, but a sarcastic edge undercuts my words.

The others, mercifully, don't comment. They exchange a series of undecipherable looks, but they don't make a peep.

"Are you sure you're going to have enough time to finish decorating and get back here to do your hair?" Izze asks, breaking the awkward silence.

"Trust me, my hair will be the easy part. Chance is setting up the big, non-breakable stuff as we speak." I dig around in my bag, pulling out a canister of hairspray and aiming it at Courtney's head. "Now," I say to my sister, "put on your gas mask."

"Chance?" I pace around the reception space while turning in circles.

I could have been a figure skater. Clearly, I have the ice dancing gene.

"Chance?" I call again.

He pops up from between two rows of chairs toward the front of the aisle. "Huh?" He blinks, clearing his eyes.

I assume you're dying to know what's going on with Chance, yes? Short answer: nothing. Like always. Long answer: I texted him apologizing for the outburst, and he responded with, *We're good. See you soon.* Courtney took mercy on me and called him about the details for Izze's wedding.

So there you are. All caught up.

"Dude, were you asleep?" Those bleary eyes are kind of cute. Mental slap.

Oy. Perhaps we're a little too good. We've fallen into a nice, playful bickering rhythm today. My defenses might be slipping. And that's bad. Very, very bad. The last time my CDS (Chance Defense System) was down resulted in a scary conversation with his father.

"Maybe. Why not? Some of us need our beauty sleep." He grins at me, and I roll my eyes. "I just figured I'd shut my eyes for twenty minutes while I waited for you. I even set a timer on my phone." He holds his phone up for me to see. Three minutes remain on the countdown.

"I couldn't find you in the reception area, so I thought I'd check to see if you were in here." Okay, maybe I was a little worried that he would bail on me. After all, we were screaming at each not too long ago.

"I finished unloading and setting up all the big stuff. Didn't dare touch anything else." Chance stands up and stretches. I avert my eyes, trying not to gawk at this handsome man who has wreaked all kinds of emotional devastation on me in the past.

Chance walks toward me, a frown covering his annoyingly cute face. "What is on your head?"

I touch the purple bandana that covers two dozen hair rollers. There was no way around it. By the time I finished Izze and Kaylee's hair, I needed to throw mine in the rollers to help the process later.

"It's a bandana." And the Most Obvious Response Award goes to...

"Yeah, I can see that. What are the bumps?"

"Bee stings?"

"Bee stings. Those must have been some really big bees."

"Ginormous. Can we get back to the task at hand?" I shift my weight from my right foot to my left.

"As long as you're not too woozy, mademoiselle." A lazy smirk tugs at his full lips.

"Save the sweet talk for someone who appreciates it," I say as my heart pitter-patters.

"Once upon a time, you did."

"Oh, what a fictitious world you live in, Chance. Now, let's decorate in here then we'll tackle the sanctuary."

Chance points towards the back of the sanctuary. "Boxes are back there."

"Wonderful." I walk to the boxes and start sorting, setting the items into piles organized by what should be done first. "Okay," I say once everything is unloaded and, frankly, quite disorganized despite my system. "Let's set the candelabras and vases up front first. Izze's father should be here soon with the flowers." Izze was in a mild panic this morning when she realized she forgot the flowers at home—uh, my home...my unused home...her former home.

Weird. It's going to take a while to adjust to that.

"Shouldn't we fill the vases with water so that they're all ready?"

"No, they're wood flowers."

Chance blinks at me. "That statement seems wrong somehow."

I snort. "Fake flowers made from delicate wood shavings." I

shrug when Chance continues to stare at me. "You'll see what I mean when they get here. Stop staring at me."

"Says the woman whose head is supposedly covered in 'bee stings.'" Chance makes air quotes with his middle and index fingers.

"Your tone made the point. The air quotes were unnecessary." I hate it when people use those. Unless it's me...then it's acceptable.

"Show me the 'bee stings,' and then they will be unnecessary."

Not on your life, buddy. "We're wasting time!"

"You're just proving my point."

I start pulling cream-colored candelabras out of the boxes lining the back wall. Beautiful glass crystals adorn all of them. I finger one of them. Not antique, but still beautiful.

Clink.

"I think one fell into the box," Chance says, holding up a candelabrum with a lopsided amount of crystals.

Goody. I lean over the deep box, straining and stretching my neck to find the missing adornment.

But apparently that little bit of straining is all it takes to loosen what Izze assured me was, "the tightest knot this side of Connecticut." My purple bandana slips from my head, fluttering into the box like it didn't just light what remained of my self-esteem on fire.

I'm burning it when I get home. In an oil drum while laughing like a Batman villain.

"Bee stings, Grandma?"

I snatch the traitorous bandana, turn away from Chance, and retie it onto my head. I take a deep breath before turning around.

Chance's eyes are exploding with mirth. "Where to start? Where to start?" He rubs his hands together.

I narrow my eyes in a warning. "You shouldn't poke the bear."

He looks me up and down, fully taking in my worn flip-flops, pink plaid leggings, yellow button-down shirt, and purple bandana covering a head full of hair rollers. "I think I can handle the bear."

I clench my fists. "You won't think that when I rip the stick from your hands and snap it with my teeth, Angry Apryl style."

"Is this metaphorical or literal? Because I have to be honest with you—I really want to see that."

I ignore Chance's goading—and you should applaud me because that makes the unicorns of my soul die—and start decorating the church sanctuary. Somehow—and I'm really not sure how—we fall into a blissful silence, only interrupted with the occasional question or direction here and there.

The decorations in the sanctuary are relatively simple. The space is made up of light and dark wood, but it works well together. Large windows reside on three out of four walls, flooding the room with lots of natural light. We've just finished placing the tiny, scent-free cream-colored candles on each arm of each candelabrum when Izze's father arrives.

"Flower delivery! *Wood* you like some?" Izze's father is one of those men who lives by the light of his obvious puns.

"Thank you! You can set those boxes on that back pew," I call from the far-left side of the sanctuary.

Chance, already at the back of sanctuary, strolls over and extends his right hand. "Chance McFarland. Nice to meet you."

"Ben Vez. Nice to meet you, son."

I dash over, eager to see these flowers that Izze has been raving about for months. They better live up to the hype. I pull open the flaps, carefully remove the bubble wrap, and gasp.

They are stunning!

"Wow, they actually look like real flowers," Chance says, only mild interest coloring his expression.

I huff in disgust. Some men...

I examine the bouquet in my hands. "I love the creamy roses and the blue delphinium. This is amazing, and oh my goodness! These roses have writing on them!" Izze had told me she wanted to incorporate her literary love into the wedding, but I never imagined this.

Ben nods. "Yes, quotes taken from *Pride and Prejudice.*"

"This must have cost a fortune." I cringe, trying to do the math. And failing.

"Actually, it was only a third of the cost of what a florist would have charged," Ben informs us. "I guess she found a company online that specializes in this sort of thing. Seems a lot of people go this route."

"Wow." I turn the bouquet over in my hands. Exquisite. That's the only word that seems to do these flowers justice.

Ben opens a smaller box. "These are the petals that are supposed to be strewn across either side of the aisle, on the tables in the reception hall as well as what the flower girls will use." Filled with the three types of petals and buds that make up the bouquet, the box probably holds a few thousand petals. My guess is that we will be looking for more creative decorating solutions in order to put all of them to good use.

Chance's eyes are wide. "That's a lot."

Poor guy looks nervous.

Hehe.

"Don't worry," I say, knowing he won't contradict me with Izze's father standing here. "*You* won't have a hard time decorating with them." Chance shoots me a dirty look.

"Oh, not at all." Ben looks at Chance. "Thank you, son! Well, I best get back to my official father-of-the-bride duties. See you two later."

Chance waits until Ben is only just out of hearing distance before growling, "You better not be leaving me to figure out what to do with all of these decorative scraps of paper."

"They're flower petals!"

"They're paper carved in the shape of flowers."

"Then why do they smell good?" I put my hands on my hips. "And is it even possible to carve paper? No. You carve wood."

Chance looks from me to the flowers back to me. "I give up. Can we get back to work now?"

"You can. I have to go." Yes, I am taunting him on purpose.

"You can't be serious."

I make a show of glancing at my phone and gasping at the time. "I'm serious."

"But... I...You..."

"I'm sorry! I am so sorry! I have to go," I call as I run out the double doors. I walk partially down the hallway and wait. I lean against the wall, studying my fingernails.

Isn't that what the villains do? Not that I'm claiming villainy, but this seems like one of those moments.

Four...three...two...one...

Chance comes barreling down the hall. "Apryl, wait! I can't do this without you!"

He stops. Takes me in.

I raise an eyebrow, not bothering to contain my smirk of victory.

Chance narrows his eyes. "You're mean."

"Only when you poke me with a stick." He glowers and I laugh. "Let's finish in there."

Chance swept the floor as he waited for Apryl to return with Izze.

They were finished. At long last.

He glanced around the room. He didn't give two figs about decorating, wedding venues, or bizarre wood flowers, but he had to admit the space looked pretty good.

And that was all he was going to say about it.

His thoughts wandered as he swept. Planning. Debating. Maybe he should have been named *Conflicted*.

Apryl and Chance had spent the last four hours working together in easy comradery. He had avoided her ever since their bizarre screaming match—but to be fair, all of their arguments were tinted with the bizarre thanks to Apryl's love of the verbal dance—like she had chicken pox, strep throat, and the flu all rolled into one germy cocktail. For weeks he had gone back and forth until he had finally convinced himself (translation: repeated it a thousand and one times) that the romantic tension had been completely imagined. Fake. A remaining tidbit of the old Chance that needed to be thrown away.

The way his heart thundered when he saw her first thing this morning wasn't helping his theory, though.

Which was why he was determined to dance with Apryl tonight since he'd never actually agreed to her no-dancing demand. Then he could decipher if there was something electric between them. It might be a flawed theory, but he was a car guy. You took the vehicle in question for a test drive when you wanted to see if it could run. Same logic applied.

He hoped.

One word flashed through his mind: *dad.*

His shoulders tensed. What about him? Chance knew his father could be...difficult. Even that tiny acknowledgment made him feel uneasy—guilty, even—like he was betraying his father. It nagged at his heels, refusing to be ignored. He couldn't see if there was anything between them when she hated his father. It wouldn't be right.

But he had to know.

He was trying not to think about what his father would have to say about it.

Ungrateful son, a voice said.

Whoa, the Old Chance added.. *A relationship? Father or not, since when did we start looking to settle down?*

Chance growled to the voices, to himself. *For once, I'm going to do what I want to do. My past is in the past, and my father doesn't get to control everything about my life.*

The broom caught something, sending it scrapping and clattering across the floor. Chance bent over. Where did it go? With a groan, he got on all fours and lowered himself onto his stomach, searching under the pews. He pulled his phone out of his pocket and turned on the flashlight app. Nothing.

Wait... There. Something glinted about three feet from him.

He army crawled forward, stretching until his fingers touched the cool metal of the object. Grasping it, he pulled his body back until he sat on his haunches.

A locket.

Chance fingered the object, running his thumb over the worn floral pattern. It looked familiar. Maybe there would be a picture on the inside that would help him figured out who it belonged to. If not, he'd give it to Apryl. She'd know what to do with it.

He slid what little fingernail he had on his thumb in between the thin piece of metal, popping the lock open with ease.

Tiny shards of papers fell into his hand. No pictures.

Each paper had a little faded heart on one side and neat, tiny cursive writing on the other side.

He wasn't trying to invade someone's privacy, really he wasn't, but one caught his eye.

A tiny piece of paper with his name.

Chance McFarland

What was this? If he didn't know any better, Chance would think he had entered an episode of *The Twilight Zone*.

He flipped the other papers over.

Courtney Burns. Charlotte Burns. Izze Vez.
Kaylee McGrurd. Renee and Davis Burns.

Chance dropped the locket. "Oh, no. Oh, no. Oh, no." He clamped his mouth shut, lest any foul language slip out. He didn't need *Swearing in church* added to his stack of sins.

Apryl's locket. This was Apryl's locket.

She was going to kill him. Death. Slow and painful. And probably deserved. The Angry Apryl of the past would be a joke compared to the Swamp Thing version of her that would emerge when she found out what he had done.

Chance started to stuff the papers back into the locket, praying that she didn't have them in there in a particular order. And that she didn't notice the extra folds and creases thanks to his shoddy stuffing job, which was ironic given his almost-Olympic ability to shove sock after sock into his top dresser drawer.

His hand lingered over the last piece of paper. The one with his name on it.

Why did she have his name in her locket?

"Chance?"

Without thinking, he stuffed the paper with his name written in pretty cursive into his pocket. He jumped up, startling Apryl and Izze.

Apryl narrowed her eyes. "Were you napping again?"

"No, I..." He ran a hand through his hair. What had he been doing? "I was sweeping. We made a mess."

Her gaze softened. "Thank you."

Izze pointed at the locket in his hands. "What's that?"

"Oh, this!" What was with all his jumping? He needed to cool it. Chance thrust his hand toward them. "Here! I found this while I was sweeping."

"What's that?" They moved closer and Chance could swear the incriminating piece of paper burned against his leg.

"Oh, my goodness!" Apryl's hand flew up to her throat, grasping for the locket that wasn't there. "I didn't realize it had fallen off. Thank you!" Gratitude flooded her expression, making him feel a quarter of an inch tall.

"Don't worry about it. Looks like the clasp broke. I didn't realize it was yours. At first." Stop talking, dude. Stop talking.

Apryl reached for the locket, and her fingers brushed against his. Fire hotter than an overheated engine burned between them. He yanked his hand back, and the locket fell into the chasm between them.

Izze eyed them, suspicion in those dark espresso eyes of hers.

Chance looked down at the locket, which had popped open between them. Apryl threw her body over the tiny papers that had fallen out again in a desperate attempt to cover them. Her movement, however only scattered them farther apart.

He just stood there like a dolt while Izze bent over, grabbing a couple at her feet. "Hey, this one has my name on it."

Apryl's face, already as red as the tomatoes from her grandmother's garden, deepened in hue. "Yeah. I, uh, keep the names of the people closest to me in my locket. To pray for you and stuff because you're near to my heart. Uh, metaphorical and all that." She coughed.

The earth should swallow him whole right about now.

"Oh, Apryl! That's so sweet!" Izze threw her arms around Apryl. "When did you add my name?"

Apryl smiled. "When Courtney and I moved into the house."

"Aww!" Izze squeezed Apryl again before releasing her.

Apryl took the papers from Izze's hand. "It's not a big deal."

"It is! Don't be silly."

Chance crouched and grabbed the piece of paper with *Charlotte Burns* written on it that rested beside his left foot. "Here you go," he said softly.

Apryl meet his eyes. "Thanks."

He was a terrible person.

Apryl stood up fast and tucked the locket into her back pocket. "Let's look around, Izze."

Chance stood and grabbed the long-abandoned broom to finish sweeping as the women looked around the sanctuary. It might sound kind of girly, but he needed to regain his composure.

"Guys, this is amazing," Izze said after ten or so minutes. Tears flooded her eyes. "I don't know how I'll ever thank you."

"Diamonds are always nice," Apryl said.

"Or food," Chance added.

Izze grinned. "The only diamonds that I have I'm not giving away." She wiggled her left hand, and her unique engagement ring shimmered in the light. "But there will be wonderful food tonight."

"Well, as a member of your bridal party, I'm feeling a little cheated."

"Count me in," Chance said.

Apryl's eyes widened in panic. Panic, eh? "You're going to stay? I told you that you didn't have to. That Courtney could help me pack stuff up tonight."

"What kind of partner would I be if I did that?" Chance crooned as if everything was normal.

Izze clapped her hands together and bounced. Bounced. The woman was a giant ball of caffeinated energy. "Great! Let's go look at the reception hall now!" Izze moved through the doors without waiting for them.

"You don't have to stay. Really."

"Do you not what me to stay?" Chance studied this woman he had known for so long but apparently knew so little about.

"No. I mean, yes."

"I have no idea what you're trying to say." But didn't he? Chance wasn't ready to pull at that thread of thought just yet.

"You can stay. I have no problem with you staying." She shifted back and forth on her feet.

"Good. I've got a change of clothes stashed in the car."

"Seriously?"

"I take my job as a wedding crasher very seriously."

Apryl shook her head. "Except you were invited again."

"Is this the part where I say pah-tah-toe?"

She smirked. "That's my thing."

Yeah, well, it seemed like Chance had taken a lot of her things lately.

Chapter Ten

I glance at Izze, the beaming bride to be.

I am so, so happy for her.

But...

But there's a part of me that wants to use my sapphire blue bridesmaid dress as a target for darts. I even have this image in my mind's eye where I rip off the scallop lace hem and tie it around my forehead.

Extreme? Sorry. Just don't tell on me. I swear it's only like two percent of me.

Izze fiddles with her lacy veil, which matches her gorgeous one-of-a-kind wedding gown to perfection. "I feel weird." She straightens the already straight veil across her forehead once again.

Kaylee frowns. "Weird how?"

"Nervous?" Courtney asks.

Izze shakes her head. "No, not nervous. Anxious maybe? Like I'm so, so ready to marry this man and start our lives that it makes me physically ache. I have no doubts, just this amazing sensation that God orchestrated all of this."

Gag me.

Courtney and Kaylee tear up—the appropriate response, I suppose. They rush Izze, clinging to her while they laugh and cry at the same time.

I grin at the sight.

Well, I *am* happy for Izze.

"Cuddles," I shout before rushing into the lacy fray.

A door swings open in my peripheral vision. "What's this?"

We, the giant ball of human satin and lace, turn as one organism. Izze's mom and aunt, Sandy and Jill as they insisted I call them, stand inside the doorway, tears in their eyes and grinning like human versions of the Cheshire Cat.

And can I take a second to point out how creepy that is?

"Well, make room for me," Jill declares, throwing her long arms around the lot of us. Sandy then encircles the group, hugging Izze in the tight way all mothers do.

"Thank you, thank you, God," Izze says, emotion thickening her voice.

"Amen and amen!" Aunt Jill exclaims.

Before I know it, we're all praying for Izze and Miles, asking God to bless and guide them. Despite my ongoing beef with God, I cannot deny that He is with us here and now. His presence is so thick, He might as well have His arms wrapped around us too.

"Wow," Izze says, blinking rapidly after we've finished our impromptu prayer session.

"Yeah," I say. Because just...wow.

Jill claps her hands. "All right, ladies. My husband didn't nickname me the drill sergeant for no reason. It's time to move Izze from the bridal room to the staging area."

"Staging area? This is a wedding, not a theater production," Izze mutters.

"I heard that, young lady," Jill says without even turning around from where she fixes the heel of Sandy's shoe.

"Yeah, you were supposed to." Izze sticks out her tongue.

"Oh, yes. That is a very flattering pose. Quick, Sandy! Get the photographer!" Jill rolls her eyes.

"Go ahead," Izze taunts. "I'll wait."

"Izze," Sandy says, smirking, "you have other things to focus on right now than a verbal battle with your aunt."

I nudge Izze with my elbow. "I don't think sticking out your tongue should count as verbal."

"I agree. What about—"

Sandy says, "Later," while at the same time Jill grabs Izze's hand and pulls her toward the door.

I grab my bouquet while the girls scurry around, grabbing everything they may need, and use it like one of those flashlight wands they use to guide planes to and from gates at the airport. The two times I've flown in my life, I've been convinced the plane was going to hit those employees. Not one hundred percent certain that we didn't, to be honest.

"Move it, ladies! Let's go! Get a move on! March! Left, left, left, right, left!" I shout.

"If you don't stop, I will throw my shoe at you," Courtney says.

I ignore her. "We have a lady getting married. This is not a drill! I repeat, this is not a drill!"

Courtney rolls her eyes as she brushes by me and into the hallway, following Jill, Sandy, and Izze, who is somehow skipping in her wedding dress.

The lyrics for "Going to the Chapel of Love" flutter through my head and I smile.

Kaylee stops just outside the doorway, pointing over her shoulder at the ceiling. "Oh, can you grab the bag of lip gloss?" Kaylee's aim isn't that great.

"No problem. I'll be right there." I wave for her to follow the others. I scan the room for the white bag that says Pucker Up in sparkly pink letters that Izze got at her bridal shower. I spot it sitting on the lumpy beige couch beside my Old Navy tote bag.

I grab the bag but hesitate as I catch sight of my locket. My clothes are just crammed into the bag, and my locket peaks at me from the back pocket of my leggings as if to say, "I'm sorry I ran away and almost revealed your secret crush!"

I pull the contrite locket out of hiding, popping it open. I haven't opened it in years. Crumpled papers fall into my hand. I take a minute, taking attendance before I expertly refold the slips.

One's missing.

The one with Chance's name.

Panic, mortification, and fear all fight for top billing.

Where did it go? Did I miss it in the sanctuary? I shake my head. No, I discreetly scanned the area as Izze and I walked around. There was nothing. I even toed through Chance's dirt pile.

Discreetly, of course.

There's only one option...

I must have gotten rid of it years ago. I'd wanted to. The day Chance's father indicated I wasn't good enough for his son. One year after realizing that I fallen head over heels in like-ish/love with Chance, so hey, why not pray for him? I must have actually done it. Given up.

It's too bad William McFarland hadn't kept his mouth shut. It's not like his son ever looked twice at me.

Old wounds start to itch and I want to scratch. The nasally voice in my head tells me to scratch. That it will help. That I'll feel better. But I know from experience that the rash will spread and ache until every inch of my soul is covered in welts.

Breathe. His whisper.

As I inhale, I try to recall one of the many verses I've learned about my worth in God's eyes. Instead the only thing that comes to mind is the seventh verse of Psalm fifty-one.

Purge me with hyssop, and I shall be clean; wash me, and I shall be whiter than snow.

Every part of me longs to have the words spoken over me, my circumstances, even my identity. To be washed away.

Leaving me new. Clean. Whiter than snow.

Instead, the same old, dingy person walks through the doorway to join her friends for a white wedding.

"Is that him?"

Courtney glanced to where Izze pointed. Heat flooded her cheeks while relief pooled at her feet.

Dallas had come.

She'd been nervous when she couldn't spot him as she walked down the aisle, but there he was, walking toward her wearing an adorable grin and a dark gray suit.

"Yes! It's about time for some payback." Izze did a little fist pump.

Courtney tore her gaze away from Dallas and twisted in her seat to face her friend. "What are you talking about?"

probably bad form to hiss at the bride on her wedding day... Oh well.

"Payback." Oh, Izze was enjoying this way too much.

Apryl snorted into her napkin.

"For what?"

"For what? For what? Are you kidding me?" Izze shook her head. "It's time for revenge."

"Oh, I want to see this. Courtney hasn't even introduced him to me." Apryl folded her arms across her chest.

"Come on!" Courtney shrieked. "Please be nice! One of the reasons I invited him was to introduce him to you guys. Don't heckle him."

"Heckling is essential to the screening process," Kaylee said before taking a sip of her water.

This was a bad idea.

"Miles," Izze called. "Come help me embarrass Courtney like she embarrassed us."

Miles raised an eyebrow. "All of them tortured us, babe."

"Oh, I plan to do it to all of them when the time comes."

"Say what?" Apryl sat up in her seat.

"Come now?" Kaylee gasped.

"You start. I'll join in," Miles said as he leaned in to say something to his best man, who also happened to be his brother.

Apryl gasped. "That's Gram's home health nurse!"

Busted.

"What?" Izze and Kaylee shrieked at the same time.

"I can't believe this! Does Gram know?" Apryl asked, mouth hanging open.

Courtney shifted. She'd just pretend that she hadn't heard Apryl...

"What?" Izze gasped.

Apryl smirked. "She probably thought it would be safer for him to meet us first."

"Wasn't it?"

"Oh, dear, sweet sister," Apryl said. "How very ignorant of you."

Courtney pushed the salad around on her plate. Nothing good would come from this. Maybe she could try to warn him, to tell him to run and save himself.

Dallas stopped in front of the wedding party's table. "Hello, everyone. Nice to meet you."

Izze stuck her hand toward him, giving it a firm shake that had Courtney gulping. "Nice to meet you. Dallas, isn't it?"

"That's right. Congratulations."

Izze glanced at Miles and beamed. "Thank you!"

Apryl jumped up and walked around the table. Oh, no. Courtney had been worried about Izze, but Apryl could be just as bad. All the stunts they pulled on Izze and Miles had been Apryl's idea, after all.

Courtney was doomed.

Apryl sized him up the same way she sized up Thomas Wallace, the most notorious bully of third grade, right before she gut-punched him for taking Courtney's Fruit Roll Up. "So you're my sister's fella." She started to walk around him.

"That's right." Dallas didn't budge thanks to Apryl's weird circling, but he caught Courtney's eye and mouthed, *"Fella?"*

She's crazy, Courtney mouthed to him.

Izze stood up and joined Apryl in her march. "It's so weird that we haven't met you yet."

"Or providence," Courtney muttered.

Apryl continued to lead the strut around him. "But perhaps it's even weirder that you're my gram's home health nurse. That I've seen you every day for the last week without figuring out your shenanigans."

"For all the love of cookie dough, you are not that good of a detective," Courtney cried. Everything within her wanted to leap over the table, grab Dallas's hand, and make a run for it.

Kaylee kicked her under the table before she betrayed Courtney too. "Is there anything we should know about you, buddy? My name is Kaylee, by the way," she said as she joined the parade route around Dallas.

What a sight they made! The bride and two of her bridesmaids circling a random guest whose panic grew more visible by the second. Three. Four. Five. Around and around they went like they were marching toward the destruction of Jericho.

"Ladies," Miles interrupted as he stepped into the fray, stopping the procession that had drawn the attention of most of the reception. "Stop torturing the man. I'm Miles, the groom. Nice to meet you."

Dallas visibly relaxed. "Dallas. Congratulations." They did that weird shake, hug, pat, chest-bump thing.

There was more than one reason women didn't do that. Ouch.

"Want to sit, man?" Miles asked.

"Uh, sure. Thanks." Dallas said.

Kaylee and Apryl returned to their chairs, but Izze remained standing, crossing her arms. "Spoilsport," she mumbled.

Miles winked at her.

Izze grinned.

Oh. No.

Dallas followed Miles, completely missing the way Courtney mouthed, *It's a trap!* The men sat down, and Izze and Miles were between her and Dallas. Courtney couldn't hear a thing.

But wait...

Dallas laughed.

A good sign. Right? Possibly?

Courtney kept a watch on them, trying to read Dallas's expression. He looked like he was having a good time talking to Miles and his groomsmen.

Courtney had just started to relax when Dallas's face paled. Actually, it looked a little ashen, matching his suit in an eerie way. He gulped, nodded, and shook Miles's hand before standing up. Thankfully, the color returned to his face by the time he reached her.

"Want to dance?" He held out his hand.

She placed her cool hand in his warm one.

"So?" she asked once they'd distanced themselves from her psychotic friends and moved onto the dance floor.

"I'm fine. They seem nice."

"I think you mean multifaceted in their craziness."

Dallas snickered as he led her in an awkward waltz. At least, she thought he was attempting to waltz. Dallas had many skills, but dancing would never be one of them. Even weakness seemed too generous of a description, but Courtney loved his attempts.

Dallas stepped on her toe. "Sorry."

She grinned. "I'm fine but I don't believe you."

A cloud crossed his face. "About what?"

"I saw the way your face paled. What did Miles say to you?"

"Ah. You saw that?" Dallas narrowly avoided swinging her into a father dancing with his daughter.

"Yes. What did he say?"

Dallas grinned. "He said he thought I was a decent guy, and that was good because he wouldn't tolerate anyone messing with his wife's friends."

"That's it?"

"What do you mean, 'That's it?' It was the way he said it, the underlying message. And he's an intimidatingly big guy."

"Miles is a financial consultant, not a wrestling champion." Courtney winced as Dallas stepped on her foot again.

"Doesn't mean the guy can't throw a punch."

Courtney giggled, and Dallas rolled his eyes.

"Hey, what did you think I was talking about? You had a weird look on your face." Courtney slid her foot out of the way this time, and she breathed a sigh of relief.

He looked sheepish. "Uh, about...before."

"Before what? Oh." Courtney stopped. An older couple bumped into them and the gray-haired woman gave her a dirty look.

He shrugged and looked at his feet. "I didn't know if he knew or not. I guess I thought maybe you'd never trust me about anything ever again."

"Dallas...no. I..." Her voice trailed off and she gave him a helpless look.

"*Do* you trust me again?"

Why did he have to ask her the one question she didn't know how to answer?

Okay, that wasn't true. She also couldn't answer any questions about the Kardashians—something she took great pride in achieving—but Dallas's question was up there.

"I see." So much weight in those two little words. Shame. Guilt. Pain. Resignation. Hopelessness. "You must hate me."

Courtney shook her head. "No, Dallas, I need to you to understand... It's not that I hate you, but you *did* break my trust. You did lie. Trust has to be rebuilt and that will take time. I can understand why you freaked out in the same way you can understand why I made those stupid claims, but it doesn't erase the fact that we need to fix a few things between us. I've spent so much of my life trying to be perfect that I've just covered up anything I deemed broken. Not anymore." She bumped her fist on his chest, the emotion from her speech making her feel quite brazen. "But you also need to understand this: I want to fix those things. With you. And in me. In both of us. You have no idea how much—"

He held a finger up to her lips. "I love you."

She blinked then kissed his finger. "I love you too. That's the truth."

Courtney snuggled into his arms, and they swayed to the music. Who cared about a picture-perfect waltz? They had a dance all their own.

And it was beautiful.

My twin senses are tingling.

Twin Sense—not to be confused with Spiderman's Spidey Senses or parents' intuition—is an unspoken language, a deep-down knowing.

I study my sister and the man I know will be her husband one day. Courtney's cornflower blue eyes scan the crowd until she spots me. Pure and utter joy blossoms on her face in the form of a mega-smile. She nods and winks.

I dip my head and wink in return.

"I'm glad they worked things out," Izze says.

"What happened?" Kaylee asks.

"There was...some drama, but they're choosing to work through it." Pride in my sister warms my entire body.

Not necessarily a good thing because it feels like a million degrees in here. I'm hot, just not in an attractive way.

Izze leans forward on the table to catch my eye. "I like him."

"I do too," Kaylee says.

I give a decisive nod. "He's a good guy. Another wedding will be in our imminent future."

"You think?" Kaylee's eyes go wide.

"I know. It's the Twin Sense." I touch two fingers to my temple.

Izze takes a bite of her salad then points her fork at me while swallowing. "Speaking of another wedding, tell us what's going on with Chance."

My throat feels like I just swallowed a dozen caterpillars. "Nothing. Ever."

"Defensive. Interesting." Kaylee grins.

"Sounds like a story to me, and if anyone can spot a story, it's the bookworm," Izze says.

"All the bookworms I know tend to suffer from an overactive imagination." I take a sip of water, but those hairy caterpillars keep wiggling within my throat.

Gag.

The DJ puts on a slow song, and Miles turns to Izze and whispers in her ear. She grins and nods. They stand up and walk to the dance floor where they take soft, swaying steps with occasional twirls thrown into the mix.

Izze's father, Ben, comes up to the table. "I would be honored if one of you would dance with me. My wife says her back hurts, and these feet were made for dancing." He looks between us.

"I'd love to dance with you," Kaylee says.

"Wonderful." He looks at me. "Would you save me a dance, Apryl?"

I smile. "Of course."

And just like that, I'm alone.

I watch my sister and friends laughing and having a good time on the dance floor. I fiddle with the lace tablecloth—courtesy of Willow Grove Antiques—and shift my attention to reading the spines of some of Izze's favorite classic books that form the table centerpieces, each stack topped with a vase and more of Izze's wood flowers.

Yeah, it's not helping. I feel a little like there's a letter L taped to my head. I wish I could say that's never happened but I can't. I rub my forehead just to make sure one hasn't been placed there again.

"Got a headache?"

I jump an inch out of my chair. "You scared me, Chance."

"It's what I do best." He looks annoyingly handsome tonight

in his black suit, crisp white shirt, and forest green tie. Oh, my—he's wearing fancy loafers, not beaten, leather work boots.

"I don't think I've ever seen you wear a tie. Not even at your high school graduation," I say.

"I was wearing a tie that day, but I had to take it off and use it as a rope to save a small child hanging from a ledge." Somehow he manages to say this with a straight face.

"I call your bluff."

He chuckles, low and deep. "Well, my father believed the story at the time."

I stiffen at the mention of his father. That man. He could make all of Batman's enemies tremble before him. Okay, that was extreme. He could make the Joker cry, though.

Chance straightens his tie again. "Want to dance?"

No, I want to faint. "Actually, I think I could use some air." Weddings are always unbearably hot.

The same principle applies to Chance.

I dash away before he can say anything else, disappearing into the restroom like the mature woman I am. What happened to the no-dancing policy? I may have apologized for my outburst, but I meant that part.

At least, I thought I did.

After a few minutes, I crack the door. No sign of Chance.

Jazz hands here.

Izze's father leads Kaylee back to the head table. I dart after them. "Here I am," I call. Air. Need air. Or exercise.

"Wonderful! A dance with you would be a delight on this cold *Apryl* night." Ben grins and wiggles his bushy eyebrows, waiting for us to laugh at his cringe-worthy pun.

I may never forgive Izze for getting married in April.

"Ha." Kaylee elbows me.

"That's a good one," I add.

Ben escorts me to the dance floor, and the DJ plays a medium-tempo song I don't know the words to, but the beat always makes me tap my toes. Once that song finishes, one of Taylor Swift's more romantic songs starts to play.

I'm about to say the perfunctory, "Thank you. I had a nice time, but I need to rest my aching feet." (There are few things more awkward than dancing to a love song with your bestie's dad.) My excellent escape, however, is ruined when someone taps my shoulder.

"May I cut in?" Chance's voice sends shivers down my spine.

"Certainly." Ben passes my hand into Chance's without a backward glance.

"You know, I may be crazy, but it seemed like you were trying to avoid dancing with me," Chance remarks once we're in the middle of all the gooey couples on the dance floor.

My heart grimaces at being caught, but I maintain my poker face. "You're right, you are crazy."

"Mm-hm."

"We said no dancing." I should just not speak ever again.

"Actually, I believe only you said it. Well, screamed it."

What do I say to that? There's literally nothing I can respond with, so I'm just going to take my own advice and keep my mouth shut. I'll get through this dance then camp in the handicap stall for the rest of the evening.

Plan failed. The uncomfortable silence threatens to choke me. Must say something—anything—to fill the void. "You're proving to be a good dancer. You haven't stepped on my toes once." Smooth. Real smooth.

"I wish I could say the same for you," Chance drawls.

Twit. I thwack his arm. "Lies and slander."

"Me? Never!"

"That's not the Chance I grew up with." But this Chance surprises me more and more.

"Well, that Chance died."

I raise an eyebrow.

He sighs. "Did you ever hear about my accident?"

I nod. I sat by the phone for hours waiting to hear from Gram, who had gone to the hospital to wait with Chance's father. But I don't tell him that.

"That's when I really committed my life to God. I'd always known about Him, had a respect for the 'dude in the sky,' but never had a real, I-want-you-to-walk-with-me relationship until then." He clears his throat.

"That's awesome, though I did kind of suspect it when I heard you praying that day."

"That day you attacked me by throwing yourself from the top of a tree?" He raises an eyebrow.

"I'm not having this conversation again." But we smile at each other.

A country crooner serenades us from the speakers now. All the couples snuggle even closer around us under the hundreds of twinkle lights on the ceiling, making me aware of the formal distance between us with a piercing clarity. No romance here.

"Anyway, it took a sleepless night in the hospital and a...I don't know how to describe it...." Chance looks toward the ceiling, struggling to find the words.

"A God thing," I gently supply.

"Yeah. You know, it's funny. My dad constantly told me I needed to get my act together and brought me to church for that sole purpose. But it took a hazy memory of the accident and a desperate prayer at 3:17 in the morning to bring about change. Afterward, I had this reassuring, stirring feeling deep within me."

"A chance meeting." Oh, great. I sound like Izze's dad.

Chance smirks. "Yeah. Despite what my dad thinks, that's what really did it."

My brows furrow in a question.

"My dad had spent the better part of the day before the accident lecturing me, and when I woke up in the hospital, it was more of the same," Chance elaborates to answer my eyebrow question.

"Always the one for lectures, wasn't he?" I mumble under my breath.

Chance frowns. "What?"

Wile E. Coyote just dropped an anvil on my foot. He must have, because that is the only explanation for why I said those words out loud. That slip-up reveals way, way too much. "Wh—Wh—What?"

"What did you just say?" There's an edge to his tone that suggests he knows exactly what I said.

Is it acceptable to say I don't remember? Make something up? I'll just say nothing. Yeah, that will work.

Because it worked out so well a few minutes ago.

"Why did you say that my father was always one for lectures? Apryl?" He looks at me with an expectant fire in his eyes. "Don't ignore the question."

And suddenly, I'm angry. I'm angrier than I've ever been. Not because his voice of steel shows no mercy for someone who would dare to speak ill of his father, despite the hypocrisy. Not because we're in this situation, having the same argument—again. No, I'm angry because I'm tired of letting that man—and I am mentally spitting right here—control me. And he's not even here!

"Your father cares more about appearances and having things his way than anything else, and he uses scathing lectures to control and manipulate everyone into his will," I hiss. Verbal venom drips from my tongue. But I'm not done. Not even close.

Chance turns us on the dance floor, his movements rough and angry. "Don't. Just don't. You have no idea what you're talking about."

I laugh, almost like the Evil Queen/Regina in *Once Upon a Time*. "I don't know what I'm talking about? Seriously? We grew up together. I know *exactly* what your father is like."

"No!" The music isn't loud enough to drown out the forcefulness in his voice. Heads swivel our way. "Don't. You. Dare," he says through clenched teeth, lowering his voice just a smidge.

Mine, however, gets shriller with each word. "Dare what? Speak the truth? I'm saying the exact same thing you just did. Your father is a bully."

"You're the only bully I see right now," Chance retorts. He backs up a step and bumps into an elderly couple who squeak a protest, but Chance doesn't notice.

"That's laughable. Your father cared more about who you saw and what you did than he did about your life, your soul. That's why his first words at the hospital when he saw you weren't 'I love you,' 'Thank God you're okay,' or even a gentle urging to turn to God, but rather a lecture on the ways you've screwed up and failed him," I snarl, finishing my scathing rant in time with the end of the song. For a moment I wish I could stuff the words back into the gaping orifice known as my big mouth.

But it's too late.

I've gone too far.

I knew it even before we skidded to a stop and Chance walked off the dance floor.

Chapter Eleven

"**I** knew you'd be here."

Awesome. Chance rammed his knuckles into the rough bark of the willow trees. "Well, you know a lot of things, don't you?"

"Fair enough." A contrite response but Apryl couldn't hide the edge in her voice. Twigs crunched as she stepped into the moonlight. "Did you get my message?"

"Yep."

"I left you a note too."

"I got your note." That Batman stationary—who knew there was such a thing?—bemused him for a moment. But then he remembered the hot iron of anger pressed against his stomach.

"That's all you're going to say?"

"Yep."

"Did you read my note?"

He did, but he didn't feel he owed it to her to say that.

"I'm sorry, Chance. I said it in the note and in the phone message."

He remained quiet.

"Did you get Courtney's message? She left one too."

Ah, Courtney's message informing him of the next wedding that he was being forced to participate in despite working his own business.

The business catapulting toward destruction, according to his father.

He still hadn't told his father about the "contractual agreement." Not even when he came over last night and looked through Chance's ledgers—just to check on how he was doing, of course...

"Chance?" his father called as he barreled into the kitchen, holding up the ledger in one hand and the appointment book in the other. His father had used the old-school system until he retired, and he insisted that Chance use it too.

Probably so he could check up on Chance whenever he wanted.

Chance swallowed, attempting to push the thought into the deep down, dark hallow of his mind. The place where ungrateful, selfish thoughts like that should go. Because his dad, while nowhere near perfect, had done everything for him.

"Yeah?"

"What's going on with your schedule?"

Big. Gulp. And not the drink. "What do you mean?"

He frowned at Chance. "I mean you rescheduled Jerry's oil change twice."

Ah, he should have known that his father's friend would rat him out. "It's not a big deal, Dad."

"It is a big deal. I didn't build this business and turn it over to you for you to drive it into the ground."

Chance ground his teeth together. "I know." He stomped over to the fridge and yanked the door open, letting the air swirl around him, but he doubted the chill would cool the temper building in him.

"Your customers come first. I thought that had finally gotten through to you." His father tossed the books on the counter. They landed with a painful thud, making Chance cringe.

"Dad, there was a situation that needed my attention. Jerry's appointment won't be rescheduled again." He hoped. Chance grabbed a bottle of water and closed the fridge.

"It's not just Jerry. Mrs. Sherman called to tell me that you would no longer be her family mechanic." His father clutched his hands into fists at his side, knuckles turning white.

Yeah, right. Mrs. Sherman couldn't hold to a threat, legit or otherwise. It's why her children were the most undisciplined Chance had ever seen.

"Lucky for you, I convinced her not to do that. Told her I'd straighten you out first."

Chance bristled. "And maybe she should have called me and talked to me if she had a problem with me."

But his father just brushed him off, ignoring him. "The customers trust me—and for good reason, it seems."

Chance slammed his water bottle onto the counter. Thank goodness he'd remembered to screw the cap back onto the bottle. "Mrs. Sherman wasn't even rescheduled."

"No, you told her that you were unable to see her the day she called."

"Which is not unreasonable." He ran a hair through his hair. This conversation needed to end.

"Except I checked and you not only had appointments available that day, you also cleared the two appointments you had scheduled."

"Why do feel the need to check up on me constantly?" Chance blurted.

His father's icy gaze froze him as he stepped into Chance's personal space. "This is my business." His tone had taken that eerily calm quality that told Chance way more than his simple statement did—that Chance had crossed a line by questioning him.

And yet Chance couldn't seem to stop the words tumbling from his mammoth-sized mouth. "You always said this was our business, and that someday you'd pass it to me. Year after year. And I guess I assumed that those legal documents in the office safe said that this business belongs to me now."

"You have no idea what I'm doing behind the scenes to help you achieve our plans!"

"Who asked you to do that?" Chance shouted. "I know I didn't. Just let things be, Dad. If it's going to happen then it will happen. I'm not going to force anything." But Chance already knew what his father would say...

"Sometimes you have to force your point to make people listen to you." William jabbed his finger into the middle of Chance's chest. "Don't make the same mistakes that I did."

Now. This conversation needed to end now. Before those beans he'd kept piled so nice and neat started to fall one by one. His father *wouldn't take kindly to the way Apryl strong-armed him into this arrangement. And regardless of their most recent dispute, Chance didn't want to throw Apryl to the wolf-like creature his father embodied when it came to his business.*

His father's face softened. "You are worth so much more than what you've got right now, Chance. I want you to achieve your full potential."

Chance sighed. "What if—"

"You've got to keep your eye on the prize."

Chance darted around his father. "There is no prize, Dad."

"We're building an empire."

He let out a cold laugh and met his father's eyes. "There's no empire!"

His father leveled him with his classic, determined stare. That stare defined him all the way to the core of his being. William McFarland would always be the man who set a goal and made it happen. And he would not budge.

"Not yet. But there will be. Soon, I'm sure. Don't screw up what we've worked for all these years."

Despite what his son wanted.

Apryl shifted, drawing Chance back to reality. That's probably why he was out here tonight. Refusing to risk an impromptu rendezvous, he had avoided Apryl and the willow grove ever since their blow-up at Izze's wedding. But he couldn't shake his father's comments from the night before.

He had needed to pray. To connect with God in the quiet of the night. And for some bizarre reason, he felt that peace out here, in the midst of the willows and their delicate branches swaying in the breeze like some sort of earthy hula dance.

Wouldn't it have been great if Apryl hadn't crashed his party?

"Yes," he finally said. "I got Courtney's message." Thankfully, he hadn't needed to reschedule anyone this time. He suspected his father would keep a close eye on things for the next few weeks.

"Are you going to bail?"

"Seriously?" He swung around to face her, scraping his already sore knuckles on the bark. "You know I have no choice. Do you keep asking that question as some sort of warped reminder?"

"I'm sorry." She turned around, walking faster than he'd ever seen her do. The moon disappeared into a sea of clouds, and her profile disappeared in the darkness.

Alone.

Just like he wanted.

Go after her.

The Voice within.

Sometimes he hated that voice and its urgings.

But he loved Who that voice belonged to.

He charged after Apryl, bursting from the grove and into the field. "Wait!" He caught sight of her only a couple arm-lengths away from him.

She kept walking.

Something rustled in the grass less than one hundred yards from them. Apryl skidded to a stop.

The moonlight caught the perpetrator, shining its yellowish glow like a spotlight that illuminated the fluffy black-and-white creature before them.

"Skunk! Get back here!" Chance whisper-yelled.

Apryl backpedaled through the tall grass of the field, hitting him in the chest. She squeaked when Chance grabbed her by the arms. "Shush."

She nodded, back to his chest. Chance released her, and together they crept back to the cover of the willow grove.

"What do we do?" she asked, keeping her voice low.

Chance looked from her to the skunk and back to her. He sighed. "Wait it out, I guess." This night kept getting better and better. Maybe lightning would strike him next to really put the evening over the top. Or better yet, maybe a bear could challenge him to a duel.

The skunk moseyed around, nosing the dirt, completely oblivious to the power it held over two human beings who didn't want to smell.

Plus, Chance was allergic to tomatoes, so the legendary tomato juice bath was out.

They were stuck.

"Oh, Gordon, why do you torture me so?" Apryl muttered.

Chance raised an eyebrow. "Gordon?"

"The skunk." She pointed to the aforementioned rodent.

Were skunks considered rodents? Right, not important. Chance shook his head, clearing away his useless ramblings. "I gathered that. Why name him?"

She shrugs. "Seemed like fun, plus he's always nosing the dirt like Detective Gordon."

The detective from the *Batman* comics? "That's who you named him after?"

"I thought the name fit him."

"He's. A. Skunk," Chance said.

Apryl stuck her hands on her hips. "I'm sorry. Would you prefer I name all skunks after the one in *Bambi*?"

"There was a skunk? I thought the movie was about antelope."

She covered her face. "No, you're thinking of a song with a line about deer and antelope grazing."

"Whatever. The name is still a bad pun on four legs."

"I thought you weren't talking to me."

"Talking, no. *Mocking*, on the other hand..." Chance allowed his lips to stretch into a villainous grin. Which he nailed to perfection thanks to all his hours—yes, hours—of practice as a kid.

Apryl ignored him and cooed to the skunk, "Gordon, time to go home. Barbara misses you."

"His daughter?"

"That would be Barbara the Second. Barbara is his wife."

Chance snorted. "I don't think that's true to the comics."

"I like my way better."

Chance shook his head. Once again, they had fallen into their easy, playful arguing. For a moment, Chance had forgotten what had happened.

Just for a moment.

Any romantic sparks between them needed to be snuffed out for good. They fought about everything. She had some personal vendetta against his father. They drove each other crazy. She drove him crazy.

Keep telling yourself that, buddy.

Whatever. He'd repeat it until he believed every word.

Despite the warm spring evening, silence settled on them like a thick layer of snow. Cold, unyielding, and covering everything. Even the sound of the cascading river, mighty in strength thanks to melting snow, sounded muted in the midst of their pure awkwardness.

"I'm sorry," Apryl whispered.

Why? Why do you hate him so much? It was the question Chance didn't dare ask aloud, fearing the answer if he kicked over that proverbial rock and gazed at the wormy truth.

Instead he said, "My father is supposed to be off-limits. He's my father, and yeah, I may have some issues with him, but that doesn't mean it's okay for you to bash him."

"I...I know. I was just stressed. It was such a long day, and some stuff caught me by surprise. But that's not an excuse. I shouldn't have said that—any of that. I am so, so sorry." Apryl's apology poured from her lips like a rushing river, threatening to sweep him away in the current.

Chance swallowed the rocky lump at the back of his mouth, but it lodged in his throat.

"Please, say something." Once again the moon disappeared under a blanket of clouds, shrouding them in darkness. Chance couldn't see her face, but Apryl sounded close to tears. "You have no idea how much I wish I hadn't said any of that."

Then nothing.

Nothing but the sound of Gordon as he rustled the grass uncomfortably close to their hideout.

"My father is a good man," Chance burst out when the urge to defend his father nearly consumed him. "He's not perfect, but he's a good man. He provided everything for me after my mother left."

"I've never heard you talk about your mother," Apryl said softly. "I mean, I knew the basics, but you've never said anything specific..."

"There's not a lot to say." Or was it that he'd never allowed himself to say it because the reminder of what he never had would be too painful? While he imagined himself to be Batman with all his cool cars, savvy skills, and playboy qualities—before he came to God, that is—every time he acknowledged what he'd lost, the devastation hit him with fresh force. Like it happened yesterday.

"She had a laugh that sounded like tinkling wind chimes and clashing cymbals all at once," Chance finally said. "Blue eyes. Long fingers. Loved to watch *I Love Lucy*. Even though Marla McFarland grew up in this town and married my father right out of high school, she had this...bohemian quality to her that I found intoxicating as a little boy. Free. Airy. Light. Gentle." Chance smiled as the bittersweet memories flooded him.

"Sounds like you guys had some things in common."

Chance flinched. "Not really. She also had a deep love for adventure and travel. She moved around with my father while he was in the military, but that stopped once she got pregnant." *With me*, but Chance didn't add the obvious statement. "She always said she loved me, but wanderlust won the war for her heart."

If it weren't for Apryl's shallow breaths, Chance would have thought she'd vanished.

He continued his story. "I'll remember the day she left forever. It's seared into my memory. I overheard them talking in the kitchen, arguing. She kept saying that this had failed. That this life was an experiment that had failed, and she needed to embrace who she really was. My father finally yelled, 'Fine! Go, but don't expect to come back!' He was never one to beg... So she left. Didn't even pack a suitcase. Just walked out the door. My father found me in my room, hugged me, and said that we would be all right. We've never spoken of it since. Divorce papers arrived a year later."

Silence.

Then a touch.

Fingers curled around his in the darkness, infusing him with strength. Or hope.

Or...love?

No, *that* was ridiculous. Comfort. That was all this was.

"I'm sorry." Her small fingers pressed, entwined, squeezed his.

Or perhaps pity. Not that Apryl and her sister hadn't also experienced devastating loss. Okay, so...mutual grief. Understanding. Solidarity.

"I poured myself into *Batman* comics after that. I could relate to him." Why did the words continue to tumble from his mouth? Heat crawled up his neck. He had shared so much. Details that he'd never even talked about with his father. "I don't know why I'm telling you all of this. To make you understand, I guess."

"I understand. For the record, I did the same thing after my parents died." While her words were soft, not a trace of pity could be found in them. She could relate.

Chance could kiss her for that fact alone.

Surprised, he turned to study the faint profile of the woman standing so close to him. Her vanilla scent floated by his nose, intoxicating him. Grateful that she couldn't see his face, Chance cleared his throat. *Get your act together, man!*

"Right. Well, like I said, it was bound to happen."

"I said that." She nudged him.

"Oh. Right," Chance murmured, leaning closer.

Her breathing vanished.

And Chance mentally slapped himself.

No! Stop! Not like this! He couldn't kiss her here, after all he'd shared. It'd look bad. Chance couldn't be sure it wasn't bad, a phantom habit from the old Chance, a man who kissed to drown his pain.

No, when he kissed Apryl for the first time, there would be no doubt that it happened because his feelings for her had over-flowed like the coolant in Mr. Shaw's overheated engine into the radiator overflow tank last week.

When.

This night was full of confessions. Or maybe revelations about what had been there between them all along.

Apryl's breath came in one big whoosh, like she had been holding it. Maybe she could sense the thoughts rampaging through his muddled brain, and the only response was a breathy gasp.

Or maybe he remained the conceited cad he'd always been.

"Chance," Apryl whispered. "I should get back to Gram, so maybe we should figure out a way to urge Gordon to go home."

"Yeah." Wonderful. A hoarse voice didn't incriminate him at all. He cleared his throat again. "Any ideas?"

"Let's throw rocks at him."

"What? Are you insane?"

"No more than usual." The moon came out from behind the clouds, illuminating her playful smile, her pale pink lips.

"That doesn't help your case."

"I'll climb into this tree. You can pass up some rocks. I'll throw them. It's as easy as one of those microwavable mug cakes."

"Why climb into the tree?"

"For a better vantage point. This way I can see which way he's running." She grabbed the lowest branch and started to climb up the willow tree.

"I guess I'll just gather some rocks," he said dryly.

"That would be great," Apryl grunted. Her legs disappeared from view.

"Please don't kill yourself," Chance muttered.

"Believe me, I have no interest in falling out of a tree again." The branches rustled their amusement as Apryl climbed through them.

Chance laughed as he grabbed every baseball-size rock and smaller in the vicinity and made a pile at the base of the tree. The smell of damp dirt clung to his fingers thanks to all his crude digging in the soft ground still moist with the remnants of winter.

"I see him!" Apryl whisper-shouted.

Chance scanned the field from the end of the clearing. Ah, there he was. At only twelve or so feet away, Gordon had gotten close. Way too close for comfort.

A small hand appeared in front of his face. "Pass me some rocks."

He handed her five. "Try to aim for behind him but far enough away that he won't feel like he's being threatened. We can hope he'll scurry away from the rocks."

"Don't hit the skunk. Got it." The branches rustled as Apryl got into position above him. "Ready... Aim... Fire!"

The first wave of rocks rained six or so feet behind Gordon. He froze and for five agonizing seconds, he didn't move.

Chance threw three more rocks the skunk's way.

Gordan scurried away from the willow grove and the house, moving as fast as his short legs would carry him to the haven of the garden.

Apryl's laughter swirled around him. "We did it!" A moment later, she hopped down from her perch in the tree. Similar to the night she fell into his arms, small twigs rested in her hair, giving her the appearance of an ethereal fairy.

This time Chance left them. He liked them. They suited her. Apryl might project a "Who cares?" attitude while she waited in the wings with a sarcastic comment, but she was so much more than that. She was delicate. Not in an I-need-a-prince-to-save-me way but rather a competent, layered woman who needed to be seen—and loved—for who she was.

"What?" Apryl interrupted his awkward staring. She patted her head. "Do I have stuff in my hair?"

"Nah. You look beautiful."

Her search froze, fingers trembling. "I'm sure I look ridiculous." To anyone else, her words would sound like they were sustained by her indifference. Not to him. Not anymore.

He shrugged. "Think what you want."

Her arms dropped to her sides. "I should get back." She turned, foregoing a goodbye or another glance, and started to walk toward the looming estate.

"Good job," he called after her. "I couldn't afford getting sprayed. A tomato bath wouldn't have worked."

"It would have killed you, but it may have gotten the stench out of your pores." She tossed a grin over her shoulder.

"Goodnight, Willow Fairy."

"I knew there was junk in my hair, you liar!" She plucked a twig from her hair and tossed it behind her as she walked.

"I call it as I see it."

She spun around and walked backward, taking careful steps to avoid falling. "You're crazy."

"Then we make a good pair." Hint, hint.

"A pair of something," she said as she whirled around again, but her laughter caught the late spring breeze and floated back for him to enjoy.

Intoxicating him in a way nothing ever had before.

Chapter Twelve

"Look! A monocle! Every, I repeat, every professor needs a monocle."

Courtney looks at the gold-plated monocle and frowns. "It's scratched."

I shake my head. "First of all, this is an antique—scratches come with the territory. It's more than a hundred years old. Second, those aren't scratches; they're etchings. They look haphazard because some have rubbed off with time."

"Isn't it a little stereotypical to associate a monocle with a professor?" Courtney motions for me to lay it flat on the top of the dresser where a cream vinyl backdrop lies. She snaps several pictures from three different angles with her digital camera. "All done."

"Azalee—our bride and paying customer—told me she wanted it to feel like them. And since the bride and groom are both professors who met in New Zealand, I think the monocle works with their vintage travel theme." I place the monocle back into the drawer where I found it, using great care not to scratch it, and make a note in my Catwoman journal.

"Are you sure?"

"It stays!"

Courtney rolls her eyes before photographing another item. In the office/bedroom, I hear Gram talking on the phone with her sister.

In true Old Faithful fashion, Great Aunt Alice has called every Monday at four o'clock, and the two of them talk for eleven minutes. She's more reliable than the postman. I think the iceberg between the two sisters has started to thaw. Or at least they've waved a white flag in their war of sisterhood to celebrate their metaphorical Christmas Day.

I inhale, sucking the musty scents of silver polish and moth balls deep into my lungs. I love this smell, as weird as that sounds. It's a scent full of past stories and the whispered hope of more.

"We should have had them pick out the pieces they wanted beforehand. It would have saved us a lot of hassle," Courtney mumbles.

"That's why we're cataloging everything—so Miles can set up a website for the couples to peruse. But so far, the brides seem to like the surprise factor. It's like that show Izze used to watch all the time. I don't remember the name."

"*My Fair Wedding*," Courtney supplies as she snaps a picture of a delicate red hand fan from China. "Maybe we should set up different decorating packages and have an adjusted price for the couples who pick out the items beforehand verses the couples who leave it up to us."

I make a note to include the hand fan too. "Whatever. That's not really my thing. My thing is the decorating." I stop writing. The admission surprises me. Almost like it wasn't an admission at all but a casual stating of a fact.

My palms start to sweat.

Courtney waves a dismissive hand. "All right, doll face."

"Since when do you say that?"

Courtney grins. "Since I just booked us a Roaring-Twenties-themed wedding three weeks after this wedding. It'll be the bee's knees!" She laughs at the ridiculous yet fun expression.

I groan.

Why?

I'm panicking. I thought the sweaty palms made that clear already.

"What?" She looks at me and frowns.

Time to engage evasive maneuvers. "It's nothing."

Courtney studies me for a moment. "Okay." She opens a drawer and paws through it for a minute. "So. What did you think of Dallas?"

I shrug. "He's nice." My stomach rumbles. I should have

grabbed some potato chips before we started this process. It groans again. I hope she doesn't hear my cantankerous meal timer. That will tip her off.

"That's it?" She stops her search and looks at me. "I'd hoped you'd be more enthusiastic about him."

"I'm not the one in love with him. What does my opinion matter?"

"You're my sister. Of course it matters. At least a little. I want you to like him." An incredulous lilt colors her tone.

"Mm-hm. Is that why you didn't tell me he was Gram's nurse dude?" The camera flashes and I swear if the lens had been aimed at her, it would have caught the guilty expression of a highly cartoonish nature on Courtney's face.

"No," she squeaks. Cartoonish indeed. She's downright mousey right now.

I raise my eyebrows at her.

She lets out a huff. "I just didn't want anyone to pop my bubble, that's all."

I look around Courtney, squinting and studying until I reach out and gingerly poke her imaginary bubble. "Whoops! Sorry! Did you mean that bubble?"

"Hardy-har-har. You're hilarious."

"So why hide it?"

"I don't know." She sets the camera on the top of the dresser and turns to face me. "Maybe I was afraid of what you would say."

"I suppose I got a little heated last time." That's all we're going to say about that. Okay, one more thing—I love my sister and just want the very best for her.

She smirks. "Just a little. I didn't know if you or the others would think I should dump him because he lied to me. But I spent a lot of time praying about what to do. I love him, but more importantly, I feel like God is guiding me...us."

"Well, then I'm happy for you." The gnawing, I-need-food-because-I'm-freaking-out hunger continues to squeeze my stomach with its cruel, vice-like grip, much like the Grim Reaper.

Side note—have you noticed that I get kind of creepy when I'm uncomfortable? Yes? Well, let me apologize in advance for any future weirdness. Because I can't promise it won't happen again.

"Are you?" Courtney gnaws on her lip. "Are you happy for me?"

"I am." I mean, I think I am. That counts, right?

"But?"

Remember, I love my sister.

So I have got to say it.

"Okay, fine. But how do you know you can trust him? How do you know there aren't more secrets buried under a pile of pretenses?" My right hand rests on my hip, like I'm all sassy and stuff, but I'm asking the question for more than just Courtney's sake.

I'm asking for mine.

My mind wanders back to the night in the willow grove. I've been called crazy many times in my life—some of them were even for legit reasons—but I don't think I'm tapping into that when I say that Chance was about to kiss me. Or perhaps the crazy part comes from wanting him to kiss me despite the four million reasons why that would be one of the worst things to happen. Like *potato chips being banned from the country* bad. This is Chance. How am I ever supposed to believe that he would like me? And that it wouldn't be a game to him? How could I ever trust him? What about the father issue?

But enough about me.

"That is something I'm struggling with." Courtney says it calmly, but I can see the war of emotions in her eyes.

"I'm not saying this to crush you, but maybe that means he's not the perfect guy for you." I insert every ounce of gentleness that I possesses into my statement. I hate being the one to say it, but it needed to be said.

You know that bubble Courtney was talking about? Turns out that was real. I watch her pop and tears meander down her checks as she stares across the room at a painting of George Washington. I cross the two feet separating us and hug her.

Courtney pushes me away no sooner than I get my arms around her. "No, he's not the perfect guy. But neither am I."

"No, you're definitely not a guy."

"Be quiet." She sniffles. "I mean that I'm not perfect either, much to my dismay. I've tried to be. I've tried to have the perfect grades, the perfect job, the perfect life. I can't do it. Our love will not be perfect. It will be filled with mistakes. But perfection isn't love, it's a cage. And with everything that's happened with Gram and the shop, my identity can't hang on my career, my accomplishments, and that elusive perfection. It's defined by God and the way I love."

I know Courtney is waiting for my stellar commentary on her heartfelt confession, but the best I can manage is, "Uh..."

"Wow. So much power in that one word."

I roll my eyes. "Okay, so what does this mean?"

She bites her lip again—which just reminds me of the . "I guess it means I'm done trying to control my future."

Wow.

She smirks. "Go ahead and say it."

"Say what?"

"That the only thing I'm not capable of controlling is my ability to not control my future."

"Are any of us capable of controlling our futures? You know as well as I do that we control nothing." Not what happened to our parents. Gram. The shop.

Chance.

"Gram would say that we control whether or not we'll choose to trust God despite what happens around us."

Who is this alien creature and what has she done with my sister? She's changing and falling in love and spiritually evolving.

But me? Yeah, I'm stuck in the mire.

And if I'm honest with myself, I think it's safer there.

"Excuse me, Professor, but can your monocle-clad eye make out how these old crates are about to collapse into a heap of broken-down boards and cloth if you don't tell me where to put them?"

I turn to Chance. "I actually can't see through the monocle, since it's so old, so the answer to your question would be a resplendent no. And those are antique traveling trunks, by the way." I squint, attempting to hold the lens in place with my brow bone and cheekbone.

It's not going well, in case you were wondering, as this is a task that should not be attempted by the faint of heart.

The monocle slips from my left eye. I catch it and secure it in my right eye this time.

"I will drop them then I'll laugh like one of the many villains who thinks he or she has won the battle for Gotham City," Chance warns. "No remorse."

I pluck the monocle from my right eye and point toward the side of a long, rectangular table. "Put them there for now. We'll probably move them later."

"Oh, goody. Nothing brings me more pleasure than moving countless heavy objects back and forth for your sadistic pleasure." Chance tosses me a playful wink, undermining his pretend annoyance.

"Then you're going to be really happy today," I quip. This banter proves to be more fun than all our years of bickering. And guys, I was good at the bickering. They crowned me Queen of Bickerton. "They" being the imaginary people in my head, but they're good people.

Chance sets the trunks down and heads for the doorway, moaning the entire time about his poor biceps. The CLOSED FOR PRIVATE EVENT sign sways as the door swings shut behind him.

Dude, I have seen those biceps. He's got nothing to worry about.

Time to return to the task at hand—unpacking and organizing. I pull several hand fans that formerly resided in China from the box at my feet. I open a red one, fanning myself as I survey the coffee house/tea shop where the wedding will be held. With its exposed reddish-brown brick walls, rustic beams, and dark hardwood floors, I can't imagine a better location for a vintage travel wedding. Delicious smells permeate the air like an exclamation point since the owners, who are also catering, are preparing the feast to come in the little kitchen.

Chance walks back into the venue with another armful, and he's followed by an older woman—Azalee, the bride.

"Hello," Azalee says. "Nice to see you again." She extends her hand, and I shake it. Though this is our second meeting, once again I'm struck with awe that for a woman pushing sixty, her mahogany skin has nary a wrinkle.

I can't help but think of the book *A Wrinkle in Time*. I barely remember the story, but maybe there's some sort of paradox at play, a connection to consider. "Good to see you, as well."

She smiles, and her lovely topaz eyes light up. "I love these items you've picked. I'm looking forward to the final product." Azalee looks around the room. "I especially love those traveling trunks. I had some just like them once."

"Thank you!" I toss a victorious grin to Chance. He just shakes his head.

"I wanted to check in with you about the paperwork that needed to be signed," Azalee says.

"Yes, I've got it right here." I pull the messenger bag that I had kicked under the table from its hiding spot and pull out a manila folder with the nice and neat, freshly printed contract, courtesy of Courtney. With each wedding we become more and more professional. "These pages are the pictures and descriptions of each item being used today, and this is the contractual agreement and liability clause. We retrieve the items at the end of the reception. I have here that you said ten o'clock tonight."

Azalee surveys the papers. "Yes, that's right."

"We either stay on premises or nearby in order to pack the items up at the end of reception quickly and efficiently," I inform her.

"I understand." Azalee looks at me and taps her chin in thought. "Will you be staying for the service and reception?"

This question makes me feel awkward, since this wedding feels like our first real event. There is no friend connection whatsoever, and thus, no loving buffer. I definitely do not want to push into a couple's private, sacred day. "It's really whatever you are comfortable with—we don't want to intrude on your special day. Today is about you and your groom."

Azalee smiles. "Thank you. This wedding is a small, intimate affair, so I don't think you would be comfortable attending with such a close-knit group of people, but I would love to have you come a little before the end of the reception, say around nine thirty? We'll just be visiting by then, and I'm sure some of our friends would love to talk with you as well."

"Thank you." I offer her a genuine smile. "We would be honored."

If Azalee senses my nervousness, she doesn't comment on it. This woman rocks.

An older dandy—the only apt description, believe me—springs into the coffee shop/tea house. He resembles KFC's Colonel Sanders with his snow-white hair, wiry glasses, and tan suit complete with ascot. He's holding a black pipe that pops against a complexion that resembles whitewashed boards.

"This is my husband-to-be, Professor Stanley Sanderson." A wide smile graces Azalee's wrinkle-free face as she introduces us to her intended.

Stanley Sanderson. Wow. You can't make this stuff up.

I bite my tongue to keep from asking if he happened to have any type of military rank to his credit. Or if he preferred his chicken original crispy, just like mama taught him.

"Hello, dear," Stanley exclaims, a heavy accent coloring his words. I can't determine what it is. Australian, maybe? Or Scottish? "A pleasure to meet you, it is." His heavy brogue sounds like he picked up a little bit of inflection from each country he's lived in, whirled it in a blender, and took a sip.

"Oh! Nice to meet you as well," I say after staring at him a few seconds too long, trying to decipher his words. "Congratulations!"

Stanley taps Azalee on her nose with the end of his pipe. "We best be disappearing now, my love, so this fine young couple can get to work. I tell you, it warms this ol' heart to see a young couple making business work."

"Oh, we—"

Chance appears beside me. "We're new to both. Honeymoon period."

"What's that?" Azalee points at Stanley's chest.

"Hm?" Stanley inspects himself. "A smudge of tobacco, perhaps?"

"What are you doing?" I quietly hiss at Chance through the smile I'm forcing for the sake of this sweet couple who are my temporary employers for all intents and purposes. Perfect timing since they're both distracted as Azalee tries to brush the offending smudge off of Stanley's lapel.

He pokes my arm, and his breath tickles my ear. "Payback."

"It's fine, my dear." Stanley Sanderson looks at us and winks. "A happy couple. Sure, sure. I can tell that's what you'll be." He directs his attention back to Azalee. "Ready to go, my love?"

She nods. "We'll be back at three thirty. The guests will start arriving around four o'clock or so," Azalee tells us, lingering. I get the impression she's the kind of woman who likes to be in control, completing important tasks with her own two hands. She snaps her long fingers. "Oh, Linda, the owner, is back in the kitchen, right? Maybe I should check on the food."

"The food will be delectable, darling. Let the love birds get back to work," Stanley calls over his shoulder with a raspy snort.

Chance laughs and slips an arm around my waist like it's as natural as the change of seasons.

My mouth runs dry yet my palms begin to sweat. Explain this to me, please?

"Coming. Coming." Azalee waves him off. "Be back later." She takes a step, stops, and wrings her hands.

"Enjoy your downtime before your guests start to arrive," I encourage. I hope I don't sound rude, but *hint, hint.*

"Yes, a cup of earl grey sounds lovely." That works the trick. Azalee turns and leaves for real this time.

The door swings shut.

Get ready for a smackdown.

I whirl out of Chance's arm and kick his shin. "Are you crazy?"

Clutching his shin, he yips and laughs all at the same time. The result sounds like a horrific dog-frog mashup. "No more than usual," he chokes between croaking yelps.

"I can't believe you said that! It could ruin our nonexistent reputation." Not to mention it's not funny to toy with the former daydreams of my inner fifteen-year-old heart.

"Relax. He knew I was kidding." Chance rubs his shin then straightens his broad physique.

"You don't know that!"

"I do. It's a guy thing."

"Oh, gag me."

"Fine. You'll just have to marry me to save your reputation," he says with a wink and a sly grin.

I choke. On air. Because I'm that talented, y'all.

"That," I rasp, "would be the worst marriage-of-convenience story ever."

Chance feigns an adorably—and utterly fake—wounded expression, complete with big, round eyes the color of willow leaves in the spring. "I'm hurt."

"Yeah, I kicked you pretty hard," I say, ignoring his typical flirty response.

Must. Protect. Heart.

I think this part will forever be the best and worst part of the job.

Azalee inspects the room before us, her face giving nothing away.

Meanwhile, my face probably shouts to everyone, "Grab a bucket! She's going to toss her cookies!"

Azalee turns in small circles, taking in the room bit by bit. The wall to our left has three long tables covered with cream-colored lace tablecloths. The first table is for gifts. The second table holds framed pictures of Azalee and Stanley from all over the world. The guest book sits in the middle. The third table has all the food, hors d'oeuvres and buffet style. Odds and ends, like the monocle and the fans, decorate all three tables.

The venue already had a mismatch of high and low tables and chairs. Azalee asked us to arrange it in an open way, with a small space for dancing in the back, where we hung silky pashminas overhead like a tent. There are no tablecloths on the guest's tables, but small kerosene lanterns sit in the middle of each. The sweetheart table for Azalee and Stanley is situated against the right wall, framed on either side by a tower of vintage traveling trunks. Each stack is crowned with a large kerosene lantern. Last but not least, a large framed painting of the world done in gold and sepia hues sits behind their table.

The only thing missing is a cracked Fabergé egg to really make this omelet.

I fiddle with my locket as I wait, preparing myself for the worst.

Side note: I'm so glad I found a new chain hidden in a random dresser draw in the shop. I needed my adult security blanket today.

Azalee touches a safari hat yellowed from age. "Exquisite," she whispers. "It's like you saw my heart's desire when I couldn't even put it into words."

Stanley, decked out in another tan suit, smiles and slaps Chance on the back. "Well done!"

Chance sputters and coughs. "Thank you, sir," he says, taking a discreet step away from Stanley.

Azalee hugs me. "Thank you," she says again, unspoken emotion dripping from her voice like the tears that threaten to leak from her eyes. She pulls away and straightens a simple, elegant ivory dress and matching jacket that looks like they came straight out of Emily Gilmore's closet.

Izze would be proud of me for thinking in *Gilmore Girls* references.

"You both are incredibly talented." Stanley remarks, studying the room again.

"It was all her," Chance says. "I'm just the handyman." He nudges me.

Heat burns my cheeks thanks to his compliment.

Stanley and Azalee fawn over the decorations some more, but once the clock strikes 3:46 p.m., Chance and I book it toward the front door. We've walked approximately one storefront down the charming main street of the urbanized town of Knight before we hear a distinctive jiggle and a hearty, "Congratulations!"

I tuck my vintage purse into my messenger bag, which I loop over my torso crossbody style as we walk down the street for a few minutes. Aimlessly.

This is weird.

"What should we do?" Chance asks.

The scent of freshly baked bread assaults my nose as we pass a bakery. "We could eat."

"For six hours?"

"It's only five hours and forty-one minutes."

"We'll barely have time to wolf down a burger in that timeframe. My mistake," Chance drawls.

A man shoves a flyer into my hands as we pass him.

A sign, perhaps?

Chance looks over my shoulder.

Inspiration has surely struck. In big bold letters, the flyer advertises a new...animal clinic specializing in neutering.

Uh... Thanks but no thanks.

I crumple the waxy paper and toss it into a nearby trash can.

"I've got an idea." Chance grabs my hand. He tugs me down Main Street before turning onto the small coastal town's boardwalk. I've only been to Knight a few times and never for long enough to explore.

Despite Chance's tugging, I skid to a stop.

All sorts of vintage and old goodness reside here, just waiting to be rediscovered for the first time. Cute storefronts from businesses that have probably been there for generations line the boardwalk, the occasional street vendor clogging the pedestrian traffic. In the distance a sandy beach winks as the ocean waves for our attention.

That song from *Moana* echoes in my head. I get it now because it really does feel like the sea calls to me with each swell and lull.

"Hurry!" Chance says, yanking my arm as he attempts to steer me.

"Dude, the arm is connected to the rest of me!"

"Move faster!"

He pulls us in a half run-walk down the boardwalk to a boathouse painted a hideous shade of yellow. Seriously, this shade makes construction-yellow look inspired. Chance tugs me inside the yellow beast and whips his wallet out of his pocket. "Two tickets for the *Queen of New England*, please."

The casher rings us up. "This is the last ferry of the day. You'll make it if you hurry. If not, I'll refund you the money."

So says the woman who's taking her sweet time. I watch the

way her hands move in time with the little arm on the grandfather clock behind her, and I hold back a snort.

"I hope we'll make it," Chance says, flashing his trademark swoon-inducing smile at the middle-age woman as she hands him his change.

Yeah, give the woman heart palpitations. That helps. Insert mental eye roll here.

She twitters in response as Chance drags me through the door and down a gangplank.

"Don't run!" a man in board shorts and a plaid button-down shirt yells. "We'll wait. Walk! Stop running!" He makes some funny hand gesture to the wheelhouse.

Chance slows our pace to a respectable speed-walk, but the guy in the shorts continues to glower at us as we make our way to him.

"Tickets?"

Chance presents our crumpled tickets. "Here you go."

"All right. Welcome to the *Queen of New England*, the finest ferry boat around." The man motions for us to get on the boat where thirty or so other people mingle on the deck, looking over the high railings into the water below us.

Chance leads me to the front of the ship—the bow, I think—with only minor pushing on his part. The whitewashed railings angle upward, towering over us like a little cage. The movie poster for *Titanic* flashes through my mind's eye as I study it.

"Is now the wrong time to mention that I'm afraid of ships and water and anything aquatic?"

"Are you serious?" Chance, who continues to hold my hand, asks. "Let's go. I'm so sorry." He yanks my arm again, panic in his voice.

Seriously, my arm will never be the same after this day.

"I'm kidding. Sort of." I rub my sore arm with my free hand. "I prefer to think of myself as 'apprehensively curious.'"

Chance growls, running his free hand through his hair.

"I am deathly afraid of sharks, though." I eye the murky water. "Are there sharks this far north?"

"I have no idea."

Comforting.

As if realizing he's still holding me, Chance lets go of my hand.

I cup the abandoned appendage, calling myself all sorts of flattering names. Why, *why* do I want his touch?

The boat lurches forward and I fall into the railing. A firm grip encircles my arms, steadying me, and Chance reclaims my hand again. "You don't have any sea legs, so this is just a precaution." But he winks and gives my fingers a squeeze.

Umm...

"Hello, everyone!" The man from the dock stands on the upper deck in front of the wheelhouse, calling to us with the aid of a squarish speaker that fits into the palm of his hand. It kind of looks like the walkie talkies Courtney and I used as kids. He waves with his free hand and clicks the speaker's button again. "We are delighted to have you join us today on this little excursion. We'll be docking at the Kensington Lighthouse in about seven minutes. My name is—"

Lost in translation. A whooshing sound drowns out every other unworthy sound as the wind whips around us, not bothering to stop and chat as it makes its way to an undisclosed destination.

Chance squeezes my hand to draw my attention away from Board Shorts once the wind calms. "Have you ever done this before?"

I shake my head. "No. I didn't even know this existed. How did you think of it?"

"My mother took me about a year before she left."

What is the appropriate response to that?

"Is this, uh, the first time since..."

Yeah, that wasn't it.

"Yes." He searches my face, and those annoyingly striking lips of his quirk into a half smile. "I'm okay. This is a good memory, and I need to hold onto those." His fingers lace though mine.

A shudder rips through me from head to toe.

It's the breeze.

Chance smiles.

It's not the breeze. Oh, man...

"Kensington Beach is one of the few sandy beaches in New

Hampshire, made by the use of jetties, those thin land barriers running parallel to the beach," Board Shorts explains as he breaks into my mini-meltdown.

"You know," Chance says, turning to face the water. "This could almost be considered a date." He glances at me, one corner of his mouth lifted as he waits for my reaction.

I have two reactions—internal and external.

My internal reaction feels like someone used the defibrillator at thrice the normal voltage.

Which explains my external reaction. Goosebumps cover my arm. My knees buckle. All breathing ceases. And...I squeak. No words. Just a very attractive—yeah, right!—squeak.

Bemusement flutters across those full lips of his and his eyes glint with...something.

Nothing.

Something?

"Why do you say that?" I try to talk like a normal person, but my words come out sounding like my tongue's numb from eating too many salt and vinegar chips. How attractive.

"We're together. In a date-like setting. Holding hands. You've yet to spit at me. And you haven't called me your nemesis." Chance holds up a finger for each reason.

"It must be the salty air." Sounds reasonable, right?

"You haven't called me your nemesis *in weeks.*"

"I've been sick?" Keep staring at the water. That's right. The water is pretty.

"Or you like me."

Everything around me shifts into slow motion. I might as well have GUILTY! stamped on my forehead. Because it's true. I like him. A lot. I never stopped. And I don't know if I'm capable of ridding my heart of these feelings, or even if I want to, which proves to be the sad part of this story. I'm a textbook glutton for punishment.

An all too familiar sorrow floods me. "You wish." I wish. Oh, how I wish!

"Maybe I do."

At this, I snort. "Don't mess with me."

"I'm not," Chance says, raising his voice to be heard over the wind, waves, and the strangers who are probably listening to our awkward conversation. "Why would you think that?"

The ship docks at the island with the lighthouse now, jerking everyone on board as the crew sets the anchor.

"I know you. I've spent years watching you flit from beautiful girl to beautiful girl. Why would I think you'd give me the time of day now?" I let go of his hand, excruciating as it is, to prove my point. "It's just a game. One I have no desire to play."

Always was. Always will be.

Chapter Thirteen

Chance watched as Apryl wormed her way through the crowd, disappearing onto the dock. At least she was stuck on this island with him. He'd talk to her again.

Right?

Could he? Should he?

A familiar feeling crept into the pit of his stomach, filling it with ice.

Your mother abandoned you. There's no way you can have a real relationship. You'll be just like her.

His steps slowed until he came to a complete stop in front of the doorway to the lighthouse. Why had he come here? What had he been thinking, coming to a place overflowing with memories of Marla McFarland that were so vivid he could practically smell her coconut-milk scent?

"Excuse me," a middle-age man said. "You're blocking the entrance."

"Sorry," Chance mumbled as the man and his companion brushed by. He wandered over to a stone bench in front of a window and sat down, the coolness of the stone barely registering in his mind.

"This is a good memory, and I need to hold onto those." He'd said that only minutes ago. What a hypocrite he was.

Just like her.

Chance hated those words.

A memory unfurled itself from the dusty corner where Chance had shoved it instead of destroying it for some inane reason. The day Marla—because he refused to call her Mom ever again—had taken him here. They sat on a stone bench just like this one on the other side of the island.

"Look at the ocean, Chance!" Marla exclaimed. "We can't fathom just how vast and wide and deep it truly is!"

Chance frowned. "What's fathom?"

She smiled and stroked his cheek with the back of her fingers. "It means we can't understand or imagine just how big the ocean is."

"Why didn't you just say that?"

Marla laughed. She sounded like Tinker Bell. He would never admit that to his buddies (eight-year-old boys could be cruel), but that's what her laughter sounded like. He loved the sound.

And Chance might not understand the fancy words his mother used, but he knew what it meant when she laughed. So he asked, "Can we get some ice cream?"

"Why do you always ask for ice cream when I laugh?"

"Because you said that ice cream was the only thing that could make a day of love and laughter better."

"I did say that, didn't I," Marla mused. "You're right. We'll get some ice cream after we climb to the top of the lighthouse."

"Awesome!" Chance bounced up and down on the stone bench.

She wrapped an arm around Chance, stilling his Tigger impersonation, and he responded in kind by wrapping an arm around her. Happiness filled his lean little body.

"Chance, don't make the mistakes that I made. Be free. Life should be freedom." Marla grasped at the ocean she could never reach from her perch with Chance. "Explore. Love. Be free. I wish I were free."

Though she whispered her last five words, Chance still heard them.

Chance frowned. "Don't you want to be with me? Don't you love me?"

"Darling, I will always love you. You will always have my love. No matter what. But one day you will understand what I mean. You're just like me." Marla smiled at him and then looked at her elusive ocean. "We were meant to be free."

Anger filled him. He was nothing like her! Chance clenched

his fists, knuckles turning cherry red, as if he could finally grasp the memory and grind it to dust. That's what he wanted to do. That's what she deserved.

Swoosh! Swoosh! Swoosh!

Blood pounded in his ears.

Swoosh! Swoosh! Swoosh!

He...could...just...

Whoosh!

All at once, he deflated and drained, emotions emptying all over the freshly cut grass.

No, anger wasn't the way to fix this or his attitude. Chance took a deep breath and let his eyes slide shut.

God, I know I've screwed up in the past... But I'm not her. Help me...

He didn't know what else to say.

But those twelve simple words must have been enough. Calmness coursed through his soul, overflowing until his body relaxed. He loosened his grip, and the redness leached from his knuckles.

Chance stood, ignoring the lingering doubt that threatened to slow his footsteps, the quiet whispers in the back of his mind.

God had made him new. Chance repeated it as he walked around the brick lighthouse.

God had made him new.

God had made him new.

New...

He gulped.

Where would Apryl be?

The island was small, and only the lighthouse and a little single-story house rested on it. Both had been turned into public museums that showcased life as a lighthouse keeper.

Chance looped the immaculate grounds twice.

Apryl would want to see the top of the lighthouse. Chance snapped his fingers. Of course! He should have checked there first.

He went inside and climbed all eighty-four steps. The top of the lighthouse consisted of a little room where the lighthouse keeper would light the beacon, signaling the threat of deadly rocks and barrier reefs. A small door led to the wraparound deck.

Chance stepped through the doorway.

Apryl stood to his left, facing away from him and leaning against the high, wrought iron railing. If she knew she had company then she didn't care.

Making her a prime target for an abduction. Uplifting, wasn't it? Sorry, he'd just watched *Taken* with his father again.

He walked to her, footsteps clanging on the metal.

Well, she knew someone had invaded now.

She glanced over her shoulder, saw him, and looked away. Despite her slight, delicate movements, Chance saw her wipe her cheeks.

"Lighthouses are timeless," she said without looking at him. "They stand here resolute and sure of their purpose even if they don't function anymore. They take you back to a simpler time when all you had to do was look for the light because it would guide you when you couldn't see." Apryl quieted and fiddled with her locket. That action alone spoke volumes.

"Apryl." His voice sounded hoarse and foreign to his own ears. "I'm not toying with you. You don't have to believe me but I'm going to try."

She didn't say anything.

"Please," Chance breathed. "Let me try." Oh, man. How the mighty had fallen! He was actually begging a girl for a date.

But not just any girl. So...worth it? Yes, worth it.

Apryl titled her head, baby blue eyes studying him through a sheer veil of blue-black hair.

Hope infused Chance. "Go on a date with me?" He held out his hand, waiting, hoping, praying she would take it.

"When?"

One word. One awesome word that infused him with a little hope—hope that he could measure on a dipstick.

"Tomorrow. And now. Both." Chance's heart thundered within him as he waited for her answer. Each second that flickered by felt like a swat at his outstretched hand.

Why was he still holding it out there like that? His brain told it to move, but someone didn't want to cooperate. Would throwing a punch at himself be appropriate?

No? Fine.

Apryl glanced back at the ocean that stretched before them.

Slim fingers clasped his.

"Let's go."

My name is Apryl Marie Burns, and boys want to date me because I'm downright pitiable.

Don't laugh or roll your eyes! I'm serious.

Whatever, let's agree to disagree and continue being friends. But when I'm proven right, I will be forced to sing, "I'm right! You're wrong! That is why I sing this song!" I think Izze taught me that song, which should give you a glimpse at the level of awesomeness contained within these lyrics.

I steal a glance at Chance. He stares straight ahead, a what-did-I-get-myself-into look frozen on his handsome face. The boardwalk ebbs and flows with a kaleidoscope of people talking, eating, and making merry. And we shuffle around like the two most awkward people on the planet.

This is how I always imagined it would be...

Gag. Did you catch my eye roll? Because I rolled my eyes.

We spent over an hour walking around the lighthouse. Over an hour filled with safe, shallow topics, sickening politeness, and no touching whatsoever once we'd left its deck.

Not that touching is a requirement or expected or wanted....

Okay, fine. *I* dropped *his* hand. It felt safer somehow. How can I feel safe and like I'm being dangled over a ledge all at the same time?

As surely as I know He lived and died for me, I know God is clucking like a chicken right now, poking at my ridiculousness.

We have another three hours before we need to head back to the wedding venue.

Three hours that snicker at me.

One hundred and eighty minutes that shake their heads.

Ten thousand and eight hundred seconds that laugh at my pain.

I really shouldn't be left alone in my head. It's a scary place with very little sympathy.

"We should probably eat." Chance rubs the back of his neck.

"Yeah." I force extra sweetness into my tone and fidget.

Does this give you an idea of what it's been like between us? I'll put my hand on your thigh in true Old Testament Abraham fashion and swear that this pathetic example has been the gist of our conversations since leaving the observation deck.

Shouldn't we be talking? Impromptu or not, people talk on dates. The undeniable scent of corndog fills my nostrils. My stomach complains in four-point-one surround sound. My stomach will talk, but we won't.

The dam of my good behavior breaks.

"Dude, this is lame."

I'm nothing if not tactful.

Chance raises an eyebrow at me. "I don't see you contributing your oh-so-brilliant ideas."

"Thanks for the acknowledgement of my brilliance when it comes to the idea department. I'm touched." Finally! We have a real verbal exchange, folks!

"Did you miss the mocking tone?" Exasperation and a hint of relief color his tone.

I clutch my hands to my chest like I'm receiving an award. "I don't know what to say in response to this moving recognition," I say, ignoring him. "First and foremost, I have to thank you, Chance McFarland, for providing a target at which to toss my brilliance."

"Ladies and gentlemen," Chance interrupts, "it appears the man in question has jumped onto the platform and started hurling tomatoes at our award nominee. Stay tuned for all the shocking details coming up after this message from your sponsor, a man who is hungry."

"Wow, that deserves the coveted slow clap." I slap the fingers of my right hand against my left palm in slow motion over and over, drawing the attention of everyone in a ten-foot radius. "Ladies and gentlemen, give it up for this guy right here! The one, the only, the Man Who is Hungry!"

"Actually, I said 'a man who is hungry.' Just butcher my words, why don't you?" Chance mumbles as I continue to clap and cheer.

Around us, my proclamation is met with seven bemused grins, six frightened expressions, three blank stares, and two mothers who usher their children away from us.

Chance rolls his eyes. "Just ignore her, folks. This mental breakdown will pass."

I stick my hands onto my waist. "So, Hungry Man, what are we going to eat?"

"Food."

"What a novel idea. I was going to suggest rocks and saltwater."

Saltwater...

"Is there a taffy place around here?" My mouth waters at the thought of the salty, sweet, chewy goodness.

"I don't think so."

A pink-and-purple awning fluttering in the breeze catches my eye. "That place may have taffy."

"Are you just going by the colors?"

Maybe. "It's one of my brilliant ideas."

"Words that could start a disaster movie," Chance mutters and shakes his head.

We reach the cute little shop. Miller's Ice Cream Shoppe is painted on the window in bold white cursive.

"Let's eat here." Ice cream is a nice substitute for taffy.

A funny look shadows Chance's face. He opens and closes his mouth. "Okay."

"Say it once more with feeling!"

He walks through the door.

Killjoy. What happened to the mandated childhood motto, "We all scream for ice cream!"?

Oh, right. Not kids anymore. The loss of the ice cream scream is yet another reason to mourn adulthood. I'm tempted to shout, "Cling to your ice cream years!" to all the nearby children, but that probably would just result in the cops being called.

The inside of Miller's is crisp and clean. White countertops, white walls, black marble floors, and vivid pictures of ocean sunsets providing pops of color with lots of pink, purple, yellow, orange, and blue. A counter with a tall, boxy glass divider separates the customers from the ice cream, and it runs the length of the entire left side of the building. A black wooden sign hangs on the wall with HOMEMADE ICE CREAM written in white block letters.

Chance and I squeeze into the long line. At least thirty different flavor choices bombard me. A man and a woman work the line, alternating between scooping and ringing the customers up.

Maybe we should go somewhere else.

Seven people squeeze into line behind us.

Or maybe we should stay right here.

Fifteen minutes pass before the woman looks at us. After the rush we just witnessed, it's no wonder her white visor doesn't contain her orange-red hair anymore. "What can I get for you?"

"I'll have a triple scoop of your orange cream chocolate chunk in a waffle cone, please." Chance looks at me.

"I'll have two scoops of your strawberry ice cream in a sugar cone, please."

"Coming right up." Exhaustion weighs her words.

The woman hands us our ice cream over the top of the glass divider, and the man rings us up. I start to dig in my purse for my wallet, but Chance shoots me a withering stare as he slides a twenty to the man.

My inner I-can-handle-myself mentality sticks out her tongue in response. My inner ice-cream-loving child licks her cone and skips into the sunset.

"There's outside seating and an exit through that door," he says, handing Chance his change.

Three more wooden signs saying exactly that hang over the door, adding a measure of credibility to his claim. That and how everyone else has disappeared through the doorway in question.

I snatch a handful of napkins, and we walk through the door, stepping onto a white deck with black metal tables and chairs. Six or seven tables have pink and purple striped umbrellas. Most of them are full with families, couples, and groups of teens enjoying the beautiful evening.

A couple stands up, tosses their remnants into a trashcan in the corner, and walks over to a swinging gate, exiting through the alley. Chance and I dash for the empty table.

I sit down, breathing in the salty air. The sun sets over the ocean, painting the waves and clouds with its Skittle tones. I wonder if the owners of the shop have taken some or all of the pictures decorating it from this deck or beach.

I lick my melting cone, catching a drop of the milky sweetness on my tongue.

"How's your dinner?" Chance asks after licking his own cone.

"Good." A rogue drip drops onto my hand. Drat.

"Strawberry is simple. I would have thought you'd choose something like Unicorn Banana Boat," Chance remarks.

"It had dragon fruit in it."

"What's that?"

"Exactly." Another errant drip attacks my hand. That's it. I bite off the top.

"Boring," Chance proclaims before following my lead and biting the top scoop of his cone.

"Strawberry is safe. And it's my favorite," I say once I swallow.

Chance swallows. "Be adventurous."

"Being adventurous gets you into trouble."

"Sometimes. And sometimes it opens up a whole new world." A story plays in his eyes. It's as if they're miniature televisions, but I'm too far away to make out the fuzzy images.

Why do I get the feeling we're not talking about ice cream anymore?

"For the record, I don't want to go for any rides on magic carpets."

Chance snickers.

We finish our ice cream in silence. My fingers are sticky but I don't lick them for two reasons. One—I'm with Chance on this quasi-date thing. Two—gross!

I set the remainder of my sugar cone on a napkin and attempt to remove the stickiness with another napkin. It rips. Great, now my hand is sticky and covered in shredded paper.

Tick. Tick. Tick.

And now I'm hearing an imaginary clock ticking down each second of this season's *Awkward Dates for Awkward People.*

Tick. Tick. Tick.

I shift. This is uncomfortable and unsettling and something else... Oh, yeah. Weird! This was a mistake.

Tick. Tick. Tick.

"Chance," I burst. "We don't have to do this."

His brow furrows. "Do what?"

"Sit here like this. I won't hold you to...what you said."

Chance leans back in his chair. "Do you really hate the idea of a date with me that much?"

"Come on," I guffaw. "This is not a date."

"Why? What makes this any less of a date than a creepy guy who stares at a girl for three weeks before he gets up the courage to ask her to dinner?"

"First of all, it wasn't planned." I hold up my index finger, counting the reasons.

"Tomorrow's will be planned, and for the record, I've been planning to ask you out."

I'm not sure what to make of that, so I dive into my next excuse. I hold up another finger. "You asked me out after we fought."

"You fought. I was serious. What else you got?"

"You can't be my boyfriend."

"Why? Do you already have one?" A seagull glides to a stop, perching on the deck railing behind Chance, its beady eyes trained on me.

Yikes. If I were the kind of person who believed by omens, this bird would have BAD! written all over him.

Chance raises his golden eyebrows, waiting for my answer.

I roll my eyes at him. "Yes, the fellas line up to date me. You'll have to wait your turn." The creepy seagull tilts his head.

"I would."

My breath catches.

"I can be a boyfriend," Chance continues. "I can be *your* boyfriend, if you'll let me. I'm not the same guy I was before I met God." Chance reaches across the two-foot wide table, taking my hand in his once again. He strokes my dry, cracked knuckles with his thumb. "I've thought a lot about this, about you. I want to try."

Gulp.

It all sounds good. Really, really good. But hiding under the not-too-distant surface of my doubts, the past remains.

I was never good enough before. Why now? What's changed? I sure haven't.

Not to mention the other little thing that's one-part man and three-parts my worst nightmare—that thing shaped like his father. "Us" is a nice idea, but it's time to pull out the argument I know I will win.

"Chance, what about—"

A wild squall rends the air between us. The creepy seagull, who shall henceforth be known as Lucifer's Pet Bird, dives toward me. All I can see is white. White feathers. A white wing. The white of his beady, horrifying eyes.

I drop Chance's hand and scream, throwing my hands over my face. That's right. When it comes to bird attacks, I live and breathe by, "Protect the face!"

"Argh!" a man—Chance, I think—growls.

I hear a thud, but it only makes Lucifer's Pet Bird angrier. "Ha-ha-ha-ha!" he shrieks.

Something hits me in the chest, followed by a wing beaning me upside the unprotected part of my head. Small, wet particles hit my hands and forearms.

I might vomit.

"Ha-ha-ha-ha!" Lucifer's Pet Bird sounds like he's laughing at me. He probably is. This is clearly a sick cosmic joke.

I do the only thing I can in response—whimper.

Something hard and sharp pokes me in the hand again and again. It's pecking me! "Get it off of me!"

"I'm trying!" Chance shouts. I think he shoved something at the maniacal seagull because the table wobbles.

Lucifer's Pet Bird flaps his wings, creating a mini-windstorm. Just as quickly as he attacked, he's gone.

I hope. I don't dare look.

Chance's large, calloused hands grab my upper arms. "Apryl, it's gone. The bird is gone."

"Is she all right?" a random voice asks.

"Yeah," Chance answers the faceless voice before readdressing me, "Apryl, it's okay. You're okay."

I lower my hands just enough to peak at the battlefield between us. The remains of my sugar cone are crushed and strewn across the table and Chance. I turn my hands over. It covers me, as well.

I keep my mouth clenched shut. Locked. Sealed.

Do. Not. Hurl.

Breathe in. Breathe out. That's right. Nice, even breaths.

At least there's no blood.

"I think it was after your cone," Chance states. You'd think we hadn't just battled a possessed bird for our lives based on his casual tone.

I'm allowed to be dramatic right now. Back off.

"Dude, look! It's doubling back!" someone yells.

Something smacks into the side of my head with a surprising amount of force.

And drips down the left side of my face.

White goo covers my shoulder.

"Guys, did you see that? The bird just pooped on her head!" a teenage guy exclaims while laughing. The camera on his cell phone flashes in what remains of my peripheral vision. I'll be the face of one of those YouTube "Fail" videos for sure.

Worst. Date. Ever.

Chance stands up so fast that his chair falls over. I watch with my non-squinted eye as he marches over to the guy. Everyone on deck holds a collective breath.

"Hey! Knock it off." While he's not as big as Miles, Chance is still pretty broad and tall. Especially compared to the lanky teenager. He stands there, hands clenched at his side, heaving breaths that say he'd love nothing more than to smack this twit upside the head.

He holds up both hands. "Sorry, man."

"I think you owe her an apology." Apryl couldn't see his face, but she'd bet it left little room for negotiation.

Not that it would stop this guy. "What? I didn't do anything."

"Apologize," Chance growls between clenched teeth.

"Whatever. Sorry, lady." The guy turns to his friends. "Let's get out of here." The group of gangly teens leave, marching one by one toward the alley exit.

Sorry, a petite brunette mouths to me before hurrying to catch up with her group.

Tears sting my eyes and blur what remains of my vision.

Chance stalks back to our table. Some people murmur and continue to stare, and others seem to decide I'm old news.

Chance kneels in front of me. "Let's get out of here."

"I need to get this stuff off of me," I squeak.

"I know. Follow me."

I hiccup. "Okay."

Chance takes my hand, and his touch is wonderfully comforting after the past few minutes of trauma. (Has it really only been a few minutes?) He leads me through the alley exit and down the boardwalk, ignoring all the people who stop and stare at me.

I'll give them something to stare at. I glare at them, and most have the decency to look contrite before looking away for a moment. But I'm sure their heads swivel back into position once I pass them, their slack jaws dangling in the evening breeze.

I don't have a lot of faith in humanity or animals at the moment.

Chance ushers me down some crumbly concrete steps that spill onto the beach. Since sunset is rapidly approaching, the beach is almost deserted, dotted with couples here and there. No one close enough to see my predicament, though.

Chance plops into the sand, takes off his socks and shoes and tells me to do the same.

"Bossy, aren't we?" But I sit, careful to avoid a jagged seashell. I remove my beat-up converse sneakers then peel off my sweaty socks. Man, I hope my feet don't smell. I set my bag on top of my socks and shoes.

Chance stands and holds out his hand. "Come on."

Our arms brush against each other as we trudge toward the water. The cool ocean air kisses my face, which is flushed from embarrassment of galactic proportions. At the ocean's edge, tentative waves lap at my toes, but their frigid greeting causes me to jump.

Chance wades into the water until his calves are submerged then turns around to face me. "Dive in."

"Are you crazy?" I sputter.

His mouth quirks to the side. "It's one of my brilliant ideas."

"I'm the one with brilliant ideas, and this isn't one of them."

"You'll feel better."

"Yeah, because within five seconds of jumping into that freezing water, I'd be at the Pearly Gates."

"It's not that cold." He lifts a foot and points at it.

I cross my arms and stare him down. "It looks blue."

"You exaggerate." Chance sticks his foot back into the water and wades farther in. It's up to his waist by the time he stops walking. He tosses a victorious grin at me, but I swear he shudders.

I squint against the blinding colors of the sunset. "We shouldn't even be out here. It's after seven."

Chance spreads his arms wide. "We won't be here long. Plus, the beach closes at sunset. The sun has not fully set yet."

"You always were one of those kids in school who skated by on your cute smile and a technicality," I huff.

"Apryl, it's not like I'm asking you to skinny-dip." Utter mortification floods my face, but Chance ignores me and continues speaking. "I figured most restaurants on the boardwalk wouldn't take kindly to you washing that junk out of your hair in their bathrooms. So short of renting a hotel room for two hours—which, believe me, would be way worse for your reputation—this is our only option."

My mouth hangs open.

Something buzzes near my ear.

I snap my jaw closed. I do not need to add SWALLOWED A BUG to the day's checklist.

"Besides," Chance hedges, clearly seeing my resolve crumble. "I know you've got a fancy change of clothes in that duffle bag in the truck. Don't tell me you'd rather go to Azalee and Stanley's reception like this."

Yeah, I brought nice, clean clothes, but I didn't bring more underwear. Didn't exactly think I'd need some... But I'd rather show up at Azalee and Stanley's reception looking like the bag lady from *Mary Poppins* than say that to Chance.

I gaze longingly at the water. Whatever. Wet underwear is a small price to pay.

A semi-translucent wall of water collides with me, stealing my breath.

"Why did you do that?" I screech. My teeth chat, chat, chatter.

An unrepentant little-boy-grin stretches across his face. "You had decided to come into the water. I could tell."

I kick the ocean, managing to get more water on myself than Chance.

He snorts. "Good job."

I bite my lip, shivers racking my body. The thought of immersing myself in this liquid ice pop appeals about as much as the cafeteria green eggs and ham did on Dr. Seuss Day in elementary school.

Chance holds out his hand. "I'll dive in with you."

I stare at his hand. Myriad thoughts swirl within my head. Warm. Wrong. Strong. Safe. Dangerous. Adventurous. All of that and more. Each time I've held Chance's hand today flashes through my mind's eye. Like they were all stepping stones to something more.

But what is this step?

And is this adventure worth all the risks?

A childlike joy blooms within my soul, and the corresponding smile reaches my eyes, my lips...which barely contain my still chattering teeth, by the way.

Chance grins, clasping my hands and weaving his fingers with mine like they're puzzle pieces reunited to form the perfect picture at long last.

Together we run and jump into the breath-stealing water. Laughing and squealing as we emerge from the water then splashing each other without mercy.

It would be a first, but maybe Chance is right. Maybe this adventure will open up a whole new world.

For us.

Chapter Fourteen

"Oh, I'll stick my hand into the drawer with the cobwebs and mouse droppings! My pleasure!"

Said no one ever.

Gram holds a handful of straws in her hand. Some short. Some long. She cups the bottom so we can't tell.

"Each of you, pull one out at the same time," she instructs Courtney and me. Yeah, we're a little juvenile right now, but neither one of us relishes the idea of a spider bite.

Spiderman was never my thing.

I rub my hands together. "Come on, babies. Don't fail me now."

Gram counts, "One. Two. Three. Pull!"

Courtney and I each yank a stick out. I examine mine—a true example of stick figure beauty—and wave it around. "Mine is long!"

Courtney holds her stick up for me to see. "Mine's longer."

"Are you serious?" I look at Gram. "My stick is over three inches. How could I have lost?"

Gram shrugs from where she leans against a pile of pillows in her bed. "I broke all the sticks into different sizes." She picks up a book lying on the nightstand then returns her attention in my direction. "Have fun, dear."

"You have a warped definition of fun, Gram."

"It'll be fun for me," Courtney says with an impish grin.

What a wonderful family I have.

I roll my eyes and march from Gram's office/bedroom to the dresser holding the drawer in question. There's no point in cleaning this thing. The chances of someone wanting to use a dresser to decorate are less than if I decided to travel to Wonderland tomorrow. But no one listens to me. "We can use it to store the smaller items," Courtney claimed. I think that means she should automatically be the one to clean the dresser.

"Gloves," I call out like I'm a surgeon while extending my right hand.

"Gloves," Courtney answers, slapping a pair of disposable plastic gloves into my palm.

I slide them on, snapping them at my wrists. "Flamethrower."

She drops a dust cloth into my hand.

Sigh. If I could, I'd pull the thing out of the dresser and hose it down. But it's stuck. Story of my life. I stoop and hold my breath as I extend my hand into the unknown perils awaiting me in the drawer.

I'm tempted to scream just for fun.

"I meant to tell you, but Miles and Izze are back from their honeymoon, and he started organizing stuff for a commercial for us."

I angle my head to look at Courtney. "Really? How?"

"I guess he's going to use the pictures you've been taking of the decorated spaces. And he'll get a professional photographer to snap a picture of the front of the store. Then he'll use a graphic designer to put our contact info on that picture. He wants it to flash at the beginning and end of the commercial. He'll hire somebody to narrate. He plans for it to run on the same channel that the Ever After commercial runs on," Courtney says, referencing the famous commercial that features Izze and Miles.

We recorded the original and watched it with popcorn (and chips for me) the first time.

"That's cool." I pull the rag out and examine it. It's nearly black with the exception of random clumps of silver webbing. Gross. "I need another rag."

Courtney makes a face as she hands me another rag. "Throw that away."

I toss it into the trash can we had on standby for this task.

"Oh, and the bride sent over the contract," Courtney informs me.

"What?" Something brushes against my bare wrist.

Oh dear.

"The bride from our next wedding. The Roaring Twenties wedding. It's in, like, three weeks." Courtney raises her eyebrows, waiting for these facts to jog my memory.

"Oh, right." My skin tingles. Okay, there's something alive in here.

"Yeah, so she sent the contract and requested that you incorporate some of the decorations she already purchased. Said she'd pay extra for that if it was necessary, so I set it up as a special package. It should be pretty simple. She claims the space doesn't need a lot, just a little extra flare, so you shouldn't need to see the space beforehand. Oh, and she wants you guys to stay for the wedding and reception. The more the merrier kind of thing." Courtney looks toward the ceiling like she's trying to remember if there's any more information that she needs to relay to me. "I think that's it."

"Mm hm," I murmur.

"Anyway- I thought I'd try to handle most of the paperwork before the actual wedding. That may make things easier for you. I'll try to do most of that from now on too."

"That's awesome. Thanks." I flinch. I really think something just licked me. Visions of a giant spider with tuffs of mouse-like fur and a snake tongue fill my mind.

It's like my nightmares have come to life.

"I'm just doing my part. I actually like handling all the paperwork and stuff for this. It's fun."

"What about after you graduate? What happens with your master plan?" I glance at my rag, which is just as bad as the first, before tossing it into the trash. "I thought your new plan involved working in a law firm and representing multiple small businesses."

Courtney hands me a third rag. At this rate, I'll use a dozen just to clean this drawer. "Maybe. Maybe not. It's up to God. I know that I want to be a part of this, and a law degree will come in handy with all the legal stuff associated with the business."

"You're freaking me out," I tease.

She snorts a laugh. "Hurry up."

I smile at her. "Thanks," I say. And I mean it.

I squat in front of the dresser, reaching deep into its depths. Man, this thing is big. My mind wanders to Chance. To splashing and frolicking in the waves. To meeting up with Azalee and Stanley in dry, fancy clothes and wet, frizzy hair. To the way he squeezed my hand when we finally got home at one o'clock this morning and how he said he would see me tonight for our second date.

My stomach takes up hula dancing within me. Tingles move up and down my arm and face. I hope Courtney can't see me blushing.

"Uh, Apryl?"

Drat. "Hm?" Play it cool.

"You...you've got a spider on your head."

"Nice try, Court. It didn't work when we were kids, and it's not going to work now."

"I'm serious. It's on your head. Touch it."

"No, I'll get this gunk in my hair." She's straight-up ridiculous.

Or so I thought.

Tiny arachnid feet tiptoe across my forehead.

For the second time in two days, I pierce the air with a blood-curdling scream, so high-pitched and frantic that dogs would beg for mercy at my hand. They would call me The Dog Screecher, not to be confused with *The Dog Whisperer*.

I fall onto my back and start smacking my face, head, and arms with a savage ferocity. It's kill or be killed. "Get. It. Off. NOW!"

It scurries down the side of my face and onto my arm. I catch sight of it and nearly faint. To think this behemoth is a descendent of that giant spider queen in *The Lord of the Rings* movies.

"I'm not touching it!" Courtney says between her squeals of laughter.

"Quiet down out there!" Gram shouts from the bedroom.

Seriously, I've got a great family.

A memory flashes. What did the firemen say to do when you're on fire? Stop, drop, and roll?

Well, it can't hurt.

I roll back and forth on the floor. The trash can falls over and empties its filthy contents on me. Gross. I hear Courtney thud to the floor beside me, presumably laughing so hard she can no longer stand.

Did I mention how awesome my family is yet?

Finally, I flop onto my back, exhausted. I'm not sure how long I spent rolling around and thrashing everything in reach on the floor, but every part of me aches. Crushed spider guts and legs cling to my right arm.

What am I doing lying here? Shower. I need to shower.

I jump—and by jump, I mean moan and groan as I grasp anything I can for leverage—up. "You're on your own, Courtney. I need to shower."

She's still giggling on the floor.

"There's a spider on you."

"Nice try."

Using the index finger and thumb on my left hand, I flick the partially intact remains at Courtney.

And run.

Her scream follows me up the stairs.

An hour later, I lumber to my childhood room wrapped in multiple towels from head to toe.

It's an art. The key is to use long beach towels.

Nudging the door open and closed with my hip, I pull out the outfit I'd selected and hidden in my closet this morning and get dressed. I grab my cell phone from the top of my robin's-egg blue dresser.

Six fifty-seven greets me.

No text messages.

Okay.

So.

He forgot. He's backing out. He's...

Just wait for it. Something, Someone, in my heart says.

I breathe I through my nose and out through my mouth as peace settles over me. I can wait.

My thumb hovers over the HOME button.

Click.

Six fifty-eight.

I'm ridiculous.

Abandoning my pretty clothes for comfy gray jeggings and a simple, sleeveless, black tunic, I turn on the music app on my phone and busy myself with cleaning my room, praying no more spiders come out to play.

Or seek vengeance.

An hour and a half passes. The sun has set. Courtney came up to ask if I wanted to watch a movie with her and Gram. I declined.

Here I sit.

Madder than the Hatter, as Chance would say.

Nothing? All day? Seriously? Why do guys do this? Is it really okay in their minds to make vague plans with a girl and then go radio silent? Every girl-power scene in all those movies and TV shows flash through my mind. It's just too bad I'm not brave enough to actually leave a message for Chance with my hotter-than-tamales annoyance.

Tap.

I shift my perch on my bed.

Tap.

Tap. Tap. Tap.

I get down low and army crawl to the wall toward the left of the window that overlooks the front yard. Resting on my hunches, I peer into the darkness.

A pebble hits the window two inches from my eye.

Huh?

I spot a male shape in the darkness.

Chance.

I stand up, stepping in front of the window. Glaring.

Another pebble high-fives my window.

I grab the flashlight I keep in my sock draw and shine it in his direction. Chance drops a handful of ammo and covers his face.

Sliding the window open, I hiss, "What are you doing?"

"Getting you for our date." He picks up something, and light bursts forth from a camping lantern.

I cross my arms across my chest. "What date?" Attitude, much? Whatever. He deserves it.

"The date we planned yesterday."

"I thought we planned a date yesterday, but I haven't heard from you. All day. Seemed like you had backed out."

"When are you going to understand that I'm not going to back out?"

Humph. I suppose that's a good answer.

Feeling like a little sheep, I lower my defenses.

"Well, are you coming or not?"

"I have to change."

"You already look great."

Aww.

"Hurry up or you'll be walking in the dark."

And end swoon.

"Fine. Fine." I shut the window. Hm... I don't want Courtney to come looking for me. I turn off my bedroom lights and turn on my TV to the episode of the animated *Justice League* series I was watching.

What? I keep the TV on when I sleep, and I can't think of anything better than superheroes to fill my dreams if osmosis works. So far it hasn't. I've dreamt of giant man-eating cucumbers for the last three nights.

I've told you before—my mind is a scary place to be.

I walk as quietly as I can on the squeaky floors. Heal to toe, heal to toe, heal to toe the entire way.

The mattress squeaks in Gram's room. My breath catches.

I strain, trying to listen for signs that Courtney's about to destroy my clean getaway.

Ryan Reynolds declares his love for Sandra Bullock.

I slip my black flats on, grab my black leather jacket, and loop a midnight-blue scarf around my neck before bolting for the door in a dainty way that would have made my first-grade dance teacher proud.

Click. I breathe a sigh of relief once the door shuts. Jogging, I make my way to where Chance stands with the lantern.

"How'd you know which window mine was?" I ask, huffing thanks to my thirty second workout.

Maybe I should lay off of the Lays...

Hehe.

"Oh, please," Chance snorts. "I've known which window yours was ever since we moved into the guest house."

Interesting. I store this tidbit away to examine later.

Chance motions with the lantern. "Let's go." He starts walking. I trot along behind him feeling a little like a dog.

"Where are we going?"

He doesn't look back at me when he answers. "The willow grove."

"You know, that's the first place Courtney will look for my body if I don't appear in the morning. Of course, she'll assume I fell out of the tree."

"I'm not surprised given your penchant for climbing trees. However, tree climbing—and falling—isn't on tonight's agenda." Now he tosses a grin over his shoulder.

Darkness covers everything. I can't see the moon or the stars, and we live in the middle of nowhere, with no streetlights until the end of our road-like driveway, so that's saying something. I inhale, thankful there's no a trace of skunk cuts into the fresh air. For now.

Chance walks away from the house, away from the driveway and any cars, deeper into the ink blot of the night.

"Chance, where are we going?"

"I told you, the willow grove."

"Why?"

"You'll see." I can hear a smile in his voice.

I repress a growl. I should be polite. Although, Chance has known me since we were teenagers. It's not like a little growl is going to surprise him at this point.

"Aren't you worried about another skunk?"

"Nah. Plus we've got a perfectly good rock-throwing system in place if Gerry decides to crash our party."

"Dude. It's Gordon. His name is Gordon," I say in mock rage.

"Whatever." Chance shoots me a mischievous grin before stopping at the edge of the willow grove. "I need you to close your eyes. I'll guide you."

I glower at him. "I am so not in the mood to trip right now, Chance."

He pulls a bandana from his pocket. "I brought a blindfold. The choice is yours."

"Fine, fine," I grumble. "At least cut the serial killer vibes."

"I knew you'd see it my way," he says in a deep, menacing tone.

"Seriously, stop."

I close my eyes. Every fiber of my being zips to life when Chance steps behind me as if I am on high alert mode. His hands rest lightly on my shoulders to guide me in my visionless state.

You know what they say about how your other senses sharpen when one is cut off? Well, it's a bunch of bologna. All I sense is Chance. His scent. His touch. His presence. Shouldn't I smell something other than his spicy cologne or hear something other than his minty breath rustling the flyaway hairs from my ponytail?

"You can walk, Apryl. I've got you," he says a few inches from my left ear.

"Really? I had no idea. I had expected some sort of levitation to take me through the willows," I quip. Best to be quippy. Quippy is natural. Expected. Safe.

"Put your snark away, or I'll steer you into the river."

I chuckle and follow his instructions. *Sometimes it opens up a whole new world.* Chance's words from the day before swirl around in my brain.

After a few minutes, his hands drop. "Okay, open your eyes."

My eyelids slide open.

I gasp.

We're in a tiny, natural clearing in the heart of the willow grove. A huge checkered blanket covers the ground, and four more camping lanterns hold the corners in place. Three things sit toward the back of the blanket.

Toeing my shoes off my feet, I step onto the blanket to examine them.

A small ice chest stands on the left. A box holding approximately two dozen snack size bags of potato chips sits in the middle. And...a stack of books? No, magazines? I peer closer. No, a stack a foot tall of *Batman* comics rests on the right side of the blanket.

Okay, this is officially better than the scene in *The Little Mermaid* with the boat ride through the willow trees while Ariel's fishy friends sang "Kiss the Girl". Take that, Walt Disney.

Chance smirks. "You should pick your jaw up. It's dirty down there."

"Well, I guess you did plan this date." I continue to gape like a flounder.

He sits on the blanket in front of the *Batman* comics, stretching out his legs and resting his feet in the dirt and grass. "My feet aren't as pretty as yours are, so I'm keeping my shoes on."

Oh, here comes the blush. "No one has pretty feet."

Chance pretends to examine mine from where he sits. "You must be the exception. I especially like the green nail polish with the gold glitter." He winks.

I don't tell him that it reminded me of his eyes. I sit in front of the ice chest, tucking my feet underneath me. "What do we have for beverages?"

"Since when do you call them beverages?"

"Since now. Seems like a moonlit picnic deserves a little extra flare."

"Well, in that case, my lady, we have a delightful assortment of bottled water and juices that sparkle." Chance pretends to bow from the waist from where he sits, but it comes across so awkward that I can't help the giggle.

Still giggling, I say, "Mr. Carson would throw you out on your rear after that pitiful attempt."

"I don't know who that is."

"*Downton Abbey.*"

Chance blinks. "I don't know what that is."

"It's like *Batman.*"

"Really?" Chance leans forward in interest. "Kind of an Alfred character?"

"No."

"You're mean." He shakes his head. "What is this and why do you like it?"

I study Chance. Wowzah! Where are those hand fans when

I need one? I hadn't really taken the time to look at him as we traipsed through the dark, but thanks to the lantern light surrounding us now, I can't help but be smacked in the face with his Chance-ness.

Yes, it's a thing.

The lanterns make his sandy blond hair shine like twenty-four karat gold. His gold-flecked green eyes are so bright that I'm not sure we need the lanterns. And the expression on his face looks tantalizingly close to the fulfilment of all my wishes. Decked out in a green-and-black plaid flannel shirt with the sleeves rolled up to his elbows, a white undershirt, dark rinse jeans, and tan work boots, there's no mistaking this handsome man for the cute boy I grew up with, despite the physical resemblance. He is different... yet the same.

Can somebody clarify why he's hanging with me and my pudgy, muffin-top stomach?

A hand waves in front of my face. "You get lost in there?"

"Sorry. Yes. My mind is a scary place. Sorry." If only I could rub the embarrassment from my cheeks. I'll have to work on that. Think of the millions I could make!

"What were you thinking about?" He raises an eyebrow, but his eyes glimmer like he already knows the answer. Cocky, isn't he?

Yeah, not going to happen, buddy. "The stars. I was thinking about the stars."

"Sure. What about the stars?" Chance reaches across the blanket with those long arms of his and pops the top of the ice chest. He retrieves a bottle of sparkling peach-mango juice and two champagne flutes then shuts the lid.

"About how they twinkle."

"Wait, let me guess. Did you also wonder where they are?" Chance pours some of the sparkling juice into one of flutes and hands it to me then proceeds to do the same for himself. I'm taking a sip as he says, "By the way, I hate these things. I'm always afraid I'm going to snap the stem in my giant bear paws."

And like a true lady, I snort.

Thank you, God, for not letting any of it squirt out of my nose.

Chance smiles but it fades, and a pensive expression covers his face. "You know what I think about when I look at the stars?"

Somehow Switchfoot doesn't seem like the right answer. "What?"

"I think about my accident."

Those five words knock the breath out of me so fast, it feels like someone took a swing at my rib cage with a baseball bat. One of the worst days of my life—and I couldn't talk to anybody about the knot of worry inside of me since I had professed to "loathe him for all eternity," in true *Pride and Prejudice*/Elizabeth Bennet fashion.

"Why?" I whisper.

Chance sets his glass in the grass and leans back onto his hands. "I've never told anyone this, but I had this moment where I was semi-conscious. I could hear the ambulance, and my vision spun around and around. I tried to look up, but it was pitch black. I remember thinking, 'God, I can't see You. Are You there? Where are You? Where's Your light?'" Chance studies my face like he's trying to gauge my reaction. "The clouds just disappeared. Then I heard, 'I'm right here.' That's the memory that came back in the hospital at 3:17 in the morning. The reason why I rededicated my life to God."

Even the crickets stopped to listen to Chance's story.

"That's intense."

His lips quirk in a partial smile. "Just a little."

I fiddle with the edge of the blanket with my free hand, sliding it between each of my fingers. "Kind of reminds me of this verse Gram would say when we looked at the stars. 'Yours is the day, yours also the night; you have established the heavenly lights and the sun.'"

"Psalm seventy-four, verse sixteen. She's quoted it to me a time or two." Chance smiles.

I return his smile. "She'd say that God was always there, and His proof was in the stars because they were there all the time. Day or night. Clouds or clear skies. So even when we couldn't see His light through our circumstances, we had to trust that He continued working, providing, and guiding."

"The accident was the first time where I felt God like that." Chance shrugs. "Probably seems weird."

"Not weird. Sometimes it's the only truth I've had to hold onto. Like when my parents died." I set my still-full glass on top of the ice chest lest I dump its contents everywhere with all my fidgeting.

Chance's right hand moves ever so slightly and covers my left hand. He strokes my thumb with his. "Can I ask you something?"

"Hmm?" I'm not capable of a more eloquent response.

He points at my locket. "Is that why you keep your parents' names in your locket?"

I press my chin to my chest to look down at the locket in question, probably providing Chance with a lovely view of my double chin. Bittersweet memories twirl and dance to a haunting melody only I can hear.

"Yeah, I guess so," I say after a weird twenty-second pause, looking at our entwined fingers instead of his eyes. "I mean, I know they're not here anymore, but I also know they *are* with God. Gram gave me the locket the first time she caught me in the willows in the middle of the night, just a few days after they died. She took me by the hand and brought me inside. I thought I was about to get in so much trouble.... Instead, she gave me the locket. That was the first time she quoted that verse to me. She told me to put the names of everyone I loved in there, starting with my parents. That I had to believe with all my heart that even when I couldn't see it, God's light was shining on them."

I look into Chance's eyes. Understanding with a hint of guilt looks back at me.

"Apryl," Chance says, his voice huskier than I've ever hear it. "I'm going to kiss you now. If you object, you'd better throw your drink into my face."

An internal earthquake drops my stomach into a chasm of nerves and longing. "That would be very *Downton Abbey* of me," I whisper.

"I still don't know what that is." Then Chance's lips touch mine.

Chance leaned towards Apryl, and his eyes slid shut only seconds after hers. With the exception of his right hand, which still held Apryl's left one, only their lips touched. Gentle and new yet the culmination of over a decade of longing, unleashing...

Fireworks? No, fire. An intense and overwhelming fire. Like someone had just dropped a match into a tank of gasoline.

As Apryl had talked, Chance had wanted to kick himself for not seeing it sooner, for not seeing what—who—was right in front of him back then. Or maybe it was because he supposed he had seen it...suspected it. But the seemingly worthless cares of life and his own stupidity urged him to brush it off, especially once Apryl started acting like she hated him.

Excuses. Time he could never get back.

That tiny piece of paper sat in his pocket even now, begging him to ask her the question. He had to know.

And...

She loved him.

Apryl loved Chance.

No woman had loved him like she must have. Waiting. Aching. Praying. The realization of which could destroy him if he let it.

Which is why Chance chose to kiss her instead.

Refusing to be that guy, the old Chance, he pulled away after less than a minute. He opened his eyes to find Apryl's still closed, lips parted slightly, barely breathing.

Her eyelids fluttered, opening to reveal those baby blues that had never left his mind's eye regardless of the number of insults she hurled his way.

Did he? Could he?

Was it possible that...that he loved her too?

"Well." He cleared his throat. "I think it's time we had some chips while we discuss which of these *Batman* comics is the best."

Her vibrant smile unleashed his heartrate, sending it racing once again. "Am I supposed to pick just one? If I have to narrow it down that far then the answer would definitely include Batgirl being a part of the story."

"What if I don't have any with Batgirl?" He enjoyed baiting her.

She gasped. "That's absurd." She tossed a bag of barbeque chips at him before taking at bag for herself. The foil crinkled and she popped a chip into her mouth.

Chance caught his bag with one hand. "You can call it whatever you want, but we all know that Nightwing is second only to Batman. Why would I waste my time with a subpar character?"

She pretended to choke on her potato chip. "Please. Dick Grayson just had to be the star of the show. He's ungrateful."

They bantered back and forth, laughing and verbally sparring until the wee hours of the morning. He wished the night would never end, but when Apryl fell over midsentence, Chance knew it was time to head to their respective homes. She insisted on helping him clean up, and Chance walked her back to the main house. He didn't kiss her again, but the way their lingering gazes danced, well, that communicated more than a simple "goodnight" ever could.

As Chance trudged back to his house, exhilarated and exhausted, a question pounded in time with his footsteps.

Did he? Did he? Did he?

Could he?

Chapter Fifteen

"I always knew you'd come looking for me. Admit it—you can't live without me."

Oh, brother.

"One kiss and you think I find you irresistible?" I've got to make him work for it, or he'll think that I'm a lovesick dope.

I am a lovesick dope, but that's beside the point.

"What?" Chance moves away from the open engine of a truck in his garage. He saunters to me. One...two...three steps before he's standing in front of me. "I already know you do." His gaze flickers to my lips before returning to my eyes.

My mouth dries. Great, now it feels remarkably similar to sandpaper in there. A texture I remember well due to a little taste test when I was five.

Chance winks. "Besides my irresistible—or as some would say, magnetic—charm, why are you here?"

Magnetic charm might be putting it lightly. A gravitational pull bent on sending me catapulting towards the cruel, rock-hard earth would be a more truthful comparison.

"I wanted to touch base with you on the next wedding." And we've hardly seen each other in the week that's passed since our moonlight date in the willow grove. I walk around Chance toward what looks like a half-assembled truck. "What are you working on?" I can't force the vulnerable, "I miss you," past my lips.

"It's the truck," Chance says without preamble, pause, or dramatic tip of the hat.

"What?" My stomach churns like I just drank a quart of yellow, chunky milk. "I thought it had been crushed into a tin can."

"Well, yeah. *That* truck is in a junkyard somewhere. I've been building a new truck, but it's the same model as the one from the accident."

"So that's why you always park your other truck outside," I mumble.

"Well, I thought it made more sense to keep it in my personal garage than in the garage where I work on my customers' vehicles," Chance teased. "Logic and all that."

His words register somewhere in my brain, but I don't focus on them. All I see is the truck. The one in which Chance had almost died. Okay, the representation of the truck in which Chance had almost died. While I know of all the parties involved, inanimate objects and humanoids, this truck is truly innocent. Yet I still fight the urge to Carrie Underwood the thing. I wonder if there's a sledge hammer in here...

The. Truck.

"Why does it look so bad?"

Yeah, that inane comment happened to be the first to pop into my brain. How could you tell? Face, meet Palm. Get acquainted. Become besties. You might as well, knowing me.

Chance snorts. "That's what I want to hear after working on it for almost three years."

"You must have started as soon as you had healed." My eyes remain glued to the truck. It needs to be painted. There are no tires. It's sitting on blocks. A door-less frame and windshield-less front leaves the inside open for inspection. There's one seat—the driver's. The hood has been detached and rests against the left wall. A jumble of knobs, hoses, and blocky things make up the engine.

I know nothing about engines, trucks, or *Transformers*, in case you were wondering.

"Can I ask you a dumb question?" Walking to the truck, I stretch my hand out like I'm going to touch it then yank it back.

"There's no such thing as a dumb question."

"You want to bet?"

"Oh, please don't do this to me."

I toss a grin over my shoulder for him to catch. "But it's fun." I rest my hand on the cool metal. There. I did it.

"What's the question?" Chance watches me from where he leans against a workbench covered in tools and (I assume) car parts.

I trace my finger over a groove that looks like metal scar tissue from some sort of surgical procedure. "What's this?"

"Part of the fender had rusted, so that's where I welded the metal I cut for the new panel into the old one."

"And welding is...hammering?"

"Welding is melting." Chance enunciates like he's a second-grade teacher reading *Cat in the Hat*.

"Oh, fire. Very caveman of you."

"I liquified the points where those metal pieces meet, fusing them together into a nearly unbreakable bond at the chemical level, so it's a little more impressive than that, thank you very much."

"Why is it raised like this?" I touch the bumpy metal again.

"I'll use a hand grinder on it eventually." He shakes his head at my black expression. "I'll sand it down, and then it will be smooth."

"I thought you could only sand wood. Like tables."

"You really know nothing about cars, do you?"

"Shop class was an elective I elected not to take."

"Yet I remember you hanging out in that hallway often." Chance pushes away from where he leans against the workbench and walks toward me. He nudges me in the shoulder with his own. "Why is that, I wonder?"

I don't look at him. "The boys were cute," I say in a noncommittal way. I try to flip my hair over my shoulder like I've seen Courtney do so many times. Which backfires. Small, blue-black daggers stab me in the eye.

"The boys?"

I blink. Oh, sweet vision, where are you? "Do you think you were the only cute boy in high school?"

"Yes."

Chance comes into focus. "Is that a note of jealousy I detect in your tone?"

"Yes." His hand brushes the errant strands of hair behind my shoulder, letting my locks slide through his fingers.

I'm so glad I conditioned my hair this morning.

A gruff voice interrupts the moment, causing my breath to disappear from my body for an entirely new reason. "Chance, what's going on?"

I'd know that voice anywhere.

William McFarland.

My body reacts. Tensing. Stilling. Freezing.

Chance whirls around to face his father. "Dad, uh...what are you doing here?" He hasn't done anything wrong, but guilt drips from his words, pooling around our feet.

I should probably turn around now, huh?

Forcing my feet to move, I face the man who has haunted my nightmares for almost a decade.

He hasn't aged. It's like Mr. Freeze from the *Batman* comics we fawned over last week froze him in some sort of animated suspension where he can walk and talk, but the physical detriment of age has no hold on him. A tall, broad build similar to Chance's. Salt and pepper hair. A wrinkled face, tan and weathered from days spent in the sun's warm glow. Brown eyes that are almost black and glaring right at me.

A warmer welcome than I would have expected.

"What's going on?" William—I don't respect him enough to mentally call him "Mr." anymore—repeats the question through gritted teeth.

"I was working on the truck. Apryl stopped by to see me. Why are you here?" Nothing Chance says is outright rude, but there's an edge to his voice that I wouldn't have expected in regard to his dear papa.

"I came by to check on the books."

"Why?" Chance asks through gritted teeth.

I really wish I had the speed of Flash. There would be an Apryl-shaped hole in the door faster than they could blink.

"To make sure you're not messing around." William might as well have tacked "Duh!" onto the end of that sentence.

Cartoon steam shoots out of Chance's nostrils. "That's unnecessary."

William shoots a pointed look at me, the only one in the room with LOSER tattooed in invisible red ink on their forehead. "Looks like it *was* necessary."

Whatever. I'm used to it. But the urge to defend Chance against his father's not-so-subtle insinuation overcomes me. "I only came to touch base with Chance about the wedding—"

Chance shoots me a look that says, *Zip it!* A look that says it all.

William's eyes flash between Chance and me before settling on his son. "What wedding? What's she talking about?"

"Nothing." Chance runs a hand through his tousled hair, something he does more than normal when he's stressed.

"Chance, you will tell me what's going on right now."

Chance crosses his arms, proving to be a worthy opponent in this round of The Staring Game.

Several minutes that bring the meaning of uncomfortable to a whole new level pass before whatever internal war that waged inside Chance finishes. His shoulders slump and all fight oozes out of him. "I'm helping Apryl and Courtney with Charlotte's new business. Wedding decorating."

William's stony expression is both the pin dropping and the bull in the china shop. The tsunami and the eye of the storm before the other shoe drops. Sorry, but clichés are the only apt descriptions here, believe me.

Scary. Very, very scary.

"Come inside. Now." With that command, William stalks through the door that leads from the garage to the house. The clattering door makes the perfect exclamation point.

I whirl around to face Chance. "He didn't know? Are you kidding me? You never told him?"

Chance runs a hand through his hair again. "No."

"What a wonderful explanation. Make sure you tell him all those details. And don't forget to include the last part. That will really clear things up for him." I rub my face. This is a nightmare. No, this is the sequel to my nightmare.

Let round two commence.

"Don't bite my head off."

"How could you not tell him?"

"He wouldn't have liked it."

A dry, this-isn't-actually-funny laugh escapes my lips. "He's going to like this a whole lot less."

"I know. I know." Chance starts to pace back and forth in the small space between the work bench and the truck.

"Seriously, Chance, why didn't you tell him?"

"He would have flipped out." Chance's green eyes flicker and spark.

"I don't think he's going to accept that explanation." I'm certainly tired of it.

"Do you think you're telling me anything I don't already know?" Chance huffs and stops pacing. "But he'll want to fight the rental agreement. He'll hate you for making me do this, for costing me business—a business he labored to build before passing it off to me."

"Yeah, he's clearly passed the business to you when he doesn't trust you to do your own books," I hurl at him, achieving a perfect growl with the snide comment.

Chance jerks his hands back and forth between us. "Okay, I need to go in there and deal with him, so can we not have this conversation again?"

"Fine." I stomp to the door that leads outside, which feels like the longest walk home in all eternity at the moment.

"Apryl..." His voice trails off but unspoken pleas fill the air between us.

They don't matter.

"By the way..." I pause at the door, but I don't bother to turn around and look at him. "William's hatred of me is nothing new. Your father already hated me."

The door thuds behind me and I start to run.

But where can I run? It doesn't matter.

My freedom is also my cage.

"What were you thinking?" his father exclaimed as he slammed the kitchen counter with his fist after demanding Chance tell him what exactly he had meant by *helping*—a nice string of spit accompanied that word—with the new wedding business.

"That Charlotte needed help to keep her livelihood from failing. Seemed like the right thing to do." Chance couldn't help hoping that last sentence would bite. After all, his father was the one who had dragged Chance to church after church where phrases like "love your neighbor" were used in response to every and all possible difficulties.

Not that many of those people actually lived it.

Oh, a father has lost his job and the family is struggling to make ends meet?

Love your neighbor. Bring them a casserole next week. One and done.

Oh, a local teen is getting in trouble?

Love your neighbor. Talk to his or her parents about the importance of discipline.

Oh, your neighbor's home business is going under?

Love your neighbor. Offer to buy their property out from under them.

An easy version of love. As long as helping didn't inconvenience you or your plans then it was acceptable to lend a hand. A version of love that made Chance sick. One he hated. One that put itself first. One that had resulted in his mother walking out on him.

One he never would have thought his father would fall prey to.

Or maybe the full truth was harder to accept—that his father had embraced this philosophy all along.

Chance didn't want to be like that—fake. He didn't want to be like his mother, but neither did he want to be like his father. Not anymore.

The realization had him stumbling backward, grabbing the counter for support. Oblivious, his father continued to rage and scorn in the background, and a deep sorrow filled Chance. A sorrow that resembled death.

The death of his father as he had believed him to be.

"Don't pretend to preach at me, Chance," his father said.

"Charlotte was talking about selling. It would be the best thing for her in the long run."

Apryl's vivid smile after each bride had thanked her flashed through Chance's mind. "You don't know that. Charlotte, Apryl, all of them seem really happy doing this decorating thing." He gripped the edge of the counter for support.—Or as a way to channel his anger. He wasn't sure.

"Wedding decorating? Seriously?" His father scoffed. "It's a worthless pursuit." He stalked over to the door that led into the garage and peered through the window. Did he really think Apryl would stick around to hear this?

"People get married every day. It's not that ridiculous." Chance threw the feeble argument out there, but it sounded weak even to his own ears.

Chance didn't know if he could win this battle.

He wanted to win this battle. He *needed* to win this battle.

"They'll go under in another year," his father predicted from where he stood with his back to Chance.

"You don't know that." The thought of what that would mean for Apryl felt like a swift, roundhouse kick to the gut. This crazy adventure brought her joy. Real joy. Chance ran a hand through his hair again, and this time he gripped it, ready to pull every single strand out by the roots.

He would, if it meant he could keep this business alive for Apryl.

She's right about him. The thought came unbidden. Not like an eerie little whisper of doubt, but like a red flashing light warning him to stop before he barreled through an intersection of death. He'd put his father on a pedestal, ignoring the dangerous flaws because he'd stayed when Marla had left. But Chance couldn't ignore them anymore.

"Perhaps not. But what I do know is that up until her fall, Charlotte was going to sell the property to us." His father leveled him with a hard stare as if Chance had something to do with Charlotte's change of heart.

Yeah, and maybe Chance controlled the wind too.

"To me," Chance interjected. "It's my business now." He clenched his fists at his sides. This was getting old. All of this.

He whirled around to face Chance. "Not until you grow up and get your head out of the sand," his father barked at him. "You have no sense of responsibility or loyalty or work ethic."

"Are you kidding me? All I've done is hoist my work ethic onto my back for all to see! But it's never been good enough for you. I'm starting to feel like all you want is for me to be your pawn."

His father rolled his eyes. "Don't be a martyr."

No acknowledgment of how Chance felt. No stopping to examine if it was true. Nope, he just pushed all the blame onto everyone else.

That. Was. It.

Time to roll up those metaphorical sleeves.

"It's my business. You signed the paperwork. It's legal. You could call every warehouse in the country, and they wouldn't have a leg for you to stand on. And you can't force Charlotte to sell her business, her property, or her home. So lay off of it already!"

Chance had just stood up to his father. Had told him off. If it weren't for the gaping stare on the man's face, Chance wouldn't believe it had happened.

His father kind of resembled Dory from *Finding Nemo* at the moment.

Exhausted and spent from the emotional stampede that traipsed through him, Chance jerked out a chair from the kitchen table and collapsed into it. Good timing too. The confrontation had leached all the strength from his bones.

"We'll talk about this later," William said, storming out of the kitchen. Chance jumped as the front door slammed shut, watching as the few pictures he'd hung up shook from the force of it.

More talking. That's exactly what he was afraid of. Chance wasn't naive enough to construe this as a victory or even a stalemate. He knew his father well enough to know this was merely the time where he'd wait with bated breath as William reformulated his moves after unexpectedly losing a bishop. His father still planned to lock all those opposing him into a checkmate.

And yes, Chance was good at chess and strategy.

Thanks to his father.

Chapter Sixteen

Silence filled the cabin of my little car. The kind of silence that could choke a person with its tangible grip.

Comforting, isn't it?

I look into the rearview mirror. Chance's truck ambles along behind me, following me to the highly anticipated Roaring Twenties wedding.

Yippie.

Why aren't we riding together? Well, I've spent the last two weeks avoiding every text, phone call, message, email, smoke signal, and pebble thrown at my window. I made Courtney help me load up my car with boxes of decorations—stuff I probably won't even use but that still works with the theme—and had her call Chance to inform him that we would need to take two vehicles.

A gust of wind hits my car on the almost abandoned highway, and though I maintain control, the wind still sends my car teetering back and forth.

Chance's lights flash three times behind me. I glance into the rearview mirror again, and I can make out the frown on his lips and his locked jaw. Then my phone that's nestled in the dashboard holder flickers from the GPS and starts flashing with a familiar name and face. He cares. It's nice.

I have to break up with him.

Although, can this really be described as a breakup? There's been one real date and one impromptu date. It's not like we were about to skip into the sunset of matrimonial bliss.

A whimper escapes my lips.

I'm not overreacting. This relationship won't work. How can it? His father hates me. William McFarland never thought I was good enough for his precious son.

And he's right.

I can't be the one who destroys the relationship between a father and his son. Breaking up is the only option.

I crest a hill, and the highway disappears into the valley of trees below. This next wedding venue happens to be located in Keene, which makes for a drive that lasts a gazillion hours in the car by myself.

We drive by the exit that would take me to my old home. My old life. The whole thing feels so surreal. I haven't been home—is it even my home anymore?—since the week after Gram fell, and that was only long enough to pack some clothes. Kaylee's visited a few times, bringing anything we wanted or thought we may want someday. She's a peach, but I also think she's lonely living there all by herself.

We arrive at the venue after another fifteen minutes. Yes, I exaggerated the distance just a wee bit. Gram's house is about thirty minutes outside of Keene.

The Grand Egg Hotel looms before us.

The name? Yeah, I thought that was weird too. I looked up the hotel's website and discovered that "egg" is Twenties' slang for someone who lived the good life with their extravagant lifestyle. The website also included a list of popular phrases from that decade.

So, obviously, I spent the next two hours of my life memorizing the list in its entirety. A necessary use of my time, I assure you. You would not believe the number of Roaring Twenties' expressions that we use every single day!

I follow the parking instructions for the hotel. Chance matches me turn for turn, practically riding my bumper. It's almost like driving within a parking garage, the path taking us underground and the little signs in the concrete maze directing me to the section for vendors.

I park in front of automatic sliding doors, and a man in what I hope is a historically accurate bell hop uniform comes out to great us. The pants and matching jacket are red and tailored to perfection. Three vertical rows of buttons extend across his chest from collarbone to waist. A little round hat that sits cockeyed on his head completes the ensemble.

Do you think those are all real buttons? I can't imagine doing all those buttons every morning. Yikes!

I climb out of my car to greet the guy.

"Can I help you?" Bell Hop says.

"Uh, hi. We're here for the Sullivan wedding. We're vendors. We were hired to decorate." I will never sound professional. Why bother?

"Of course. We've been expecting you."

A good thing, I suppose, but those words sound so creepy. I don't want strangers expecting my presence in any way, shape, or form.

"You're welcome to park here while you're unloading, but afterward please move your vehicles to an available parking space in the vendors' section until it's time to reload your equipment." Bell Hop nods, turns on a heel, and marches away.

Rap, tap, tap plays in my head.

Where's a drum when I need one?

A door slams shut. "Well?" Chance says, standing just outside the door of his truck.

"Let's unload. We have to park over there after we're finished." I jerk my thumb toward the dozen various vehicles parked thirty or so feet away from the unloading area.

"Okay."

A man of few words. I mean, I know I've been freezing him out, but there's a part of me that says since we're stuck together now then he should be trying to talk to me.

It's girl logic.

We each grab an armful and enter the hotel through the automatic doors. A man dressed in what looks like a butler's uniform greets us inside the doorway from behind a narrow podium. He guards another set of automatic doors and types something into a computer that sits on top of the podium.

"The Sullivan wedding is located in the Abbey." The man looks and sounds just like Mr. Carson from *Downton Abbey*. In fact, I'm sure it is him.

I glance at his nametag, which reads, "Mr. Ames."

It's a lie. Or his twin brother.

"What?" Chance asks. "What abbey?"

"The event room," I say. "It's called 'The Abbey.'"

According to the website, the Grand Egg Hotel specializes in modern conveniences and vintage flare. The guests aren't deprived of computers, televisions, and hot showers, but the staff is dressed in uniforms that would be typical of the era and are taught popular Roaring Twenties' slang. The hotel restaurant, modeled after a speakeasy, only serves and caters food from that decade. The décor resembles some of the popular, ritzy hotels of the day from across the country.

"It's the grandest event space in the Grand Egg Hotel," the butler informs us. . A frown wrinkles his forehead, matching his serious tone. "The Sullivan wedding is sure to be an extravagant affair indeed."

I bite my lip. Regardless of his loyal devotion, it's hard not to laugh at the idea that a ritzy hotel has "Grand Egg" in the name.

Chance doesn't try as hard as me. He snickers to my left.

The wrinkles on Mr. Ames's face deepen.

The *whoosh!* of the automatic doors draws my attention away from his frown, and the sound of wheels rolling on the marble floor in the unloading area fills my ears. The same bell hop from before and a second man who is decked out in a similar uniform but done in black and with only two rows of the vertical buttons steer what look like fancy versions of those small flatbeds in hardware stores.

"You can load your equipment on these. Robert is a bell hop, and Jack is a footman. Jack will also be serving at the reception. They will show you to the Abbey." Mr. Ames says, "The Abbey," with a little flourish in his words.

The snort slips out this time.

I glance at Mr. Carson—Ames—to see if he noticed. He did. He outright glares at me.

Jack—the footman in black—winks at me. "Let me take that box, miss." He retrieves my box and sets it on his flatbed, the tails of his suit jacket fanning out behind him.

"Take my box? No, thanks. I've got it," Chance grumbles, setting his box on the second flatbed.

I don't dare try to make eye contact. I'm not completely clueless. I can tell he's annoyed at Jack's flirting. But our situation is...complicated. Unresolved. Ending. Soon. Ish.

"Let's unload your car first." Chance says. His words might as well be named, "Curt." He storms through the doors toward the parking lot.

Thanks to the fellas, Chance and I make quick work of unloading the vehicles.

"Right this way," Jack says, adding an extra hop to his step and shooting me another wink. I follow Jack, Chance follows me, and Robert the bell hop follows Chance with his flatbed. Jack leads us through the automatic sliding doors and down a labyrinth of hallways. He looks over his shoulder. "No worries. I'll make sure you don't get lost."

Can you guess what happens next?

That's right. Jack winks.

Poor guy. Too bad only Chance's winks have any effect on me.

And too bad for me.

The hallway's cushy tan carpet with its hideous floral pattern dampens the sound of our footsteps and the rolling wheels of the flatbeds. Jack pushes through two double doors that automatically lock behind us, and the hallway with all its modern industrialism transforms into something grand.

A rich wood makes up the half wall of wainscoting and the wallpaper above it is an emerald geometric Art Deco pattern, broken up by the doors to the hotel suites, which are painted a solid shade of the deep green. Glancing over my shoulder, I see that even those simple double doors are decorated in the same way. Gold fixtures that have been polished to a brilliant shine glimmer at us from every imaginable angle. Golden doorknobs, golden side tables, golden lamps, golden picture frames.

King Midas would be very comfortable here.

"Here we are, miss," Jack says, stopping in front of two tall doors.

"Yeah, I'm here too," Chance grumbles. The heat from his glare permeates through my hair to the back of my neck.

Jack pushes the heavy double doors open for us.

A gorgeous room done in shades of cream, gold, pale green, and emerald green—similar to the elaborate hallway but so much grander—welcomes us. It's as if a fairy from a Disney movie has drifted some sort of enchantment over me. The heels of my Converse sneakers click on the marble floor like I'm wearing three-inch stilettos. An enormous chandelier hangs from the middle of the high ceiling. Hotel staff scurries to and fro, setting up dinnerware on the sea of tables.

"This is the reception space," Jack tells us. "Those doors open into the ceremony space." He points to two more double doors in the center of the far wall.

Magnets pull me to them. I've got to see this.

Without bothering to wait for anyone, I push through the doors. A similar color scheme delights my eyes, but instead of the half wall of wainscoting, the wainscoting trims—no, acts—like a frame. A garden mural in muted shades has been painted within the wainscoting on each wall. Stepping into the room, I turn in slow circles, discovering that the mural continues on the doors. The ceiling has been painted to look like a cerulean blue sky dotted with puffy clouds. Another chandelier that matches the one in the previous room hangs from the middle of the ceiling mural.

More members of the hotel staff move around me, busy setting up white wooden chairs with golden accents for the ceremony. They face the far wall, which has an epic fountain painted in the middle of its mural. A physical dais with a flowery arch atop it awaits there, presumably where the bride and groom will stand as they say their vows in front of the preacher and witnesses.

Why did this bride hire us? Seriously?

"Why are we here?" Chance's breath tickles my left ear.

I jump. "Where did you come from?"

"Do you mean physically or spiritually? Both are lengthy answers." Chance grins.

It's the first time he's cracked a joke all day.

I steer the conversation back to our mutual question. "I don't understand why we're here. This place is incredible."

"Yeah. This is weird but it was fun watching you explore." Chance keeps his words soft, for my ears alone.

This is so not the time, but I can't do this to him anymore.

"Chance, I..." My words trail off. I open my lazy mouth to start again, but someone shouts my name from across the room.

"Apryl? Oh, there you are." A petite redhead in her early thirties saunters toward me. Her short hair has been styled in a perfect bob. "I'm the bride, Monica Sullivan." A graceful hand extends towards me.

"Nice to meet you." I grasp her lovely hand in my rough one. The hangnail on my thumb proves to be particularly alluring, doesn't it? "This is Chance."

Monica smiles and shakes his hand too. "Nice to meet you as well."

"Likewise," Chance says.

Monica turns her undivided attention back to me. "I think I've only spoken with your sister. Connie, was it?" She taps her chin with a long manicured fingernail.

"That's right. Courtney," I cough. It's really awkward to correct someone when they mess up a name. Especially when they're paying you.

"Right. Is this the first time you've been to the Grand Egg Hotel?"

"It is." I glance around the room again. "It's lovely."

"It is, isn't it?" Monica smiles. Her beige satin shirt crinkles in that splendid way that tells you it's top-of-the-line material. Her slacks have a straight crease down the center of each leg, and she's wearing red, peep-toe pumps. Her outfit screams haughty, but she seems nice. Not like an outright snob with condescension for perfume. More like, well, an egg, to use Twenties' slang.

"I must confess, I'm a little confused why we're here. It seems like everything's covered," I say. Against my better judgement, I didn't meet with Monica beforehand since the newly named Connie claimed this would be an easy job. If I had met with Monica myself, we wouldn't be in this predicament. I won't make that mistake next time.

"It's a beautiful hotel, but I didn't want my wedding to look like every other wedding that's been held here, you know? Courtney sent me pictures of the other weddings you've worked on, and I loved the unique touches you've been able to incorporate." She shoots me a conspiratorial wink. "I love the Roaring Twenties. They're unique. I've always loved unique things. And the weddings you've decorated are unique."

Blood drains from my face. What exactly did Courtney say to this woman? I can't make this venue into something more marvelous and glamorous than it is. It's the epitome of luxury.

My sister might want to change her name to Connie and go into hiding.

Monica must see my internal conniption fit. "Relax, darling. I don't expect you to transform the room. I just want unique touches and decorations. I know what you've brought will be lovely."

Sure. Lovely.

Just like my vomit.

Monica glances at her watch. "Well, I best be going if I'm going to make my hair appointment." She gives me a quick side hug before she leaves. "Don't worry, doll. It'll be darb."

"What is 'darb'?" Chance whispers once she's out of earshot.

"It means a great person or thing," I whisper, staring at the double doors. I wish I could disappear through those same doors.

"How do you know that?" Disbelief colors his tone.

"I spent a few hours memorizing slang from the Twenties the other night."

"Why?"

I turn to look at Chance. His expression matches his incredulous tone. "It's fun." I shrug.

Chance raises an eyebrow at me. "Darb? Darb is fun?"

"No, darb is great. Like Jake."

Annoyance flickers across his face. "You thought he was great?" Chance frowns. "I thought his name was Jack."

"Yeah, it was." I chortle in glee at his confusion.

"Why'd you call him, Jake?"

"'Jake' was slang for everything's great."

He shakes his head. "That's just wrong."

"Or all wet." This is fun. I love talking circles around people, but I should probably refrain from rubbing my hands together.

"Okay, that's enough. Can you please stop giving me an earful of Twenties' slang? I really, really don't care," Chance pleads.

"Did you know that 'earful' was slang for 'enough'? Ironic, right?" I grin and thread my fingers together.

It's not the same as rubbing my hands together. It's not.

"Please, stop. I'm begging you."

"Don't be such a flat tire." A bore.

He moans and grabs his hair.

I laugh but it fades. How on earth am I supposed to do what Monica expects of me?

"Hey? What's your beef?"

"I don't have any beef," I whisper. "By the way, that's slang too."

"You can do this." Chance ankles—uh, walks—to stand in front of me. "And you've got me."

No. No, I don't.

They say everybody fails. Sure, whatever. I can accept that fact. What I can't accept is always feeling like *the* Supreme Commander of Failures who raises the bar on what it means to fail for all the other failures in the world. A fate that seems to have been doled out to me since birth.

I wonder if I've reached some kind of record.

"Would you relax? She's going to love it," Chance claims.

I snort in derision. "Oh, go tell it to Sweeny."

He sighs. "You really need to stop with the Twenties' expressions before I lose it."

"Hello, darlings!" Monica calls as she burst into the room. "What do we have here?" A critical eye scans the ballroom.

I inhale the crisp, odorless air. Yes, the room has no smell. Explain that to me.

"Well..." I start.

Chance nudges me with his shoulder.

Gulp. Here we go.

"I, uh, incorporated the crystal candelabras that you already purchased, making them the centerpieces on all the tables. I also used the ones that we brought with us. Those are on your sweetheart table as well as the unique tables, like the one with the guest book and the gift table." My words come out in a jumbled rush.

"Mm hmm," Monica murmurs while studying the hodgepodge of decorations around us.

Time to continue. "The items I brought are technically all older than the Twenties, but they were still widely in use during the period."

Monica walks over to the nearest table and points. "And what's all this?"

I'm a DC Comics fan. Sure, I'll throw in the occasional Marvel reference here and there because, let's face it, some things they just get right. However, I'd renounce DC and switch to Marvel for life if it meant I could suddenly possess the abilities of the Invisible Woman. Namely, the invisibility.

My tongue, or at least my ability to speak, has disappeared. Why does this always happen to me? Hey, maybe I do have superpowers! Malfunctioning superpowers but superpowers all the same.

Chance jumps into the conversation, probably sensing the destruction to all mankind thanks to my damaged abilities. "Apryl thought the best way to incorporate that special touch would be to make the guests feel like they were part of that world."

The song about being a part of the human world that Ariel sings in *The Little Mermaid* starts to play in the background of my mind.

Also, there are dragons attacking my faculties.

Chance shoots me a look.

Oh, right. Real world.

"We've set items like fedoras, top hats, cloches, opera glasses, monocles, stoles, hand fans, beaded shawls, and pipes on each of the chairs. There are some other random items, but those are the most common around the room. The guests are welcome to use them during the reception."

Monica nods once but her eyes twinkle. "Would I need to sign anything more in the contract regarding damages or theft?"

"No, that's all covered in the contract that you've already signed. There's always the risk of either, but we do have photographs of all the items being used today included in the copy of the signed contract that I've brought for you." Sweet relief bathes me in warmth from head to toe. I shove the papers I'd forgotten that I'd been clutching in my hand toward her.

Monica grabs them and twirls around, taking in the room. "Perfect. It's just perfect. The guests are supposed to come in Twenties' garb. I knew you'd come up with that extra little punch." She beams at me.

A rare shot of courage infuses me. "I also spoke to the staff and instructed them to turn the lights down in the reception hall. It will add to the atmosphere."

Monica snaps her fingers. "Ah, yes. Like the hotel restaurant."

Uh, sure. "I'm afraid I haven't seen the restaurant, but maybe we'll have dinner there while the ceremony and reception are in progress," I offer.

Monica whirls to stand directly in front of me. "What? I mean, you should definitely visit the restaurant because it is absolutely darb."

Chance groans behind me, but he covers it with a cough. "Sorry," he apologizes.

Monica frowns at Chance for a moment before looking back to me. "But you're supposed to come to the ceremony and certainly the reception," Monica finishes. She tilts her chin up, up, up. "I insist." There's that upstage—snobby—edge.

Time to press the panic button. The last thing I want to do right now is hang out with Chance at another wedding. We settled into a comfortable rhythm while we worked, but things are still awkward between us. And I purposely did not pack any fancy clothes. There's no way I'm going to a wedding as ritzy as this in jeans.

"We would love to attend. Thank you for your hospitality on this special day," Chance says.

I laser him with my one-of-a-kind death glare, one for which a patent is currently pending.

She claps her hands. "Wonderful. You're absolute darlings. Now, I've got to go. I'll see you two later." Monica blows a kiss and away she goes.

I glare at Chance.

"What?"

"I'm not even going to bother asking if you're crazy. At this point, I know you are. But we can't go to this wedding."

"That's the deal, Burns. We wedding crash."

"We were technically invited again, you dork."

"Why, you're right! That simplifies the problem, doesn't it?" Sarcasm drips from his overly cheerful—and fake—realization.

"I didn't bring any fancy clothes with me. There's no way I can go like this." I gesture to my dirty clothes. "But thanks to you, I don't have a choice. And when we are thrown out of the wedding, I'm going to blame it on you. You'll be the one left holding the bag."

"As a matter of fact, I am holding the bag."

Well, that was a comment worthy of a head scratch, if I do say so myself. "Say what now? And kudos on not groaning at the slang that time."

"When it comes to you, Apryl, it's best to steer into the skid." Chance smirks. "Which is why when Courtney called me to confirm the details for today, I asked her to make sure that you had a change of clothes available. She agreed to take care of it. I believe if you look in your trunk, you'll find a duffle bag with the necessary items pushed to the very back." Chance delivers his explanation with all the poise of a super villain giving his I've-won-and-this-is-why speech.

My sister. For as well as I know her, I keep underestimating her. Courtney had pestered me a few times to tell her why I was being a wet blanket, but I told her that it was none of her beeswax.

Guess that worked out well for me.

And this slang is kind of addictive.

Chance moves to stand directly in front of me. His presence has an agonizing yet soothing effect on my traitorous body.

I look everywhere but into those beautiful eyes.

Chance uses the index and middle finger of his right hand to lift my chin, engineering the collision of our gazes.

Resist. Resist. Resist...

And fail. So much for not looking at him.

His breath tickles my face, but it's his words that send shivers down my spine. "Whatever this weird thing between us is, it gets resolved tonight."

Chapter Seventeen

This is the point in the story where everything goes wrong.

I know this story.

It's my life.

My shoulder rams into the wall of the bathroom stall. I growl and the bobby pin that's in my mouth slips from between my lips and lands in the toilet.

Umm... I'm not sure what to do about that....

Usually public restrooms are a level of disgusting that's not fit to be talked about in any situation. However, like everything else in this hotel, the public restrooms are things of beauty. White marble floors and countertops. Bright lighting. And best of all, bathroom stalls with actual locking doors and side walls that go all the way to the floor. I could live in this bathroom.

But I still don't want to stick my hand into the toilet. And I will not be putting that thing back into my hair. My overgrown bangs can fly free.

I'm hiding out in the handicap stall. After retrieving the bobby pin—a traumatizing story that I'm not even going to share with you, dear friend—I unzip the duffle bag and find deodorant, black flats, socks, nylons, body spray, makeup, clean underwear (I told Courtney about the incident with Lucifer's Pet Bird), and a dress.

Pulling my phone out of my pocket, I hit the speed dial.

"Hello?"

"I'm not wearing this," I say to my sister.

"Apryl?"

"Of course it's Apryl. Who else would call you saying they wouldn't wear the crazy clothes you packed for them?"

"Maybe I pack clothes for a lot of people."

"Are you being cute?"

"Sorry. Now, what's the problem?"

I point at the dress sitting in my bag even though she can't see me. "I can't wear this!"

"Yes, you can. I even asked Gram to make sure it was okay. That's actually her pick. I had picked out a brown one, but Gram thought that one would look better with your complexion."

I groan. "You are no help."

"I beg to differ. Without my help, you'd be attending a swanky wedding with the guy of your dreams, and you'd be in jeans streaked with dust," Courtney chides.

"What?" I gasp.

"You heard me. You and your feelings are not as much of a mystery as you think, sister dear."

"What? What did you say? I can't hear you. The hotel is going through a tunnel." I make a few gargling noises and hang up, tossing my phone into the duffle bag.

Let's get something straight.

I like dresses. Sun dresses. Tunic dresses. The bridesmaid dress Izze made me wear. I prefer pants but the occasional dress and skirt brings out a girly side of me that I like to show every so often. I have no issue with getting dolled up from time to time.

But this flapper dress pushes my boundaries of comfortable.

Bending over, I loop my fingers through the thick straps of the sleeveless dress. I hold it up. It's pale pink with black beads that have been sewn on in the familiar craziness of the Art Deco style. Repositioning the dress, I hold it against myself. High neckline. No definable waist. The hem stops about three inches above my knees, but there are long, beaded tassels on it that shimmer and shake for another foot.

Something else glimmers in the bag. Bending over again, I discover a golden circlet that's decorated with black pearls and some type of black jewel with a long black feather behind it.

My options consist of wearing the uncomfortable, albeit beautiful, outfit or trying to sneak out of here.

Chance is probably guarding the bathroom door. Though he might expect that I expect that. Which means he may be guarding the cars instead. Unless he expects that I've expected that. Clearly I cannot trust either of those escape routes. Window it is.

Unless he's already anticipated that.

When did I turn into Vizzini from *The Princess Bride*?

Grumbling, I get dressed. I slip my feet into the black ballerina flats and push the stall door open a little too hard.

It comes back and whacks me in the kisser.

And that's as close as it gets to kissing tonight.

I blink at the woman standing in the mirror.

The dress does look nice. It accentuates all my best features more than the dresses I usually wear, but it's not so tight as to be considered a second skin. It's actually still loose enough to hide my ample muffin-top.

Using a wide toothed comb, I attempt to fix my limp locks. My hair needs to be dyed again; the blue-black color looks a little faded.

I put the circlet on, adjusting it so that it runs across my forehead.

There.

I twirl and the beaded tassels spin with me. I look like a flapper. Giggling with girlish glee, I gather my things and repack them into the duffle bag.

Time to find Chance.

Opening the door to the bathroom, I glance around the hallway. Hmm, I don't see him.

In true Apryl fashion, I kick the door open the rest of the way and almost fall over as I wrestle the duffle bag through the doorway. Huffing, I free it. Rolling my shoulders and standing a little straighter, I ankle down the hallway like I hadn't just flashed my Batman shorts at the world.

Yes, I wear those shorts (or similar ones) under all my skirts and dresses. I'm a bit uncouth but that's probably obvious to you by now.

A man leans against the wall on the opposite side of the hallway. A low whistle escapes his lips as I walk by him.

I drop my duffle bag.

Chance leans against the wall looking swankier than a gnat's whistle. His vintage suit—a plaid, oak-colored tweed—looks dashing on him. The matching vest fits him perfectly, and an espresso-colored tie caresses his neck.. He's wearing a fedora that matches his tie over his slicked back, long hair. Very news-paper man.

Basically, he's a handsomer, light-haired version of Cary Grant. Don't throw rotten tomatoes at me. I'm entitled to my opinion, and my opinion is that I'll never be able to watch *His Girl Friday* again without seeing Chance dressed up like this.

"I know. My already stunningly good looks are nearly un-recognizable in this getup." Chance winks at me.

Unlike Jack the footman's winks, Chance's sets me swooning right here in the hallway.

Does anyone see a fainting couch nearby? What about smell-ing salts?

Chance pushes away from the wall. "But you, well, I don't think there's a word in existence that could be uttered from any man's lips that would describe just how beautiful you look."

Someone catch me. I'm going down.

"Here." Chance grabs my abandoned duffle bag. "I'll carry this to the car." His eyes pop and crackle a new kind of green energy, and I notice threads of forest green are woven into the plaid of his suit.

Words. Need words.

"Swell."

Well, I used a word. That counts for something.

I follow after Chance like a lost little puppy to the vendor's parking garage. I'm glad he was paying attention to where we were going before. I'd have taken us to the roof or something.

Mr. Ames continues to guard his station. He inspects us as we pass by him and nods once. It seems like we've earned his approval.

After taking care of our stuff, Chance grabs my hand and we dash by Mr. Ames. I don't need to look over my shoulder to know our quick-footed jaunt resulted in our loss of favor.

The appalled gasp said it all.

But the wedding ceremony will start in less than twenty minutes, so in the grand scheme of things...

We make it back to the Abbey where two footmen now guard the door. They pull it open, and smoke pours out of the space we'd spent a couple hours decorating.

"Is there a fire?" I jump back lest I pull a Katniss/"Girl on Fire" impersonation. And I am not wearing the dress for that.

"No, miss," one of the footmen says.

My nose wrinkles. "Is it actual smoke?"

"No, it's fog," the other footman says.

Huh?

Without explaining, the footmen urge us forward as other people form a line behind Chance and me.

"Hello." A woman dressed like a flapper greets us just inside the doorway. "If you would just step this way, I have the seating arrangements for the reception right over here."

"First, can you tell us what that fog is?"

"Don't worry, miss. The Grand Egg Hotel has several fog machines that we use in the restaurant on the main level as well as for the occasional event on premises."

Chance raises an eyebrow at me. "That's interesting."

The hotel flapper puts a hand on her slender waist. "Most people think it's fun." Her voice holds a flirtatious challenge.

I want to flick this woman right in between the eyes.

So this is how Chance felt. Props to him for not tripping Jack—whose name I can't separate from his title—the footman.

"Well, my gal and I aren't most people," Chance says while slipping an arm around my shoulders.

I shoot her a triumphant smile.

But this changes nothing between Chance and me.

She glares. "Names?"

We tell her, and after searching a moment, she hands each of us a small card. "Table seven. You can put your belongings there now. There may be items on your seats. You're welcome to use them during the event, but make sure to leave them here. Otherwise, you'll be charged for the cost. And they are expensive," she says with pursed lips and snot dripping from her delightful attitude.

I snicker. Clearly the woman doesn't know who we are. "Thanks." I make sure to use a little extra syrup in my tone.

Chance leads me to the table, which is located to the left of the reception space and set directly in front of the platform where a jazz band completes soundcheck.

I start to giggle.

Chance looks at me like I've lost all knowledge of social decorum. "What's so funny?"

"It's the slush table."

"The what?"

"The slush table." I laugh even harder at his flummoxed look. "It's the table where you put unexpected guests."

"Is that more slang?"

"No idea. I learned it from *Gilmore Girls.*"

Chance shakes his head.

I set the beaded clutch purse that Courtney packed for me in front of my chair before grabbing the black furry stole from my seat. I drape it around my shoulders like I'm a lady of leisure about to enjoy a night on the town with my beau.

"How do I look?" Chance is scrunching his face to hold one of the few monocles that I brought over his eye. Its little gold chain dangles from it.

I snort. "Here." I pluck the monocle from his face. "It's too small. You're not supposed to squint. The natural tension in your relaxed face is supposed to hold it in place." It slips into my hand again, and my fingertips brush the skin of his cheeks. "Why don't you just keep it in your pocket. Let the chain loop down all dapper-like."

"And a dapper is?" Chance raises an eyebrow as he waits for my response.

"A flapper's dad." I tuck the monocle into the empty pocket where the pocket square would go, careful to touch his broad chest as little as possible.

"How many hours did you spend memorizing all this?"

"It's irrelevant."

There. My hands drop but Chance catches them in his. He opens his mouth.

"Ladies and gentlemen, please make your way to the ceremony space. The wedding is about to begin," one of the footmen announces from his position at the front double doors.

The guests converge on the entryway as soon as the footmen open the doors, forming the type of crowd bottleneck that gives me panic attacks. Chance slows our pace so that the impatient party-goers push around us. We end up being some of the last people to take our seats.

The wedding passes in a blur. If someone quizzed me on the details, my blank expression would be the only answer that I could give them. It's not that it wasn't beautiful. It was. But focusing on anything other than Chance's arm—which he slung around the back of my chair—proved to be impossible.

The guests make their way back to the reception space where the jazz band plays with vigor. The bride and groom make their grand entrance. All the special dances are completed. The servers start to deposit plate after plate of delicious food in front of us. I eat everything but pay little mind to the taste of it all. Deviled eggs—the hotel special, if you couldn't guess. Brie with crackers. Caesar salad. Mushrooms stuffed with crab and parmesan cheese. And for the main course—as if the previously served food wasn't enough to test the strength of the stitching in my old dress—a plate of assorted popular Chinese food, a favorite food in any decade.

"I don't think I'll be able to eat anything for the next two days," Chance mutters from where he sits next to me at the slush table.

"Please. I've seen you eat two pizzas in a single sitting," I scoff.

Chance pretends to be aghast. "I haven't done that since I was eighteen."

"Sure. I believe that," I tease.

Our conversation has been easy and polite. Chance hasn't addressed the elephant of the conversation that's sat between us all evening. Though I suppose the elephant has been on his best behavior. He's just so stinking big that he makes everything awkward.

I kind of hope that we'll be too busy to talk. I can write him a letter about all the reasons we won't work as a couple.

I kind of hope that we do talk and that he ignores all my reasons and kisses me.

The only other couple at our table takes to the dance floor. They've made some polite small talk with us, but mostly they've kept to themselves. Which was fine with me. People stress me out.

"Let's dance." Chance tips his fedora and raises both of his eyebrows at me.

"Are you sure that's wise? Remember what happened last time we danced?" Maybe reminding him of our nasty fights will deter him. Be mean to him so that he'll leave. One day he'll understand that I had his best interest at heart.

I think that's in a book or a movie, so it's legit.

"Let's go." He stands up and drops his hat into his vacated seat with one hand while extending the other for me to take.

"Fine. Fine. But if you get mad at me again, I'll be sure to tell you that I told you so." I drape the fur stole on the back of my chair.

Chance shakes his head as he leads me onto the dance floor in the center of the room.

It hums with energy as the guests—who dove into the Roaring Twenties' theme without any scuba gear—shimmy and hop. Women twist in their beaded, fluttery dresses. Most of the men look a little awkward as they step and clap to the beat, but they seem to be having fun. The dim lights and the fog machine really do add to the atmosphere. It's like a happier version of *The Great Gatsby*.

I hated that book in high school. Depressing on so many levels.

The band finishes playing the Charleston, which I only know because Gram happens to be obsessed with everything related to dancing. I'm pretty sure that she would have married Fred Astaire if she could have.

The saxophonist starts to croon a slow song, and the other band members join in after a couple of measures.

Chance pulls me close to that brick chest of his, swaying to the music.

This feels like a sick cosmic joke.

"So," Chance says. "Now that I have your undivided attention, are you going to tell me why you've been avoiding me?"

"I haven't been avoiding you."

He twirls me. "Lies," he says when I'm secure in his arms again.

"And we've been really busy."

"More lies."

"Seems like your father thought you should be really busy." Might as well say it.

"I'm busy enough. You may have been right about some things. I talked to him. He won't be a problem anymore. I won't let him be a problem anymore."

I scoff.

"Really. I promise." He spins us with a little extra force, as if that will convince me.

"You can't stop him from causing problems."

Chance tips his head down to meet my eyes, and a loose lock of hair falls into his face. "If he causes a problem, tell me."

"You really want to be in the middle of this?"

"I don't know what *this* actually is. I just know that you don't like him." His eyes search mine.

Yeah, I'm not about to disclose *those* details. "He doesn't like me, Chance."

"He will once he gets to know you."

I shake my head. "How cliché is that?"

"I like you and that's all that matters. You make me happy. You make me want to be more...better. And yes, I know that's a cliché too."

Oh, sweet man, you have no idea how much I ache for that to be true...

I angle my head back to look him in the eye. "How can you know all that? We've only been whatever we are for a couple of weeks."

"We've known each other for years." Chance dips me, and I clutch his arms with both hands. I will never star on *So You Think You Can Dance*.

I wait until I've been returned to an upright position before responding. "We don't really know each other." Except we do. I know Chance as well as I know my sister and friends.

"That's absolute bunk." Another twirl.

"Bunk?" I grin.

Chance gives me a cheeky one in reply. "I may have looked some stuff up while you got ready earlier tonight."

"Oh? What other expressions did you learn?"

"Cat's meow. Beat one's gums. Hip to the jive." His expression grows intense and his voice deepens. "Cash or check. That's my personal favorite."

My breath lodges in my throat. I might choke.

Choking on air. Ironic, eh?

Cash or check—do we kiss now or later? My checks burn at Chance's unasked question disguised in Twenties' slang.

"We can't," I whisper.

"Do you think that God brings two people together like this after all this time for no reason? Because I don't. Give us a chance." He winks.

"That's such a bad pun." I chuckle. My reservations weaken. I can only remember one point on my twenty-page list.

Granted it's a big point. Even has a name.

Chance dips me back over his arm, showing off his dancing prowess for everyone to see. I can hear some women titter behind me, likely giggling over Chance. I add a little pizazz this time and extend my free arm above my head. Or is it behind? The vertical position is messing with my sense of direction.

He flings me upward again and catches me with ease. "Apryl," he murmurs, a pleading question in the aching way he says my name. "I choose you. Let me choose you."

My heart races. Could God really, truly be bringing us together? With all my heart I want to believe it's so.

Got anything You want to add? I whisper internally. *I know I don't always put a lot of faith in Your good will towards me, but is this for real? Can we—You—make this work?*

Warmth floods me.

I'll take that as a positive endorsement from on high.

"Cash."

With that one word, Chance stops us in the middle of the

dance floor just as abruptly as all those weeks ago at Izze's wedding. But this time, he slides his fingers into my crazy hair and frames my face, kissing me for all to see.

Chapter Eighteen

"So, how was your night?"

"Get out of my room." I yank the Batman-logo throw blanket that Kaylee made for me a few years ago over my head.

"I need details. Lots of them." Courtney's voice is far too cheerful for what I can only assume is far too early in the morning. She's a morning person. I'm a night owl. Being twins didn't seem to put us on the same internal clock.

Courtney tugs the blanket from my face, exposing me to a horribly blinding light. I squeeze my eyelids together as if that will prevent the acidic light from burning my corneas.

"Spill." She hops onto the bed, and the mattress tosses me up and down. Great way to wake up.

"No," I whine while trying to burrow underneath the blankets and pillows.

"Fine, but I have something I want to talk about with you."

"Don't you always," I mumble with my eyes still closed.

"I'm serious."

I open my eyes, blinking against the light until I can make out Courtney's face. "What's wrong?"

"Nothing, I just…I'm not sure I want to be a lawyer anymore."

I blink more and then open my mouth to scream for help.

Courtney slaps a hand over my mouth. "Stop being dramatic."

"Whu oo me ont yer?" I attempt to say around her hand.

"What do I mean I don't want to be a lawyer?" Courtney expertly translates. "I don't want to pursue the corporate path anymore. I mean, I'm not going to drop out of school, and I'll still take the bar exam. But I'm not sure I want to work for a law firm anymore. It's still something I'm praying about."

I point at my mouth, and she removes her hand. "What are you going to do then?"

"This." She waves her hands around. "I want to really do this business with you. I'm all in. And like I've said before, a degree in business law could be helpful."

"Yeah, I will concede that point," I say. Truthfully, it already has been helpful. "Have you talked to Gram about any of this? Or Dallas?"

"I've talked to Dallas, and he'll support me no matter what I choose."

"I should hope so," I mutter.

Courtney purses her lips but doesn't comment on my jab. "But I haven't said anything to Gram. I wanted to talk to you first."

Uh? What? Since when?

Probably shouldn't say that. The you-woke-me-up-early excuse will only cover so many faux pas.

"I just don't understand. Why the change?" I push myself into a sitting position on my bed.

Courtney shrugs and looks out my window. "Because... I mean, there's nothing wrong with pursuing the corporate career path if it had been God's plan. But it wasn't."

I've said it before and I'm going to say it again: who is this alien creature and what has she done with my sister? The Courtney I know firmly believed the life of a corporate lawyer was God's call. Suddenly *Lilo and Stitch* doesn't seem so ridiculous.

"How do you know that?" I need to know or the sheer strength of my curiosity will kill Miss Jeremiah, and Gram would be beside herself at her cat's death.

She grabs a gray throw pillow and hugs it to her chest. "Because there was no joy in it," she says after several minutes.

Oh, yeah. That simple answer just clears everything up.

"Think about it. Gram's accident was awful, but look at all the good God has brought in the wake of it. Dallas and I are closer than ever. Gram and her sister spoke for the first time in years, and now they talk every week for a few minutes. I'm excited for the first time about my career path because I get to work with you and Gram. And look at you."

"What about me?" Are my palms starting to sweat? I can't let her see, or she'll know she's struck a nerve. Maybe she won't notice if I discreetly wipe them on my blanket. Come here, blanket. Yes, thank you for your fluffy drying abilities.

A new pool forms in the palm of each hand.

"I've never seen you so alive with creativity before this. I mean, don't get me wrong, you're amazing with hair, but this taps into a part of your soul I've never seen. You look alive when you talk about each new setting you've created with these old pieces. The pictures you've taken are amazing."

Instead of bringing me comfort or pride, her words bring me panic.

Pure and utter panic.

My hands start to tremble, and a bead of sweat drip, drip, drips down my back.

Gross.

I press the back of my T-shirt against my damp back to stop the drip.

A voice whispers a message into my ear over and over again, pounding like a drum solo at a Skillet concert.

There's no way you can do this.

Chance looked up from the engine of his 1958 Ford pickup. "You aren't here to tell me why we shouldn't be together again, are you? Although, that usually ends with us kissing, so never mind. Go ahead."

Apryl blushed, something Chance rather liked. "You're not making me want to kiss you, that's for sure."

"Somehow I doubt that." Chance wiped his hands on a rag hanging on the side of the truck, but oil and grease clung to his fingers regardless of the coarse material. "I figured you would be bursting at the seams waiting for our next kiss."

"I just think we should talk about the specifics." She wrung her hands.

"Like how often we should kiss?" Chance winked at her, hoping to calm her fidgety state.

"No... I mean about what this is."

"O...kay," Chance said. Why did he get the sense that something bad hurtled toward them as they spoke?

Thud.

"Well," Apryl started, but Chance held up his hand.

He strained, listening.

Apryl arched an eyebrow. "What?"

"Did you hear that?"

She looked around the garage. "Is this a joke?"

"No, I thought I heard something."

Chance walked to the door that lead to his kitchen and paused. He listened for creaking boards, soft thuds, or shallows breaths, but he only heard the staticky sound of silence.

He shook his head. "Must have been the house settling."

"Or you're paranoid. Either is possible."

Chance smirked. "Says the woman who wants to convince me that my kisses don't make her dizzy."

She shook her head. "Not dizzy. Just weak in the knees."

Chance chuckled. "You may proceed with your vague, ridiculous argument now."

Apryl smiled but a sigh followed. "I'm not going to pretend that I don't have fun with you, or that I don't care about you. I'm just tired of the pretense. I do...like you."

"I'm going to ignore that you sounded pained when you said that and focus on the good." The paper with his name on it burned against his upper leg, telling him a whole lot more. This was a step in the right direction "The feeling is mutual, by the way."

"Hush now. I'm still talking." Apryl tilted her chin up in that saucy way of hers that Chance loved. "But this is new, and I would be equally as foolish to pretend that we don't have a fair amount of baggage between us."

"Baggage?"

"Enough to fill a cargo ship."

Ouch. True but it stung his pride a little. A guy didn't want to be looked at as a basket case. He knew he had some issues. He wasn't delusional. He just preferred to think that they fit nice and neat into a small knapsack.

He sighed, resisting the urge to bury his fingers in his hair and pull. "Continue."

She shrugged. "I think we should take this slowly."

"I wasn't about to propose marriage, Apryl."

She turned the shade of a cherry tomato. "That's not what I meant."

As he studied her red face, realization struck him and the thorns of his past stabbed his gut. "I'm not the guy I was before, if that's what you mean," Chance said, hoping that his wild past hadn't reared its ugly head in another attempt to ruin his life.

"No. I know that." Apryl said, shaking her head with as much force as she said the words.

Relief more divine than water in a dusty desert flooded him.

"But." Hesitation, angst, and decisiveness came off loud and clear in that one word.

And just like that, the mirage faded, leaving him dirty and thirty once again.

"But?"

"I'm worried because I've watched you, Chance. You've never really been in a relationship before. Not that I'm, like, Mrs. Relationship, or anything, but I, well, you..."

"My Bruce Wayne impersonation was a little too on par," Chance finished for her.

"And I'm worried about your dad..." Apryl paced back and forth between the truck and the work bench.

He sighed. "That's not going to be a problem. I told you that."

"You don't know that."

"If he causes a problem, tell me and I'll deal with it."

She glanced over her shoulder. "Have you told him about us?"

Chance ran both hands through his hair. "No." He hated that it made it seem like he was hiding something, but he hadn't actually spoken to his father since the big blowup three weeks ago. So...not entirely his fault?

"Good."

"What?" Chance guffawed, staring at her. That would have been the last response he expected.

"I just think that maybe you should wait to tell him until we know what we are." Apryl stopped pacing and watched his reaction.

Outside, he looked fine.

Inside, a thousand piranhas feasted on his limbs.

Each word from her pretty lips stung him more than the last. And there was a part of him that said he deserved it. He had screwed up and he didn't deserve to have this beautiful, amazing, kind, vulnerable, fiery woman in his life. Not after all he'd done.

You're just like your mother.

Turning away from Apryl, Chance squeezed his eyes shut. He grabbed the abandoned rag, balling it between his hands and squeezing it tighter and tighter.

You're just like your mother.

Oh, yeah? he taunted the sinister voice. *Would my mother do this?*

Taking a deep breath, he turned to face Apryl. "I understand. I do. But please understand this—I'm not who I was before. I'm not my mother. I'm not my father. And I do care about you." He knew he sounded desperate, but, well, he *was* desperate. Desperate for her to see him as the man he wanted to be, not the jerk—because, frankly, that's what he had been—who hadn't seen, hadn't cared.

Tears filled Apryl's eyes, and Chance ached to wipe them away. Physically ached. Was this what love felt like? It was about more than just wanting her to be happy. If he could, Chance would take all her pain and bear it for her, carrying it on his back until he could cast it in the ocean.—

"Chance..." Apryl blinked a few times, closed her eyes and took a deep breath, then reopened them and watched him with an uncertain expression. "I just think it's going to be a lot harder for you than you think it will be when you're stuck in the middle and forced to choose."

Chance shifted. Was she right? "Is there a knife to my throat or something? That usually makes the decision."

"I'm serious."

"I know. I'm sorry. I guess we'll just find a way to...coexist." Chance ran a hand through his hair. His father wasn't known for coexisting, preferring to live by his my-way-or-the-highway philosophy.

Apryl studied him before looking away. "What if there isn't?"

"I already chose you."

"How can you just say that? He's your father. If you can say that about him then what will you say about m...me?"

Answer—he loved her too.

Chance opened his mouth then smashed it shut. Nope. Not ready to say it yet.

"I'm scared," she whispered, no longer waiting for his reply.

"You think I'm not?" Soft but so truthful. So truthful that his pride felt a little wounded. But for the first time in his life, he was in love, and that was more than a little scary.

"I just...I've cared about you for so long. I don't want to get hurt. I've never been the right kind of girl...for you." Apryl's broken explanation halted but that didn't stop Chance from hearing the defeat in those words.

"What do you mean 'the right kind of girl'?"

"I'm a failure."

In three steps, Chance crossed the room and pulled her into his arms. She didn't resist. "Why would you ever think that?" How could she believe that for even a second?

"Look at me compared to my sister. Courtney is beautiful, smart, talented, and successful. She had good grades in school. She's the one all the boys liked. Everyone liked Courtney better." Bitterness laced her words.

Chance tilted her head back. "First of all, you are just as smart as Courtney." He held up a finger to silence Apryl's scoff. "You are. I happen to know that your grades were good too. Your grandmother has spent hours talking about how well you both did in school. It may have been harder for you, but you still succeeded, and there's something to be said for all the students who worked at what didn't come naturally for them."

A sniffle was her only response.

"Second, while all that paperwork and legal stuff comes easily to Courtney, you have a talent, a God-given gift for creating."

"I don't create." Her wistful and forlorn tone pierced his heart.

She'd resigned herself to a definition that couldn't begin to describe her.

"Look at what you've done with the weddings."

"That's called decorating, Chance," Apryl interrupted, rolling her eyes.

"Hush now. I'm still talking," he teased. "You have a deep, intimate sense of people, seeing their hopes and passions. You take that, and you make something beautiful for them. You take old, forgotten things and give them a new purpose, a way to be treasured forever. A lot of people wouldn't look at this business as something inspired, but I've seen you. You touch the heart of God by touching the hearts of people. That's incredible." He squeezed her shoulders.

Apryl tried to catch her tears with rapid blinking, but a few escaped, cascading down her face.

Chance caught them with his thumbs. When had his hands moved to frame her face? "Last but not least, you are beautiful. And for the record, I never, ever wanted to date your sister."

Apryl laughed through her tears. "I'm not sure I believe you."

"I could kiss you. You may believe me then." Chance wiggled his eyebrows.

She tapped her chin, pretending to think about it. "That would have to be one special kiss."

"All of them are." His voice dropped, along with his eyes, landing on her mouth.

"Always the charmer," Apryl murmured.

"I only want to be *your* charmer," Chance whispered before gently kissing the rest of her tears away.

"Nice to see you again, Apryl."

I freeze. The tone belies the words, but more importantly than that, this is not nice.

Not nice at all.

William McFarland stands just inside the doorway of Willow Grove Antiques.

I wonder if we should change the name. Willow Grove Weddings has a nice ring to it.

I mentally slap myself. Focus! Or scream for help. Probably the latter. Definitely the latter.

I open my mouth then clamp it shut. Courtney and Gram aren't here. My sister and Dallas took Gram to a doctor's appointment, and the three of them won't be home for hours.

This is the point in the horror movie where I die.

His salt-and-pepper head turns, studying the dysfunctional room with its pieces strewn everywhere, some piles so precariously balanced that one well-placed stomp will send the whole tower crumbling to the ground. "Seems like I've interrupted your...work." Polite but his words hold their usual judgmental sting.

I lick my lips. "Just organizing, cataloguing, a little dusting." *Not that it's any of your business.*

Way to go inner tough girl! What a help you are!

He nods. "That's nice."

Nothing about this is nice, you liar.

William looks as immaculate as he did when I saw him a couple weeks ago. Ageless with an easygoing demeanor but I've always secretly suspected that he hangs out in abandoned warehouses and interrogates people with less-than-approved methods in his free time.

Each second dredges by us like sand in a giant hourglass. And I'm frozen, trapped under William's disapproving gaze. Why does this man have that effect on me?

Chance's face flashes in my mind's eye, and his words from the night before play in my heart. Drawing courage from his belief and support, I stand a little straighter, ready to do battle.

"Do you really expect the business to continue like this?" William throws the words out, the first thrust of his double-edged sword.

Angry heat boils in the pit of my stomach. "Like what?"

He raises an unrelenting eyebrow at me. "Unprofitable. I was somewhat aware of your grandmother's financial status. It would take a lot to turn that around. Much more than you have to offer."

I flinch. "I have plenty to offer." *Do I?* The words sound unbelievable, even to me.

Courage. Courage. Courage.

"Don't be so sensitive. I only meant that there's not enough weddings—or whatever it is your *business* caters to—to really support this endeavor." His icy smirk doesn't help support his endearing claim.

Right. I'm sure that's what he meant. Just like I'm sure I'll suddenly sprout scales and a siren's call that I can then use to lure him into a giant box far, far away.

"It doesn't matter what you think. So, why are you here?" *Rude? Yeah.* Gram probably would threaten to wash my mouth out with soap despite the fact that she can barely walk. However, I'm long past the point of polite with this man.

Insert mental spitting here.

"Why do you think?" William raises an eyebrow in a way that is far too similar to Chance's.

I huff. "I don't know. To berate and belittle me."

"Is that what you think I want?" He turns from me, walking farther into the store.

"Seems to be what you're doing."

William gives a humorless chuckle. "What I want is what's best for my son. His future matters to me more than anything else."

"And I'm not good enough. I remember the speech. I can repeat the speech word for word. You, however, don't get to control who Chance loves." The room starts to spin as soon as the word slips from my lips, and I don't think it's the overpowering scent of Orange Glo.

William's casual perusal halts. "Loves?" The question clings to the icicles of his tone.

Way to go, you colossal fool! Chance hasn't even said the word, yet I give the supervillain the greatest weapon of all time. So awesome.

"I, uh..." A few words too late for my disappearing speech superpower to kick in again. Always a disappointment, my superpowers.

"Ah, my son." William shakes his head. "Always one for sweet talk. Never one to stick around."

Just like his mother. William doesn't say it, but his pointed look leaves little to be interpreted.

"That's not true," I spit with, yes, real spittle. The flying spittle was an accident, though I can't help the immense pleasure I get from the way William wipes his face in disgust.

Sorry, God.

"I know my son. He needs the right woman by his side in order to settle down."

"And it's not me. Like I said, I remember the speech. You don't like me."

"I want the best for my son."

"And it's not me." Each time we do this particular dance step, my technique becomes sloppier, and William's cruel statement drowns out Chance's sweet words in my heart a little more.

He studies me. "Are you agreeing with me?"

Am I?

"Don't take it personally, Apryl. Obviously, I can't stop Chance from making mistakes, but I don't have to pretend that I'm okay with it."

I shake my head, attempting to clear my way through the fog and tell him off, but his next words halt my trek.

"Like I also don't have to pretend that not selling the business and property to Chance isn't a mistake. It was the original plan, after all."

Dizziness overtakes me, from my comprehension, to my ability to stand, to the roiling within my stomach. I grasp the edge of an antique desk for support. "What are you talking about?"

"Charlotte had been considering selling the estate to us. Once the sale was complete Chance was going to move forward with our plans to expand the family business."

A veil is pulled away from my eyes, shining light on what I hadn't seen. Gram's admission in the hospital room before Courtney convinced her to give this hairbrained scheme a go. The way Chance resisted at first. The guilty look on his face that night I fell into his arms in the willow grove. The way William reacted when he found out.

I know that Chance said he believed in me. He's faithfully helped and supported me—us, Gram—in this venture. But a part of me feels betrayed. I can't help it. It's there.

"Let's be frank, Apryl. I know you care about my son." William studies me, and my heart pounds like it is under a microscope for observation. He nods. "Yes, you do. Shouldn't you want what's best for him?"

"I do," I whisper. God help me, I do. Seriously...help.

"Excellent. Let me share something with you that will help you understand." He pulls an upside-down chair off of a bureau and sits. He takes a long breath then says, "I loved Chance's mother. I loved her with every fiber of my being. Any foolish description that you can find in a love song paled in comparison to my love for her. She, however, wasn't fit for this life, the life of a wife and mother. And sadly, we didn't find that out until far too late. In the end, I had to let her go follow her dreams. I had no choice because forcing her to live a life that she hated would have crushed her spirit, which would have destroyed me in the long run. It tore me up, but I had to let her follow her heart."

I stare at him in morbid fascination. This is a rare crack in the facade I've always known as William McFarland. For a moment, I can see his heart bleeding over the woman he loved and lost.

Moment's over. William sits up straighter and pins me with his lethal glare. "Apryl, do you understand what I'm saying to you?"

"No." I shake my head, panicking as his implied meaning becomes clear. "No! No, I can't."

He holds my gaze with his unrelenting one. "If you love him then you'll do what's best for him. I think you're a nice girl, but you are not it. This business is not it. I've been where you are. If I had known, I would have saved myself a lot of heartache. I wouldn't have given up my dreams for a woman who would give up on me. And once your business venture fails, please reconsider selling the estate to Chance. It's for the best, especially for him. I know that matters to you. Just like I know you'll do the right thing."

With that, William stands up and walks out the door without

another word or cursory glance at the wreckage he's left in his wake.

As soon as the door slams shut, I'm released from the spell his presence placed on me, and I collapse on the floor, too weary to stand up under the weight of my doubts anymore.

And that's the end of round two.

Chapter Nineteen

"For a moment I thought you were avoiding me again," Chance said.

Apryl jumped and the moonlight highlighted the guilty look on her face. "No," she lied. A lie Chase recognized because he could see the truth in her darting eyes and skittish demeanor.

He narrowed his eyes. "What's going on?" It had been two weeks since the Roaring Twenties wedding. Everything had been amazing between them for the first week, but this most recent—and unexpected—week of radio silence had left him drained. If God was attempting to teach him patience then Chance thought God should wash His hands of him.

Lather. Rinse. Repeat.

"Nothing. I was just praying. That's all." She kicked at the moss growing on the trunk of the willow tree.

"Shouldn't you be sitting in a tree if you're praying?"

She gave him a weak smile in response, the light missing from her normally bright baby blues.

"Courtney left a message for me about the next wedding. Surprised me that it was in a week, but I didn't even need to reschedule any of my appointments this time, so that was good," Chance rambled, hoping she'd say something if he talked long enough.

Apryl nodded, continuing to kick at the now moss-less tree trunk.

"Is this about my dad?"

Her head snapped up. "Wh—What?"

"He told me that you guys talked." Chance folded his arms

across his chest and tucked his hands underneath his armpits. "He said it was a good conversation."

For one brief second things had looked hopeful. William had appeared at his door the night before with a rented DVD in hand. Okay, so his father hadn't apologized for anything, but he'd said that he had worked things out with Apryl. Claimed that it was a good conversation. William had been kind, and he and Chance had settled into their old rhythm. Maybe everything would work out.

"Yeah," she mumbled, but something about how she uttered that word sent bolts of worry through his heart.

And maybe not.

"Apryl?" He squinted, as if that could help him discover the truth in her eyes. If only.

She looked at him again. "Yeah?"

"Did he lie?"

"Does your father lie?"

Chance swallowed hard, avoiding the answer. "Is there more you'd like to add to the story? If there is, I'll deal with it. I promise." *Please God...*

She stared at him, blank, unseeing, unfocused. "No." And resolved.

Okay then...

Chance ran his hands through his wavy blond hair. It had grown out a little more than usual in the last few months. he hadn't cut it since all of this started. It rested on his shoulders when he left it down, so lately he'd tied it back. Chance occasionally utilized the infamous manbun when he was working, but most of the time he rocked the ponytail.

"Why didn't you tell me?"

He frowned. "Tell you what?" Chance took a leather strap from his pocket and tied his hair back.

"That you were going to buy my grandmother's estate."

The sound of rushing blood filled his ears. Chance started shaking his head so fast that he probably looked flat-out ridiculous. "No, my father broached the idea with her, but nothing had been decided. I didn't say anything to you because it wasn't my responsibility."

What had his father done?

"Your...responsibility." Apryl shook her head as if she couldn't believe those asinine words had processed in his brain, let alone tumbled from his lips.

"That came out wrong." Frantic, Chance grabbed her hands and clutched them in his. "It wasn't my place. The land belongs to Charlotte to do with as she pleases."

"Okay." These emotionless answers scared him more than if Apryl morphed back into the Angry Apryl of their childhood and started hurling all kinds of choice names at him.

"What did my father do?" So much for working things out. If William had divulged this information to guilt Apryl, then blast it all—

"What if it were for the best?"

Chance's eyes widened and the air disappeared from his lungs. "It's not."

She tilted her head to the side. "How could you know that?"

"What's best is this, right here. The way things are right now." Chance jerked their joined hands back and forth between them.

"Things change," Apryl said, shrugging.

"They don't have to change."

Apryl snorted. "Things always change. There's no getting around that. Once upon a time I watched VHS tapes. Now toddlers can explain the merits of streaming on demand."

"I don't want these things to change. Not when I have a choice," Chance said forcefully.

"What if you didn't have a choice?" She looked away from him.

Chance inhaled, the sharp intake of evening air dizzying him with its earthy scent. Although, last he knew, fresh air didn't intoxicate. People always used it to clear their heads. So the dizziness could only be a result of the sheer panic this woman's words had sparked inside of him.

What if he didn't have a choice? Then things would be far too familiar. Then he'd have to say goodbye to another woman that he loved.

And then his belief in love might never recover. Not this time.

Chance opened his mouth, prepared to dive into the lengthiest explanation (also known as begging) of his life. "Apryl—"

A mechanical jingle and buzzing in his pants' pocket cut him off.

Followed by a weird song about peanut butter and jelly that blasted from somewhere on Apryl's.

Apryl pulled her phone from the pocket of her hoodie while Chance did the same. His phone buzzed once in his hand, indicating that someone had sent a text message. Clicking the home button, he saw that the text and call were both from Courtney.

Apryl gasped as she listened to the voicemail, a message that probably said the same thing as the text message that showed from his phone, bathing them in harsh light as cruel as reality.

Gram fell. Get Apryl. Meet us at the Keene hospital.

Where was her paper bag when she needed it?

"Babe, calm down. Otherwise, I'll get the OB/GYN and make him teach you some Lamaze breathing technics."

"Not funny." But despite her words, Courtney smiled.

The smile fled from her lips just as quickly as it had come. It felt wrong to smile in a place that smelled of disinfectant and broken dreams.

Dallas wrapped an arm around her shoulders. "It'll be okay."

She shifted in her seat. "You don't know that." She'd never admitted it, had even extended the placating gesture herself a time or two, but it drove Courtney bonkers when people said that. They didn't know. No one could know.

"I don't know what's going to happen or what's going on, but I do know that ultimately God has the final say. Everything will be okay because He overcame everything a long time ago."

Courtney bit her lip. "What if she dies?"

"Then you will see her again because He's already overcome every form of death." Dallas squeezed her shoulder. "I know that's not a perfect answer, but we need to have faith that God is good. No matter what happens in this world."

Courtney choked back a sob. She knew he was right about all of it. But she wasn't ready to say goodbye for now to her surrogate mother. Not in the least. Not now. Not ever.

The memory of Gram's latest fall played in her mind, all the details fresh and in place.

Courtney jumped. Where did that thud come from?

Visions of her grandmother lying on the floor in extreme pain flashed before her eyes.

"Gram, where are you?" She strained, listening for her grandmother's answer.

Gram was getting more and more mobile, using her walker any chance she got, much to Courtney and Apryl's dismay. Thanks to some research from the resident Web MD junkie, Courtney learned that Gram shouldn't be pushing herself so hard. But whenever she or Apryl tried to tell her to take it slow, Gram just harrumphed and said that she would be using a cane in no more than two weeks.

The wild look in Gram's eyes didn't bode well either.

Creak. Squeak. Squeak. Squeak.

Not a mouse. If only she could be so lucky.

"I'm going to the water closet, dear," Gram called, voice stronger than ever. The door clicked a moment later.

Courtney just wished her hip was stronger...

"Gram, let me help you!" She rushed from the front part of the shop, through the office/temporary bedroom, to the connecting private bathroom.

"Courtney Elisabeth Burns, if you so much as touch that door knob, you will get a verbal lashing you won't soon forget," Gram growled from within. "I am a grown woman and then some. Its high time I started handling myself in the restroom again."

Courtney's hand froze, hovering over the door knob. One wrong flinch, and she'd touch it. "Gram, you shouldn't be doing this by yourself."

"It's bad enough that you still need to help me bathe," Gram muttered loud enough for Courtney to hear. "Now stop talking to me. That's just plain rude. And weird."

Courtney huffed.

"Go away!"

She quieted her breathing. *Leave? Not on her life.* But Courtney plugged her ears and counted to fifty Mississippi in her head to give Gram a measure of privacy.

Removing her hands, Courtney heard the toilet flushing. After twenty-six agonizing seconds, she heard the facet turn on.

"I did it," Gram called. Water continued to splash.

Courtney kept her lips pursed shut and held her breath.

"Stop holding your breath, Courtney." The facet turned off.

She grinned and let the stale air out of her burning lungs.

A minute later, the old oak door swung open. Gram looked exhausted. If Courtney hadn't known better, she'd have thought Gram had attempted Parkour again. She clutched the walker, her already pale hands looking whiter than Courtney had ever seen. Her arms shook and her hair looked far more mussed than her grandmother's particular standards allowed. A bead of sweat dripped down the right side of her face. Water stains covered her clothes and the tile floor at her feet.

"Are you okay?" Courtney reached out but Gram swatted her hands.

"I'm fine. I'm fine. I'm fine," she muttered through clenched teeth.

Courtney bit her lip, drawing her hands to her sides.

Gram slammed the walker down, the force of which caused the wheels to slip against the wet floor. The walker jerked forward, hitting Courtney and knocking her onto her backside. Gram wobbled, grasping for anything to keep her upright. All of her frantic movements, however, sealed her fate.

Courtney watched as Gram fell down, down, down. Time slowed, stretching the horrible moment into a torture that lasted for hours.—You'd think she had fallen into the same abyss as Gandalf the Grey. Courtney sat frozen underneath the walker, powerless to do anything to help her grandmother in time.

Thud.

"Ahhh!" Gram's face contorted in pain. Rapid breaths came out in short little puffs. Her eyes rolled back into her head, leaving a blank, horrific whiteness in their wake.

"Gram!"

"Babe," Dallas murmured, shaking her out of the memory of her living nightmare with a light touch.

"Sorry," she mumbled. Maybe if she rubbed her eyes hard enough, she could rid the memory from her mind.

"You don't need to be sorry. I'm here for you." He drew her farther into the crook of his arm and squeezed her shoulder again.

"Thanks." She smiled at him, a real one this time, and snuggled into his chest.

His voice rumbled through his chest into her ear. "What were you thinking about?"

Courtney ran her hands over her face and sat up to face him. "The fall. It's awful but I'm kind of glad I wasn't there the first time. I don't think I could handle two memories like that. This one won't stop playing in my mind. Like a scratched CD that repeats the same line over and over until you finally skip the song."

Dallas shrugged. "You could hit the eject button and toss the CD out the window."

"Not exactly the wisest thing to do when you're driving on a highway," Courtney said, shaking her head.

"Oh, were you driving with care in this delusion? Sorry. You can toss it onto the backseat then. Problem solved." He winked at her.

She raised an eyebrow. "Ah, but then I'd have to find a new CD, and my hands would leave the prime ten-and-two position."

Dallas shook his head. "I'm pretty sure this analogy fell apart about three exits back."

"It's not my fault you decided to pass my mental car with your odd logic."

Dallas smiled, sweet and with a cherry on top, and pressed her head against his chest again. She could hear his heart beating steadily. He kissed the crown of her head and started murmuring against her hair. Praying for her.

A calm settled over her. Slowly. Surely.

"Courtney!"

The glass dome of calm shattered around her.

Apryl ran toward her, frantic. Chance walked a pace or so

behind her, his long legs making up for most of the difference in speed between them.

"Where is she?" Apryl wheezed and folded at the waist to catch her breath. "What's going on?"

Courtney stood up and Dallas followed her lead. "She fell."

"I know she fell," Apryl snapped. "Do you have any more pointless information for me, or is there an update on how she is?"

"Apryl," Dallas said, stepping in front of Courtney like he was shielding her with his body. "Apryl, calm down. There haven't been any updates, and we are not sure what's going on because the nurses insisted that we move into the waiting room. The on-call doctor is tending to her now. Dr. Rothman. I know him. He's a good man and will take care of her."

"Why did they make you leave?" Apryl's eyes swung from Courtney to Dallas and back . "Is it bad?"

Dallas sighed. "They're...concerned. They were having trouble stabilizing her, which is why they made us leave."

Courtney resisted the urge to cover her ears to drown out another horribly vivid memory—the doctor counting to three, defibrillator in hand. Unfortunately, that memory had better acoustics than a Broadway theater. She let out a small sight of relief that at least the doctor had announced that they'd found her pulse right before the nurse pushed them through the door.

Tears sprung from Apryl's eyes, and her accusing glance landed on Courtney. "Where were you?"

Similar tears flooded Courtney's eyes, and she threw her arms around Apryl. But Apryl shrugged out of her grasp, covering her face with both hands.

"Where were you?" Apryl asked again as she sobbed into her hands.

Courtney didn't have a good answer. No answer would be good enough right now, at the height of Apryl's panic.

Chance cupped Apryl's shoulders and steered her away from them. Courtney watched as he drew Apryl to his chest, holding her as she sobbed her fear and anger into Chance's plaid shirt.

Courtney collapsed, remembering at the last second to look to see that no one had moved her chair. She'd developed the paranoid habit when they were kids. Long-ago giggling echoed in her ears, the resulting sound each time one of them high-fived the floor with their rear end. Courtney was vaguely aware of Dallas sitting beside her, interrupting her sweet musings.

If only they could go back to those good, simple days...

But they couldn't so they did the only thing they could.

They waited.

Hospital chairs are incapable of being anything other than hard, stiff, and awful. Anyone who says otherwise is probably jacked up on pain meds.

I huff. seriously should invest in better chairs for the waiting room. The people here are distraught enough. Adding a bruised tailbone and a stiff neck to the list of whatever trauma happens to be afflicting them seems cruel. Like from the pit of—

Well, you get my point.

I wiggle in the seat, trying to get comfortable for the fifty-seventh billionth time.

Courtney shoots me an impatient look from where she sits in the chair across the narrow aisle from me.

I glare at her. After glancing around to make sure no one happens to be watching us, I stick my tongue out at her.

Courtney gasps and crosses her arms over her wrinkled T-shirt.

It's been over eight hours since I got here around ten o'clock last night, twenty or so minutes after Gram's arrival. Almost two hours after I arrived, Dr. Rothman finally came out to tell us that Gram was stable now, but after running some tests and X-rays they were taking her to emergency surgery for a total hip replacement because the second fall had damaged the blood supply to the ball part of her hip joint.

Regardless of the fact that it was another two hours before she was taken to pre-op, giving the evil hospital chairs more time to grind my tailbone into dust, we weren't allowed to see her. The staff *claimed* that she was heavily sedated and needed to rest.

At least a nurse comes every two hours to update, as regular as Old Faithful. Small mercies and all that.

Or they remember me and my craziness is the stuff of legend at the nurse's station.

Unfortunately, Gram's been in the operating room for over three hours due to complications from a hematoma.

I lick my dry and cracked lips, trying not to think about Gram...bleeding...

Something I've had as much success with as a tap dancer trying to tiptoe on hardwood floors.

Tap. Tap. Tap.

Sunlight peaks through the closed blinds on the windows in the waiting room. I swear the early morning light highlights the tension in the room. That or the lack of sleep. Neither of the guys are here to act as a buffer, though they did spend part of the night slumped in the painful chairs of the waiting room with us. Both left around two o'clock in the morning. Dallas has an exam, and Courtney insisted that he didn't miss it. I asked Chance if he had appointments later today—the memory of my most recent conversation with William being the driving factor behind my relentless questioning—and urged him to go when he reluctantly confirmed that he did indeed have several appointments.

Old Faithful opens the door to the small, surgical waiting room. "Hello, dears. The doctors successfully closed the surgical site without further complications, and your grandmother has been moved to a recovery room. Dr. Rothman will be out to speak with you about the particulars posthaste." The kindly nurse offers each of us a reassuring smile before shutting the door.

Posthaste? Who says posthaste anymore?

I'm going to start. Watch out, world. Posthaste will be my new middle name.

I sigh. Crazy might be my new middle name.

Courtney rolls her eyes.

And something inside of me snaps.

"What is your problem?" I lean forward in my seat. It squeaks underneath my sudden movements.

"What is *your* problem?" Courtney snarls.

I snort. "Nice comeback. You'd fit right in on *Gilmore Girls.*"

"Nice deflection. You'd make a good linebacker." A hard glint flickers in her eyes.

"We are in this situation because of you!" I spit. "That's my problem."

Courtney swings both of her feet to the floor from where they rested on an empty chair. "How could you possibly say that?"

"You weren't watching her!"

"Have you met our grandmother? Obviously you two need to be reacquainted if you think for one second that Gram would put up with me watching her every move. She'd have eaten me alive," Courtney hisses and points at her chest.

I swallow. My saliva feels as hard as a rock. Have I met our grandmother? Have I met our grandmother! Delivering one of those smacks that the actresses always did in old-fashioned movies sounds quite appealing right now. Unfortunately, I need to settle for a verbal smackdown.

"I'm sorry, but weren't you the one who said that we do what we need to do for family in that delightful, heavy-handed, manipulative way of yours?" I'm yelling now but I don't care.

"We do need to do anything we can to help family!" Courtney bellows, skootching forward in her seat to match my posture.

"But I can't do this," I scream, standing up and throwing my hands into the air.

She huffs a cruel, humorless laugh. "What? Scream like a two-year-old? Seems like you're doing that just fine."

Pent-up emotion spills out of me faster than a river runs at the peak of thaw. "I can't do this! I can't handle worrying that each morning I see Gram is the last morning. That whatever drivel I managed to sputter on my way out the door will be my last words to her forever. That I will destroy her legacy and drive her business into the ground because I'm an incompetent fool."

"What are you talking about? You love this!" Courtney cries, jumping up in angst.

I jab my index finger at her, hangnail and all. "No, I love Gram, and you made me feel like I had to do this for her."

Courtney gasps and covers her mouth, crumpling into the chair behind her.

And I swoop in for the kill.

"I've had no choice, but I'm taking my choice back now," I say through clenched teeth. "And. I. Can't. Do. This. I'm done!" My ultimatum reverberates through the small space.

"Ladies," a man clad in a security uniform says as he steps through the doorway. "I understand that emotions run high in the hospital, but you both need to calm down. Right now. Otherwise, I'll be forced to ban you from the premises."

I stare at him, clutching my hands over my rapidly beating heart.

He gives both of us the evil eye, waiting.

Getting weird...

Oh, he's waiting for us to respond!

"Okay," I mumble.

"Yes, sir," Courtney says, contrite.

"Good." But he continues to eye us as he shuts the door in two-inch intervals.

Suddenly I feel like I'm about five years old again and can't be trusted with the telephone because I'll dial 9-1-1 at the slightest creak.

Courtney pretends not to watch me from where she sits in her chair. I collapse into my still-warm seat, weak in the knees now that rushing adrenaline isn't holding me upright any more. Clearly I'm not in good enough shape to keep having these emotional outbursts. I'll probably give myself a heart attack if I keep it up.

But what are the physical consequences of keeping everything pent up inside? Rising levels of fury that build until I finally burst into an emotional explosion that destroys everything around it? That doesn't sound good either.

"Truce?" Courtney mutters, not bothering to look me in the eye. Not that I blame her.

I don't answer. Pulling my legs and feet into the chair, I bury my face in my knees.

Go away, world.

Chapter Twenty

You know when you get déjà vu, and you're wracking your mental files of memories trying to figure out why this moment in the present echoes with memories of the past? Most of the time no one can figure it out, no matter how much their memory resembles large tusked mammals'.

Well, there's no need to wonder right now thanks to the familiar scent of chemicals that permeates everything.

I might burn these clothes.

Courtney and I sit in Gram's hospital room again. Monitors beep around us. Nurses scurry in and out. My intense stare doesn't leave her face, watching for each rise and fall of her chest. Really, the crushing weight of my certified, registered, and trademark creepy stare should wake her faster than a pillow over the face.

Sorry. Hospitals make me a little morbid. The point is that she continues to sleep.

Gram's been in and out of it for the last day. She's woken up a few times, but that pep that makes Gram the feisty woman I love continues to sleep within her. Her soul sleeps. And mine weeps. Just when I didn't think I could break anymore, another piece of my heart shatters as it collides with the cold, hard floor.

I feel eyes on me, but when I glance at my sister, she's focused on Gram. A tiny fork pokes what remains of my heart.

Courtney and I have capped all communication with each other at five words max. If I hadn't been so cruel, maybe my best friend and I could support each other during this tortuous waiting. Instead, each second that ticks by equals another emotional mile between us. For some ludicrous reason, I can't seem to form Those Words.

"If you girls are going to continue to stare at me while I'm trying to sleep then I may be forced to send you packing," Gram rasps. Two weary eyes flicker back and forth to where we sit on opposite sides of her gray hospital room.

Courtney gets to her first. "How are you feeling, Gram?" She grabs our grandmother's blueish hand in her healthy tan one.

I hang back. I don't deserve to be by her side. Not now but especially not after I speak my piece. Destroying all their dreams.

"I'm..." Gram takes a deep breath. "...fine."

Tick. Tick. Tick.

"This is all my fault," Courtney bursts out and bites her lower lip.

"Where would you get a ridiculous idea like that?" Gram sputters.

Courtney tenses but she doesn't tattle on me. "I'm the reason you fell."

"Did you trip me?" Gram's eyes burn with intensity.

Courtney doesn't say anything.

"Courtney Elisabeth Burns, did you trip me?" There's the no-nonsense tone that I love. Sort of.

"No," she mumbles.

"I see." Gram raises an eyebrow. "Did you insist that I push my physical limitations and go to the restroom myself?"

Courtney sticks her free hand on her waist. "Gram, I'm a little old for this."

"Answer the question," Gram says, gaining strength with each word.

"No."

"No. In fact, you tried to convince me to accept your help."

"You're not saying it's your fault, are you?" Courtney's voice and expression are so incredulous, it could almost be funny.

If it weren't really all *my* fault.

"If I use your logic then it's definitely my fault. Although, you pumped me full of tea, so maybe I can blame you." Gram quirks an eyebrow at Courtney.

Her eyes fill with tears.

Gram clasps her hand around Courtney's hand. "I'm sorry, dear. That was a poor joke. My point is simply that it was an accident. You had no control over my actions, so don't let anyone throw flaming arrows of accusation at you."

"She's right, Courtney." I look at the floor, but the magnetic strength of Gram's gaze forces me to lift my head. "I never should have said that."

Instead of disgust, Gram offers me a sympathetic smile and extends her hand toward me.

I grab it, desperate to feel her love for me despite my cruelty toward my sister.

She squeezes my hand and looks into the depth of my eyes, my soul. "And don't let the enemy whisper lies to you, my dear. He'll throw flaming arrows at your wounds and convince you to do the same to others. Remember that God's strength makes you strong. No matter what."

My throat burns. I nod rather than speak, lest I turn into the blubbering dolt that I am.

My heart cries out to God, begging Him to forgive me, but I feel...unforgiveable. *I'm so sorry, God.*

"Do you both understand?" She looks back and forth between us. Apparently satisfied with whatever she sees written on our faces, she squeezes both our hands again and lets go. "Good. Let's talk about something fun. Anybody kiss anybody lately?" She wiggles her wiry, white eyebrows.

Courtney's complexion matches Strawberry Shortcake's dress.

I clear my parched throat and look away.

Gram chuckles. "Interesting. Very interesting."

"Uh, I spoke to Aunt Alice," Courtney says. Smooth, sis. Smooth.

Gram shakes her head. "That was a rather obvious change of subject, dear, and I don't think it qualifies as fun."

"Well, I just thought you should know. I called her to let her know what happened, and I've been keeping her up to date."

"Thank you, dear, but I assure you, when it comes to my sister, she is more than capable of getting information herself." Gram shifts her head against the single pillow on her flat bed. "So girls, one of you tell me about the next wedding while the other one hits that call button above my bed. I can never find the right button on this remote thingy, and the pain in my side is what woke me up."

There it is—an opening so wide, I know God listened to my countless pleas. And answered.

So why does it feel like the Grim Reaper beckons me from the corner with his scythe?

I gulp and resist the urge to protect my throat.

Gram raises an eyebrow, and Courtney ignores me, fussing with Gram's comforter with her back towards me.

Here we go. "Gram, about the wedding decorating..." Mental slap on the back. Nothing like a false start to make a tense situation even better. Actually, make it a slap in the face.

Courtney whirls around to look at me, and I swear at this moment, she could be her own disturbing—though I'm not sure that's a strong enough word—version of Two Face from *Batman*. But instead of half of her face looking normal and the other half permanently marred from explosive chemicals, the right side of her face flashes with panic while the left side thrums with resignation. I drop my gaze to Gram's bed, the guilt Courtney's anguish stirs in me proving to be too much to handle.

This is the right decision. I know it is.

Gram tilts her head to the right. "What, Apryl?"

"I can't do this anymore. The weddings... It's...it's just not right," I whisper, studying the paisley design on Gram's blanket.

"What, sweetheart? Is the client not a good match?" I don't need to look to know that Gram has raised another eyebrow as she waits for me to meet her gaze and answer her question.

Courtney squeaks, interrupting us. "Excuse me, but I need to go to the restroom." I jerk my head up to see her rushing toward the door.

"Stay right there, Courtney." Gram's head swivels to look at her. Courtney stops in her tacks and stands stills, straight as a board, as she provides us an exclusive view of the back of her head.

Gram's penetrating gaze shifts back to me. "Go on, Apryl."

"I'm so sorry, Gram. I'm so sorry," I rasp as tears stream down my face. The barricade on my emotions will never be the same, possibly altogether irreparable. "I can't do it. I'm not good at this."

"Yes, you are!" Courtney bursts from where she stands by the door, spinning to face us. Her chestnut hair whacks her in the face thanks to her little spin. "You're amazing!"

I shake my head and try to focus on them, but my vision is too distorted from my tears. It's like I opened my eyes underwater. Nothing looks right.

"Courtney, I want to hear what Apryl has to say," Gram says softly. "Go on, Apryl."

"I can't do this, Gram. I'm not right for this. I screw everything up," I gasp through my tears. I hope that was understandable regardless of the sobs punctuating every other word.

Gram squeezes my hand. "I find that hard to believe."

"I'm not right for it, Gram. Please, please believe me! I can't do this anymore." Every doubt, every cruel comment, every disbelieving look thrown my direction plays on the big screen of my mind, threatening to pull me into its cruel grasp.

And I let it.

Collapsing onto the side of Gram's bed, I wail like I've never wailed before. I don't see or feel or hear anything but my own pain. I don't see Gram direct Courtney to make me sit. I don't feel the way Courtney wraps her arms around me, her tears mingling with my own. I just weep.

And weep.

And weep.

I have no idea how much time has passed, but eventually the suffocating wails subside. I blow my nose into the wad of tissues someone shoved into my hand.

Who needs a gym? Ugly, snot crying gives your upper body a workout. It's all that gasping for breath.

A hand caresses my face. Gram. I lean into it.

"Apryl," Gram says. "I'm sorry you feel this way, sweetheart. I don't believe it. You are fearfully and wonderfully made. You just don't know it yet. I know it, but I can't force you out of your comfort zone. I can't force you to become the woman in the beautiful future I see whenever I look at you. Only you can decide to walk God's path. No one else."

My breaths quicken. Those cursed tears might be ready for an encore performance.

Gram captures my chin in her wrinkly hand, her hold remaining gentle yet firm. "But know this—no matter what road you choose, He will still love you, child. And so will I."

"What will we do?" It might just be because of Gram, but I can tell Courtney's trying to understand. Bitterness, however, laces through her words.

"I'll sell the estate like I had been considering." Gram's voice leaves no room for argument. She's decided. That's it.

All because of me.

Oh, drat. Here come the waterworks again.

"I'm sorry. I'm so sorry for letting you down," I moan, tears cruising down my face again.

"No, dear. No," Gram coos, stroking my face until I calm down again.

"We'll need to tell Miles so that he stops production for the commercial and can pull the ad from the newspapers. Let's just hope we haven't already lost money," Courtney grumbles.

"Yes, we'll need to tend to those details immediately," Gram agrees, ignoring my twin's attitude.

Silence. Unbearable silence.

"What about you, Gram?" Courtney finally asks. "Where will you go?"

"Oh, there's a facility where I could live." The flippant way she says this suggests that I heard her wrong, that she just asked what show Patrick Dempsey was on until they killed his character off.

"Facility" sparks all kinds of negative thoughts. Visions of white hallways, white rooms, and men in white suits and with no sense of humor dance around in my mind like white flags of defeat.

"Gram, just move in with us!" Courtney exclaims.

Gram shakes her head. "No, I couldn't do that. One day you girls will each have homes of your own. I can't be that kind of burden to you."

"You're not a burden to me," Courtney says, stumbling toward the bed and reclaiming Gram's hand.

But her subliminal message comes across loud and clear. She should have just used a megaphone and proclaimed for all to hear that I thought my grandmother was a burden.

It's not true. It's so not what I meant. Not that Courtney will ever believe me. That old breakup cliché has never been truer. *It's not you. It's me.*

"Come on! I don't want you living in some weird facility," Courtney says, pulling her lawyer voice out of her pocket. Too bad she doesn't have an argument that will work against *THE* Charlotte Burns, Queen of Stubborndom.

"It's actually rather a community, with little apartments for those who can live on their own and spacious rooms for those who need more assistance. I've already seen the place, Courtney. It's lovely. I'll be well taken care of and have plenty of fellowship."

"But I don't like the idea," Courtney whines.

"Unfortunately for you, I'm the one who gets to decide. Anyway, I already have a room," Gram announces.

I gasp. "What? So you did expect me to fail!" Doesn't that kind of seem like she doubted me too? I recoil from her, and that familiar pain buoys to the surface again.

"No!" Gram grunts in frustration. "When I toured the facility, I put my name on the waiting list. At the time, I'd been planning to sell the estate to the McFarlands. Or just Chance. He's the owner of the business now." Courtney gasps but Gram ignores her and continues talking. "Nothing was final. I thought I'd wait until a room became available or temporarily move in with you girls. The waiting list looked longer than the Ammonoosuc River, so I never expected anything to open up so soon. After the accident, I forgot all about it. But I received a call shortly before this most recent fall."

Courtney's mouth hangs. "That call? Seriously? I...I thought that was a bonus call from Aunt Alice," Courtney stutters.

"That's what I wanted you to think. I needed time to think and pray about it. But it seems like God has opened up the doors, and it's time I step into this new world." Gram catches my eye, then Courtney's, with her weary gaze. "This is a private facility that's run by a Christian organization. I felt at home there, and I think that's because my Father is guiding me. This is for the best."

The door swings open. "How's my favorite patient?" a young woman asks as she comes into the room. "What can I get for you?"

Gram squeezes each of our hands once more, accompanying it with a loving smile. "I'm in quite a bit of pain," she tells the nurse.

Everything rolls around in my head as Gram talks with the nurse.

This is all my fault.

I've destroyed everything.

It's for the best.

Right?

Chapter Twenty-One

Voicemail. What a surprise.

Chance huffed as the familiar words played in his ear. "You've reached the voicemail of Apryl Burns. You can leave a message or try texting me, but I recommend showing up in person with a pan of brownies."

Chance loved being ignored. Okay, perhaps not. It had never actually happened before now, and he wasn't loving the sensation so far. Trial run over.

He clicked the END button and tossed the phone onto his kitchen counter. It slid across the granite countertop before it collided with his microwave. Walking toward the window, Chance peeked through the blinds. Apryl's car sat in the driveway. Multiple lights shone in the main house. His ragged breathing formed a circular spot of fog on the window.

Great. Now he felt like a creeper.

Chance let the blinds slip around his fingers and spun away from the window, stalking through the kitchen into the living room. At least in there he couldn't look out the window and see Apryl's blatant snub.

His hands burrowed into his hair, and he yanked on the ends a little. Maybe he should just pull it all out and go for the bald look. Seemed to work for that prince in England. Of course, he probably hadn't pulled his hair out because of a stubborn woman.

This constant avoidance whenever something went wrong had started to grate on Chance's nerves. He hadn't seen or spoken to her since he left the hospital. Pretty soon he'd have a whole new woman complex that he could lay at Apryl's feet alone.

His phone rang and Chance leapt for it. "Hello?" Wow, did he sound desperate or what? Chance didn't think his voice could sound any breathier.

"Chance?"

His father. And his hope drained away like old oil sludge dripping from an engine.

His father spoke again. "You there?"

"I'm here, Dad," Chance mumbled.

"I just got a call from Arnold."

Chance looked at the ceiling. "Who?"

"The lawyer."

"You mean my lawyer," Chance snapped.

"My lawyer. I'm the one who pays him."

Chance kept his mouth shut. So they were back to this. Whatever.

"Arnold got a call from Charlotte. Says that if we're interested then she wants to sell the estate to us. We did it, son."

The call went dead.

Thud.

He'd dropped the phone onto the floor. It lay in pieces around his feet. He'd probably need a new one, and no doubt his father would chew him out for the abrupt end to their conversation.

His announcement rang in his ears, growing louder and louder until that was all he could hear. *She wants to sell the estate to us. We did it, son.*

Chance bolted for the door and flung it open, not bothering to shut it behind him. He sprinted across the long yard that separated the two houses. "Apryl!" Chance yelled as he ran, not caring that there was no way she could hear him yet. "Apryl! Apryl!"

He was about to collide into the front door and start pounding when it opened.

Apryl stood there looking confused. "What—"

Chance had tried to slow his speed but it was too late.

Smack.

They tumbled into the storefront, barely missing the clawfoot dresser.

Apryl groaned from where she laid next to him. "Nice landing." She rubbed her right elbow.

"What do you think you're doing?" Chance demanded. His knee pulsed with pain, but he ignored it and shifted his body back to rest on his haunches.

She narrowed her eyes and sat up. "Uh, making sure nothing's broken since you ran into me like a maniac."

"Why did my father receive a call about the estate being sold?"

Apryl glared at him. "Because Gram decided to sell."

"Oh, really?"

"Yes, you dolt."

"Stop it. You convinced her to sell, didn't you?"

Her face contorted into a mask of guilt. Bingo. "Why would I do that?" Right, like that lame deflection could distract him.

"Why have you been avoiding me?" Chance countered.

"Because there's nothing to say!"

"Nothing to say? There's plenty to say. Entire TV stations would be able to compile breaking news reports due to all there is to say!"

"Well, aren't we vain," Apryl grumbled as she stood up, dusting herself off with her left arm. She kept her right arm cradled against her torso.

"Why would you do this?" Chance demanded again. "This business is your calling." The pain in his knee started to subside, and he rose as well.

Apryl scoffed. "Don't be idiotic. I don't have the capability to run a business like this."

Chance smacked the doorframe with his open palm. "Not true." The sting made him tighten his fist.

"It is true and it was time everyone stopped pretending otherwise," Apryl huffed.

"Now who's being idiotic?" His rage was turning this into a bickering match. Chance should have waited until he was calmer to confront Apryl. But like a fool, he'd sprinted over here and started yelling at her. Smooth. Real smooth.

"Oh, good burn," Apryl mocked. "Does *Saturday Night Live* know about you?"

"Stop pretending!"

"Fine! I convinced her to sell! Are you happy?"

"Deliriously," he growled.

"I don't want to do this anymore. I'm tired of pretending. This whole thing was a mistake. A big mistake. And it needed to end before everyone got hurt."

Similar words from Chance's past played in tandem, but try as he might, he couldn't snuff the painful fire either set of words brought to his soul.

He'd thought this was different. He'd thought Apryl was different.

Fool me twice...

Apryl continued, oblivious to his internal struggle. "I didn't want to tell you, so I guess I've been avoiding you."

"You've been avoiding me longer than the past couple of days," Chance mumbled. "You get doubts and you avoid me."

"You don't have doubts about a relationship between us?"

His vehement response caught in his throat.

Did he?

"That's what I thought." Apryl looked away from him but not before he caught the pain in her eyes. "I just...I just need time to think."

A lie. She might as well end things right now.

That blasted piece of paper burned in his pocket again. Reminding. Taunting. Lying some more. "Think what you want. You usually do," Chance spewed, his anger rising, rising, rising, and spilling.

"It's the truth." The steel edge to her tone still cut into him.

He laughed. Bitter. Angry. Done. "You want to know the truth?"

Apryl remained silent, but man, if glares could talk...

"Fine, I'll tell you the truth. You're afraid. You're afraid of everything. For some reason, you've bought into this lie that you're not good enough for anything or anyone. So instead of proving that lie wrong, you just run away."

"You're right." Apryl's calm tone stopped him in his verbal tracks, and Chance's mouth slammed shut.

What just happened?

"I am running away. I'm running away because I know that I will fail. I know that I'm not good enough. Period. So why bother trying? Why try and fail?" She shook her head. "It's time to get back to real life. The lives we were supposed to live. And it's not this."

Apryl walked out of the room, ending the conversation. Everything about her demeanor and declaration stated this was the end.

But how could that be?

Chapter Twenty-Two

This is the part in the fairytale where the hero fights for his one true love.

But that's not going to happen. This is so not a fairytale. And I am so not Chance's one true love.

Insert Taylor Swift song here. There's at least a dozen that would fit.

The early morning breeze carries the loving scent of home. I inhale the familiar fragrance of dirt, moss, and river. But like a Sour Patch Kid, the breeze also whips into me, slashing me with its familiar chorus of "He's not coming." The encore performance will probably contain the line, "You've cast your pearls before swine."

Sigh.

Why am I standing out here? I should just get into the truck I rented and drive to the wedding venue.

The last wedding I will decorate.

Chance's lack of appearance stings, but I don't blame him. Not really. I don't want to work with me either. If I could, I'd get out of this wedding. But when I asked Courtney about canceling and refunding the bride's deposit, she flipped out. And, unfortunately for me, Gram agreed, claiming we should honor the commitments we'd already made.

Courtney spoke to Miles about the...developments. We lost a little money for the commercial, but not much, and the newspaper ads are in the process of being pulled.

It's almost over. I can make it through one more wedding.

I glance at my phone screen.

He's not coming. The truth settles around me like an itchy blanket that burns my skin with each movement. If only I could let it drop onto the ground.

I have to leave now or I'll be late. It's a long drive to Jefferson, New Hampshire. I climb up and into the huge truck—think armored-vehicle huge—that Miles had helped me load. Thank goodness he had taken pity on me. The alternative would have been dastardly.

A familiar truck cruises down the dirt driveway, casting dust clouds in its wake.

Chance.

He stops next to my imposter of a truck. Thanks to the height of his monster-sized vehicle device, I can still see into his truck cab. Gulp. His face is a mix of anger and hurt.

Why couldn't he just stay home? It would have been so much easier to move on if he had been *that guy*. Everything about our last conversation screamed that the end was nigh. If he hadn't come, I could have considered that a breakup. Now we're going to be in some weird limbo tournament all day.

I'll fall, guys.

I stay in my truck. He stays in his truck. It's a standoff.

A marshmallow gun would be nice right about now....

Chance rolls his window down. Drat. I couldn't even be the one to break the silence. He came. He's here. And I'm still a flimsy twig in the face of his steadfastness.

"We going or what?"

I press the button on the door, lowering the window three or so inches. "I didn't think you were coming."

"I don't break *my* promises."

Nice emphasis, dude, but I think the venom in your tone conveyed your meaning quite clearly.

I just nod and roll up my window.

A day filled with fun for one and all.

If painfully awkward could be defined by a day, this would be the day scholars studied.

Clack. Chance drops another chair in place. I bite my tongue to keep from reminding him that these are antiques.

One more wedding. One more wedding. One more wedding.

A blessing and a curse.

Thud. Another chair clings to its four-legged life. His icy silence fills the lulls when he isn't slamming furniture. He walks through the barn doors without a word.

I'll just talk to you.

Welcome to our *Anne of Green Gables*-themed wedding! It's too bad this is the last one. I have a feeling this wedding will be especially beautiful.

Sorrow fills me.

Ahem.

The little farmhouse and barn look how I imagined Matthew and Marilla's homestead. The buildings are painted white with a green trim that resembles the first blades of grass that poke through the soil after the long winter. And if the smell of manure didn't alert you, then look past the buildings to see fences that keep cows and pigs from coming to visit. Said fences, however, don't stop the chickens from coming by to peck, peck, peck.

Like the stinking fowl pecking my foot right now.

I kick (the air, not the bird), sending it scurrying toward the double barn doors just as Chance walks through them. The chicken bumps into Chance's legs, stumbles backward a few steps, and resumes its scurrying.

In that chatty way of his, Chance grunts in response.

Again, not that I blame him.

George Campbell (not the soup) walks into the barn. The father of the bride and owner of the property looks around his revamped space. "Looks so strange like this," he murmurs.

"Dad, it looks beautiful," Anne (the bride) says, following her father into the barn. "It's exactly like I imagined it." Explains the *Anne of Green Gables* theme, doesn't it?

"You didn't want anything to match?" George asks, sweeping his hand around to indicate all the mismatched chairs, tables, and miscellaneous paraphernalia.

"Nope," Anne says with the perfect amount of sass. "I wanted it to look like Matthew and Marilla threw a wedding for Anne and Gilbert, and the neighbors pitched in with anything they could carry over."

I hide a grin. It's the country version of shabby chic.

George just shakes his head.

Anne grabs my hands in hers—no easy feat considering I'm holding a floral vase. I press it into the crook of my arm to keep it from crashing and shattering. "Everything is beautiful," she says. "I don't know how you do it."

Chance clears his throat, shooting daggers at me with his eyes.

Just...shut up.

I follow her gaze around the room. Mismatched plates, tea-cups, saucers, doilies, and tablecloths are set on the tables, and in the middle of each one a vase sits on three L. M. Montgomery books. (The bride supplied all of those. She collects different editions of the beloved author's stories.) The vases will be filled with daisies once the florist arrives. All the mismatched furniture creates such an endearing atmosphere too. Even the chairs for the ceremony, which will be held to the right of the barn surrounded by a dozen or so apple trees, are mismatched. It's a small wedding but not any less beautiful than the one at the Grand Egg Hotel.

The memory of Chance's lips on mine at the Roaring Twenties' wedding takes my breath away in a loud whoosh.

Everyone stares at me, and I swear Chance knows exactly what memory just ran through my mind. There's a hint of a sad smirk on those lips of his.

"Anne! We've got a problem!" Martha (the panicking mother of the bride) comes running into the barn. She grabs George's arm to keep from falling over, puffing as she catches her breath.

"What's wrong, Mom?" Concern covers Anne's face.

"Darla slipped and fell in her tub!" Martha pants, still gasping for air.

Anne frowns. "That's awful but what does that have to do with us?"

"Prudence has to travel all the way to Exeter to help her sister! She won't be able to do the hair for the wedding!"

Understanding dawns on Anne. "Oh, no!"

"I know!" Martha exclaims. "What are we going to do? Your bridesmaids will be here in half an hour."

"I can help." The offer slips out before I have any time to think it through.

Chance raise his eyebrows, shakes his head, shrugs, and nods. Uh? I guess that means it's okay?

"What can you do?" Martha eyes me, a familiar criticism in her expression.

Back off, lady. I actually know what I'm doing here. "I use to be...uh...am...sort of...a hair dresser." There's the spunk I crave.

Martha doesn't look convinced Her eyes scan me up and down.

Anne, however, jumps on the wagon. "That's wonderful!"

"What about in here?" Martha asks, waving her arms around like a giant flapping bird.

"It's basically finished," Chance says. "Apryl can tell me what's left to do, and I'm sure she'll be able to check in later."

Anne nods like a dashboard bobble head on a backroad riddled with potholes. I'm getting a headache just looking at her. "Sounds perfect to me! And of course we'll pay you extra for this."

I quickly go over the remaining details with Chance. Awkward since I'm trying to pretend—at least in front of these strangers who are depending on me to save the day—that all is fine. That The Talk that Changed Everything hasn't happened

Mental snort here. If they only knew...

Once I'm finished with Chance I follow the Campbell family into their modest farmhouse. George holds the front door open for us. My eyes adjust to the light, and I take in the framed pictures, handmade quilts, and pure love that welcomes you like a warm hug from a dear friend.

If my parents had lived, would our home have resembled this one? Something squeezes in my chest for the parents I lost, a pain so many people don't quite understand.

Chance does.

His voice. I'm sorry, God, but it's too late. I ordered my entrée, and I'm not the kind of person to send their food back because I changed my mind.

That's just rude.

And what if you received exactly what you didn't know you wanted, compliments of the chef? All you have to do is accept it.

I'm not going to tackle that one, God.

Martha and Anne bustle up the stairs, and that feeling of intrusion continues to gnaw on my leg. I'd get fired if I tried to shake this feeling off my leg like I did with that Terrier in sixth grade, right? Yeah.

Hmm... Apparently, I don't have a good rep with animals in general.

Martha uses her hip to push open the door to a surprisingly lavish bathroom. Like large enough for a clawfoot tub, a separate shower, *and* a chaise lounge. Martha marches over to the chaise lounge and sits before grabbing a few printed pages from the coffee table that stands in front of the seat.

She thrusts the pages at me. "Can you do this?" She leans back and crosses her arms across her chest as if expecting me to admit at any second that I'm a phony.

I study the picture and instructions for all of seven seconds before smiling sincerely with just a touch of condescension. "Not a problem. That's a simple braided bun. The braid will weave around the crown of her head like a laurel wreath before twisting into an elegant bun at the base of her head. It will look lovely."

Martha blinks. "Okay."

Anne smirks. "See? Everything is under control."

Martha purses her lips. "I suppose," she admits then stands up. "I best be tending to the rest of the food."

Anne gives her a quick hug. "Thank you, Mom."

Martha smiles. "Always, my heart," she says before trotting down the stairs.

Oh, there's that pinch again.

"Take a seat," I say, pointing to a dainty chair in front of the vanity. I start prepping Anne's hair, asking her vague questions about her husband-to-be, a skill I've perfected over the years. Yes, all human interaction is a skill. One that I don't normally excel at. Except here. In this element. My element.

My fingers move like they've got a mind of their own. And maybe they do. It doesn't seem so illogical once you take the disturbing factor out of the equation. I could do this braid in my sleep, and that's not an inflated exaggeration. I've braided my hair in my sleep. It's like a nervous habit for me or something.

Using a pick, I pull a few tendrils of Anne's stylishly layered hair out of the braid/bun to frame her face. Looking around, I spot some hairspray sitting on the vanity. "Cover your eyes," I instruct Anne as I pop the top from the canister.

The toxic cloud dissipates, leaving a stunning bride in its wake.

Anne touches her hair with the lightest movement then looks at me in the mirror. "Seriously, are you an angel or something?"

I grin. "Nope."

Just a girl who knows her one and only talent.

Chance surveyed the crowd at the reception, happy and celebrating the love between the bride and groom.

Would it be inappropriate if he shouted that this love was all a big lie?

Mental slap. Chance wouldn't allow himself to think like that. He shouldn't. He couldn't. He wouldn't.

He scanned the room once again. His fruitless search for Apryl was proving to be the *Where's Waldo?* of weddings.

Stranger. Stranger. Creeper. Crying toddler. Aha. There she was.

Apryl had avoided him most of the day. He'd only caught brief glimpses of her since she had left to help the bride. And yeah, he kind of wanted to avoid her too.

But God never let him give up that easily.

How could she look around all of this and not see how incredibly talented she was? Chance had spent the better part of the night praying, begging God to let him flake out on this one. The way he saw it, Apryl had made her decision. Just like his mom, she was leaving. Chance didn't want to keep pining for women who didn't want to stay for him.

Then he'd found his Bible opened to the book of Hosea. Funny how that always happened.

For the record, Chance wasn't insinuating that Apryl was... *that*! Far from it! But as he read the short book, conviction of the example of God's love settled over him. No matter how many times Gomer had fled, cheated, and hated him, Hosea continued to love her.

Didn't God do that for him?

Chance had swallowed an extra-large cup of shame with a turbo shot of guilt after reading through Hosea. No longer high and mighty in his anger, his heart lay like a deflated tire after a dirty, rusty nail had been pulled from it.

If he really wanted to reflect God in all areas of his life, shouldn't Chance love others like God loved him? Shouldn't he be steadfast in his love despite the pain and heartache and disappointment? Because yeah, Chance had come to love Apryl. Not a perfect love but a real one. One he prayed to God it would be allowed to grow.

The admission seemed underwhelming, but Chance needed to save the real romantic declarations for a certain stubborn woman standing by the gift table. Thus far he had failed to keep his attitude in check, so this would not be easy. But when it came to love, nothing was.

The sneak attack seemed like his best option. Moving into the shadows, Chance made his way to Apryl. He ducked through one set of barn doors then bobbed back into the barn through the second set of doors without her noticing. Now she stood with her back to him.

Stepping behind her, Chance waited for her to flinch or run, but Apryl remained still. "I'm not sure standing with your back to an open door is the best way to avoid someone," he said near her ear.

But instead of whirling around to face him and say something snarky, she stiffened and plunged her elbow into his gut.

Oomph!

Man, that hurt! Chance clutched his gut, and then realized her leg was about to make solid contact with a rather sensitive part of his anatomy. He dodged her spiky heel before it could do any damage that would leave him sounding squeakier than a preteen boy going through puberty before collapsing on the barn floor. Maybe this steadfast love thing wasn't a good idea. Had Gomer beat up Hosea?

"Apryl!" Chance rasped. "Please stop hitting me!"

Now she looked at him, covering her mouth with her hands. "I thought you were some creep!"

"Just a creep that you already know." Regardless of his aching abdomen, Chance forced himself to stand up. In a weird way, knowledge that she could land a mean elbow jab filled him with pride. He just wished he hadn't been the test subject. "I thought you knew it was me."

"How was I supposed to know that? Someone whispered in my ear, and I interpreted it as a random guy preparing to hoist me over his shoulder and murder me in the corn field."

"Do they grow corn too?"

Apryl rolled her eyes. "Not the point."

He gripped his midsection and groaned as pain pulsed through the area with vengeance. Apryl reached for him then stopped herself. She looked like she wanted to touch him, do something to help, but she lowered her flinching hands to her sides. "What's up?"

Oh, that's cool. Does the Fonz know about you?

Chance took a deep breath. He needed to chill or he'd screw this up. This might be his only chance to convince Apryl to stay.

Deep breath. "Can we go outside and talk?"

Apryl bit her lip and glanced around the room, undoubtedly calculating if she could make a run for it. She sighed. "Okay, that's fair."

One point for Chance.

Resting his hand on the small of her back and ignoring the obvious flinch, Chance guided Apryl outside to a nearby picnic table resting under a large acorn tree. The scent of manure filled his nostrils, not exactly creating just the romantic atmosphere he craved.

Apryl circled around the picnic table and sat on the far edge of the bench. The boards shifted and settled with her weight.

Well, two could play at that game. Chance climbed over the bench and sat in the middle. His left knee bumped into her right knee.

Two points for Chance.

She cleared her throat, keeping her gaze focused on her folded hands that rested on top of the picnic table. "Okay, let's do this."

Chance raised an eyebrow. "Do what?"

"Yell. Complain. Give me a guilt trip that could take me around the world in a hot air balloon." Apryl rubbed her face, avoiding his eyes.

"Is that what you think I want to do?"

Apryl shifted. "Isn't it?"

"No."

"Well, then what?"

"I want you—to be with you, to have you in my life." Whoa, better tone it down, buddy. Chance gulped. "I love you."

Nice move, dolt.

Apryl snorted. "You do not."

That could have gone better. Might have lost a point there.

Chance didn't say anything. He just reached into his pocket and pulled out the piece of paper that he grabbed from his nightstand each morning. He laid it in front of Apryl, letting the moonlight illuminate the truth.

She frowned at him in confusion before snatching the paper.

Then gasped.

"I love you, and you love me," Chance said softly.

She looked at him then. "This is from my locket! How did you get this?"

"At Izze's wedding. I found the locket while sweeping, dropped it, and everything spilled out. I wasn't trying to invade your space, but I saw my name." Chance shrugged. "When you dropped the locket again and told Izze about it, I thought you'd be upset. So I kept it hidden."

"Upset doesn't even begin to cover what I'm feeling right now." She dropped the paper onto the wooden table top. "Mortification. Rage. And this does *not* mean that I love you." A light wind invited the paper to play, dragging it along the rough wood toward adventure in the great and wide.

Chance slapped his palm onto the top of the table and caught the runaway paper. He held it up between his thumb and index finger. "I know the significance of this piece of paper, Apryl."

"Okay, so I've cared about you for a long time. That doesn't mean it's love."

"I don't believe that."

"Well...you're crazy."

He laughed. "Maybe. You keep pushing me away, but I keep trying to show you that I'm there for you. That I love you too."

She jumped up, nearly tripping as she untangled herself from the picnic table's grasp. "Stop saying that. You don't love me. You don't know the first thing about love."

Ouch. One point for Apryl's evil twin (not Courtney) and her well-placed barbs.

He gulped and stood up too but stayed on his side of the picnic table. "I know that God's love is steadfast. That it's there for you, believing in you even when you don't. I know that it doesn't give up. I know that love speaks the truth even when it hurts."

Apryl shook her head, but she didn't say anything.

"Don't give up on this. Don't give up on us. And don't give up on the business. Your calling."

Only crickets answered Chance's plea.

Nothing.

Silence.

Failure.

The silence stretched from one minute to two minutes. From two minutes to five minutes. From five minutes to, well, you get the gist. He might as well pack a bag and hit the road. Game over.

"Chance," Apryl said, startling him from his stupor. "When I was doing Anne's hair before the ceremony, I remembered how good I am at styling. I have a system. I have creativity. I create and see and express all with that." She gestured toward the barn where everyone danced the night away. "It's no different than what you say I do with the decorating."

Another point for Apryl.

"Then why not do both?"

"I can't do both." She swatted at something on her arm.

"Why?"

"I just...can't."

"Convincing," he said, rolling his eyes.

Apryl balled her fists and slammed them onto her hips. "Well,

I hate to break it to you, but I don't need to convince you. I don't need your blessing. And I don't need you to believe in me. I'm just fine on my own."

Chance ignored the gash from her verbal dagger, but the sting from it might cripple him if he made it out of this encounter alive. "You can say that all you want, but it doesn't mean it's true."

"I *am* fine by myself. I don't need you. And I really, really don't need—"

Chance threw his hands up. "My dad, right? Just tell me! I want to know. I want to help! I love you! *You.* So as far as I'm concerned, the rest of the world has disappeared because you're my world now."

Silence. Well, silence punctuated by Chance's heavy breathing. He'd put everything out there for her to see, and he felt more vulnerable than the time Marla had hung his Batman underwear on the clothesline when his buddies had come to the house.

He chose her.

Would Apryl finally choose him over the skeletal heartache stashed in her closet?

"You can't help me," Apryl finally said, voice colder than negative fifty. "Besides, Gram made her decision. There's no going back now." She crossed her arms across her chest and glared like she was being paid six figures for it.

"Except you're the one who convinced her to sell. You're scared. You told me that you thought you'd fail. You admitted you didn't want to bother trying for that reason, but I can't figure out why."

Her face hardened. "It's not your job to figure out why so you should just leave. I don't need your help here." She pointed toward the car, hard and furious. "I'm serious. Go."

"Fine, go through life empty and die alone. That sounds like the plan God has for you." He turned around and stalked away from her. So much for the Hosea theory.

"Chance." Her voice pleaded for him to stop.

Oh, how he wanted to go...and be done...

Chance stopped, exhaled, and turned to face her.

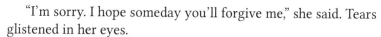

"I'm sorry. I hope someday you'll forgive me," she said. Tears glistened in her eyes.

How could he be filled with both tenderness and anger toward the same person? Longing and revulsion? Love and hate?

Chance forced the words, the truth, the goodbye from his hoarse throat. "I believe in you, even if you don't believe in yourself. I hope that someday you'll see that. That you'll stop being afraid to try. That you'll follow God's tug."

"I am following God," Apryl said in a quick beat, like it was a reaction, not a fact.

"You're playing it safe. But that's between you and God. He'll love you no matter what, right?"

She gulped. "Right. And...you?"

Chance swallowed. He had tried and tried and tried again. Now he needed to be done. "I hope that I can forgive you someday too."

She sniffled and turned her pale face away from him. "It's for the best. I'm not right for you." She took a deep breath. "Goodbye, Chance." She ran for the barn.

Chance shuffled back to his car. He'd loved and lost. Again. Was it worth it?

Nope. Another lie.

Chapter Twenty-Three

Do you know what it's like to have a stranger's hair lodged so far up your nose, it's probably embedded in your brain? No? Well, let me tell you about it: it ain't good.

Do *not* correct me about that word either.

All I've done today is snip, snip, snip. First thing this morning, this incredibly obnoxious person decided to shake their hair clippings off like they were a dog, hence the hair lodged into the part of brain that's responsible for eye twitching. One woman sneezed on me as I was cutting her bangs. A small boy kicked me in the shin. A man had hair so greasy, I almost lost my hand in it.

Now I need to boil said hand. Or find gloves. I need gloves, a mask, and a giant clothespin to go over my nose. Body odor is real and unrelenting.

Oh, you could tell that I'm having a rough day, could you? What gave it away? The tirade or perhaps it's how my left eye twitches every five, four, three, two, one...

My left eye spasms again.

Now my client, who sits in the shampoo chair, looks around the room for help. She must think that the psychotic woman (aka me) plans to drown her in the shampoo sink once she lays back.

I'm really more of a pincher.

"Apryl," my boss, Jayden, says, "why don't you get something to eat? Doree can finish Suzanne's shampoo." Her dark eyes convey the order-like nature of this suggestion from across the room where she stands by the register.

Doree nods, brushing her blond hair out of her eyes and hanging the broom on the hook on the back wall. "Yeah, go eat."

Fresh out of cosmetology school and eager to please, Doree will do almost anything as the resident goody-goody. Okay, in all fairness, she's actually really nice and just an easygoing person.

Suzanne has the audacity to nod her agreement. Grrr.

There goes my eye again. Sigh.

By the way, I really wasn't going to hurt the woman, but I think you guys should all know that *Suzanne* is the person who shook like a dog and stabbed my brain with her hair daggers. She had an appointment first thing this morning, left, and reappeared an hour ago claiming that she needed another inch trimmed off.

"Thanks," I mumble. After drying my hands on the nearby towel, I lumber to the back room. I plop into one of the four chairs that sits around the small table in the center of the room. The chitchat from the washer and dryer in the far-left corner accompanies my unpleasant thoughts.

I've been back at the salon for almost two months, but I just can't seem to...settle.

What's going on, God? Care to enlighten me?

Silence.

I'm used to that.

A little hint would be nice. I mean, I know I ran away. Regardless of what you may think, I'm not an idiot. But what choice did I have? How could I build a life with a guy whose father seeks to destroy us? Or save a failing business? Or constantly top what I had created with the previous wedding? I could have morphed into a diamond for all the pressure placed on me to succeed or fail.

It felt so right at Anne's wedding. The familiar comfort of hair. Something I knew I could do and do well. Confirmation. Why wouldn't I go back to that?

My stomach rumbles, interrupting my thoughts. Oh, yeah. I'm supposed to be getting food. Well, I do have one of those mini canisters of chips stashed in my purse.

I bury my face into my crossed arms, and the familiar bleach scent that clings to them turns my stomach. Food is overrated, anyway.

"Hey," a familiar voice says. Someone taps my shoulder. "Are you all right?"

I look up at Jayden. "I'm fine."

A deep frown replaces the usual cheerful expression on her bronze face. I don't think she believes me. "Is everything okay with your grandmother?"

"Yeah." I rest my chin on my folded arms.

"Mm hmm. She's all settled?"

"Yeah." Jayden glares at me, so I elaborate. "Courtney and I helped her move in last weekend and celebrated our birthdays with her, and I went by again last night. It seems to be like living in a community. All's good." I forced Gram out of her home, I pushed Chance out of my life because his father hates me, and Courtney and I are barely speaking but yeah, *all's good.*

"Some of the regulars live there. They say good things about it."

"Glad to hear it."

Jayden flicks my wrist. "Girl, what's your problem?" She yanks out the chair next to mine and proceeds to make herself comfortable on the vinyl seat.

"Ouch!" I cup my wrist with my right hand. "I've probably lost all function of this joint, so I'd say that's a problem."

She points a well-manicured finger at me. "Quit your whining and spill."

"I'd rather just whine." It's a good thing I've worked for Jayden for so long. She's more family than employer. The fact that she's old enough to be my mother doesn't hurt either.

Jayden shakes her head. "Honey, you're not yourself."

"I am...myself. It's not like I can just change personalities." This is who I am, who I'm meant to be.

She frowns. "You know," she says after a moment, "I love this business."

I offer a sincere smile. "I know." The volume of her love for this place could be cranked to the max, but it would still only sound like a whisper to the mere mortals around her.

"But I love this business because it's my heart and soul. It's my passion." She studies me for a moment. "Is it still your passion?"

"Jayden, how can you ask something like that after all this time? I've worked for you for almost seven years!"

"Honey, you're good at this, make no mistake about it. But

being good at something doesn't mean it's your passion or your calling. I'm good at eating cupcakes, but that doesn't mean it's my passion." She chuckles and points at her ample hips. "Maybe that was a bad example, but you catch my drift?"

"What are you saying? That you don't think I should work here anymore?" Great, I'm about to lose my job. Awesome sauce on a cracker.

Jayden sighs. "Please. You know that's not what I'm saying."

"Well, I think I need you to translate to dunce for me. Maybe include some stick figures so I can follow your thought process." The dryer buzzes, signaling the end of its cycle, but the washer protests his abandonment as it continues churning the load of bibs and towels that I started before I was ordered to take this delightful break.

She pats my arm. "Honey, you've always done well here, but do you want to keep working here? I've known you a long time, and I saw the pictures of the weddings you decorated. I honestly didn't expect you to come back. You have so many talents, and I know you would flourish in any of them if you'd let yourself."

I really wish people would stop bringing this up. "I'm good at this."

"We've established that. Answer my question."

"I...don't know. This is all I've ever known." The admission escapes from my heart for the first time. I just don't know.

Jayden clucks her tongue at me. "Or is it all you've ever allowed yourself to imagine? Are you playing it safe instead of letting God work new things through you? No one is just one thing. I'm a wife and a mother. A hairdresser and a business owner. An avid reader, ministry leader, and former singer. Doors open and doors close. Seasons change. We stumble into adventures we never dared to imagine could be ours only to realize that they were our heart's desire all along. Think about it, sweetie." She pats my hand and gets up, leaving me alone.

Great. Another question that I don't want to think about, let alone try to answer.

I knock on Gram's apartment door.

She lives in the main building, but her small space is like a one-room apartment. Manhattan-style in that it's tiny but at least there's no refrigerator-stove-toilet combo. I haven't decided if that's a good thing or not. On one hand, obviously good. On the other hand, I kind of want to see how that would work...

I take it back. A combination like that can only lead to disaster. And burns. Awkward, painful burns.

Gram opens the door, keeping one hand firmly clasped on the walker she's using again. "Hello, love! I didn't realize you were coming by too."

"Too?"

"Too." Courtney glares at me from the couch.

Excuse me, I'm going to internally rage for a few seconds...

...

...and I'm back.

Time to employ evasive maneuvers. "I just wanted to check on you and give you a hug." Leaning in, I hug her, quick and to the point. "I'm going to head home now." The word feels foreign on my tongue. When did our beautiful little house stop feeling like home? So much has happened... Gram's falls and surgeries. Living in our childhood home for all those months. Izze getting married and moving out. The wedding decorating. The dissolution and pending sale. The iceberg sleeping in my sister's bed.

Chance.

Everything changed. I changed.

Oh, dear. Was Jayden on to something? And how can I change back to the person I was before all of this happened? There's got to be a way that doesn't involve Marty McFly. Clearly that's the reason I'm having a hard time readjusting to my old life, and I *have* to get back to my old life.

"Get in here. The three of us need to talk," Gram orders, using her walker to help her step backwards.

I sigh. This is the part of the story where something is going to change. Whether that's good or bad...well, that remains to be seen. There are, however, no unicorns present, so that's not a good sign.

Gram points at the couch where Courtney squirms. "Sit."

I'd rather do the worm over a bed of hot coals, but I know there's no use in arguing about it. Gram will drag me in here if she has to, and I'd rather she didn't break her hip for the third time this year. I walk in and sit on the edge of the sofa as far away from Courtney as possible. She scoots closer to her arm of the couch. Sisters are nothing if not passive-aggressive.

"Oh, good grief. Do I need to force you girls to kiss and make up?" Gram grunts as she walks to where we sit. She's being extra cautious with a side of pain.

"She's got cooties," I mumble.

"And I'm allergic to shots," Courtney grumbles.

"Enough." Gram gives us a stern look. "I've been here before, and I've seen how it ends. Trust me, you don't want that." Gram finally sits down on the worn loveseat across from us.

"What?" Courtney and I ask in unison.

We glance at each other.

Courtney's brow furrows. "You've seen how what ends, Gram?"

"Do you mean Aunt Alice?" I gulp. That won't be us.

Will it?

"Yes, I do," Gram says, weariness coloring her demeanor.

"What happened?" I ask. "I mean, can you tell us?" Can you tell my curiosity is getting the better of me? But I've never heard what happened between them, so color me nosy.

Gram sighs and leans her back against a little pillow with a Bible verse cross-stitched onto the white canvas-style material. "Girls, it was a long time ago. While it doesn't make what happened meaningless, there comes a point where you have to let go and let God...or be consumed. I confess that I haven't always had the greatest attitude when it comes to my sister, but I've never tried to turn anyone against her either."

I nod as I think. It's true. Memories of Gram talking about their childhood and encouraging us to send Christmas cards or photos to Aunt Alice pop into my mind. I even remember our mom talking on the phone with her. Whatever happened, Gram tried.

I can't help but wonder, though, if Aunt Alice did the same. So much was never...reciprocated. Or even acknowledged.

Gram continues talking, oblivious to my musings. "You're going to disagree. You're going to fight. Some of them will be humdingers. And maybe the pain of those instances will last far after an apology is uttered. Some wounds won't heal until we're all with God. But they *will* heal. That's a promise from Him to you."

She pauses, letting that sink into our hearts.

"But I don't want to see the pain of a hard heart and unforgiveness impact you like it has your Aunt Alice and me." Gram snaps her fingers. "Now, I want you girls to go into the bedroom and really talk, maybe even start to heal. I'll be praying for you out here."

I stand up, but my legs feel like they're encased in cement blocks. Is it too late for Courtney and me?

Is it too late for any of us?

Following my sister into the bedroom, my heart pounds with anxiety. On the bright side, I must be a lot stronger than I realized to walk with cement blocks for legs. Olympics, here I come.

We sit on the bed next to each other. Neither of us squirms or fidgets as the weight of our hurting relationship—and its potential consequences—settles on us. A relationship that's been moaning with pain far longer than we've dared to acknowledge.

Silent minutes tick by...

Until...

"I feel like I'm not good enough compared to you," I whisper, laying my deepest insecurity bare for Courtney to poke. "After Mom and Dad died, you threw yourself into being the best, and compared to you, I failed in every way."

She nods, accepting my truth—my pain—for what it is. "Sometimes I feel like you think I'm stiff. That because I excel at all my intellectual stuff, I'm not your emotional or creative equal."

I open my mouth to argue with her then smash it shut. It's her hurt. Her pain. And unfortunately, not entirely untrue. My head hangs low, wobbling to and fro.

"I carry pain and insecurities around too," Courtney says. "It may not have been the best reaction to their deaths, but I've always had this need to be seen."

"While I've always tried to hide," I say.

She sniffles. "I never wanted to disappointment them or Gram, you know?"

I nod because I do know. It's like we've been feeding off of each other. Responding and reacting based on our hurts without really taking the time to understand the other person or acknowledge our part in the pain.

Touching my face, I realize that I'm crying. I guess that explains the head wobbling.

No, wait. It's more than that.

Creak. Creak. Squeak. Creak.

The bed shakes beneath me.

Bits of information about earthquakes, doorframes, and bath tubs play tug of war in my mind, but before I can call my feet to action, I realize that Courtney sobs next to me.

The leaking dam of emotions breaks then, drenching each of us in salt water as our tears cleanse the rift between us.

When it comes down to it, Courtney and I are exactly the same. Two women who love God but who view the world from the brokenness of two orphaned girls, girls just trying to be seen and loved for who they really are.

Throwing my arms around her, we continue to cry together. "I'm sorry," I croak.

"No, I'm sorry," she hiccups.

I don't expect that Courtney and I will ever become those sisters who hold hands and skip into the sunset with their matching outfits and perfectly contrasting lollypops. Honestly, the mental picture that image paints terrifies me. (Like, where did all my clothes go?) But for the first time, we understand each other.

I don't know what will happen after today. It may be too late for me to fix the other dilemmas circling me like vultures, but we can still fight for this, for us.

And I will fight for my sister.

Chapter Twenty-Four

"Congratulations, Chance. I'm sure your father is very proud of you."

Chance could only grunt and snatch the keys from the outstretched hand of the lawyer before he fled—manly, right?—from the bank office where the closing took place.

Twenty-five acres that now belonged to him.

"We're building an empire."

"If you wanted to build an empire, Dad, you shouldn't have sold the business to me," Chance grumbled. He wouldn't step into that house ever again. Not even a scene straight from *A Christmas Carol* would do it.

Done. Finished. Over. For all he cared, the place could burn.

Chance burst from the air-conditioned building into the late summer heat that had extended its unrelenting grasp into September. A car blasting rap music drove down Main Street. Across the street, a family walked, each of them holding an ice cream cone. He walked to his car, which was parked in the back of the empty parking lot.

Except not really. While he didn't want anything to do with the place anymore, Chance couldn't bare the idea of lighting a match and watching his memories of Apryl turn to ash.

It was funny, really. Chance had spent so much time welcoming affections he never intended to return, but he never imagined he'd turn into the kind of guy to buy an estate from his ex-whatever simply to keep someone else from destroying it.

Behold the power of love.

Or the idiocy. That's what his father would undoubtedly say.

Chance climbed into the truck cab. A rotten scent from the dirty fast food wrappers he'd left in there pummeled him. He should probably clean out this thing before a mouse took up residence.

Chance snickered. He could just imagine Apryl's face if she found out a mouse lived in his truck. She hated rodents with a vengeance, a fact he'd known since high school. And a fact that he might have used to his advantage a couple times back then.

Just as quickly, the smile faded and the pain returned.

Abandonment. Again.

He needed to focus on something else.

Yeah, like that had been working out for him. Thoughts of Apryl plagued him, sticking to him like the motor oil staining his hands.

Chance drove home, ignoring the private road—his private road—that would take him by the grand Victorian house. He pulled into the driveway and spotted the restored 1957 Ford Thunderbird he knew would be there.

Chance parked and got out of the truck with the odor of stale French fries clinging to him. He so did not want to deal with him right now.

"Chance." His father leaned against the hood of his precious Thunderbird.

"Dad."

"Well?"

"Well what?" Go. Away.

William grunted. "The keys, Chance. Did you get them?"

Chance rolled his eyes and held up the keys, letting them dangle from his index finger.

A delighted gleam lit William's eyes, but the way he rubbed his hands together creeped Chance out more than any campfire tale ever had. What on earth? How could Chance have been so blind to this for so long?

He already knew the answer—because he didn't want to lose someone else that he loved. But this warped version of love was never what God intended, so did he ever really have his father?

"Wonderful," William rasped. "Shall we?"

Chance closed his hand around the keys, locking them into his palm. "No."

"What? Let's go check out the space and start making plans." William took a couple steps, clearly hoping that would persuade Chance.

Think again.

"No," Chance declared. "I'm done."

"What are you talking about?"

He pocketed the keys. "I won't be doing anything with the house or the rest of the land."

William shook his head once then twice. Did he think that would delete Chance's plan from his memory? "You've got to be kidding me! That's not the plan. Why buy the property if you aren't going to do anything with it? I can't believe that you would do such a stupid thing."

"I've got plenty of business here, Dad. I like being a small-town mechanic. That's always been what I've wanted but you had no interest in listening to me. I won't be remolding the buildings, expanding the business, or selling antique cars." Chance took a deep breath. "Not when it's my choice. And it *is* my choice."

"I can't believe I'm hearing this. Why would you change your mind after all this time?" His father ran a hand through his hair.

Like father, like son, apparently.

Chance walked toward the front door, refusing to answer him.

"It's because of her, isn't it?"

Chance's foot caught on a groove in the sidewalk. He straightened himself then turned around to look at his father. "She has a name." What was wrong with him? How could he be so caustic and unfeeling?

The comparison between father and son would not include that. Not if Chance could help it.

"What? Did she ask you to keep it for her?" William spat the question, disdain and anger dripping from his accusation. "To keep it safe until she could come back?"

"*Apryl*," Chance stressed her name. "Her name is Apryl. And she's not speaking to me. Hasn't spoken to me in two months."

"Well, at least someone can follow a plan," William spewed.

His father could have slapped Chance and stunned him less. "What?"

William didn't answer, just continued to glare at Chance.

Fine. Chance would make him answer.

Storming over to him, Chance got right in his father's face. "What did you do?" He clenched his fists at his sides. Only the fact that this man was his father kept Chance from grabbing his flannel shirt and slamming him against his precious car.

"I saw a problem, and I dealt with it." So cool. So calculated.

"She was *not* a problem!" A red haze tinted everything and blood pound, pound, pounded in Chance's ears.

He'd like to do some pounding with his fists too.

Chance took a step back, lest he be tempted to follow through with the pounding notion took over. "What did you do?"

"I told her to convince Charlotte to sell. I told her to stay out of your life," he said through clenched teeth. William swept his hand towards the grand home. "We had a plan, and she didn't fit into it."

"I never wanted anything to do with your plan!" What was happening? How could this have happened? "You are nothing like the man I thought you were, the man I was proud to call my father," Chance spat.

William flinched like he'd been slapped, but then his face hardened again. "You can think what you want about me, but I was only trying to do what's best for you."

"Driving away the woman I love was the best thing? Are you kidding me?"

"Oh, please. You don't love her. You have no idea what love is, what it requires. And neither does she. That girl isn't right for you. It wouldn't have lasted, and you would have been heartbroken and alone, thinking that it was your fault."

"I'm already heartbroken and alone!" Harsh and angry pulses of sarcasm released on the beats of Chance's false laughter. "But it turns out it's your fault." Words couldn't describe how messed up this was. The rolling in his stomach might be able to give it a try, though.

Why hadn't Apryl told him about this?

Would he have believed her?

Sure, he'd come to see that she was right about his father, but was she right about him? He'd wanted so badly to settle into that easy comradery that had defined his relationship with his father. So much that he'd kind of ignored the signs when put to the test. No, not kind of. Had. He had. Chance had wanted to see things work out so much that he ignored what his gut told him.

Around and around his stomach rolled.

William stood taller, positioning himself so that *he* was in *Chance's* face. "I wanted to spare you, to save you from experiencing what happened with your mother all over again. I always knew that Apryl cared for you. When you guys were in high school, I thought you cared about her too. And I could just see it, history repeating itself in you and Apryl. Fortunately for all of us, she listened to me then, and she listened to me now."

Chance stumbled backward. His stomach wretched harder this time, and Chance lurched for a nearby bush.

His father had driven Apryl away.

Again?

His throat stinging from the bile, Chance wiped his mouth on his sleeve. "How could you do that?" .

"I only did what I needed to do in order to keep you safe and help you achieve our plans."

Safe? His actions had destroyed Chance's life as he forced his dream onto him. Some father he'd turned out to be.

Chance stood up straight, bringing himself to his full height of six foot one. He needed every bit of leverage he could gain here. "I'm only going to say this once. The house stays the way it is. Period. I loved Apryl, and you destroyed that. And I'm sorry that Mom left and broke your heart, but that's not a good enough reason to destroy mine. So help me God, I will not take part in whatever twisted plans you have for me. And if that ticks you off, well, that's just an added bonus."

Only the increased rate of William's heavy breathing signaled that he heard Chance's speech.

But Chance didn't need him to say anything anymore. He stormed to the house, William's words slowing him down but no longer stopping him or determining his actions.

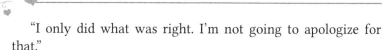
"I only did what was right. I'm not going to apologize for that."

"Continue to think that," Chance growled over his shoulder. "I know differently. Goodbye, Dad."

The slamming door echoed its agreement.

"Yoo-hoo? Anybody here?"

Chance straightened, smashing his head against the hood of his truck. He groaned. Rooky mistake.

The voice called again. "Hello?"

Chance growled under his breath. Did this person have to pound on the door to his private garage? "I'm coming," he called to the intruder.

Opening the door to his garage, he discovered an older woman, mid-sixties if he had to guess, standing there. "Sorry about that. This is actually my private garage. Can I help you with something?"

"My car took to sputtering about two miles outside of town. The guy at the gas station said you're the best and gave me directions here." She shot Chance a big smile and wiggled her bushy eyebrows.

He repressed a sigh. Today was his day off, but he couldn't send her away. "Sure. I'll open the first garage door on the right for you and meet you in there."

"Thanks, hon." The woman winked at him. Her eyes made her look old enough to be his grandmother, but age didn't affect the rest of her. Her light brown hair only had a smattering of silver streaking through it. Deep laugh lines framed her mouth and eyes, but otherwise no saggy jowls or flopping skin.

"Sure thing." Chance shut the door behind him while the mystery woman bounced to her truck. Her youthful appearance made him think of his dad, who had also aged well.

He glowered. Chance didn't want to think about *that man*, just the latest addition to the list of people who had betrayed him.

He pressed the button to open the motorized garage door, a

change he had made as soon as his father had signed the dotted line, relegating the business to him.

Grrr. There he went again, thinking about his dad.

The woman drove her car, a little blue Subaru, into the garage and climbed out. "Well, that's a sour look if I ever saw one. I'm Lou, by the way."

"Nice to meet you, Lou. I'm Chance." He nodded, ignoring her first comment.

She handed him the keys. "Care to share?"

"What?"

"Care to share why you look angrier than a goat?"

He smirked, hoping she didn't see the way his breath hitched at her all-too-accurate guess. "Do goats get angry?"

"Honey, you've got no idea." Lou shook her head. "Goats are mean. But enough about them. Tell me about yourself."

"Oh, I'm really all right." A lie but why would he spill his guts to a stranger? Thanks, but no thanks.

Lou raised an eyebrow. "Mm hmm. I know I'm a stranger, but sometimes talking to an objective third party who has a love for God is the perfect remedy for an ailment of the heart."

Chance cleared his throat. "So about the car. You said it was sputtering?"

Lou waved her hand without a care. "Something like that."

Chance climbed into the car and turned the key in the ignition. No noise. Leaving it in park, he tried pressing the gas pedal gradually. No noise. Chance shut the car off and looked to the left of the steering wheel, searching the dashboard and floor for the button to pop the hood.

Ah, there. *Thump.*

Climbing out of the compact car, Chance started his perusal of the engine.

So far, he'd spotted nothing. Odd...but not impossible.

"This is an impressive place," Lou said from over her shoulder. "Must keep you and your family busy."

"Don't have any family," Chance mumbled.

"Really? No family? Hmm... I thought the sign said this was a father-and son-business."

Ah, the blasted sign. Another item Chance needed to burn.

"My mother walked out on me when I was a kid," Chance said as he tried to get his eye on the spark plug. "My father isn't a part of my life anymore." Betrayal had consequences and all that.

"I'm sorry to hear that," Lou said.

Chance glanced at her and saw the sincerity in her expression. "Thanks."

"No wife?"

"What?" Okay, uncomfortable again.

"Are you married?" Lou lifted an eyebrow suggestively.

Ah, one of *those* ladies. "Um, ma'am..."

Lou chortled. "Not a suggestion. Just old-fashioned nosiness."

His face burned. "Right. Sorry, ma'am."

She shook her head. "I told you to call me Lou."

"Right. Sorry, Lou." Chance glanced back at the engine. The sooner he found the problem, the sooner this odd, albeit nice, woman would leave him alone.

Lou grinned. "Well?"

"What? Oh, right. No, I'm not married. No girlfriend anymore either."

"Anymore?"

Not good! Chance had said too much. "Yeah, single again." He'd add an extra edge of annoyance to his tone. Not that it was hard. A relationship status that used to make him happy now left a sour taste in his mouth.

Chance stared at the engine, but the parts had lost all their shapes. He really needed to get a grip. So he was alone again. Big deal. Chance didn't need anyone. Not a mother. Not a father. Not Apryl.

"Listen, son," Lou said, grabbing his attention. "I know you didn't ask, but I'm one of those people who's just going to give it to you." Chance would click his heels for joy at that, but Lou continued to speak. "Whenever I've ministered to people with this particular ache in their heart, I always direct them to the book of Hosea."

Chance snorted. Been there. Done that. "I don't think that's going to help. I'm no Hosea."

"Nope, you're Gomer."

Chance's jaw dropped. "Excuse me?"

"You're Gomer." She pointed to the stools in front of his workbench. "Mind if we sit?"

"Okay." Stunned, Chance followed Lou to the stools, waiting as she positioned herself just so on the rickety thing.

"Have you ever wondered why Gomer needed someone to be there for her no matter what?" Lou raised an eyebrow at him in question.

Chance shrugged. "I just assumed it was part of God's illustration." Brilliant insight, right?

"God used the situation to show His love and speak to His people, but Hosea and Gomer were also real people with real hurts. God knew that Gomer needed to be loved unconditionally, that she needed a person to stay with her no matter what."

His breath caught. "I get that."

She nodded and pointed an index finger at his chest. "And you're Gomer."

Flattering, but Chance had been called worse. "So, what? You're saying someone will eventually stay with me? No more betrayal? No more abandonment?"

Lou shook her head. "No, I'm saying that Someone *has* stuck by you through every moment. Someone who will never abandon you. Someone who has seen all the bad you've done or will ever do, but He's here to stay."

Chance gulped as her meaning became clear.

Lou continued speaking. "You see, we are all Hosea *and* Gomer. We're called to love relentlessly like God does. But we also need to *be loved* relentlessly. So many have felt the pain from broken love." Lou clutched her hand against her chest. "People fail. God doesn't. People leave. God doesn't. People reject you, but God doesn't."

Chance lowered his face until it rested in his open palms, grappling with the truth Lou had proclaimed with ease. A truth that completed the half picture Chance had been living with all these years.

Love had been with him all along.

Chapter Twenty-Five

Marriage changed everything. Making things weird, good, awkward, sad, and wonderful.

Courtney glanced at Izze and Miles, who sat cuddled on the large sofa. They had come over for dinner, but frankly, the evening had been a little uncomfortable. The PDA of newlyweds tended to do that. And she kept thinking about one thing over and over—she had lived with Izze, Kaylee, and Apryl in this house for so long.

No duh. Way to state the obvious, right? But the obvious had a way of being unapologetically stated when everything had drastically changed.

Courtney thought about the last few months, the good and the bad, before her mind settled on Dallas. Warmth bubbled inside of her. What other changes awaited their little group? What changes awaited her and the man who had taken hold of her heart? Because, to be frank, she was ready. More than ready. Brought-a-bridal-magazine-and-hid-it-in-her-purse ready.

Kaylee nudged Courtney's foot with hers. "I know stuff didn't work out the way you wanted, but I'm glad you guys are back. Even if it's not for long."

Courtney frowned. "You make it sound like we're going to move out again tomorrow."

Kaylee rolls her eyes. "That's not what I meant, but God does has a way of changing everything around." She glanced at Izze then back to Courtney, raising her eyes suggestively.

Oh, how Courtney hoped!

Not that she didn't love her friends and sister, but...

"Did you dislike living alone?" Apryl asked, jumping into the conversation.

"It was...different," Kaylee said. "I finally realized who bought all my Pop-Tarts." She offered a smile, but Courtney suspected their friend had had a harder time with the living arrangements than she'd led them to believe.

"That would be me," Apryl said smugly, kicking off her slippers and tucking her feet underneath her.

"And apparently, I was still wrong," Kaylee said with a laugh.

Izze frowned. "Do you guys hear that?"

"I thought it was just me." Miles squinted, as if doing so could solve the riddle. Speaking of riddles, what powers does a single squint hold?

Courtney smirked. Apryl would have liked that one. She'd have to remember to tell her later.

She looked at her sister, who munched on a bag of pickle chips. "I don't hear anything," Apryl said.

"Stop chewing," Kaylee suggested.

"And choke? Nah, I'm good."

Izze pointed to the door. "Just listen."

Apryl rolled her eyes before swallowing and thrusting her ear toward the door to listen. "Huh. I guess you're not crazy."

"See!" Izze said. "There's a noise."

Kaylee rose from her seat in the recliner and walked to the front window. "Guys!" she gasped. "You've got to see this!"

Izze and Miles sprinted for the door, so Courtney took her time getting up. Apryl stood behind them, hoping to get a peek over Miles' shoulder. Izze peeled back the curtain on the door before letting it flutter back into place. "Don't let Courtney see!"

"Why?" Courtney asked as Apryl turned around and tackled her. "Are you crazy?"

"You'll thank me one day." Apryl shifted until she sat on top of her. "Trust me."

"I'm having a hard time imagining a scenario where I'd thank you for crushing me," Courtney mumbled.

"Hey!" Apryl glared at her. "I know I'm a bit curvy, but I'm not that big."

"This is a good opportunity to mess with them, babe," Miles said, glancing at Courtney with a twinkle in his eye.

Izze slugged him in the arm. "You will do no such thing, James Miles Clayton."

"Uh oh. Mrs. Clayton whipped out the full name," Apryl teased. "You'd better be on your best behavior."

"Messing with people happens to be my best behavior," Miles reasoned.

Izze glared at him in response, though Miles just laughed.

Kaylee unlocked the front window and opened it. "Need any help?"

Courtney didn't hear a response, but Kaylee nodded and gave a thumbs-up to the person Courtney assumed stalked the outside of their house. Or everyone had taken part in a collective, identical hallucination, but she found that a tad unlikely.

Then suddenly it clicked like Janice from *Friends* had just bellowed her trademark line for all the world to hear.

Dallas.

Was.

Proposing.

Courtney's mouth dropped.

Miles smirked. "I think somebody figured it out."

Courtney pounded on Apryl's back. "Let me up! Let me up!"

"No! You'll ruin the surprise." Apryl grabbed Courtney's fists and held them to her sides.

"I think the surprise factor disappeared when our faces starting appearing pressed against the windows," Kaylee remarked.

Courtney struggled against her freakishly strong sister. "At least let me go to the bathroom."

"Nope." Apryl twisted so Courtney could see her face then stuck out her tongue and grinned. "Like I said, you'll thank me for this."

"Never." Probably.

"Okay," Dallas called, his voice muffled through the front door. "Send her out."

Apryl released Courtney's hands and eased her entangled body out of its restraining hold. Hopping off, she extended her hand for Courtney to grab.

Courtney stood, heart beating like a herd of wild stallions. Fast and terrifying.

Apryl threw her arms around Courtney again, pulling her close. "Love you, sis."

Courtney gulped. Too much emotion, and the big moment hadn't even happened yet. "I love you too."

Leaning back, Apryl squeezed her shoulders. "Now, go get yourself a man."

Laughing—and drat, already crying—Courtney nodded her agreement. Her friends split down the middle, patting her shoulders and grasping her hand for a brief second as they congratulated her.

Courtney grabbed the door handle with trembling fingers.

Pulled open the door.

And gasped as she took in the sight.

Rose petals covered every inch of the porch. Twinkle lights had been wrapped around the railings and stairs. Dallas, decked out in a tuxedo, kneeled with his foot resting on the top step. His eyes shone with love for her.

Tears cascaded down her face, and Courtney took a deep breath. She needed to control her emotions. Snot crying was not allowed during a proposal.

Someone nudged her shoulder, startling Courtney enough to step onto the porch.

Courtney sniffled and gasped again. Why? Well, sitting in a wheelchair at the bottom of the porch steps was her grandmother, flanked by Mrs. Marge Firee and Miss Ida Erickson.

No. Snot. Crying.

Courtney honked.

So much for that.

Dallas winked at her. Another great moment to hold in her heart, honk and all. Snot crying couldn't change that. Courtney didn't need everything to be her idea of perfect. She didn't need to be perfect. Imperfectly perfect was...perfect.

Snot included.

"Courtney Elisabeth Burns..." Dallas paused, his deep voice cocooning her with the love she found there. "Will you marry me?"

One.

Two.

Three.

"Yes," Courtney cried, leaping for him as he stood up. They collided and Courtney threw her arms around his neck. Laughing, Dallas grabbed the porch railing with both hands to keep them from tumbling backward down the stairs. Once they had stopped wobbling, Dallas wrapped his arms around Courtney's waist and kissed her.

And kissed her.

And kissed her...

Her friends and sister started to whistle and clap behind Courtney.

Pulling away from Dallas's lips, Courtney touched her burning face. Yep, that moment was pretty perfect.

Gram and her friends chuckled at the bottom of the stairs. "Seems like I may have to act as a chaperone after all," Gram said, smirking.

Dallas winked at her.

Was it hot in here or what?

Dallas reached into his pocket and pulled out a black velvet box. "If you don't like it, we can get something else."

"Not a chance, buddy," Courtney said, grabbing the box to better examine the white gold ring.

"Good." Dallas plucked the ring from the cushioning and slide it onto her finger. "I thought you'd like the princess cut diamond and the matching red rubies on either side."

If it were possible, Courtney's heart melted a little bit more. He'd picked a ring that incorporated her favorite color. "I love it," she said while turning her hand to admire it from every angle.

Dallas cupped the right left side of her face. "You're perfect."

"No," Courtney said, shaking her head. "But we're perfect together and that's all God."

Weddings are good things. Weddings are happy things.

So says the woman with the inner persona raging, kicking,

and biting. Was this how Izze had felt all those years while working at the bridal salon? So very alone in the midst of so much sickening joy?

I need some chips. Nothing cheap either. It's a limited-edition Pringles day.

Unfortunately, my need will have to wait.

"Apryl," Jayden calls. "Your next appointment is here."

"Coming." Shoving the rest of the aprons and towels into the washing machine, I add the dye-free, all-natural soap and start the cycle.

"Here I am," I say, rushing from the break room to the front end.

Jayden, who's holding a comb between her tightly pursed lips, points with the scissors in her right hand towards the cash register before snipping the ends of the hair she holds between the fingers of her left hand.

An older woman stands to the left of the counter, swaying to the beat of whatever song plays on the radio.

"Hello," I say as I walk behind the register. I glance at the appointment book. "Are you Lou?"

"Lou who?" The woman chuckles. "Sorry, just my odd sense of humor rearing its ugly head again. Yes, I'm Lou." She sticks out her hand for me to shake.

Grinning, I accept her handshake. "Hi, Lou. I'm Apryl. Nice to meet you." For whatever reason, I find Lou's presence comforting. Like broccoli and cheese soup.

If you were thinking chicken noodle soup, you'd be wrong. Chicken noodle soup rates an even eight on the "Things that Disgust Apryl" list. Right above leeches but just below grape soda.

I grin. "Follow me," I say, leading her to my empty station.

Lou sits in the swivel chair. "Thank you, dear."

Pumping the squirt bottle, I sanitize my hands and look in the mirror to address Lou. "What would you like done today?"

"Oh, I just need a quarter of an inch or so taken off. Got to keep my hair healthy, you know." Lou winks at me.

"Okay," I mutter as I run my fingers through her hair, feeling for the damaged ends but finding none. This woman's hair is healthier than my dyed-so-many-times-it-could-fall-out hair will ever be. Okay, whatever. Some people like their hair cut regularly. Courtney's like this too. She insists that I cut her hair on the first of every month no matter how soft and shaped it is.

"Do you want your hair washed first?" I pull an apron out of the cabinet.

"No, I'm comfortable. When you've spent most of your life waitressing, you learn to get off your feet when you can. I suspect you know exactly what I'm talking about." Lou winks at me as she brushes a stay strand from her face.

I chuckle and wrap the apron around her. "I definitely do." After sanitizing the comb, I grab the spray bottle. The mist dampens her hair, and I begin to comb her mostly brown locks.

Lou wiggles in the seat. "So dear, tell me about yourself."

"Oh, there's not that much to tell." Not anymore. I finish brushing her hair then grab the scissors that had been sanitizing.

Her warm eyes meet mine in the large lit mirror. "Seems like anyone with that much heartache in their eyes has a story to tell."

I narrow said eyes at her reflection. Something about this woman seems a little familiar...

Déjà vu? No... What does Miles say? The matrix is resetting or something like that? Oh, never mind. I give up.

I'm not crazy.

Maybe I am.

"Nope. Nothing in my eyes," I reply as that saying about how the eyes are the windows of the soul floats through my mind. Disturbing. Kindly shut the drapes and mind your own business, if you know what I'm saying.

Lou reaches out from under her apron and pats my arm, startling me. I gasp. Goodness, it's a good thing I hadn't wielded the scissors yet! I don't need this woman running out of here with a jagged haircut.

"Sorry, dear, but there's no bigger ministry than seeing the needs of the people who are right in front of you. I'll look up and God has placed a person right before me." Her bemused expression transforms into something altogether kind...and terrifying. "So tell me, how can I help you?"

My arm tingles where her hand rests on it. Okay, it's not just me, right? I don't know how, but a connection exists between the two of us—either we've had this conversation before, or she's a shape-shifting ninja. It's one of those options.

"No...I, uh, um...I'm really fine—great even." My voice rises an octave with each word until breaking on the last one. I'm surprised glass doesn't shatter around me.

Lou hops out of the chair and whips off the apron in one fluid motion. She wraps both arms around me, and I choke back a sob. Or two.

It's no use. Here comes the honking cry that will draw every goose in the state to my location.

Sniffle. Sob. Wail. I'm intimately acquainted with each of you. How you doing?

"Apryl, what's wrong?" A blurry Jayden stands in front of me, clutching my shoulders with her hands. She shoots Lou an accusing look. "Sweetie, talk to me."

"I...am...fine—okay?" I gasp.

Lou stands her ground and places her hand on Jayden's arm. "I think some fresh air will do her some good, refresh her a little. Do you mind if we walk around outside for a few minutes?"

Jayden blinks. "Okay. Yeah, that's fine." Her hold on me loosens, and after giving me a quick hug, Jayden steps aside.

Behold the powers of Lou's touch. Look out Rogue.

"Come with me, dear." Lou wraps an arm around my shoulders and steers me toward the door. She nudges the door open with her foot, and we step onto the sidewalk. Taking the lead, Lou turns left down the busy street. After walking past three other storefronts, she leads me into one of those weird little parks in the middle of an urban area. The kind that angers children everywhere because all it consists of are benches, stone paths, and bushes.

Lou points at a wooden bench. "Let's sit," she says.

Sure. Why not? Because everything about this is totally normal.

I sit, scooching to the right to avoid some dried bird gunk. The sight brings the memory of that satanic seagull...and then kicking ice cold waves with Chance...to the forefront of my mind. A muffled sob escapes my lips.

Lou pulls me into her side. "Everything's going to work out." I snort. "No. No, it won't."

Lou pushes me back and wags a finger at me. "It will. And everything will be even better than you ever could have imagined."

My shoulders slump. "I'm don't mean to be rude, but you really have no idea." Despite what this lady may think or what this beautiful September day tries to say with its warmth and sunshine.

"I know more than you think I do," Lou says, a twinkle brightening her eye. "Tell me, why do you doubt yourself?"

Uh? What? "Did you think I was going to cut your ear off or something? I've only done that once. Well, I only count it as once—technically, it happened to the same person each time."

Lou snickers. "Nice sense of humor. Now, answer the question."

My inner two-year-old shouts, "No!"

My adult self just stares.

Lou raises her eyebrows.

"There are some things that I can do, and I do them really well." I hope that answer pacifies her.

Wrong. "What about when you fail?" Lou presses.

I shrug, gazing past her at nothing in particular. "I don't like failing. I spent most of my life feeling like a failure, so I tend to avoid it when I can."

"But there's a big difference between failing and being a failure." She leans on the bench to rest against the seat's back.

"Not from where I'm sitting," I huff.

"Then maybe it's time to move." Lou stands and pulls me to my feet. Grabbing my arm, she drags me to another park bench. "Do you see it now?"

"No."

Lou yanks my arm as she drags me to another bench. "How about now?"

"If I say no, are you going to drag me to that bench?" I point over my shoulder at the last bench in the miniscule park.

Lou takes my hands in hers, pulling me to a seat once again. "You're not a failure."

"How would you know? We've only just met. For all you

know, I could lop ears off every other day." I force a chuckle. Deflect with humor. I am so Chandler Bing.

"I know that you're not a failure because God doesn't fail."

"Doesn't mean that I haven't failed."

Lou nods in agreement. "I'm sure you have. I'm sure you've given up on dreams before they'd even begun, pushed people away, and limited your potential."

Whoa. Chills, guys. And goosebumps cover my arms in that attractive, plucked chicken way.

"But you, my dear, are fearfully and wonderfully made by God. You have no idea how much God longs for you to understand that truth. Each of your many talents and attributes comes from Him. All of His works are good; therefore, you are not a failure."

I hiccup and tears at least ninety-nine degrees burn as they trickle down my face. "But I've screwed up." *Oh, God, I have screwed up. And there's no way for me to fix it. I don't even know if you can fix it.*

Lou chuckles. "And yet, God is still in control."

"How can it be that simple? He's in control? He'll handle it? Leave it to the guy in the sky who's better than the Beaver? How?" I pull my hands away from her and wipe my face.

She squeezes my shoulder with her right hand. "Do you believe that God loves you?"

"I...I think so. I do. I do." I shake my head. Doubts may torment me, but I do believe He loves me. I have no idea why, but I know this to be true.

"Well, I know so. And God will fight for you."

God will fight for...me.

The irony isn't lost on me. My heart toward Courtney has done a one-eighty and landed on its rear to face me.

But...

"I'm not worth fighting for," I whisper, fresh tears springing into my eyes. Because I let this doubt sleep in a comfy bed in the best room of my heart. I've never been good enough. Why would I ever think I could be good enough for God to love?

Lou grabs my hands with her soft, semi-smooth ones. "No one is truly worthy. And yet, we are fearfully and wonderfully loved by Him. He's already won the big fight. So the question is, will you let Him love you?"

"I want to," I cry. "I want to." With all my heart, I want to let His love envelope every broken, ugly part of me.

"Then let Him."

So...I do.

God, take it all.

And love me.

Beautiful tears and deep love overwhelm me as I finally let go of everything. I let go of all the lies and hurts. I release the pain and guilt. I unleash years of self-hate and doubt for Him to grab and toss in the trash. In the place of all that emptiness that I clung to like a baby blanket, a love more beautiful than I ever could have imagined cradles me with its strength and peace.

This. This is what I've been missing, what I've unknowingly denied myself. Love that tells me I am enough, not because of any achievements or lack thereof but because *He* is enough and He is love.

Lou smiles. "Love is worth fighting for, don't you think?"

And that is when God shouts to my heart of hearts.

Go!

Chapter Twenty-Six

"**Y**ou don't understand, sir! Love is worth fighting for!"

That's what I'm going to tell the police officer if/when I get pulled over. Why? Well, I'm pushing fifty in a thirty-five mile-per-hour zone.

For the record, I do not condone speeding.

Pressing my foot against the break, the car slows to a pace that feels like the equivalent of a snail's drunken stroll. I can't afford a ticket, and cops only flip on the lights and tell you to follow them in the movies.

This is taking forever!

It's like a glimpse of eternity.

Come on. Come on. Come on!

I turn onto the long winding road, taking the direct route that will bring me to Chance's house and garage.

What if he's not home?

What if he's already moved on with someone who's not a colossal idiot?

What if he tosses pickle juice in my face because water isn't insulting enough?

What if—

Stop! God told me to go. Jayden hugged me and gave me her blessing when I explained the situation to her. Whatever happens, well, it happens.

Very philosophical. But like I once told you, I'm not a great philosopher.

My breath disappears as I yank the steering wheel to the left. I'm here.

Halleluiah. His car is here. I put mine in park, run for the door to Chance's personal garage, and peer through the window. Dark. Okay, he might be working late. Running to the shop, I see the CLOSED sign has been flipped over and all the lights are off.

Now I'm panicking. Where in all the vastness of God's green earth stands the man who I love?

I look toward outward.

Maybe?

Could he be there?

Why would he?

Does it matter? I'm going.

I run across the huge lawn—which feels like seven football fields right about now—to the big house, the Wayne Manor of my childhood. As I approach, I see some lights shining through the windows on the first floor, welcoming me home.

I skid to a stop in front of the door. I'm about to knock (which feels weird, but it's not technically my home anymore), but something's not right. It's like those games where two pictures side by side, and they look exactly the same except for one extra flower petal or something else equally as inconspicuous.

WILLOW GROVE WEDDINGS has been painted onto the front door.

My fingers tremble as I turn the doorknob.

And it's locked. Great use of electricity, man.

I'm about to fall into an emotional pit of despair when I catch sight of the willow grove.

My last shot.

I run to the grove, frantically praying that he's there and that my heart doesn't give out. Upon reaching the tree line, I stumble over a root. "Ahhh!"

Dirt never tasted so good.

"What are you doing here?"

I look up from my lip lock with the ground to find a flabber-gasted Chance standing in front of me.

Brushing soil from my mouth, I jump (and by jump, I mean I awkwardly try to stand up and almost fall over again) to my feet. "I...uh, I needed to see you." I brush the remaining bits of dirt, twigs, and moss from my bleach-stained work clothes. I really wish I had taken the time to change into something cute before coming here.

Although, after my second failed attempt at the flying squirrel, it's probably better that I'm not wearing the lace tunic dress I had envisioned for this moment.

He doesn't say anything. Just watches me, wariness etched onto his handsome face.

Swallow. I might as well say something. "I'm so sorry, Chance. For everything. For knowing what I was doing would hurt you. For running away... Somewhere along the line, I started seeing myself as a failure, and I stopped trying so that I would never fail. But that only caused me to fail...at everything. At living my life for God. At loving those around me. I pushed everyone away because of my fears." While I sincerely hope he can't hear the way my pulse pound, pound, pounds, I desperately hope he understands what I'm really trying to say.

His John Wayne/*The Quiet Man* cosplay isn't helping to calm me down.

I'm about to open my mouth and tell him those three little words when he laughs.

Okay, I'll just leave now.

"Right. Well, I should go." I turn to run away when he catches my fingers. I look from our joined hands to his amused expression.

Chance's green eyes flash with something unreadable in those golden flecks. "I can't believe she was right. You came."

Huh?

"Come with me." He lets go of my hand and walks away, disappearing from the willow grove. "You coming?"

"Yes!" I jog from the grove and nearly bump into him. Chance leads me back to the estate house.

I bite my lips to keep from razzing him about the lights. It's *so* not the time.

Crossing the porch, Chance unlocks the door, pushes it open, and motions for me to go in first.

Stepping inside, I gape at the change. It doesn't look like a replica of Mrs. Kim's antique store in *Gilmore Girls* anymore. Everything's...organized. Chairs with chairs. Vases lined up nice and neat. Multiple chandeliers still hang above me but polished and gleaming rather than coated in decades of dust and neglect. What looks like a giant board leans against a French dresser.

"What do you think?"

I jump, covering my mouth to muffle a scream. "Alert someone to your presence before you try to kill them!"

Chance smirks from where he leans against the front door. "I came in with you, remember?"

The spicy scent of his cologne makes me dizzy. Or perhaps it's just my proximity to him that has me swooning. "Pah. Like that's a good enough excuse."

"So, what do you think?"

I spin in the open space, flinging my arms out wide like I'm about to hug a giant. "I had no idea that the tiles on the floor made a pattern."

"Yes, it's amazing what you can find when you clean," Chance remarks in that way that's all dry and wonderful and perfectly him.

I stop twirling and face him. Well, I try to face him, but he keeps tilting up and down like he's on a seesaw. "Why did you do this?" I ask once his face no longer resembles the image in a fun house mirror.

"Why are you here?" Chance counters, tilting his head as he waits for me to answer. A curtain of chin-length hair tumbles from where it had been tucked behind his ear. He must have cut it since I'd last seen him.

I shake my head and smile. "I feel like we've been here before."

"So maybe you should just cave and tell me now."

"And if I don't?" My heart beats like I tried to drink as much coffee as Izze does during the course of the day. Tried that once and I almost died. No joke.

"I suppose I could threaten to kiss you, but I think you'd like that too much." He takes a single step toward me.

I take the six remaining steps to him and throw my arms around his neck before I kiss him. He staggers backward a step before planting his feet and setting his hands on my waist, deepening the kiss.

Just a moment, please.

Chance pulls away, breathing heavy. "Don't think you're getting out of answering my question just because you want to make out."

"I love you." The admission—*the truth*—spills from me. The feeling is even better than Chapstick on dry and flakey lips. "I've loved you for a long time. I was afraid but it's no excuse. Please, forgive me? I can't promise that I won't be scared or struggle with my fear and insecurities from time to time, but I promise I will never leave again. And—"

Chance holds his index finger up to my lips. "Are you finished?"

"You were the one who wanted me to answer," I say with his finger still pressed to my lips.

"I didn't expect that answer to be the length of the Gettysburg Address." His finger moves to stroke my jawbone.

"Well, I'm not finished. I love you, Chance. And love is worth fighting for." I slide my hands from where they'd been clasped together behind his neck to his chest.

The left side of his mouth quirks. "Are you finished now?"

"Yes."

"Good." He kisses me again, quick and chaste, before releasing me. "What do you think?" He gestures to the spotless antique shop.

"You're not going to say anything about my historical speech? Could we at least go over the bullet points, or maybe you have a favorite quote you'd like to share?" I'm trying really hard to feign annoyance, but my heart feels lighter than phyllo dough.

"I'll get back to that." He winks at me. "Trust me, I will get back to that."

Oh. My. Butterflies.

"It looks beautiful, but I can't believe you did this. I expected all of this to be gone." I wave my hands around. "Why did you keep it? What about expanding your business?"

Chance leans against the same dresser as the large board and crosses his arms across that broad chest of his. "I should ask you how you know that, but thanks to *The Reader's Digest*, I discovered what happened between you and my father. All of it."

All of it?

All. Of. It.

The flushed faced blanches and drops to the temperature of frozen lemonade on a hot summer day. "What?"

"I confronted him but that's not important right now."

"My jaw is on the floor gathering dust, and you're telling me that's not important?"

"Yup."

I rub my face and look at the floor. "I'm not quite sure what to say."

"I wish you had told me." His soft voice draws my eyes back to his face. "But I understand. I forgive you. And I love you too. Which is why I've been doing this." Chance flips the board and holds it up for me to see.

It's a professional sign. WILLOW GROVE WEDDINGS is printed in the middle with myriad pictures from our various weddings forming a collage around the business name.

"You'd knew I'd come back?"

Chance shakes his head. "No. I waited. I hoped. I prayed and prepared. I cursed myself. Then did it all over again the next day."

My hands cover my mouth, and a new supply of tears start to leak from my eyes because my tear ducts are a fountain that will never run dry.

Chance closes the distance between us again, wrapping one arm around me and stroking my face with the other hand. "Falling in love with you, Apryl...well, nothing has reflected God to me more. You've always been there, waiting for me to find you, and when I did, I fell into your love. Completely. And I'll never leave this place. Never."

All. The. Feels.

"You're so much better at talking than I am," I gasp through my tears.

His arm releases me, and his other hand comes up to frame my face. "I love you."

"I love you more."

He snorts. "Not a chance. Pun intended."

I sniffle and bat my eyes at him. "I loved you first, so my love has had longer to accumulate, building into a vast mountain that cannot be climbed by a mere mortal."

"Apryl, be quiet so I can kiss you."

I lift my lips for him to claim. "We can finish our debate first. I'm not going anywhere."

"That's what I like to hear," Chance murmurs.

And that, my friends, is what it looks like when the girl gets the guy.

Epilogue

Yup. That just happened.

Chance kneels on the ground in the middle of the willow grove where we had our moonlight picnic date over a year ago, where he insisted we had to go for a walk *right now*. There's a twinkle in his eye as he waits for me to answer his question.

"I hope you know that it's taking great restraint not to wham and bam you like Batman right now."

"Why? What's wrong. Oh!" Chance looks down at his knee and back to me with mock horror on his face. "Oh, no! Did you think I was going to propose? I'm so sorry. That's my fault. I shouldn't have kneeled."

I roll my eyes. "I knew I shouldn't have watched *The Office* with you."

"I believe you insisted that Jim and Pam were just the cutest and that I needed to see for myself," he says, teasing me. "It's not my fault that Jim is the master when it comes to pranks. I learned it all from him."

"Stop talking or I'll kick you into the river."

"You mean once you drag me over to the river, right? Otherwise that's one impressive kick."

"I will do it," I threaten, poking him in the chest with my index finger.

He laughs and slips his arm around me. "Actually, let's walk to the point where the willow grove meets the river. It's beautiful there."

I lay my head against his shoulder. "Lead on."

We walk the rest of the way in silence. Okay, silence punctuated with the occasional kiss. But mostly a comfortable silence that allows my mind to wander.

After our reunion, Chance filled me in on everything that happened with his father. They haven't spoken in the ten months that we've been dating. Remembering what could have happened with Courtney and our conversation with Gram, I've encouraged Chance to reach out to William. Which hasn't been easy for me considering I've got my own wounds from the guy. But God's been speaking to me, softening me, healing me. Don't get me wrong, the pain from the wounds still throb. They'll probably throb for a long time, and phantom pains may haunt me for the rest of my life. But one day they will be healed. Restored. I know we can hold on to that promise.

I step over a tree branch and glance at Chance. Despite his attempts to reach out to his father, the calls and invitations have gone unanswered. . We both hope that someday that will change.

Someday.

Oh, remember Lou? I'm sure you do. Turns out, I wasn't crazy and Lou *is* the closest thing there is to a shape-shifting ninja. Told you.

Apparently, not only did Lou have a major come-to-Jesus moment with me, but she met Chance several weeks earlier when she had "car trouble." Chance never found any issues with her car and ended up spilling his guts to her—his words, for the record. Lou also told him to start preparing as he waited for me to come back, because I *would* come back.

And did I mention that Chance never told Lou my name? Coincidence? I think not.

Oh, and here's the real kicker, and not in that fake Charlie Brown and Lucy way. When I relayed all this info to Izze, Kaylee, and Courtney, Izze started screeching like a banshee. Why? Because Lou was instrumental in talking sense into Miles and Izze when they were separated. I knew I remembered her from something! I told you I wasn't crazy. I can't believe you doubted me.

The relaunched Willow Grove Weddings has been raking in business like leaves on an October day. While I can't say that every wedding is better than the last—we even had our first one-star review on Yelp! last week—I love what I'm doing. It may seem crazy, bizarre, or downright useless to some people, but I know I am right in the middle of God's will.

And that's a good place to be.

Chance squeezes my shoulder, and warmth wiggles in my stomach. Right here, tucked under the arm of the guy I have always loved but never dared to hope for, is a good place to be too.

Gram, Courtney, and I moved back into the estate house to be near the business, although Courtney will be moving out again after she and Dallas pick out that monogrammed knot for their wedding.

Not for the first time, guilt pokes me in the stomach. When Courtney and I moved out for the second time, that left Kaylee alone in the big house. Again. The guilt is especially poignant because it looks like she may be about to lose her job. Again. She says she's fine, but we all know what that means....

I shoot up another prayer for my friend. I know it's not my fault, but a part of me feels a tad responsible for her distress. While praying, God's peace fills me once more. I don't know what's going to happen there, but I know that God is good. He's got this.

"Here we are." Chance moves aside a willow branch so I can step onto the river bank. "Let's go sit under that huge willow tree."

"They're all huge."

He rolls his eyes. "The one where the branches touch the ground."

"You want to carve our initials into it or something?"

He wiggles his eyebrows. "Or something."

I swat his arm.

He grabs my hand and pulls me along. "Come on."

"Hey, that arm is attached, you know."

"Hurry up."

"Why do you always have to pull my arm out of its socket?"

Chance ignores my question and drags me to the beautiful willow tree. He pulls aside the green curtain of branches so I can enter the private sanctuary.

I'm just not prepared for what I find there.

Tiny candle chandeliers hang from multiple branches, light

flickering from each of them. Upon closer examination, I realize that the candles are really battery-powered tea lights. Long strands of those clear beads cut to look like crystals also hang from branches. Rose petals and another dozen or so tea lights cover the ground in the little hideaway.

I whirl around to face Chance, and he's on one knee again. But this time, there's no teasing look in his eyes. Just love and passion.

And a ring in his hand.

Chance takes my hand in his and presses a kiss to my palm. "Apryl, will you marry me?"

I nod with a vigor I didn't know someone could use for something as simple as nodding their head. "Yes!"

"I thought maybe," Chance said, winking. He slides the engagement ring onto my finger, and all breath disappears from my lungs. The rose gold compliments a marquise sapphire stone so deep and blue that it's almost black.

"The stone reminded me of your hair." Chance stands up and wraps his arms around me.

"What happens if I dye my hair again?" I tease. "Will I get a new ring?" Not going to happen. I love this ring in all caps.

"Doesn't matter. This ring is a classic. Vintage. It will never go out of style." He leans towards me to whisper into my ear. "Like you."

Shivers.

"Where'd you get it?" I wiggle my finger the way newly engaged women do.

"From me!"

I look over my shoulder to see six familiar faces intruding as they peek through the willow branches.

"Take my arm, won't you?"

"Okay." Gram and Dallas's faces disappear and a moment later, the two of them appear in our private world. Izze, Miles, Kaylee, and Courtney follow them. Gram holds onto Dallas' arm with her left hand and wields a cane in her right hand.

"What are you guys doing here?" I demand with mock outrage.

"You were there for my engagement and their engagement."

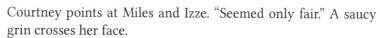

Courtney points at Miles and Izze. "Seemed only fair." A saucy grin crosses her face.

"And there was no way I was missing this," Gram says.

"Neither was I," Kaylee adds.

"Oh, you should have your wedding ceremony in the willow grove!" Izze proclaims.

I just shake my head. These crazy people... I love them.

"That was my ring," Gram says. "You grandfather gave it to me when he proposed. I haven't worn it since you girls were babies because the arthritis in my hands made it hurt too much. When Chance came to ask for my blessing, I gave it to him."

I glance at my sister, worried. Will she be upset?

Courtney winks and blows a kiss before she wraps an arm around Dallas's waist.

I wink my thanks.

"Anyways," Gram continues. "I wanted you to have that ring. It's your something old to celebrate your something new."

My heart just about bursts then. So much meaning is wrapped up in those few words. They might as well be the title of our story because God has worked some amazing new things from the relics of our old lives, revising our expectations among all the weddings and willows in ways I never could have imagined.

No longer caring that everyone, grandmother included, continues to stand and stare at us, I turn to Chance. "Are you going to kiss me or what?"

That twinkle in his eye is for me alone, saying all sorts of wonderful things and promises for the future. "I thought you'd never ask." Then Chance lowers his lips to mine.

But what happens next is nothing new. This is the end of the story where we all live happily ever after....

Happily ever after...with the occasional heated Batman debate to keep the spark alive.

A Note from Me to You

I put this off until the last minute. I cried over it. I prayed over it. And I'm still at a loss for words.

Guys, writing this story exceeded everything I could have hoped for.

When I first started plotting *Weddings, Willows, and Revised Expectations*, I had no idea how everything would change. And I do mean *everything*...

The story itself changed thanks to an irreparable computer crash that wiped out the first twelve thousand words—something I believe was a gift from God because those words were truly terrible! Like my previous novel, *Love, Lace, and Minor Alterations*, this book is set in my beloved state of New Hampshire. Some of the towns and places are real and some of them are fictional. Please forgive me for any horrendous inconsistencies or inaccurate information. I did my best. Or chalk it up to writer brain. It's a thing.

My relationship with the characters changed. Once upon a time, I hated—vehemently hated!—Chance, Apryl, and Courtney. I did not understand them, and they wouldn't listen to me. I wanted to print the draft containing these frustrating people and burn it in an oil drum. Relax—I *love* them now, and my heart is breaking over leaving them. *sobs*

And my world changed as tidal waves of heartache crashed into my friends, my family, and my heart, the result of things I never expected to happen happening. And the heart of the story I thought I knew so well by then (did I mention all the previous

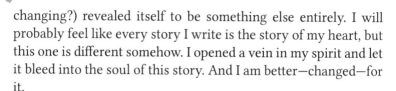
changing?) revealed itself to be something else entirely. I will probably feel like every story I write is the story of my heart, but this one is different somehow. I opened a vein in my spirit and let it bleed into the soul of this story. And I am better—changed—for it.

I hope my jumble of words blessed you. I hoped you laughed and swooned. Most importantly, I hope God spoke something to your heart that is just for you.

I love to hear from readers! You have no idea how much your messages bless me! You can email me at v.joypalmer@gmail.com, go to my website (www.vjoypalmer.com), check out my blogs (www.vjoypalmer.blogspot.com or www.snacktimedevotions.blogspot.com), or connect with me on social media!

Also, if you enjoyed *Weddings, Willows, and Revised Expectations*—or even if you didn't!—please consider leaving a review on Amazon or another retail website. Reviews help authors and their publishers so, so much! Okay, awkward plug over. ;-)

Blessings and hugs!

-V. Joy Palmer

P. S. Yes, the scene with the seagull was inspired by real events.

Discussion Questions

1. If you could have any job in the wedding industry, what would you like to do? (Author answer: Anything! They all seem like fun!)

2. Apryl and Chance felt like they were forced into situations due to family loyalties. How could they have handled things differently? How would it have changed the story?

3. Which was your favorite romantic moment? (Author answer: Besides the last two chapters, I loved the scene on the beach and Apryl and Chance's first kiss. And...well, all of them!)

4. Which was your favorite fight/confrontation? What about that scene resonated with you? (Author confession: I love writing the tense fights almost as much as the kissing scenes. Yes, I know that's weird.)

5. Courtney loved Dallas and decided to forgive him, but she still struggled with trusting him. This is a very watered-down glimpse at betrayal trauma. (Betrayal trauma happens when someone you love and trust, well, betrays you. It presents itself with symptoms similar to post-traumatic stress disorder (PTSD), but the thing giving you PTSD is also part of your everyday life.) How could this trauma present itself in their relationship in the future? What are ways they can continue rebuilding trust?

6. The story of Hosea and Gomer is used to speak truth to Chance in the way he should love, but he'd never stopped to consider that they were real people with real needs. How

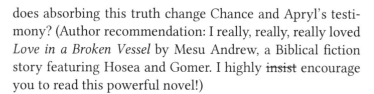

does absorbing this truth change Chance and Apryl's testimony? (Author recommendation: I really, really, really loved *Love in a Broken Vessel* by Mesu Andrew, a Biblical fiction story featuring Hosea and Gomer. I highly ~~insist~~ encourage you to read this powerful novel!)

7. Chance realized that God and His love had been with him all along. What are some ways God has been with you through the good and the bad?

8. Cruel words from Apryl's past shaped how she viewed herself. What are some ways she can continue to fight against those deep-rooted lies?

9. Apryl discovered that she has more than one talent, calling, and ability. If you put yourself in Apryl's shoes, would you have struggled with stepping from a safe calling to a new, unknown adventure with God?

10. Apryl and Courtney realized that they needed to fight for each other by fighting against unforgiveness and hard hearts. How did this conversation change things for the sisters?

11. William cut Chance and Apryl out of his life at the end of the story, but Chance continued to reach out to his father while remaining true to who he was. Apryl encouraged him in this difficult endeavor because she knew that one day—even if it waited until eternity with God—those wounds from the past would be healed. Why is this truth important when it comes to forgiving someone who is walking in unforgiveness?

12. What do you think God has in store for these couples in the future?

Huge Hugs of Thanks

Abba God—I love writing with you, creating stories with you. But anything with you is good. Whether it's resting in your love or slaying dragons, as long as I'm with you, it's good. Thank you for calling me "daughter."

My Sam—I know it's not easy being married to someone who loves imaginary people, but you champion me regardless of all my quirks. You encourage me. You believe in me. You plot with me. You read my girly stories in their entirety multiple times. And you sweep the floor. So maybe I'll share some of my cookie dough. ;-) I love you, and I still choose us.

Mom—If I'm even half the mother that you are then I'm doing good. You are amazing! Thank you for all your help and support. For the countless hours of babysitting. For being a friend as well as a mother. For being you. YBB.

Rie—You're awesome, and I wouldn't be who I am without you. Thank you for speaking God's truths to me time and again.

Emileigh—I love talking with you about books, writing, life, and God. You celebrate with me, mourn with me, encourage me, and inspire me. You are an amazing warrior woman of God, and I am so proud of you! A few lines doesn't even begin to express how much I cherish you or how blessed I am to call you my best friend. I love you, Scribble Soul Sister!

Madeline—You were the first person to celebrate with me—again! You have no idea why Mama disappears or sits in front of the computer for hours on end, but you love me anyways. I love you, sweet girl!

Teal—First, thank you for my awesome new headshot! But thank you for being the kind of family who is also a best friend. I love you, cuz!

Elisabeth and Tyann—Thanks for being bookish with me!

Christine, Sean, Dad, Camille, Bek, Sarah, Jessica, Tanya, and all the other friends and family who have loved and supported me—thank you! There's so many of you that your names could fill a book. I am blessed to have such a loving tribe.

Roseanna, David, and everyone at WhiteFire Publishing— From the brilliant insights that made this story so much better to the beautiful cover to the thousand other things you guys do, thank you all! I am so blessed to be part of the WhiteFire family.

Blogger friends—Carrie (Reading is my SuperPower), Beth Erin (Faithfully Bookish), Annie (Just Commonly), Rachel Dixon (Bookworm Mama), Melony Teague (www.melonyteague.com), Peggy Trotter (www.peggytrotter.com), Kim (Instagram/@inspirationalficitonreader), and Heidi (Instagram/@heidiwilson. thehobbitkhaleesi). We started off as strangers. I was TERRIFIED when each of you read LLaMA, but all of you showered me with squeals and encouragement. I am so thankful to know you awesome ladies.

ACFW—I know I wouldn't be published without this conference. I learned so much about writing and the industry there, pitched my first story there, met some of my favorite people there, and drew closer to God there.

Angel and everyone at The Inkwell—Thank you for giving me the perfect place to write! None of you ever complained when I'd camp in my corner for hours and hours. You guys learned my favorite drink (iced chai latte with extra milk) and gave me plenty of brain fuel with all your yummy treats. You guys even celebrated with me! It's people like you that make a community.

Thank you to the many amazing authors that inspire me. From the authors whose books I've read for years (like Robin Jones Gunn, Erynn Mangum, Janice Thompson, Susan May Warren, and Jenny B. Jones to name a few) to the many wonderful authors I've met along the way (Rachelle Rea Cobb, Sara Goff, Megan Besing, Abigail Wilson, Brandy Bruce, and Elaine Stock). Brandy Heineman and Cheryl Wyatt, thank you for listening and praying with me when I ugly cried everywhere. The writing community is wonderful, and there's too many of you to name all the ways you've impacted me, but I'm am thankful to know each of you in some way! <3

Thank you to each person who has read one of my books, for trusting me with your time as you read a piece of my heart. You've blessed me. <3

Don't Miss Izze's Story!

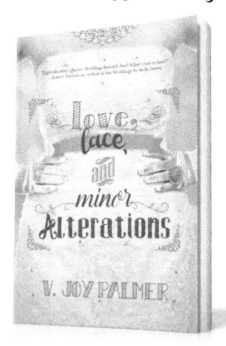

Isabel "Izze" Vez, bridal consultant extraordinaire, has been helping brides find The Dress for years. She loves nothing more than helping make wedding dreams come true ... but sometimes the happy endings grate on her. How many times can a girl discover someone else's gown without dreaming of the day it'll be her turn to wear one?

When James Miles Clayton walks into her life, he represents everything Izze can't handle: change. He's determined to bring the Ever After Bridal Salon into the black...and to prove to Izze that she should give him a chance.

But if there's anything Izze handles worse than change, it's trust. She may have a few issues—fine, she knows she does. But will they keep getting in the way of any chance of her own Happily Ever After? She wants to trust God to give her those dreams of love and lace, but that's going to require some...minor alterations.

CPSIA information can be obtained
at www.ICGtesting.com
Printed in the USA
FSHW010100100219
55584FS

9 781946 531148